PRAISE FOR THE WORK OF

𝔖tephanie 𝔏aurens

"When it comes to dishing up lusciously sensual, relentlessly readable historical romances, Laurens is unrivalled." *Booklist*

"Laurens's writing shines." *Publishers Weekly*

"One of the most talented authors on the scene today…Laurens has a real talent for writing sensuous and compelling love scenes." *Romance Reviews*

"Stephanie Laurens never fails to entertain and charm her readers with vibrant plots, snappy dialogue, and unforgettable characters." *Historical Romance Reviews.*

"Stephanie Laurens plays into readers' fantasies like a master and claims their hearts time and again." *Romantic Times Magazine*

Other Titles By Stephanie Laurens

M. S. Laurens

Desire's Prize

SAVDEK MANAGEMENT PTY. LTD.

SAVDEK MANAGEMENT PTY. LTD.
P.O. Box 322, Macedon,
Victoria 3440, Australia.

DESIRE'S PRIZE

Cover design by Robin Ludwig Design Inc.,
http://www.gobookcoverdesign.com/.
Cover photograph by Jenn LeBlanc/Illustrated Romance.

For information, address Savdek Management Proprietary Limited, Melbourne, Australia.
Website: www.stephanielaurens.com
Email: admin@stephanielaurens.com

First print publication: December 2013

Dedication

This work is dedicated to all those who have contributed to the e-book r-evolution—from Mark Coker and Smashwords, Amazon with their KDP platform, and all the other retailers who followed suit, and most especially all the authors who marched fearlessly into the evolving world and shaped it into the thriving—and still evolving—enterprise it now is.

I especially wish to thank all my fellow authors who have so generously shared their experiences and knowledge—my colleagues on the Author Friends loop, and also those who widely share their wisdom via blogs, both in the posts and the commentary. Your contributions, large and small, helped this book reach my readers.

Why? Because being a medieval historical romance penned by an established author whose name is synonymous with Regency-era historical romances, adequate publication via any traditional route was never going to happen.

But that was then, and this is now.

With sincere appreciation to all those who have made "now" what it is.

Desire's Prize

Prologue

Versallet Castle, on the Hampshire/Wiltshire border
June in the 12th Year of our Sovereign Lord, Edward III (1338)

He'd been a fool—an abject fool.

Whump!

The force behind the mace thudding into his leather shield buckled Alaun's knees. Dragging in an agonized breath, he pressed exhausted muscles to his bidding and hauled himself upright—just in time to meet the next punishing blow.

Thurrump!

The sound of the blows was becoming monotonous, but he could do nothing to stem the tide. Sweat trickled beneath his armored skull-cap, stinging his eyes. Blinking as he positioned himself to meet the next Herculean blow, he glimpsed his opponent's eyes.

Henry de Versallet was enjoying himself.

At just over forty, Henry was heavy and barrel-chested, with arms like rough-hewn oak, yet what he'd lost to the years in speed and agility he more than made up for in skill. He wasn't in any hurry to bring the beating to an end.

Alaun's shield shuddered again; the impact jarred his shoulder plates. He swore, wishing he'd been wiser. *He'd* suggested the bout, confident his advantage in height and reach would be decisive. Instead, Henry was having the time of his life, doubtless grinning from ear to ear behind his visored helm.

Thump!

Strength waning, Alaun braced himself for the next mighty wallop. His broadsword hung useless from his fist; he was too weak to raise it. Knowing

Henry would favor the mace, he'd worn both plate and mail, while Henry, with only the blunted edge of his tournament broadsword to deflect, had appeared clad in mail hauberk and surcote alone. Without the additional weight of plate armor, the older man had a telling advantage, provided the bout revolved on endurance.

Henry had made sure that it had, refusing to offer a blow until Alaun had been wild with impatience and half-exhausted to boot. Then the thrashing had begun.

Crump!

Alaun staggered. Had it been any other man, he'd have yielded long since, but nothing—no amount of punishment—would ever be sufficient to make him cry quarter of a de Versallet. He'd never fully understood the long-standing, somewhat subtle enmity that had brewed for generations between their two families—some insult over the de Versallets' pure Norman ancestry as opposed to the de Montisfryth blood, tainted by Irish Norse, Celt, and Saxon, had reputedly started it. The countering response was the success of his family, appointed by the Conqueror as Marcher lords, all-powerful in their domains.

Thrump!

Pain shot up his left arm; he gritted his teeth. His unwise challenge was about to come to an inglorious end. Still, while Henry might win Alaun's late father's stallion, no one could take from him his pride.

He didn't see the blow that felled him; he hardly felt it. The horizon suddenly tilted and spun, then the dust of the arena enveloped him. His last coherent thought was that it was lucky the wedding was but a few hours away; there were no ladies and only a few nobles present to witness his ignominious defeat.

Blessed blackness engulfed him. With a sigh, he surrendered, honor intact.

Mailed legs planted wide, his mace gripped in one ham-like fist, Henry de Versallet stood over his opponent, staring down unmoving, until, assured de Montisfryth was beyond further chastisement, Henry harrumphed and raised his visor.

Squinting through the glare, he scanned the arena. Catching sight of an appalled face above the de Montisfryth livery, he roared, "You, boy! Come tend your master!"

Thus abjured, no fewer than five white-faced de Montisfryth retainers rushed out to attend their young lord. Inwardly reflecting that that was just as well, for the boy, young and lanky though he was, doubtless weighed a ton, armor and all, Henry grunted and turned away.

It had been a most satisfying morning.

Raising his eyes to the battlemented keep of his castle, two hundred yards distant across the tournament ground, his smile broadened. The morning had gone well, and the afternoon would crown his day.

Pulling off his gauntlets, he joined his old friend Albert d'Albron at the entrance to the arena.

"Was that really necessary?" Albert, a fine-boned aesthete with a forked black beard, his thin frame enveloped in the billowing folds of a red-and-green checkered houppelande, eyed Henry with resigned disapproval.

"An excellent way to start the day, teaching the young some manners." Henry handed his helm to his squire and drew a deep breath. The morning air was crisp, spiced with the tang of wood smoke spiraling upward from the village cottages. He tossed his gauntlets to the squire. "Check on Lord de Montisfryth and report to me. And be sure you pick up that stallion."

"Aye, m'lord." The squire grinned.

Henry narrowed his eyes. "I want no fighting between retainers, mind."

The squire's grin faded. "No, m'lord."

With a snort, Henry started for the castle. "That's the last thing I need—scuffles disrupting the wedding feast. Elaine will be at me enough as it is."

Albert's brows rose. "I wouldn't have thought you'd tell her."

"I hadn't intended to." Raising a hand to his left shoulder, Henry winced. "But be damned if I don't need some of that magical salve of hers."

Albert's brows rose higher. "I thought it was *you* did the teaching?"

Henry growled. "That whelp has enough damned weight behind his arm to sheer a statute in two. Just give him a few years to grow into that body of his and he'll be a match for any man." Henry grinned wickedly. "I'm just glad I caught him in time."

About them, the morning mist rising off the River Bourne, flowing steadily southward on their right, thinned as the sun rose triumphant above the royal forest of Chute, to the east beyond the river. Behind them, the tournament field lay peacefully serene, the pavilions of the competing knights planted like jeweled blooms on the green slope beyond, identifying pennons snapping in the breeze. The curtain wall of Versallet Castle rose before them; a stream of country folk delivering produce requisitioned for the festivities hurried along the road, jostling as they crowded across the drawbridge and on through the castle's gate tower. With respect tinged with awe, they gave their lord a wide berth.

"What do you plan for the stallion?"

Albert's question had been idle. Henry's answer was not. "I'll breed from him. Had my eye on him for years, but de Montisfryth—the last—would never have parted with him."

"Aha!" Albert glanced, narrow-eyed, at his friend. "You're an evil man, Henry de Versallet. You may have gulled young de Montisfryth into believing *he* challenged *you*, but you had it in mind all along."

Ferociously smug, Henry grinned.

Albert snorted. "You should be ashamed of yourself. Your time in purgatory has doubtless just doubled."

"Fear not." Henry's grin deepened. "I'll endow another chantry with the profits I'll make from having a Montisfryn stallion at stud. The Good Lord, I'm told, makes allowance for such things."

Albert snorted again.

The outer bailey was alive with scurrying humanity, ants provisioning a mound. The carter had brought a load of wood; lads hurried back and forth, unloading the logs. An army of women were scrubbing the church steps. Amidst the country drab, the gaudy clothes of lords and ladies invited to witness Henry's daughter's nuptials glowed brightly, declaring their owners' gentility. Henry paused, viewing the scene with open satisfaction.

"I take it de Cannar accepted your terms?"

Albert's question sliced through Henry's distraction. "Oh, aye—eventually." Henry resumed his progress toward the keep. "The income from half his estates as jointure against the dowry I offered."

Albert's brows reached his hairline. "He must have been keen to secure the alliance."

"Keen as a Saracen's blade." Henry frowned. "The man's got his eye on quick advancement and he doesn't expect to die along the way. I'd say I've got my girl well-settled."

"And what of Eloise? Does she approve your choice?"

Henry shrugged. "She's easy enough. I'll give my lady that—she's never encouraged any silly notions in the girl, even if she did insist that I sent Eloise to that blessed convent. Cost a small fortune, but the outcome's been satisfactory."

"So Eloise gets security, de Cannar fills the only vacancy as son-in-law to the de Versallets, and you—" Albert broke off. "What do you get from this, Henry?"

"Buggered if I know. De Cannar's wealthy enough, but his lands don't march with mine and he's Warwick's vassal." Henry's frown matched his growl, then he brightened. "The Montisfryn stallion, perhaps? Who knows—perhaps God was rewarding me for my selfless act in providing so handsomely for my daughter."

Albert choked.

* * *

Five hours later, Albert d'Albron was one of the many nobles who danced at Eloise de Versallet's wedding feast. In the ornately carved chair at the center of the lord's table, raised above the rest of the hall, Eloise saw her father's old crony and smiled and nodded politely. Her elbows on the table, hands cupped about the golden wedding goblet, she forced herself to take a slow sip.

Around her, the revelry was scaling new heights. The great hall was overflowing with guests. A smoky haze hung low, rising from the central hearth to veil the hall's massive beams. The aromas of rich food and spilled wine overlaid the freshness of the new rushes on which the extravagantly garbed guests, as colorful as peacocks, strutted and posed.

Noise blanketed the shifting scene; the strains of a pipe and the rhythmic thump of a tabor were buried beneath it.

"Aye! An excellent win—that stallion will be worth a fortune at stud! Be interesting to see if de Cannar shapes up as well!"

Her father's bellow was greeted with salacious laughter and ogling glances; Eloise ignored them. Her sire was in fine fettle; she wondered if marrying her off was really such a feat. The settlements had been explained to her, but she'd yet to divine what her father gained. Something, she was sure. She might be his daughter, yet he'd never given her reason to believe she was anything other than an encumbrance, a dependent he needs must dower and establish.

Perhaps that was it? Her marriage would get rid of her, and seal an alliance with the wool-wealthy de Cannars.

The point was no longer of any great relevance given she'd married Raoul de Cannar that day. Eloise caught her mother's eye. Elaine of Montrose, lady de Versallet, sat beside her lord, her calm face betraying no comprehension of the increasingly ribald comments flying about her ears. Equally composed, Eloise returned her mother's smile, then allowed her gaze to drift over the knights, squires, ladies, and maidens who milled before her, some dancing, others chattering, a fluid, jewel-hued tapestry carpeting the hall.

Soon it would be time to retire.

Suppressing a shiver, she reiterated, yet again, the arguments with which she'd resigned herself to her fate. As the daughter of a noble, her marriage had been arranged for worldly considerations; her family gained by the connection, as did de Cannar's. In addition, he gained her sizeable dowry and the use of her body in which to plant his seed, while she gained security and position, which, to a lady of noble birth, was all.

Or should be. Unfortunately, she'd yet to convince herself of that. But on returning from Claerwhen, the convent she'd attended for the past five years, she'd been presented with a fait accompli—the settlements had been signed, her only role to play her prescribed part.

"It's natural to feel hesitant," her mother had said, "but from all we've learned, de Cannar will make you a good husband. He's inherited his father's estates, and he's not, so I hear, unattractive." Her mother had paused to snip a thread, then had added, "At twenty-six, that's a reasonable recommendation. Who knows? With the right management, he might even turn out as well as your father."

Eloise had smiled and accepted her lot with equanimity if not enthusiasm—until two days ago she had come face to face with Raoul de Cannar. Her misgivings had returned with a vengeance. Her mother, when appealed to, had listened, not without sympathy. Even though she had reassured Eloise that de Cannar would treat his wife with all due respect, her mother, too, was uneasy.

Eloise forced down another sip of wine.

Beside her, in the carved chair matching hers, Raoul de Cannar lounged, his heavy warrior's body imperfectly disguised by the blue velvet of his fashionable jupon. Replying to a ribald jest offered by one of his knights, Raoul grasped the moment as the knight moved on to turn to his bride. Raoul's dark, sharp-featured face would have done justice to a satyr; his eyes, of a color that was no color at all, narrowed as he considered his new acquisition. As he watched her sip, the ends of his thin lips lifted.

Eloise appeared calm, serene, her ready smiles those of a young wife pleased with her new position. Her composure was faultless, as were her features, smooth, ivory cheeks barely touched by the sun, a broad forehead without line or wrinkle to mar its perfection, her lips full of promise despite her youth. Not even the graceful arch of her fine dark brows gave a hint of her underlying tension.

Raoul's smile deepened. He knew that tension was there. Her eyes gave her away. Dark, lustrous, fathomless, they held too much intelligence, looked on the world with too clear a vision to fit the mold of unwary innocence. So large and wide they should have imparted a doe-like vulnerability, their startling vitality left the careful observer with an impression of unchartered depths.

A subtle change rippled through Raoul, distorting his handsome façade. His lips twisted, his expression momentarily one which, had she seen it, would have shaken Elaine of Montrose. But neither Eloise nor her mother had yet seen him clearly; Raoul had made certain of that. The taking of Eloise de Versallet to wife was a goal he would not jeopardize. The haughtiness of those females descended from Montrose was a byword throughout the kingdom. It was there in Eloise—an indefinable quality that showed itself in her carriage, in the set of her head, in the regal sway of her slim hips.

Pride—women's pride.

Raoul ached to crush it.

Smoothly, he leaned forward and ran a blunt fingertip down the back of Eloise's hand, molded about the wedding goblet.

Eloise didn't jump; her control held firm, despite the rigidity that gripped her.

She turned to face Raoul, her lips curving, her eyes wary. "Yes, lord?"

Pale, almost opaque eyes held hers. "How now, wife?"

When she made no reply, Raoul reached for the goblet. Lifting it from her hands, his unnerving eyes holding hers, he drained the goblet in one gulp. Setting it aside, he returned her smile. "Tis time to retire. Summon your lady mother and do so."

Eloise knew, then, that her amorphous, ill-defined fears were not groundless. The coldness in her husband's eyes promised some terror she couldn't comprehend beyond the fact that it frightened her. But never would she show him or any man fear; she inclined her head in an unconsciously regal manner. "As you wish, lord."

As Eloise turned away to catch her mother's eye, Raoul's expression hardened, but he was smiling good-humoredly when the ladies, with light laughter and smiles, stole her from him. The men closed about him, eager and raucous.

Eloise allowed herself to be led upstairs. She let her mind flow into the chatter of her mothers' ladies and the high-born guests who had been invited to take part in the ritual.

In the bridal chamber, she stood silently as they removed her headdress and unplaited and brushed her long hair, then removed her wedding gown, the gold embroidered surcote trimmed with ermine and pearls and the tight-fitting silk cote. There were giggles as her garters and hose were rolled down; the giggles died as her chemise was removed and she stood naked, tall and slender, her body not yet fully formed.

Her fifteenth birthday was a month away; while her bones had finished growing, flesh had yet to soften the contours. She was painfully aware of her adolescent body; a soft blush tinged her cheeks. Then a fine linen nightrail, embroidered by her mother, was dropped over her head and pulled down.

Soft hands urged her into the big bed plumped high with featherbeds and covered with satin and furs. She moved in a daze, distanced from the proceedings. Mayhap if she held fast to her mental sanctuary, the nightmare lurking in her husband's eyes wouldn't reach her.

The touch of her mother's lips on her forehead, the unexpected sight of tears in the dark eyes so like her own, forced her to return to earth. She managed a weak smile.

The door burst open.

Chaos invaded, along with a host of drunken knights who had carried her husband, stripped to nothing more than his braies, up the stairs. It was plainly their intention to deposit him beside her, but to her surprise, he broke free, and, aided by her father, turned the rowdy crowd, ladies and all, from the room.

The melee retreated, leaving Raoul leaning back against the door. Seeing a bolt beside his head, he slid it into place, then straightened.

His pale eyes found Eloise, sitting primly against the pillows.

Raoul let his lips curve cruelly; he was no longer restrained by the need to ensure the wedding took place. Eloise was his now—his to tame, his to break.

Coldly viewing her, he untied the girdle of his braies, then stripped off the linen folds. Flinging the garment aside, he stalked, naked, across the room. He halted a yard from the bed, hands on his hips, feet apart, legs braced.

Eloise could not tear her eyes from him. With four brothers and the run of a castle packed with warrior males, she'd seen naked men aplenty, but few had been as aroused as Raoul de Cannar—none as menacing. She forced her gaze upward, over his chest, broad and covered with a pelt of black hair, to his hard, shadowed jaw, to his contemptuous smile. His eyes were as cold as a winter's fog.

"Get out of bed."

The words were steely, the command inflexible. Eloise obeyed, as she'd vowed that very afternoon to do. Slipping from beneath the covers, she stood before him. With an effort, she kept her head high.

That action sealed her fate.

Rage welled behind Raoul's dark mask, but he'd learned to control and conceal his emotions. Every instinct impelled him to sink his fingers into the rich mahogany tresses spilling down Eloise's back, to rip her nightrail from her and take her as violently as he wished; her screams would be heard, but no one would intrude, not even her family, the haughty de Versallets. The satisfaction would be great—the idea was sorely tempting.

But Raoul needed this alliance. If her family ever learned that he had mistreated her, he would receive none of the military support he was counting on. If he showed her less respect than they expected, then went out on a limb, they would let him hang. He hadn't gambled half his income for that.

Plumbing the dark depths of Eloise's eyes, he allowed his features to contort with the lust he no longer needed to conceal. "Take it off."

Eloise blinked then obeyed, forcing her stiff fingers to the laces. The tension gripping the dark body towering before her was palpable. Raoul didn't move as she tugged the fine shift off over her head and laid it on the bed. Inwardly quivering, she turned back to face him, pale, composed, her gaze distant.

Raoul's gaze touched hers, then he looked down, boldly assessing.

Eloise held herself proudly, the fine bones of her shoulders and long limbs outlined beneath her delicate skin. Her breasts were small, mere suggestions of what was to come. Her waist was indented above slim hips, not narrow so much as unformed. The long sweeps of her thighs were sleekly muscled; she was tall as women went. Overall, her figure was boyish, yet distinctly feminine.

The sight pleased Raoul immensely. With a smile of brutish anticipation, he raised his eyes. "Turn around."

Eloise obeyed.

From behind her came silence.

Eloise's senses pricked wildly, trying to gauge Raoul's intentions. Oddly, the sight of her girlish body had, if anything, aroused him further. It was a struggle to keep her limbs from shaking—to keep breathing—yet she refused to give way to her fear.

Hard, calloused hands reached around her, capturing her breasts.

Eloise suppressed a shocked start.

Raoul kneaded firmly, then with thumbs and forefingers captured her nipples and squeezed. She frowned. Before she could decide on any comment, he released her nipples; hands surrounding her breasts, he pressed against her.

She sucked in a breath. With a powerful motion, he ground his hips against her, his thrusting manhood, hard and hot, riding in the cleft of her bottom.

Taut, tense, her thoughts chaotic, Eloise stood stiff and unmoving.

To her relief, Raoul stepped back; she drew in a quick breath. His hands shifted, one lowering to splay across her belly; with the other, he gripped her nape, then, slowly, traced callused fingertips down her spine.

Eloise's eyes widened, then she let her lids fall. Fists clenched, rigid yet quivering, she forced herself to suffer her husband's touch.

Coldly, clinically, Raoul appraised the smooth, ivory globes of his wife's bottom, fondling, probing. His lips lifted in a satyric leer. She would serve him well. He would get heirs on her; she would also give him great pleasure. Satisfied, he looked up, and noted her clenched jaw; his eyes gleamed.

Smiling coldly, he released her. "Get into bed."

Eloise complied. She reached for the covers; rounding the bed, Raoul pulled them away.

"Not yet. I want to look at you."

Stiffly, Eloise lay back and wondered if she dared close her eyes. Raoul sprawled beside her, then came up on one elbow to examine her. After a long, thorough inspection, his eyes lifted to hers, his gaze penetrating, then he flopped back on the bed. "Go to sleep."

Slowly, Eloise turned her head. He lay on his back, one arm across his eyes, the other at his groin. Caution suggested she obey unquestioningly, but she had to ask; she couldn't bear not knowing. "You wish to sleep first?"

He raised his arm. His eyes searched hers, then he lay back, his arm once more screening his face. "I'm not going to take you tonight. I've decided to train you first."

"T-train?"

"I'm a demanding lover. I'll teach you what I expect before I take you."

Eloise lay back and stared at the canopy. Gradually, it dawned that, given the choice, she'd rather lose her maidenhead tonight, knowing her mother would be near in the morning. Tomorrow, they were to leave for Cannar Castle, many miles distant. Besides, she'd been keyed up to play her part, to lie dutifully beneath him regardless of whether he pleasured her or not. "It won't do. What about the sheets?"

Her calm question drew Raoul from his absorption. After a moment, he heaved a sigh and rose. Crossing the room to where his squire had left his clothes for the morrow, he located his belt knife. On the way back to the bed, he noticed a songbird tethered to a perch. "Perfect."

In a second, the songbird was dead.

Stifling a cry, Eloise scooted back against the pillows, watching, horrified, as her husband held the dripping carcass so that blood artistically splattered the sheets.

"There." Raoul strode to the window, pulled back the shutters and flung the dead bird into the blackness outside.

Eloise thought her heart would choke her. She watched Raoul stride to the chest, swiping up a towel to wipe his hands and knife. Struggling to breathe, she reminded herself she'd never liked songbirds, not tethered ones, anyway. By the time Raoul returned to the bed, she'd stifled her reaction sufficiently to ease down, avoiding the bright red splotches on the sheets. She made no further attempt to argue his intentions.

When he fell back in the same position as before, and said nothing, Eloise risked closing her eyes. Subduing her inner trembling was imperative.

Raoul had left the shutters open; a cool breeze wafted in, raising goosebumps. Cracking open her eyes, she spied the covers tangled at the foot of the bed. Half sitting, she reached for them.

"Not yet. I'm not finished."

Finished? Eloise glanced at Raoul. The hand at his groin was curved about his thick member, moving rhythmically up and down the turgid length. For a moment, Eloise simply stared, then her cheeks flamed.

From under his arm, eyes agleam, Raoul watched her.

Wrenching her gaze away, Eloise lay down. Rigid, her arms at her sides, she stared at the canopy.

Raoul laughed; the harsh sound shredded the silence and echoed through the chamber. His hand left his groin; he reached for her hand, then hesitated.

"Turn over."

Eloise obeyed.

Grinning coldly, Raoul changed hands, lowering the one he'd used to shade his eyes to his groin, while with his right hand he reached for his wife's delectable bottom. She went even more rigid, but, as he'd expected, she made no demur. Feeling her flesh beneath his hard fingers, he closed his eyes and gave himself up to his quest.

Her crimson cheeks pressed to the pillow, Eloise suffered his pleasure in silence. He didn't hurt her, but his probing fingers filled her with shame. Even when, with a deep groan, he achieved his release, his fingers didn't leave her, but continued to play until, finally, apparently satisfied, he turned over and went to sleep.

One by one the candles guttered; blessed darkness blanketed the room. Even so, it was many hours before, exhausted, Eloise fell asleep.

A single question had dominated her mind.

What manner of marriage was this?

Chapter 1

Versallet Castle
Late August, nine years later

"By all the saints! What's *wrong* with dancing girls?" William de Versallet, broad as a destrier's rear and equally uncompromising, planted his feet on the battlements and glared at his sister.

Eloise glared back. "I am trying," she enunciated witheringly, "to ensure the celebrations in honor of your marriage maintain an appropriate tone."

"Tone?" William looked thunderstruck. "There's nothing amiss with the tone of dancing girls—it's what the men expect."

"Aye—what the *men* expect. But what of the ladies?" Eloise whirled to include the woman standing behind her. "What do you imagine *your wife* thinks of dancing girls?"

William glanced down at the pale, sweet-faced child he'd married a month before.

Suddenly finding herself at the center of this typical de Versallet dispute, and not being a de Versallet but a much more timid sort of mortal, Julia wrung her hands. Like a startled fawn, she stared at her huge husband.

William smiled perfunctorily. "You see nothing wrong with having dancing girls at the banquet tonight, do you, Julia?"

Blue eyes darting from one overpowering de Versallet to the other, Julia blinked. "I...that is..." She swallowed. "If that is what you wish, my lord." Submissively, she bowed her head.

For a long, silent moment, Eloise stared at that down-bent head, at the sheen of blond hair showing through Julia's veil. She resisted the urge to grind her teeth, and remembered to relax her fingers from the fists they'd curled into before turning back to her brother. She met his gaze coldly. "I'll tell Sir John to hire the troupe presently in the outer bailey."

William beamed. "Good." Still grinning, he added, "You won't be disappointed."

The glare Eloise hurled him sizzled. Chuckling, he lumbered off.

Lips compressed, Eloise turned to her sister-in-law. "Truly, Julia, if you're to make any mark in this castle, which, one day, will be yours to run, you must start acting as its lady. You know you will not enjoy seeing the men ogling and pawing the dancing girls."

Julia lifted a face so disarmingly mild not even the devil could remain irate. "Oh, but…if it pleases my lord…"

Smothering a snort, Eloise refrained from further expostulation. Chiding Julia was pointless. She would let William clomp roughshod over her as long as that was the easiest course, then, years from now, she would carp and complain that he paid her wishes no heed. Julia's future was Julia's concern—Eloise had a castle to run.

"I must find Sir John." Sir John Mattingly, her father's steward, would not be surprised by her order. Eloise left the castle-side of the battlements, but instead of heading for the stairs, she glided to the northwest corner, to where the rising expanse of Salisbury Plain hid the distant Welsh hills.

Timidly, Julia followed. "You often look out that way—what can you see?"

"'Tis the direction in which my old convent lies."

"Claerwhen?"

"Aye—in the shadow of the Black Mountains, in the valley of the Dore."

"Do you pray for assistance?"

"Nay." Eloise smiled wryly. "Merely for strength." Patience, actually, but then, these days, that was often the same thing.

"You spent years there, didn't you? After your husband died, I mean?"

"Aye, twas my sanctuary." A place to heal and grow. To recover from her month-long marriage, a marriage ended when the saints had heard her prayers and had released her from purgatory in the only possible way. With a lightning bolt, they had removed Raoul de Cannar from this earth, and had set her free. As free as a woman could ever be. "As a wealthy widow, there was much they could yet teach me, and I was eager to learn."

So she could remain free, and retain control over her own life.

Leaning on the battlements, she gazed at the distant horizon. "There was also the matter of my jointure—my husband's family tried to deny it me, but Claerwhen came to my aid."

Faced with a writ and the threat of a Chancery suit, the de Cannars had capitulated. For the past nine years, Eloise had received half the yearly profits of their extensive estates. As the brother who had succeeded Raoul had proved remarkably talented in commerce, her accumulated wealth—much to the de Cannars' disgust—now approached the legendary.

Almost enough to make her forget the month she had spent with Raoul.
Her expression blanking, she straightened.

Julia was still frowning. "But you must have been quite young—did not
your parents wish you to return here?"

"Aye, they did." But Eloise had been too wary to risk it—to risk being
given in marriage again, used as a pawn to cement some other alliance. "But I
wished to remain in the peace of the cloister."

Julia's glance was shy. "You must have loved him very much."

Eloise didn't answer.

"And you only came back when your mother died?"

"Not immediately. But when my father came and begged me to return, I
could not say him nay."

That still surprised her. Her mother's death five years ago had rung in
the changes. Eloise had already begun questioning her continued presence at
Claerwhen. The peace and quiet had grown monotonous; a curious
restlessness had gripped her. Her studies were long completed and there was
nothing to fill the void. Even so, she had ignored her father's and brothers'
written pleas. Then, unheralded, her father had arrived. On seeing how deeply
her mother's death had affected him, and hearing how sincere was his plea,
she could no longer deny him. She had returned to Versallet Castle.

"And you've been chatelaine here ever since." Julia made it sound like
the triumphant ending to a tale.

Her expression hardening, Eloise inclined her head. Despite William's
marriage, despite her father remarrying two years ago, *she* was still chatelaine
of Versallet Castle.

The fact filled her with no joy—neither Emma, the new lady de
Versallet, nor Julia, she of fawnlike fright, could stand up to her father and
four brothers. She, on the other hand, could, and did. She might lose a few
battles, such as the one this morn, yet overall she managed the castle much as
she wished.

As her mother would have wished.

Elaine of Montrose had had very definite ideas, frequently and clearly
stated ideas, on how far the male of the species could be allowed to run amok
before the sobering hand of a lady was brought to bear. Eloise had discovered
that she was very much her mother's daughter.

Glancing at Julia, she ventured, "Once you're ready to take up the reins,
I'll gladly pass them on."

"Oh! *Nay!*" Eyes wide, Julia all but flapped. "You do such a…a
remarkable job—why, no one would want you to stop."

Eloise grimaced. *That* was true. Everyone, from her father to the
villeins in the fields, turned to her, and, far more than she, would resent any
incompetent replacement. "Twill have to happen someday. As I told you this
morn, you—and Emma, too—must learn to treat with your men. I'll allow
they are oftimes thickheaded, but if you insist, they'll come to terms."

Leaning against the battlements, she frowned sternly at Julia. "It may be an effort, but it must be made if you're to forge a partnership—tis the only true measure of successful marriage." Her mother had been her father's right hand, and, to give the devil his due, he had always treated her as his queen.

"But there's no real need." Julia smiled placatingly. "While you're here, everything will run smoothly."

Eloise bit her tongue. Something would have to be done. Unfortunately, it was now impossible for her to live at the castle and not be its chatelaine. Perhaps it was time to return to Claerwhen.

Straightening, she drifted along the battlements to glance down at the bustle in the courtyard below. Julia trailed after her.

This time, Claerwhen could not be the answer, not permanently. She was not cut out for the cloister; that much she knew. Unfortunately, thanks to Raoul, the only other acceptable career for a noblewoman was no longer a possibility for her.

Once, she had dreamed of being the lady of a castle, her children about her, a strong husband at her side.

Her dreams had turned to dust.

With a brisk shake of her head, she resettled her veil. "Come—I must find Sir John."

Together, she and Julia headed for the stairs, nodding to the guards as they passed. Eloise led the way down.

She had vowed she would let no man take her dead husband's place.

Her lips curved, cynical humor returning. Adhering to that vow had cost her no pain, and had provided hours of entertainment through the years.

Raoul's private legacy to her.

Pausing by an arrow slit, she peered down, and drew a determined breath, forcing her mind from the memories that still haunted her, dwelling instead on the amusement she felt at the continuing interest in her as a bride, and the bewildered frustration she delighted in placing in so many men's eyes.

Amidst the bustle in the courtyard, she spied her father striding through the melee, bellowing orders right and left. His harassed steward scuttled in his wake. Turning from the sight, she continued down the stair.

To give her sire his due, he hadn't pressed her to remarry. Neither had her brothers. They continued to introduce the subject along with potential suitors, but she only had to shake her head and they would retreat. Puzzled, but accepting.

Julia murmured an excuse and parted from her, heading for the solar.

Smiling wryly, Eloise stepped into the hall. She suspected her brothers thought they were doing her a favor by offering up all the eligible males they could find. They couldn't fathom how she, their sister, could stomach a celibate life. They, poor souls, driven by their apparently unrestrainable urges, simply couldn't understand her.

But she understood them. Very well.

She knew that the service of the castle whores was not restricted to the de Versallet men-at-arms, but, on occasion, was solicited by their masters. To her mind, if neither Emma nor Julia felt inclined to protest, then she could hardly do so. Her father and brothers were only men, after all.

Men. She could see that they might serve some purpose in the greater design of the cosmos, but, for her, they were largely redundant. There was very little she needed of them. Yet women of her station had to pander to their whims, and today their whims meant dancing girls.

Halting at the top of the keep steps, she saw her father still bending his steward's ear. Rather than expose herself to her sire's innumerable questions on duties she had already performed, she summoned one of the pages.

"Tell Sir John I wish him to hire the troupe of dancers waiting in the outer bailey." Absentmindedly, she pulled the young page's jupon straight and settled his girdle more levelly. "The usual rates. We'll need them immediately the last course is cleared."

"Aye, lady." The page suffered her ministrations with resignation, flashing her a smile when she released him with a nod.

Eloise watched him wriggle through the crowd. Hands rising to her hips, she surveyed the noisy courtyard. The tournament announced by her father to celebrate his eldest son's nuptials, formalized a month before at Julia's father's keep, was due to start tomorrow. The guests would roll up through the afternoon; she had already organized the evening banquet. The rooms were prepared; dinner had been served and cleared. There was nothing more to do, to oversee.

Glancing at the sun, Eloise estimated that it was just after midday. The notion of sitting with Emma and Julia in the solar, quietly embroidering until the sound of arrivals summoned them, did not appeal.

With a last glance around, Eloise turned inside.

Twenty minutes later, garbed in nondescript brown, she nudged her palfrey through the postern gate. She had avoided her father and brothers; they would insist she take a full escort even though she wasn't going far. Her drab cote was sufficiently like those of merchants' daughters to pass without comment; her telltale hair was hidden beneath a simple wimple and veil. Her palfrey, of course, bespoke her station, but she wasn't trying to fool anyone, just avoid notice. The guards at the postern knew her too well to question her.

A plank bridge had been rolled out to ford the moat, giving the serfs bringing in produce easier access to the bailey. Within minutes of leaving the castle, Eloise was cantering along the ride leading south along the Bourne, skirting the outliers of the forest.

There was another, more practical reason for her drab clothing. She had recalled that the swineherd had gone to round up his charges. The main herd with the fattening pigs had been taken to pannage in the forest, an annual treat. Rounding up the piglets was a game for many; most of the castle children would be helping the swineherd today. There would be laughter and plenty of innocent play.

She felt sure that, by the time she found the herd, she would have invented a reason for joining them.

* * *

Deep in the forest where the boughs of old oaks intertwined overhead, a group of horsemen plodded along, followed by three swaying wagons.

"There." Alaun de Montisfryth, first earl of Montisfryn, pointed to where the stream they were following widened into a deep pool.

"Perfect." The rider alongside him craned his head to look. "Sweet water to wash away the dust." Roland de Haverthorne slanted a glance at his cousin. "Of the road and, perchance, from your memory?"

Alaun grunted.

The party dismounted, tethering their palfreys close by the pool. Within minutes, all ten knights had stripped and plunged into the clear water. Their squires scurried about, collecting discarded clothes and laying out their masters' armor.

With smooth, powerful strokes, Alaun swam to the pool's center, dove, then resurfaced, and slicked back his wet hair from his face. The water was cool on his sun-warmed skin. They'd ridden hard from Amesbury; the wagons and destriers, sent out before dawn, had been overtaken on the road. Now, with his party gathered, he was intent on ensuring they presented a suitably imposing spectacle when they rode through the gates of Versallet Castle.

Looking around, he saw the squires, their chores completed, hanging back in groups. "You, too."

The order was greeted with dismay, but obeyed instantly. Noting the reluctance with which his own squire, Bilder, a veteran of numerous campaigns, stripped off his short cote, Alaun shook his head. "Why is it that a man has to reach knighthood before he'll willingly bathe?"

"The saints only know," Roland returned, stroking past. "Still, the poor bastards have been up half the night polishing our armor until it gleams, so perhaps you should let them off lightly."

"They can have an early night tonight."

"What? And miss the banquet and all the excitement?"

"What excitement?"

"Why, the excitement that's bound to ensue when you challenge someone, or run someone through, or whatever it is you have in mind to pay back old Henry Hardnose for beating you into the dust nine years ago." Eyes half closed, Roland tensed, waiting for some response to that taunt.

But Alaun merely humphed and turned to float on his back. "It's just a tournament."

"Ah, I see. Just a general, run-of-the-mill tournament, which just happened to hold sufficient attraction for you to turn aside from our long-awaited journey home—to your estates, which, as you well know, are crying out for your attention. This despite the fact that you, not to say we, have had a bellyful of tournaments in the recent past, having had to sit through a year of siege in company with a king who reaches for a lance on the way to the garderobe."

A rumbling chuckle vibrated through the water. "Edward's not that bad."

"I'll remind you you said that when you receive your next royal summons. How long do you imagine that will be after our esteemed sovereign returns to these fair shores?"

Alaun groaned, but didn't open his eyes.

When his liege lord remained silent, Roland prompted, "Just to appease my curiosity, *are* you going to challenge de Versallet?"

Alaun sighed. "Why do I put up with you, Roland?

"Because I amuse you," Roland replied. "And because you know you can rely on me to cover your back."

Rolling over, Alaun met Roland's eyes, then turned and stroked for the shore. Roland followed. As they rose, water coursing down bodies hardened by two years of almost constant campaigning, let alone the years before that, Alaun stated, "I have no plans to challenge de Versallet. I'm not even sure I'll enter the lists."

Roland accepted the rough towel his squire, also naked and dripping, hurried to hand him. These days, Alaun frequently sat out from tournaments, his experience and enormous strength making him a formidable opponent at even the highest levels of chivalry. No one in their right mind would look him in the eye and call him coward for it. Yet Roland would have sworn that competing was the purpose behind their present excursion.

They'd landed in England four days ago, having departed for France more than a year before. As Earl of Montisfryn and one of the Marcher lords, Alaun had joined Edward in most of his recent campaigns, this last proving no exception. The Montisfryn banner had flown to the left of the Prince of Wales's standard at Crecy, the commanders in charge of the Prince's battle having specifically requested Alaun to take that position. As their request had been followed by an essentially identical one from the Prince's father, an old and valued friend, there they had been, in the thick of it.

While at Crecy the result had been glory for all, Roland, for one, considered his cousin's pre-eminence a mite hazardous. That had proved true when Edward had moved on to lay siege to Calais. While many of the other commanders of rank had been allowed to retire from the field, Edward had requested—such a diplomatic way of describing it—Alaun and a number of his similarly experienced vassals to remain and provide the mainstay of his besieging force.

A full year spent outside Calais had tried their courage in ways battle never had. In the end, however, even boredom and sickness had been defeated, along with the burghers of Calais. Even Edward had had a change of heart, dispatching Alaun back to England immediately the town's gates had been opened and the booty distributed.

Roland hadn't believed it until he'd learned that Edward, as canny as ever, had realized that, with Roger de Mortimer a mere lad of sixteen, with Alaun still away, there was a large section of the Welsh border defenses which had been without strong leadership for nearly two years. The Welsh border was not a district it was safe to leave poorly tended for long.

So they had commandeered four ships and set sail, the cogs wallowing deep with the weight of their accumulated booty. The saints had smiled and the crossing had been peaceful. From Southampton, they had commenced their long trek, a line of heavy wagons rumbling between detachments of archers and men-at-arms. With over one hundred knights and men-at-arms, and more than five hundred archers, together with the inevitable camp-followers of assorted trades, their cavalcade resembled a small army.

They'd camped outside Amesbury last night. A squire, released to visit the town, had returned hotfoot with the news of a noble tournament, open to all comers. Alaun had shown little interest—until the squire mentioned the name of the castle hosting the tournament. Then, of course, the orders had come; no drawing straws this time, just the pick of Alaun's knights.

Handing his towel back to his squire, Roland accepted his braies, then his hose. He was shrugging on his shirt when the first shrieks drifted through the trees.

Every man in the clearing froze.

The shrieks continued, high-pitched, feminine, clearly shrieks of enjoyment.

Roland glanced at Alaun. His cousin, still bare-chested, slowly rose from the rock on which he'd been sitting. Hands on his hips, he listened to the sounds of high-flown revelry percolating through the forest. Every one of his men was watching him.

Alaun slanted a questioning glance at Roland.

Roland sent the glance right back.

Alaun's lips curved. Shrugging lightly, he headed for the festivity.

His men were right behind him.

* * *

In a forest clearing two hundred yards away, Eloise held her aching sides as yet another of the swineherd's rowdy helpers landed on their backs. While the heavy sows were placid and easily herded, the piglets were running amok. Every time one struggled free, squealing at the top of its lungs, it spurred the others on to greater efforts. Despite the sizeable force the swineherd had assembled, the pigs were winning.

Just then, a pink bundle on tiny legs streaked in her direction. The cobbler's son, in hot pursuit, tripped over his own toes and went sprawling. Infected by the gaiety, Eloise dispensed with dignity and pounced on the piglet. She trapped it between her skirts, which it had tried to run right through.

Within seconds, she discovered why it was taking so long to capture a few piglets. Every time she tried to gather the squirming bundle to her, it wriggled out of her arms. Determined to conquer, she bent over the piglet; bracing her legs, trapping its undulating body between her feet, she gripped its front trotters.

She was about to straighten and hoist her captive into the air when a very large, definitely masculine hand stroked slowly, leisurely, and all too knowingly, over her bottom.

Eloise shot upright, pig and all. Her breath stuck in her throat—she couldn't even gasp. Furious, panicked, and a great deal more, she rounded on her attacker, purposefully swinging the piglet before her. As she completed the half circle, she let go.

Alaun barely had time to register a pair of flashing dark eyes, and the fact the woman was uncommonly tall, before thirty pounds of squealing piglet slammed into his chest. Instinctively, he caught the beast, stepping back with the impact.

His heel caught in a tree root; the piglet heaved.

The next thing Alaun knew he was measuring his length on the forest floor, a virago—she was definitely his vision of a virago, her hair tumbling loose from beneath her veil, rippling in a dark river all the way to her hips, with lightning in her eyes and scorn on her lips—standing over him, hands on her hips, pointedly inquiring, "One of your relations, I presume?"

With that, she swung around and stalked off.

Eloise marched a good ten paces before what she'd seen impinged on her brain.

She halted, raised her head. She blinked, then swung around and stared.

The piglet, released, ran off, squealing, to join its fellows. Slowly, her attacker sat up. Muscles rippled under golden skin stretched over a stomach resembling one of her serving women's washer boards—ridged and rock-hard. Her gaze traveled upward across what seemed acres of tanned flesh, a generous dusting of golden hair gilding the smooth contours. His shoulders seemed impossibly large. Her palms prickled. The thews of upper arms and thighs were all in proportion, yet, for all that, he did not seem overly muscled. She decided he was just plain huge. He was wearing braies and mailed hose, which observation answered several questions. He was doubtless a knight on his way to her father's tournament.

Suddenly realizing what she was doing, she jerked her gaze up to the stranger's face.

His body had stopped her in her tracks. His face hit her like a blow—she couldn't have breathed to save herself. His forehead was broad under a mane of wavy, golden-brown hair. His nose, and the set of his mouth and chin, informed her that he was no mere knight—this man commanded. His eyes, well-spaced under straight brows, were tawny golden, too.

They were watching her, a speculative glint flaring in their depths.

As the full impact of his presence registered, Eloise watched one tawny brow rise.

A slow, thoroughly suggestive smile softened the line of his lips.

Eloise stiffened. She let fly with a scorching glance, then turned on her heel and stalked off.

She'd tethered her palfrey out of the way, beside a fallen tree close by the edge of the forest. It was the work of a minute to regain her saddle. Her composure would take much longer.

Muttering curses beneath her breath, she swung her horse toward the ford. Minutes later, she was cantering across open ground heading straight for the safety of the castle.

From the shadows of the forest, Alaun watched her go. Predictably, Roland materialized at his elbow, chortling uncontrollably.

"One of your easier conquests?" Roland eventually managed.

Alaun turned and met his gaze. "One of my more intriguing conquests." Without another word, he headed back to the stream.

Chapter 2

"Indeed, Sir Percy. Tis a pleasure to see you again, too." Summoning one of her minions, Eloise directed, "A chamber in the west wing, Alwyn."

With a regal nod, Eloise dismissed Sir Percy, mentally as well as physically, and returned to her position behind the keep door. To carefully peer out.

It was not general practice for a chatelaine to thus efface herself, but she'd insisted that today only Emma and Julia should stand at the top of the keep steps, flanking her father and William as they welcomed all those who had answered the call to arms. Her tone had been sufficiently shrewish to ensure none had argued.

From her vantage point, she had screened each party of guests, but had yet to sight the stranger's face. Or his body. She wasn't sure which had made the greater impression. Never in her life had a man affected her so; she was anxious to discover if the affliction was permanent, not least so she could take appropriate steps to counter it.

She'd ridden back to the castle in an uncharacteristic dither, nearly riding down one of the guards in the barbican. All the way back, and for hours later, she had felt that knowing hand on her bottom. The predatory curve of the stranger's lips was indelibly imprinted on her mind. Yet what truly puzzled her—what had sent a wary shiver through her normally unshakeable resolve—was that while both touch and seductive smile had evoked strong memories of Raoul, that hadn't dampened her interest.

For the last nine years, the lightest caress, the veriest hint of such a smile, had sent her rigid. Even this afternoon, while she'd been greeting the lord of Hightham's party, one of his knights who knew her not had candidly looked her over. With luck, the hapless fool would thaw out before the banquet.

Peering through the shadows, she frowned. The sinking sun was gilding the gray stone of the keep. The courtyard was still crowded, the newcomers leaving their allotted quarters to chat and watch the later arrivals, while the serfs and craftsmen who had labored all day drifted home. The incoming stream, however, had dwindled to an intermittent trickle. And the stranger hadn't appeared.

Beneath her breath, she swore. Relief was not what she felt, and she didn't like to think why.

Disgusted with her unlooked-for sensibility, she gathered her skirts. Her father and brother might as well abandon their positions and retire to make ready for the banquet. She stepped forward—

A horn sounded.

The single brazen note echoed from keep and wall, a clarion announcing the arrival of some significant noble.

Just what she needed—unexpected nobility. Swallowing her curses, Eloise swung about. "You—Eadith." She pointed to a maid. "Run and prepare the main chamber in the south tower. Find some others to help— quickly now!"

It was the room below Eloise's own, the one she had hoped to keep free as a ladies' bower, but that couldn't be helped. She couldn't rearrange the entire keep for one man. There was space in the barracks and lower floors for lesser knights, but their master, whoever he was, would have to be well-quartered.

Turning back to the courtyard, she was just in time to see a pennon, dipped to pass through the tunnel leading from the outer bailey, emerge into the sunlight. As the banner was raised, she, along with everyone else in the assembled throng, struggled to make out the emblem. A dragon? Entwined with a lion rampant? The primary colors were scarlet and gold.

Eloise tried to recall the device. It was not local, that she would swear. The shape of the banner declared the owner an earl. The Earl of what?

Montisfryn.

The name came to her on whispers, rising from the crowd like startled butterflies. The rider carrying the standard rode forward; he was followed by more, carrying pennon and banner. The crowd was fairly awash with whispers now. A glance at her father and brother was uninformative, other than telling her they knew who this was. Both men stood proudly erect, feet apart, fists on hips, towering over their diminutive ladies. This was no ordinary unexpected guest. Both Emma and Julia had sensed the expectation in their husbands, yet, from their faces, knew no more than she.

Who *was* the Earl of Montisfryn?

The knights made their entrance in half-armor—richly embroidered surcotes over mail, their heraldic arms emblazoned on their shields, specific features of their devices repeated on each surcote and on their destriers' magnificent caparisons. Plumed, crested helms covered the warriors' heads.

The setting sun caught their lance-points, adding more gold to the show.

Dragging her gaze from the spectacular sight, Eloise glanced at the crowd. They were, one and all, mesmerized. Whoever he was, the Earl of Montisfryn knew the value of a grand entrance.

Returning her gaze to the knights as they approached at a stately walk, the heavy thud of chargers walking in unison reverberating like a drumbeat between the walls, Eloise felt the faint stirrings of respect. The gesture had been gauged to a nicety. Her father had straightened perceptibly; it was an honor to have a great knight appear in such style. It would ensure the tournament was talked of for months, if not longer.

Her gaze fastened on the knight in the lead. The Earl of Montisfryn had a magnificent pair of shoulders...

Eloise froze. Eyes widening, she scanned the rest of the knight—the arms, the thighs—it *could* be the same man. Her heart thudding in her throat, she waited, barely breathing as the earl halted his destrier before the keep steps.

Alaun let a pregnant moment pass while through his visor he eyed his old adversary. Henry de Versallet had grown older—too old to fight. His son, however, looked to be a prime specimen, an opponent capable of giving him a fair match. Moving with his habitual deliberation, Alaun reached up and removed his helm. The nine knights at his back did the same.

Behind the door, Eloise pressed a hand to her lips, choking back her exclamation. She closed her eyes, uttered a quick prayer, then opened them again, but the sight before her remained unchanged. Stiffening, her heart thumping, she swung about and stalked deeper into the hall.

Out on the steps, Henry gestured grandly. "Welcome, Lord de Montisfryth. My house is honored to receive you."

Alaun allowed one brow to rise. He dismounted; his knights followed suit. With him at their head, they trooped up the steps.

Alaun attended the introductions with half an ear, lazily scanning the crowd. He took note of William, measuring the heavily-built knight even as William returned the compliment. After greeting Lady de Versallet and William's wife with courtly courtesy, drawing awed glances from them both, he gave his attention to his host.

Henry was frowning, peering into the shadows about the keep door. "My daughter, Eloise, was about." Henry glanced at him. "You might remember her—twas the tournament for her wedding you were here for last."

"Ah, yes." Alaun smiled coolly. "The time I lost my father's palfrey. To you." He paused, but Henry made no response. "Lady de Cannar, if I recall aright." He vaguely remembered the skinny girl whose nuptials had cost him his father's prize stallion.

Henry snorted. "Not any more. De Cannar died. Eloise is chatelaine here—she'll attend to any needs you might have."

Alaun inclined his head. Introduced to Sir John Mattingly, he consented to be led to his chamber.

As the other guests dispersed, Albert d'Albron joined Henry at the top of the keep steps. "Your prediction of nine years ago has come true, it seems. Your old sparring partner's son has certainly grown into that body of his."

"Aye, and from all I've heard, he's learned to use it most effectively." Henry rubbed his hands together, anticipation lighting his face. "His presence is a coup, no doubt of that. The man's a born fighter. I've heard tales aplenty of Montisfryn's prowess—it looks like at last I'll see the phenomenon in the flesh."

Gleefully, Henry clapped Albert on the shoulder. Together, they entered the keep.

* * *

In a chamber off the entrance hall, Eloise pored over a slate, a chalk gripped tightly between her fingers.

The door opened, and she glanced up.

Blanche, Lady of Selborough, Albert d'Albron's daughter and Eloise's oldest friend, looked in. "Problems?"

Eloise returned to the slate. "May the saints fly away with the man—he's *ruined* my table!"

Blanche chuckled and closed the door. "I'd have thought he'd *make* your table."

"He's an *earl*—curse his golden hide. He's the ranking nobleman. I'll have to put him at the lord's table, and at Emma's side."

"Lucky Emma."

Eloise snorted. "She'll probably turn green when she realizes."

"Surely she's not still so nervous?"

"She is." Eloise paused, then smiled. "In fact, it won't surprise me if she can't find two words to say to him."

The door opened to admit Sir John. Eloise waved him forward. "Here is the new seating for the lord's table. There are to be *no* last minute alterations, no matter *what* any knight—or noble—might say. Is that clear?"

Sir John, who had served at the castle since Eloise was a child, smiled. "Aye, lady. I will see to it."

With a heavy sigh, Eloise rose. "Come, my Lady of Selborough." She waved Blanche toward the door. "Tis time for us to change."

Blanche's husband had been detained—a little matter of a rebellious vassal. He was unlikely to be free in time to appear at the tournament, so Eloise had arranged for Blanche to share her chamber.

They left the room arm in arm, but Eloise was waylaid by the cellarer. Blanche, absorbed with thoughts of sartorial significance, went ahead. The sun had disappeared behind the walls before Eloise finally followed.

Her foot was on the lowest step of the tower stair when a squire, a man of indeterminate years, came hurrying down. Seeing her, he immediately halted and flattened himself against the wall. Stepping back, Eloise motioned him on. "Nay. Continue. And then I may pass easily."

The squire bobbed respectfully and dashed past. Only as Eloise started up the stair did the man's livery, scarlet with a golden lion and dragon entwined, register.

She froze, then looked up. The door to the chamber below hers lay ahead, mercifully closed. Her gaze on the panels, she climbed steadily past, then went quickly up the next flight. When her door latch fell behind her, she quietly exhaled.

"At last!"

Eloise turned to see Blanche holding up two richly embroidered surcotes, one in peacock blue, the other in vivid green.

"Which do you think? Both go with scarlet."

Blanche's silk cote was a delicate sea-green. Eloise frowned. "The green." As she headed for her chest, she added, "We won't be sitting anywhere near him, I warn you."

Her head popping up through the wide neck of the green surcote, Blanche pulled a face. "A pox on this formality. Still, there's always the dancing."

"Dancing girls."

"Eloise! How *could* you?"

"Against my better judgment." Eloise wondered if her temper would survive the night. She frowned at her stock of embroidered surcotes.

Commonsense, along with propriety, dictated that she should wear her best, yet she refused to pander to Montisfryn's vanity, as Blanche and doubtless half the other ladies would. A dusky lilac surcote she had never favored was the least likely to complement his scarlet. Unfortunately, it didn't complement her, either. With a sigh, she reached for it, then glimpsed the black velvet beneath.

For what felt like the first time in hours, she smiled. "Where's Jenni?"

Even as she spoke, the door opened and her little maid slipped in. The girl was flushed and breathless. Eloise waved her forward. "Come, Jenni. I must hurry."

With Jenni's assistance, Eloise stripped and washed, then, clad in her fine linen chemise, she sat on a stool while Jenni brushed her hair. After pulling on a pair of soled hose and gartering them above her knee, Eloise stood and donned the ivory cote she'd chosen. The garment fitted the upper half of her body snugly, the neckline so wide it left her shoulders bare. Long folds fell from her hips to the floor; the sleeves fitted like a second skin, extending beyond her wrists.

Jenni wound a finely wrought gold girdle about Eloise's hips, then climbed on the stool to lift the black velvet surcote over Eloise's head.

As the weight of the sleeveless surcote settled on her shoulders, Eloise imagined it her armor. The black was relieved by intricate gold-and-silver embroidery bordering the neckline and the elongated armholes that extended to her hips, revealing the richness of the ivory cote and gold girdle beneath. Denser embroidery filled the surcote's center panel, which narrowed to her waist before the surcote widened into the long skirt, the velvet flaring over her hips, then hanging heavy to the floor.

Settling her skirts, she straightened. "My hair. Quickly, now."

Jenni's fingers flew. The long tresses of deep, rich brown were braided and looped, with ivory ribbons entwined in the plaits. Suspended from a worked gold fillet, a gold-encrusted divided crespine, simple but elegant, enclosed the two vertical loops of plaits, one on either side of her face.

"Just my ring," Eloise called as Jenni darted to her jewel casket. Placing the single emerald on her finger, Eloise smiled smugly. Her attire was positively austere.

Finally satisfied with her own toilette, Blanche turned. "By the sainted Virgin, Eloise! You can't wear black!"

"Indeed, I can. I'm a widow, remember."

"Yes, but..." Blanche frowned.

"I'm to be the raven," Eloise informed her as she headed for the door. "The raven amid all you gaily plumed lovebirds."

With that, her head held defiantly high, she majestically swept down the stairs.

* * *

In the chamber below, Alaun lounged on the bed. He was dressed for the festivities, a heavy silk houppelande in deep forest green sheathing his shoulders, its full sleeves caught at his wrists. Soled hose of a softer green provided a subtle contrast. Short, the houppelande concealed nothing of his powerful thighs, while the goffered neckline of his fine shirt showed above the furred collar. In one hand, he clasped a chased goblet; a blood red ruby gleamed as he raised the cup to his lips and idly sipped.

From his perch on a stool by the bed, Roland, in a blue jupon over parti-colored hose, viewed his cousin with misgiving. Alaun appeared sleepily content, a relaxed lion ready to roll over and have his stomach scratched. Roland trusted the illusion not at all. "You're going to make quite a few ladies very peeved."

Alaun shrugged. "What they wear is none of my concern."

Roland raised his eyes heavenward. Alaun's casual attitude toward the fairer sex, occasionally verging on the negligent, was a byword at court. In Roland's opinion, his cousin was spoiled. Spoiled by the fact that, having been blessed with a manner both easy and courteous and a body beyond compare, the ladies flocked to his side. And his bed. The constant procession of beauties, some well-born, others less so, through the flaps of his pavilion outside Calais had spawned innumerable ditties.

But none of the women lasted long; none had proved capable of fixing Alaun's interest for longer than it took him to bed them.

However, given that the king's orders to Alaun to secure his domains had included a command to secure his succession, it was time and more, in Roland's opinion, that his cousin paid the ladies' wishes more heed.

He was about to say so when the door opened.

Bilder, Alaun's squire, entered. An unprepossessing individual with lank fair hair brushed over his head to conceal the bald patch forming on his crown, Bilder's oftimes vacant expression led the unwary to consider him wanting—an impression as erroneous as Alaun's laziness.

Alaun drained his goblet and fixed Bilder with a glittering gold stare. "Well?"

"Ain't no woman of that description in this entire castle."

Alaun grimaced. He knew Bilder too well to question his accuracy. Could she be one of de Versallet's serfs? The last thing he wanted was to have to reconnoiter the old man's nearby manors. Looking down, he studied the goblet; his fingers tightened on the stem as the image of her rose in his mind—the flashing eyes, the scornful tone. True, she'd been more amenable later, even shaken; she'd realized by then that he was knight, if not lord…

He stilled, eyes narrowing. What if it wasn't that—and it had simply been him that had done the shaking? Her horse, he would swear, had been better bred than the rouncys serfs rode.

He looked at Bilder. "Forget women. What about ladies?"

Bilder nodded. "Rovogatti checked that out. He's right quick with the maids, what with all that Latin charm. Only one possibility, though from all we can gather, she fits your bill right well."

"Who?"

The word was a command; Bilder hesitated no longer. "The old lord's daughter. A real hoity one, she is. Runs the castle, which, if I may make so bold, operates like a well-drilled army. Lady Eloise, she be."

Stunned, Roland glanced at Alaun. And the hair on his nape lifted. Alaun's expression remained relaxed, but his eyes were alight with an unholy golden flame.

"What else did Rovogatti learn of this lady?"

Bilder shifted. "I don't know as how I've the whole story, mind, but she's not married—by all accounts she's disinclined to take a husband. Too used to being her own mistress, seemingly. It's she who's the real lady here."

Alaun's eyes gleamed. "You interest me greatly."

Bilder cast him a cautious glance. "Rovogatti did say as how it seems she has no great opinion of knights, nor men in general. Wasn't actually interested, if you get my drift. Much sought after, but she brushes them all aside."

Roland smothered a groan. In his frenzied imagination, he could quite clearly see Alaun licking his lips.

His fancy was made all the more real when Alaun all but purred, "Better and better."

It was all too much for Roland. "Devil take it, Alaun—she's old de Versallet's *daughter*!"

"Sweet saints, she is." With a smile of leonine anticipation, Alaun uncoiled his long length and stood. He handed his goblet to Bilder. "She's a widow, did you know?"

Muttering curses mixed with imprecations, Roland followed Alaun out of the room.

* * *

From her seat at the end of one of the two smaller boards added at right-angles to each end of the lord's table, Eloise surveyed the hall. All was as it should be, the fire in the huge hearth already blazing while the steward's staff scurried about filling goblets. She'd given her orders; there should be little to demand her attention during the meal.

The guests, dressed in their finery, were drifting in, but the seat beside Emma remained empty. On Eloise's left, the Chevalier d'Osceux, a Gascon knight, was chattering animatedly to Blanche, beyond him.

From the gallery above the far end of the hall, the trumpeter gave a single long blast, the summons for latecomers. Of course, the sound would penetrate the thick walls only so far—a typical male conceit.

From the corner of her eye, Eloise saw movement beside Emma, and turned, prepared to witness another example of man's folly.

A single glance informed her that she'd misjudged.

Montisfryn smiled lazily down at Emma and made some remark; Eloise grasped the opportunity to study him. His choice of attire, she reluctantly conceded, was masterly. Just as she stood out—or rather, she hoped, back—from more gaudily-clad ladies, so he, with his restrained elegance, eclipsed men of lesser stature who relied on their clothing to make their mark. Montisfryn, nude, would yet look better dressed.

Unbidden, the vision of his naked torso, gleaming in the sunshine as he'd sat on the forest floor, flashed into her mind. She glanced away, annoyed to feel heat in her cheeks. Disgusted, she forced herself to look back, to prove that she could view him dispassionately—without any ridiculous fluster— only to find his gaze on her.

Despite the distance, she felt its touch. And his warm approval as his glance swept her exposed neck and shoulders. His eyes returned to her face, sleepy sensuality in the golden depths. Their gazes met—and she knew beyond doubt that what stirred behind those golden orbs was not sleepy at all. It prowled, hungry, infinitely dangerous, frighteningly fascinating.

With an effort, she tore her gaze from his, only then realizing that she needed to breathe. Dragging air into her lungs, she turned to the Chevalier. "Have you spent much time in England, sir?" She ignored Blanche's frown.

Her father entered and took his seat, and at a signal from Emma, the banquet began.

Alaun bided his time. Given the number of eyes on him, he was careful not to let his dwell overmuch on Eloise de Versallet. Other men, he noticed, were not so restrained. She was the most stunning woman in the hall. The graceful arch of her neck, exposed by her hairstyle and gown, drew male eyes like a beacon. In her black, ivory, silver, and gold, she was the raw material for any number of fantasies. The black called attention to her widowhood, the richness of the fabrics to her station, while the elegant cut of the robes set the imagination to dwell on the ripe fullness of the charms concealed.

She was temptation incarnate.

Resisting manfully, he smiled and charmed the sweet innocent at his side, for thus he saw Emma. She might lie beneath old Henry on occasion, but it was plain her lord had not married her for sons.

Memories of the previous lady de Versallet returned to him; *she* had had Henry's measure. A strong woman, a woman to bear a warrior's sons, to rule in his absence and support his position. Alaun glanced at her daughter, sitting chatting seriously to the Gascon by her side. Was Eloise de Versallet of the same ilk as her mother?

"Can I serve you some of this spiced pork, my lord?"

With a lazy smile, Alaun returned his attention to Emma.

Henry also bided his time. He waited until the fourth course of the six scheduled, the meal being of but medium size given the contests tomorrow, before taking advantage of a lull in the conversation to lean back in his great chair and, over his wife's head, address his principal guest. "The lists have been drawn, my lord of Montisfryn, yet I did not see your name among those wishful of joining the contests."

Alaun met Henry's gaze, his most urbane smile to the fore. "I fear, my lord, that I rarely enter the lists these days. Not without a royal command."

Henry humphed. "Your knights seem keen enough to joust for gold and honor—do not such prizes tempt you?"

"Nay." Laying aside his knife and reclaiming his goblet, Alaun settled back. "There was gold and honor aplenty on the battlefields of France. I fear I've had a surfeit and am unlike to be tempted more."

As all England was ringing with tales of the grand exploits of Edward's recent company, Henry realized that might well be true. William had embarked with the king from Southampton, but had been left as part of the force garrisoning Caen, the first major town taken, thereby missing both the glory and spoils of later events. Henry shrewdly regarded Montisfryn; the desire to see William measure up against him grew. "There must be something will stir you from your lethargy?"

Alaun's lips twitched. He'd already decided to be a late entrant, quite why he hadn't decided, but there was no need to tell old Henry yet. Considering his next words, he let his gaze stray to Eloise de Versallet. As if sensing his regard, she looked up.

Calmly, coolly composed, she returned his look with one of haughty disdain.

He did not look away. "What else could a knight rightly aspire to claim by such means?" To any casual observer, it would appear he was staring across the hazy chamber while considering his host's words.

"Why—whatever was offered as prize." Henry leaned forward. "A jewel, perhaps? One with meaning."

Alaun arched a brow. Eloise continued to meet his gaze, but distantly, as if acknowledging him at all was beneath her dignity. Within him, something primitive stirred.

Determined not to lower her eyes again, Eloise fought to hold Montisfryn's steady gaze while ignoring her fluttering pulse and giddy head. She'd been certain she could simply outstare him, and drive him to acknowledge her lack of susceptibility by looking away. Instead, his golden gaze held hers, the pressure of his will steadily escalating, increasingly compelling, as if he would force her to submit, to lower her eyes and thus acknowledge some fundamental right over her. His intent reached her clearly. Grimly, she kept her gaze locked with his, refusing to yield, to admit to any womanly consciousness of his powerful presence.

"I have in my keeping a certain sapphire, worth a duke's ransom."

Henry's words reached Alaun, but distantly. Ten minutes before, he would have settled on the famed Aladdin's Stone, captured by a crusading de Versallet, as a sufficiently tempting prize. Now, his mind was no longer on the material plane. "Nay," he replied shortly. "I have no need of gaudy gems."

"A destrier, then. Or perhaps a colt from your father's stallion?"

Alaun's gaze didn't waver. "There are many strong stallions in the fields around Montisfryn. I have many prime destriers—I need not more."

Henry couldn't hide his exasperation. "Name your prize," he growled, "and if it's within my power, it'll be yours for the taking."

His words dropped into Alaun's mind, crossing the train of much deeper thoughts. Eloise's defiance, the unspoken challenge in her haughty gaze, consumed him, aroused him, taunted him as little else had for years. He was determined to have her, to feel her arching, naked, beneath him, frantic in her need, her nails scoring his back in urgent entreaty, her long legs wrapped about his hips as he conquered her. What price her haughtiness then? Her surrender would be a prize worth fighting for.

Slowly, he raised his goblet. Sipped. "Your daughter."

Silence engulfed the high table. A tangible presence, it spread through the air and held, quivering with anticipation.

Stunned, Henry glanced at Eloise, the first of the rest of the company to do so. Only he was in time to witness the seething glare she flung across the chamber, directly at Montisfryn. Visions of hell, surging fire and brimstone, contained less heat than her furious response. Then, as if the episode was no more than a joke entirely beneath her notice, she turned gravely to the Chevalier and engaged him in conversation.

Alaun fielded her fury, triumph surging through him at having finally breached her walls. As she looked away, haughty to the last, he shifted, easing the fullness in his groin. Slowly sipping his wine, he allowed his gaze to drift idly over the hall, and patiently waited for Henry to draw back from his ridiculous suggestion.

The idea was, of course, ludicrous. Even had she been unmarried and within Henry's writ, the days of tournaments being fought for a fair damsel's hand were long past. Besides, it wasn't her hand that had tempted him, a fact he was certain Henry understood. True, if she agreed to stand as prize, there was no reason the absurd couldn't come to pass, but the chances of her doing so were, Alaun would wager, rather less likely than that the heavens would fall.

No—the entire concept was the fruit of his disordered brain. The only excuse he could find for having voiced it was that, at the time, he'd been wholly intent on subduing her and had seized on any avenue to victory.

"This prize…" Henry sounded pensive.

Alaun turned to find his host regarding, not him, but Eloise. Then Henry's head came around, his gaze piercingly acute.

"I would want it understood," Henry stated, his voice even, its volume undimmed, "that any prize we agree on would be for you alone to claim, should you be declared overall victor of the tournament."

Surprise flashed through Alaun; intense interest immediately swamped it. "I had thought," he said, his gaze locking with Henry's, "that that was what we were discussing."

"Just so. The rules of the tournament have already been declared, the victor to be decided by the final joust."

Alaun had assumed as much; he inclined his head, and wondered what Henry was up to.

Playing for time was the answer, while Henry feverishly considered every angle of his plan. The plan that had, entirely without warning, burst upon him but moments before.

For the first time in the past five years—in all of her life, if it came to that—Henry had seen his daughter respond to a man. She was, did she but know it, the bane of his life. A hardened warrior, he'd loved his first wife dearly, and held all their five children very close to his heart. But Eloise had confounded him from the first. He had never known how to show his love to her; with sons, it was easy, but with daughters…daughters, so Henry believed, were sent by the saints to keep a man humble.

He'd arranged her marriage to Raoul de Cannar believing it the best he could do for her, but de Cannar had died and Eloise had retired to her convent. After visiting her there, Elaine had returned, suspicious that Eloise had not enjoyed her brief marriage. Elaine had gleaned nothing specific to support her belief, which, in retrospect, was just as well; if she had, he would have roared north with his men to descend on the de Cannars, even defying the king's edict to do so. Just the thought that de Cannar had not done right by Eloise was enough to make Henry see red, even now.

Through the smoky haze, his gaze rested on her; unshakably serene, she gave no sign of being aware of it. She was a daughter an old warrior could be proud of, with her matchless beauty and indomitable pride. Her hand was sought by the rich and powerful, as well as by the warrior clans. In vain. She spurned all her suitors with chilly disdain—he'd heard more than one complain of frostbite. Yet he would swear she had her woman's dreams, along with her woman's pride.

She remained an enigma, one that worried him well-nigh to death.

Men were nothing to her—that much, he understood. Why it should be so was another matter. Yet here, today, before his very eyes, he'd seen her respond to Montisfryn with a look Henry understood very well. The devil had baited her; his suggestion of her as his prize had been a ploy to rattle her defenses.

The wonder of it was, it had succeeded.

Memories of his courtship of Elaine of Montrose remained vivid in Henry's mind. Eloise was Elaine's daughter through and through. Which meant that, if handled correctly, this joust with Montisfryn might just hold the key to his salvation.

"And this prize?"

Montisfryn's casual, almost bored tone deceived Henry not at all. The man's golden gaze seemed unable to remain long from Eloise, and his hunger was imperfectly concealed, at least from Henry, who knew the feeling well. There was a danger, of course, that his scheme might go awry, yet it seemed as if Elaine stood at his shoulder, urging him on. "Ah, yes. My daughter, I believe you said?"

The tension about the high table was palpable; every soul present was hanging on his words. All except Eloise, who continued to ignore it all, and the poor, confused Chevalier, who struggled to emulate her calm.

Henry glanced at his principal guest. The intent expression in Montisfryn's eyes, the faint suggestion he could not believe his ears, delighted Henry. Nevertheless, in those last, vital seconds, he paused long enough to run through his plan once again.

At the worst, if Montisfryn lost, Eloise would have received a salutary shock; Henry could use that to illustrate the dangers of her position and the advantages of taking another husband.

But if all went well, the match would be an excellent one. Old Edmund would have been delighted; in retrospect, it was a pity Henry and

Montisfryn's father had been so busy preserving the fiction of their enmity that the possibility of linking their families had never entered their heads.

Henry glanced at Eloise. If he played his cards right, he would see her well-settled, Montisfryn well-served, in more ways than one, and his sainted Elaine well-pleased. The potential gain was far too great to ignore.

Reflecting that God preserved the valiant, he met Montisfryn's golden gaze. "Should you compete in this tournament and be declared its victor, when you leave this castle, my daughter, Eloise, will be in your care."

Montisfryn's lashes flickered, then his golden gaze returned to Henry's face. Talk erupted on all sides.

Unlike the majority of those about him, Alaun did not miss the subtlety of Henry's phrasing. "In my care?" He'd lowered his voice; none but Emma, between them, could overhear his words.

"Aye." One of Henry's brows rose. He, too, now spoke quietly; only deep rumbles carried to the many ears straining for details. "I hear Edward's suggested you find a wife and get yourself an heir without delay. And with that monstrous pile you call a home, you'll need a first-class chatelaine. Eloise could be your route to filling all three positions, provided, of course, that you can convince her to agree." Henry's eyes gleamed. "Think you can handle the challenge?"

For a long moment, Alaun held Henry's baiting stare, then he looked at Eloise, talking animatedly to the wilting Gascon. A glance down at Emma confirmed that she was trembling like a terrified rabbit; he doubted she could even make out their words, let alone follow their drift. "I gather that your daughter has shown some reluctance to take another husband."

Henry snorted. "She treats all those who approach with disdain—her untouchability is legendary. However, with her in your care, living in your household, you'd have an advantage all others have lacked." Henry paused, then, a knowing glint in his eye, innocently added, "Of course, her walls are said to be unbreachable."

Alaun shot him a narrow-eyed glance. He understood very well the challenge Henry was, with determined provocativeness, laying before him. His body reacted powerfully even while his brain grappled with the details. But all Henry had said was true—he could not hope to find a candidate more suitable to take to wife than Eloise de Versallet.

He shifted his gaze to her dark head. She was still deep in earnest discussion, her apparent obliviousness a blatant insult in itself.

If he won the tournament, he would win…a chance to win her—an effective chatelaine, a wealthy and well-born lady of fertile stock, no vapid girl but an experienced woman.

A woman who defied men, who held his sex in contempt.

A woman who could heat his blood to simmering with a single haughty glance.

Viewing the unquenchably regal, openly defiant tilt of her chin, he made up his mind. His gaze steady, he raised his goblet and, with calculated deliberation, saluted Henry. "You may add my name to your lists, my lord." His voice carried through the hall, hushing the whispers. Then he looked at Eloise. "I will fight."

At the end of the table, Eloise calmly reached for a platter. "Do try one of these onions, Chevalier. They're remarkably succulent this year." Behind her serene mask, her jaw was aching; icy rage consumed her, turning her glance so frosty the Chevalier shivered. An impulse to murder and mayhem lanced through her, fading as the possibilities of prolonged torture superseded it. Regretfully, she banished the notion. Behind her glacial façade, she reined in her seething fury; an explosion would only play into Montisfryn's hands.

Besides, none of it mattered one jot.

Frigidly contained, she continued to chat at the thoroughly distracted Chevalier.

Those who knew her not wondered at her understanding; those who knew her well waited, agog.

She had no intention of pandering to their ill-bred interest. Within her hearing, lords and ladies both were congratulating themselves on their foresight in having come. Raising her head, she swept a coldly superior glance about the hall, then commented to Blanche, "It seems my father has achieved his objective. His tournament bids fair to being remembered for years."

"Indeed," was all the reply Blanche, wary, consented to make.

Eloise saw out the last two courses with unshakeable calm, but when the dancing girls entered, she had had enough. The tone of the gathering degenerated rapidly. The salt was virtually at the other end of the room, so great had been the turnout of knightly nobles, yet despite the fact that the majority in the hall were well-born, and there were many ladies deployed among their ranks, the dancing girls quickly reduced the men present to the status of elemental male. Disgusted, Eloise grasped the opportunity of a query from the cellarer to quit the table, and then the hall.

The door from the dais gave onto a corridor. She turned left, strolling through the familiar dimness to where a deep embrasure surrounded a window—a mere slit for bowmen. The window faced west; a cooling breeze wafted through.

Free of the stale, smoky air of the hall, the tension in her temples, the inevitable reaction to her self-imposed control, made itself felt. Instead of further stewing in her fury, she determinedly put it from her. Resting her hands on the sill, she drew in a deep breath. It was peaceful outside.

* * *

In the hall, Alaun slowly stood, his action noted by few. Both Emma and Julia sat with eyes downcast, trying to ignore the increasingly licentious activities in their hall. All the men had their eyes fixed, feasting, on the scantily-clad girls writhing in time to a tambor and a naker drum. He, however, had a different woman in his sights.

The corridor was empty. He paused, silent and still, his eyes adjusting to the poor light. This was not the main corridor leading to the hall; the only illumination came from small cresset lamps, high and widely spaced along the inner wall. To his right stood steps, presumably leading to the solar. He hesitated, then turned left, his leather-soled hose making no sound on the flags.

The faintest stirring of air at her back alerted Eloise to his presence. She whirled, gasping, her hand rising to her throat. Just so had Raoul approached her, like a stalking cat.

"Nay, lady." Montisfryn frowned. "I meant not to startle you."

Wide-eyed, she stared up at him. The deep, rumbly resonance of his voice lapped about her; an odd little quiver ran through her. Irritated, she sucked in a breath and lifted her chin. "Then you should cultivate a firmer tread, my lord. I like not men who creep up on ladies in the dark."

With the lamps behind him, she couldn't see his expression, but his reaction, a stilling, as if he'd clamped a lid on his response, suggested her barb had found its mark. Unfortunately, instead of growling and going away, he propped a shoulder against the wall, effectively blocking her exit, and silently looked down at her.

His quiet scrutiny was unnerving. The sense of facing a predator at very close quarters was strong. She wished she could gather her skirts and sweep past him; instead, as the silence lengthened, she held herself rigid, hands clasped before her, her head high. It was his move.

"I would apologize, lady, for my gaucherie in naming you in the hall as my prize."

Eloise blinked. Those were, quite definitely, the very last words she'd thought to hear. Stiffly, she inclined her head. "I'm glad, my lord, that you realize such an outcome can never come to pass."

"Lady, if so you think, you have not thought enough." His face wreathed in shadows, Alaun studied her intently. "Your sire and I have moved too far for that."

She drew herself up, straightening until her forehead was on a level with his lips. Even in the poor light, he saw her eyes flash.

"If you believe I am such a mouse as to feel obliged to honor a wager made without my consent, you'll find yourself done out of a prize, my lord."

His lips twitched. "Nay, lady. I stand in no danger of thinking you a mouse." Anything less like the incipient virago bristling before him was, indeed, hard to imagine. "Yet three days hence, you will leave here with me."

The wry humor in his first statement was not repeated in his second. That was imbued with sufficient determination to send a shiver of disquiet through Eloise. "Nay, my lord—you will find you're mistaken." Intending to cut short the interview, she nevertheless felt compelled to ask, "But why, if you are still intent on this foolish wager, apologize for naming me as prize?"

"Not for naming you, but for naming you in the hall. The matter could have been dealt with with greater discretion."

She couldn't resist—she cast her eyes heavenward. "You'll forgive me, my lord, an' I do not feel much appeased. I fear I, in common with the majority of my sex, place little value on such nonsensical nuances. In staking my honor as prize, you do me grave insult. Apologizing for mentioning my name in so doing is hardly like to ease my ire."

Alaun looked at her sternly. "Lady, tis not your honor that is at stake."

Her eyes flamed. "My hand, my honor—for me, tis the same. I know well that many men consider widows to possess but the barest remnants of honor. Permit me to tell you that such men are varlets and fools!"

With an effort, he held onto his temper. "Tis—"

"Nay, my lord." With an imperious gesture, she cut him off. "I see no benefit in arguing the matter further. I view this wager you have made as contemptible; there is nothing like to change my mind."

Pleased to have been able to vent her feelings, Eloise condescended to issue a last warning. Gathering her skirts, she looked up at him. "Regardless of the outcome of the tournament, I respectfully suggest, my lord, that you prepare for disappointment. Even should you win each and every contest, an unlikely event you'll allow, I will not be leaving Versallet Castle in your company."

She'd intended the statement as a parting shot. Unfortunately, Montisfryn showed no sign of shifting, despite her clear wish to escape. He remained rocklike before her. His expression was lost in the shadows, yet she got the impression he was studying her, gauging her, making some decision.

"Do you care to wager on that certainty?"

She blinked. "On which certainty?"

"That I won't win each and every contest."

She narrowed her eyes. "Each and *every* contest?"

When a nod came in answer, she drew in a slow breath. The chances of a single knight winning all contests, including such diverse activities as archery, fording in full armor, and tilting, were so slight as to be negligible. She was not pleased with Montisfryn for a host of excellent reasons. Indeed, she had a number of scores to settle with him—here, perhaps, was the way.

Tilting her head, she boldly studied him, taking in his broad chest and the heavy bones of shoulders, arms, and legs. To her not-inexperienced eyes, his chances of winning each and every contest appeared slim indeed. No one with a body so large could exhibit the dexterity required for excelling with the longbow. There was a race, too, and there was no doubt he moved slowly. She'd yet to see a rapid movement from him.

Her lips curved. There were many satisfying boons she could ask of him—like being her slave for a week. Her eyes narrowed in anticipation; she would enjoy making him rue the day he had first disrupted her peace.

Lifting her head, she met his gaze. "Very well—I will wager with you, my lord. But as we have three days, why not three, separate wagers?"

He smiled; even through the dimness, the curving of his lips drew her gaze. "If you wish it, lady."

"I do." She forced her reluctant gaze upward, to his shadowed eyes. "For my first prize, I will have from you a signed and sealed statement that you will not attempt to hold me, now or ever, to the bargain you have made with my father."

He inclined his head. "And for my part, should I succeed in winning all the contests held tomorrow, I will have from you...a kiss."

She stilled. Wariness intruded. Then again, where was the danger? One little kiss, a single quick peck, hardly constituted any great risk. Regally condescending, she nodded. "Done."

He smiled sleepily down at her. Then, stepping back, he bowed gracefully and held out his hand. "Allow me to return you to the hall, lady."

The tambor and naker drums had ceased. Her interest in her father's tournament amazingly restored, Eloise inclined her head, a cool but gracious smile on her lips.

Alaun gritted his teeth. St. George's bones!—just her smile had the power to make him rise. As she placed her slim fingers across his, he steeled himself against the contact, uncomfortably aware of the ache that was growing, minute by minute, in his loins.

Turning her toward the hall, he shot her a sharp glance. She appeared coolly distant, aloof, blithely disinterested. Henry's words echoed in his brain. The urge to shatter her chilly façade—the desire to have her heated and panting beneath him—hardened to solid intent.

The need to conquer had never been so strong.

In a courtly manner, he conducted her to her seat at the end of the bench. She sat and graciously dismissed him, then, with unimpaired serenity, took up her part in the conversation.

To the blank astonishment of all in the hall.

Resuming his seat, Alaun picked up his goblet. Sipping, he saw Roland, seated down the hall, openly staring at him. He returned the stare blankly.

Then, straight-faced, he turned his head and looked at Henry, the hint of a question in his eyes.

Henry met that look with one of frosty, distinctly paternal uncertainty. He knew Eloise too well to imagine that during the last twenty minutes Montisfryn had soothed her ruffled feathers in the time-honored way. Yet there she sat, calmly chatting, no trace of the arctic remaining.

Deciding not to question the benediction of the saints, Henry raised his goblet to his unexpected guest, and drank.

Chapter 3

The first of the three days of the tournament dawned bright and clear. The river mists had dispersed by the time Eloise, with the rest of the ladies, emerged from the castle to take up her position in the stands.

Gaily-striped tents housing raised benches had been erected alongside the tournament ground, affording the ladies and other noble spectators an excellent view of the arena of hard-packed earth. The rest of the perimeter of the large, roughly circular ground was bordered by grassy slopes dotted with the pavilions of the competing knights. The lists, directly before the stands, were cordoned off with thick rope.

Calmly claiming a seat on the front bench of the center stand, Eloise inwardly delighted in the bafflement apparent in a great many eyes.

In the general fuss as others found seats, Blanche, settling beside her, whispered, "I didn't believe you when you said you would attend. I can't believe you're here now."

Eloise smiled. "I wouldn't miss today for anything."

Blanche frowned at her, but Eloise ignored the invitation to explain. With unexpected eagerness, she scanned the knot of knights making their way to the field.

None of them was Montisfryn. Buoyed by good humor, she settled to watch anyway.

The judges—the sheriff, Sir Geoffrey Harcourt, Albert d'Albron, and her father—all too old to viably enter the lists, were seated in the middle of the same bench as she.

"Papa mentioned they'd arranged the contests differently this time." Blanche wriggled, skirts rustling. "I only hope there's something more enthralling than just jousting."

Eloise scanned the pavilions. "No jousts today or tomorrow, you'll be pleased to hear. Single combats only on the first two days. For light relief, there'll be archery contests, both longbow and crossbow, this afternoon, and a race tomorrow."

"A race?

"Aye. Fully armored through obstacles they use in training—fording, vaulting to the saddle, the quintain."

"*Fully* armored?"

Eloise smiled. "My father called it an endurance race—you know he favors understatement."

Blanche looked impressed. "And on the third day?"

"They've arranged the bouts so only sixteen knights will remain unbeaten on the final morn. All sixteen will joust in the usual fashion, the winner of each contest progressing to the next round until the victor emerges."

Blanche frowned, counting on her fingers. "That means the two knights in the final joust will have already faced three opponents that day."

Eloise let her smile deepen. "Aye. Twill be a grueling trial just to get that far."

"Indeed!" Blanche blinked, then glanced at her. "Montisfryn will be in the final joust."

Raising a brow, Eloise fixed her gaze on the first two combatants, walking forward to salute the judges. "We'll see."

* * *

Behind the knights' pavilions, screened from the arena, Alaun had his eye fixed on a circle inscribed on a tree trunk some two hundred paces distant. In his hands rested a heavy wooden crossbow; carefully, he sighted along the stock. His finger tightened on the trigger; the bolt thudded into the trunk just wide of the mark.

Lowering the weapon, he grimaced. His youngest squire hared off to retrieve the bolt as Roland strolled up in company with the Genoese crossbowman, Rovogatti.

"I don't believe it." Halting, Roland blinked in exaggerated surprise. "The last time I saw you with one of those in your hands you were trying to hit the side of Gloucester Castle."

"Don't remind me," Alaun growled. Both he and Roland had been squires under Gilbert of Gloucester. Frowning, he reprimed the bow. His aim was good, but at least every third bolt went too wide of the mark for comfort.

"Why's it so important—the crossbow? You don't have to win that to win the tournament."

Alaun sighted, then released another bolt. It thudded into the center of the circle. Lowering the bow, he reprimed it again. He had an hour before meeting his first opponent. "Let's just say I've a vested interest in winning."

Roland's eyes opened wide. "A wager?"

Alaun nodded, sighting again.

"With the lady Eloise?"

The bolt flew wide, missing the tree altogether.

"*Roland...!*"

Responding to the menace in Alaun's growl, both Roland and Rovogatti perched on a nearby wagon—in silence. He shot them a warning scowl, then continued with his practice.

On learning the details of the day's contests two hours ago, he'd been gripped by an entirely unexpected reaction—one perilously close to panic, compounded by chagrin, self-disgust, and not a little surprise. When he'd wagered with Eloise, he'd assumed the contests would encompass nothing more than the usual single combats and jousts. While he was confident of his skill with the long bow, the crossbow had never been his weapon; there was every chance another knight would better his score.

Which meant he might lose. Not only his wager with Eloise, but any chance of winning her to wife.

Swallowing a snarl, he loosed another bolt. The damned witch had tricked him. Unfortunately for her, defeat was not in his lexicon. Frowning, he reprimed the bow.

He had followed her into the corridor last night with the objective of building on his earlier success. After their visual duel, let alone the little matter of his prize, she should have been quivering with reaction, uncertain, vulnerable to a subtle, more gentle assault. He'd expected to find a woman primed for seduction.

What he'd found was a woman only one step removed from the virago of the woods. Instead of melting into his arms, she'd tried to summarily dismiss him.

He wasn't used to being dismissed, summarily or otherwise.

The next bolt lodged off-center; he growled, then, lips compressed, brows knit, fell to repriming the bow again. Eloise de Versallet was costing him more time and effort than any woman before; he would make sure she repaid him—for every minute of his time, for every tithe of his effort.

His next bolt flew wide. Smothering an oath, he grimly applied himself.

After a few more minutes of enforced silence, Rovogatti rose and disappeared around the tents. Roland remained, his grin wide.

Alaun concentrated, yet his skill seemed unwilling to improve. He was scowling blackly when Rovogatti returned.

"Try this."

Turning, Alaun's gaze fell on the arbalest Rovogatti was offering. It was the Genoese's own crossbow, an engraved steel bow easily drawn by a detachable winch. The work of a craftsman, it was easy to fire and perfectly balanced.

Rovogatti took his acceptance for granted and reached for the other bow.

With a grateful grunt, Alaun released it and hefted the arbalest, gauging its weight, then loaded it.

The next six bolts pierced the target's center.

Lowering the arbalest, he smiled at Rovogatti. "Friend, you've just earned your life."

* * *

Up in the stands, Eloise shifted impatiently.

Blanche smothered a yawn. "I vow, tis almost as bad as jousting."

"Did your father mention the order of the bouts?"

"He ran through them this morn, but I paid no heed."

Eloise glared at her.

Blanche shrugged. "We're fixtures here anyway—what matter who falls in the dust first?"

Just then, one of the pair presently slogging away at each other did. The winner was declared, the up-ended knight carted away.

Eloise glanced to the edge of the field—and straightened. Montisfryn stood by the ropes, surrounded by his squires, accoutered and ready for battle. He had yet to don his helm; his eyes were turned her way.

A most peculiar thrill shot through her. Excitement stirred within her, certainly the first she'd ever felt at a tournament. As it gripped her more firmly, she allowed her serenely distant mask to slip long enough to smile.

Alaun stifled a groan. His body had reacted instantly to the sight of her, and even more to that smile. Reaching for his helm, he settled it in place, visor up, and grimly marched forward. It was, he was certain, the first time he'd entered the contest arena aroused. As he approached the stands, Eloise's lips lifted lightly again. Gritting his teeth, he fastened his gaze on the judges, and, with his opponent, a local knight, saluted them.

Henry leaned forward to recite the usual cautions. Behind him, the interest of the assembled ladies was marked, a sibilant twitter ruffling their calm.

Eloise sat back, determined to show no especial interest. Then she noticed Montisfryn's badge. Like most knights, he did not carry his heraldic coat of arms, his 'arms of war', into jousts, which, by law, were fought with blunted weapons and with sport and honor as their aim. Instead, both surcote and shield carried a different device, his 'arms of peace'.

Blanche leaned forward. "The badge is a sleeping lion—that's plain enough. But what's the motto?"

Inscribed around the edge of the shield and again about the hem of his surcote, Montisfryn's motto took a little deciphering. Eloise finally made out the Latin words, then mentally translated them.

Fearsome when aroused.

Abruptly, she sat back.

"Can you make it out?" Blanche, short-sighted, was still peering.

"No," Eloise lied, irritated by the warmth in her cheeks. Clearly, Montisfryn possessed an untrustworthy sense of humor.

Her father finished his instructions. Both knights saluted again, then stepped back and squared off. They lowered their visors, saluted each other, then started swinging their broadswords.

Eloise had watched many such a bout, but never before had she felt any real interest. Now, she sat on the edge of her seat, hands clasped in her lap, her eyes never leaving the armored men laboring in the dust before her.

Swords clanged on plate, thudded and sheered off shields, and shook the links of their mail. The broadswords, heavy, single-edged affairs, were swung in broad arcs at the end of the arm or thrust with the force of the shoulder.

Montisfryn made short work of his opponent. When, beaten to his knees, the de Versallet vassal yielded, Eloise let out a tense breath and unlocked her fingers. Only then did she realize that she had, albeit inwardly, been cheering on Montisfryn rather than her father's knight, who, in the circumstances, stood as her champion.

"Well!" Blanche sat back, no trace of ennui in her face. "What did you think of that?"

"Tis no more than one would expect from a knight of Montisfryn's experience." Eloise rapidly reassembled her usual haughty demeanor as Montisfryn drew off his helm. The glance he cast her could only be described as victorious—she met it with an expression carved from stone.

A slow grin transformed his features; she could have sworn there was a twinkle in his eye.

Frostier than ever, she joined the other ladies in repairing to the castle where the noon meal awaited them. The knights, meanwhile, retired to their pavilions. When the ladies returned, the bouts resumed.

By the time Eloise had watched Montisfryn beat his third opponent, this time a knight-banneret, into the dust, she was prepared to acknowledge that he was, indeed, a knight of considerable prowess.

"What do you say now?" Blanche asked, determined to gain more than a shrug.

She shrugged. "Twas clear from the first that he's very strong." Calmly composed, she rose and flicked out her skirts. "But tis the archery next."

Blanche frowned. "So? He doesn't need to win that to win the prize."

Eloise smiled.

* * *

The archery contests were held late that afternoon, once the knights had refreshed themselves after their exertions on the field. The butts were set up on the village green, close by the castle walls.

"We'll have the crossbow first," Henry declared. "If the breeze strengthens, twill make the longbow more difficult."

All the knights nodded, a more difficult contest being infinitely preferable.

Standing with the other ladies, Eloise couldn't stop smiling; it was rare, indeed, to find herself in accord with such knightly subtleties.

The marks were set and the crossbow contest commenced. The first round winnowed the novices from the experienced. The second round saw six contestants stand out from the crowd, all notching perfect scores, Montisfryn among them. The judges conferred, then moved the targets back another ten paces.

"Damn!" Alaun muttered. The range was now pressing the limits of accuracy. "It'll be a matter of luck who wins."

"Well, luck or no, you've the best chance with that bow." Roland nodded at Rovogatti's weapon. "None of the others have anything half as accurate."

Alaun grunted.

As matters fell out, he was the last to shoot. When he stepped up to the mark, there was only one man to beat, a knight from Salisbury who had hit the eye twice, with his third shot but slightly wide. Sighting the arbalest, Alaun felt his nerves quiver for the first time in years. His palms were slightly damp. He did not appreciate the sensation. Gritting his teeth, he got on with it, sending first one, then two, then three bolts into the heart of the target.

Cheering erupted; Henry was grinning from ear to ear.

All Alaun felt was a sense of ill-usage.

Thankfully, the longbow competition was a mere formality; there was a saying at Montisfryn that he'd been born with a bow in his hand. It was quickly seen that he was unbeatable and the contest declared in his favor.

Eloise was disgusted—and not a little flustered. A situation not improved by her father, who paused beside her to comment, "Truly remarkable. He always was a wizard with the bow."

Through the softening dusk, she stared at him. "You *knew* he was that good?"

Henry frowned. "Of course. It's the Welsh blood."

Welsh blood. Eloise swung on her heel and marched back to the castle. She'd made a pact with the devil, thinking him clumsy, only to be defeated by his Welsh blood. Perhaps she could protest the result on the grounds of her ignorance?

With a humph, she marched on.

Supper that evening was a much simpler meal than the banquet of the night before. Nevertheless, everyone dressed just as grandly. Eloise held fast to her black velvet, scorning the competition rampant among the ladies, each vying to most perfectly complement Montisfryn's attire. As he appeared in a soft houppelande of ochre wool trimmed with sable, few even came close.

The conversation revolved about the contests of the day; by the end of the meal, Eloise had heard Montisfryn's name too often for her liking. He was the darling of the ladies; many found some reason to stop by Emma's chair, until, with an unprecedented spurt of decision, Emma moved to sit beside Eloise.

"That poor man," Emma exclaimed, settling on the end of the bench. "Truly, some of those ladies are no ladies at all. Their forwardness quite made me blush. Why, even your father disapproved."

That last surprised Eloise. Whatever else her father might be, he was no hypocrite.

"But Montisfryn is so much the true knight," Emma rambled on, "he made not the slightest push to take advantage of their offers. I hadn't thought to find him so strict in his ways."

Eloise stared at her. The idea that Montisfryn—he who was "fearsome when aroused"—did not dally when the mood took him was so ludicrous she was lost for words. Luckily, the players she'd hired were then ushered in, and the company settled, content after their day of endeavor to be entertained with ballads of battles long past.

The guests drifted early from the hall, most knights opting for a sound sleep in preparation for the morrow's decisive events. Eloise retreated to the solar to confer with Sir John, then headed for her tower. Gliding along the dimly-lit corridors, she was aware of distant footsteps, the creaking of doors opening and closing. Some knights, she fancied, would get less sleep than others. Lips curving in cynical acceptance—she'd lived among warrior males too long to be shocked—she started up the tower stair.

Passing the door to Montisfryn's chamber, she cast the oak panels a disgusted glance. He'd won his kiss; she had, indeed, expected him to make some effort to speak with her, to set their wagers for the morrow. Perhaps he, too, was occupied. Perhaps he'd even forgotten her forfeit, sufficiently satisfied with the rouged lips of some other lady.

Frowning, she rounded the curve of the stair, lit by torches in brackets on the wall. Her gaze on the treads, the first she saw of him was his feet. Like the rest of him, they were large. She blinked and halted. Slowly, she let her gaze travel upward, up the long length of his legs, past his hips and the broad acres of his chest, until, finally, she reached his face. "Good even, my lord."

His lips curved, but his gaze remained intent.

"Lady." Alaun acknowledged her greeting with an inclination of his head. "You hadn't forgotten our wager, I trust?" Taking her hand, he drew her into the alcove of an archer's station.

"No." She faced him. "I was just thinking that we should meet to set our terms for tomorrow."

"And settle for today."

Her gaze flew to his face. "I thought we would settle at the end of the tournament."

Her startled expression assured him more surely than any protestation that she had, indeed, thought just that. The suspicions he'd harbored for the past half hour evaporated; he smiled lazily. "Ah, no, lady. Forfeits fall due when the wager is lost."

"Oh." It wasn't, perhaps, the most intelligent reply, but Eloise could think of no other. She couldn't refuse him and have him think her without honor. Ignoring her skittering pulse, she called her senses to order, and nodded. "I see."

When he made no move to claim his prize, but simply stood smiling sleepily down at her, she mentally gritted her teeth and, inching closer, placed one hand lightly on his shoulder. Stretching up on tip-toe, she touched her lips briefly to his.

She retreated.

His eyes opened wide. "That's it?"

She blinked. "What do you mean?"

The smile that curved his lips made her long to take a step back, but the alcove was only so wide.

"Lady, if that's a sample of what you bestow on your lovers, you're in danger of being arraigned for shortchanging."

She blushed, embarrassed, irritated, but wary. She'd never actually kissed a man. Raoul had ravaged her mouth; she'd submitted, but had taken no active part. And none of the men who had wooed her since had ever got so close.

The idea of admitting ignorance occurred only to be dismissed, yet if she didn't do or say something soon, Montisfryn would. That he'd trapped her in such a revealing situation pricked her temper.

Then she saw the way out.

She threw him a haughty, openly challenging glance. "If you're so particular, my lord, perhaps you should instruct me in your requirements?"

It was a bold throw, a sultry, brazen invitation.

He caught her gaze, held it. "Aye." His voice was gravelly, low. "A commendable notion."

Shifting so he blocked the entrance of the alcove, he gathered her easily into his arms.

She fought to dampen her instinctive stiffening. Her palms met the solid wall of his chest, covered by the fine wool of his houppelande. His arm tightened about her waist, drawing her closer; his long fingers glided over her nape. Her lungs locked. When his thumb slid under her jaw, tilting her face upward, a sudden tremor shook her; by dint of sheer will, she subdued it, forced herself to let go and acquiesce, to let her body follow his directions without resistance. His head lowered; she let her lids fall.

And braced herself for an assault, for the brutal ravishment which was all she'd ever known.

His lips touched lightly, experimentally, then settled more firmly, warm and assured over hers.

The sensation was pleasant.

His lips moved, the pressure definite, yet pleasing. Gradually, she relaxed, tension flowing away. His solidity, and the warmth of his large body, were comforting. Tentatively, she moved her lips under his. He approved—his lips firmed; she met the increasing pressure. His arm tightened; his fingers curled about her nape.

Willingly, she closed the distance between them, letting her body meet his. The contact sent a wave of prickling sensation spreading over her skin; the surging warmth that followed soothed like the caress of a flame. Pushing her hands upward, she encountered the sable edging his neckline. Spearing her fingers through the luxurious fur, she followed the trail up over his shoulders. Something softer, silkier, fell over her fingers. His hair. It was incredibly soft, a cross between silk and sable in texture. Her fingers played, her senses delighting in the tumble of the heavy locks.

Engrossed in a slow, thorough exploration of her lips, Alaun felt her fingers thread through his hair, a gentle, very feminine caress. Her lips were warm and pliant under his; she rested, soft and supple, in his arms. But he wanted more; he needed to taste her. "Open for me, Eloise." He breathed the request against her lips, his voice low, urgent.

The words jolted Eloise—they were words Raoul had often used. Yet she didn't break away; this wasn't Raoul. Montisfryn's kiss held nothing but warmth and pleasure—it had never been so with Raoul. Would what she was experiencing change if she granted what Montisfryn asked?

Alaun sensed her hesitation. He increased the pressure slightly, then was about to draw back and repeat his request when her lips opened under his. Not parted slightly as women were wont to do, in shyness or thinking it more alluring, but fully open, a gifting so complete it stole his breath.

He took instant advantage, yet exercised restraint, too experienced not to know such a gifting was an honor, given in trust.

Decision made, Eloise yielded in the only way she knew; Raoul had never encouraged shyness nor coyness. Yet she fully expected to feel revolted; she was only engaging in the exchange in the interests of her own understanding.

Instead, the slow surge of Montisfryn's invasion was pure magic; her senses reeled—she'd never imagined such pleasure. His tongue found hers and stroked, heavy yet gentle. Then he set about a typically thorough, predictably slow, devastatingly sensuous exploration that left no part of her softness untouched, uncaressed.

Unclaimed.

A slow shiver shook her—she wondered what manner of conquest she'd invited. She felt boneless in his arms, her breasts nestled against his chest, her hips brushing his thighs.

Then he shifted, both arms closing about her, trapping her against his hard frame. She knew she could resist, that if she wished to call a halt she had only to struggle. Instead, she gave herself up to his embrace, eager to understand, to more fully experience the unlooked-for pleasure. Boldly she drew her tongue along his, and felt him shudder. Delighted, she kissed him back, inviting, then returning increasingly intimate caresses. She sensed tension rising within him, tightening his muscles until they locked. Then his lips shifted, his head slanted over hers, and she tasted the dragon's fire.

The lion and the dragon.

Through the heated mists that fogged her brain, she recognized the imagery. If she'd been able, she would have smiled. Instead, she savored the heat that flowed from him, the inexorable tide that seeped into her blood until it thudded in every corner of her being. Behind the heat lurked a hunger she had not before encountered; it hung back, hardly shy, but not yet ready to fully reveal itself. The brief glimpses teased and tantalized.

Alaun was similarly fascinated. God's teeth! she was a heady piece, a potent mixture of siren and saint. Her very deliberation—in daring him to take what he wanted, in opening so completely to him, and now in participating so boldly in an exchange that was setting them both aflame— was challenge and surrender combined. Nothing could have more completely convinced him that behind her chilly façade, she was as experienced, and as hungry, as he. The knowledge fueled the flames that licked through him, greedily seeking release.

So caught up were they in their enjoyment of each other that neither heard the soft slap of leather-soled feet mounting the tower stairs.

Henry had finally decided that he needed to know his daughter's mind. Her incomprehensible behavior was too much for him to accept. She could not approve his actions, so why, then, was she smiling so much? He knew she wasn't devious, so her inexplicable attitude worried him all the more.

Looking ahead as he rounded the bend in the tower stair, Henry saw Montisfryn's back filling the recess—from the angle of Montisfryn's bent head, it was easy to guess his occupation.

For an instant, Henry saw red.

Damn the boy! Ladies had been throwing him lures all evening—Henry had thought they had been rejected. Now, just when he'd thought he'd found a man for his difficult daughter, he discovered that man was the sort to risk an advantageous connection for a quick kiss and a poke! Chest swelling with righteous indignation, he looked down at the skirts showing between Montisfryn's braced legs.

Black skirts.

Henry blinked, then glanced up. Even as the stunning realization burst upon him, green fire flared amongst Montisfryn's tawny locks. Eloise's emerald. As he watched his daughter's fingers twine in Alaun de Montisfryth's hair, Henry's jaw dropped. Eloise, quite obviously, was a very willing participant.

With the reflection that he'd badly misjudged Montisfryn—the man was a wizard, forsooth!—Henry carefully retreated down the stairs.

Alaun couldn't get enough of the woman in his arms. The soft cavern of her mouth was sweetly mysterious, her body, pressed wantonly to his, beckoned and enticed. Yet when he raised his head, ending the kiss, and watched her lids slowly rise to reveal the dark, fathomless depths of her eyes, he immediately sensed her retreat. Bemused, he watched as she composed herself, then gently drew back, although she remained within his arms.

"I hope you found my forfeit satisfactory, my lord."

Satisfactory? All but giddy with need, he stared down at her, tempted to tell her, baldly, exactly how he'd found her—how she'd tasted, what he now wanted of her. He ached so badly he could barely think. The urge to sweep her up and carry her to his chamber, to lay her on his bed and find his ease in her, was almost overpowering.

With her hips pressed to his thighs, the evidence of his desire a burning brand against her belly, Eloise needed no soothsayer's crystal to read his mind. She smiled lightly, inwardly amazed at her assurance. Boldly, she trailed a finger along the edge of his jaw, then traced the firm curve of his lower lip. "Nay, lord. I have paid what I owed."

His eyes blazed. She'd noticed the odd light in his golden eyes, flickering and elusive, ever since he'd raised his head, but with the torchlight behind him, she couldn't define it.

Alaun knew the flames were there; the fire she'd ignited burned fiercely within him. He bit her fingertip, hard enough to hurt, but not hard enough to damage, and her eyes flared. He captured her hand and soothed the hurt finger with a kiss, drawing the sensitive tip into his mouth and sucking lightly before releasing it. Along with an aggravated sigh.

"As you wish, lady." His voice was deep, darkly turbulent. Jaw clenched with the effort of tamping down the lust she'd raised, he forced his mind to her conquest. "But we have yet to set the terms of tomorrow's wager."

Shaken by the sensations his odd caress had evoked, Eloise drew back. "My terms stand. What do you ask against them?"

He hesitated, looking over her head, then his golden gaze dropped to her face. "One of your garters."

"A garter?" Again, he'd surprised her. Try as she might, she could see no danger in agreeing. As she stepped from his arms, which fell reluctantly from her, she shrugged. "If that is what you wish, so be it."

"It is not what I wish, but, tomorrow, I'll settle for that."

Disconcerted by his tone and the very clear statement he'd left unsaid, she sent a startled glance his way.

Frustration riding him, Alaun felt his expression harden. Standing back, he gestured up the stairs. "I suggest you get to your bed, lady." He met her gaze. "Unless you wish to warm mine."

The widening of her dark eyes assured him that she was not yet ready to surrender that far. With a parting nod, which she still managed to make regal, she stepped onto the stair.

He watched her climb toward her door, beyond the curve of the wall. The last sight he had was of her curvaceous rear, cloaked in silk and velvet, swaying gently as she climbed the steep steps.

Suppressing a growl, he turned away, and forced his feet in the opposite direction.

Chaper 4

Alaun entered the lists in a foul mood the next morn.

What sleep he'd had had been filled with dreams of a sleek, elusive siren with long dark hair and deep, mysterious eyes. After waking for the third time only to find himself stiffer than ever, he'd cursed and flung a pillow across the chamber. Bilder had sleepily inquired whether he'd wanted one of the castle whores. He'd considered the offer long and hard before grumpily rejecting it.

The reason why had made him grumpier still. Not only was the lust gripping him unexpectedly intense, it was completely focused on one particular woman. Never before had desire been so thoroughly female-specific.

On waking heavy-eyed and heavy-blooded, he'd been ready to swear off ladies for life. Then Eloise had passed him on the stair, her smile assured, her gaze wary. He'd smiled easily back. Appalled, he'd left for the pavilions before she could further bewitch him.

He vented his bad temper on his opponents, dismissing them with such ruthless ferocity that his third opponent resigned the bout before it had begun on the grounds of a faulty shield strap. His offer of a replacement shield was waved aside with a startled look. Denied the opportunity to ease the tension still coiled within him, he accepted the judges' award with a churlish grunt.

Before turning away, he glanced up at the stands. Eloise was there, as she had been all day. She seemed to have forgotten he could see through his visor. Each time he'd vanquished an opposing knight, he'd looked up to see her smiling beatifically. Yet on every occasion, by the time he'd raised a fist and lifted his visor, she was sitting stone-faced, as prim as a nun. Her antics, for some reason, sweetened his sour mood.

In mid-afternoon, he lined up with most of the competing knights for the armored race.

"I won't ask if you're looking forward to this." Roland stood beside him. "Not even in your present state could you possibly be that senseless."

Alaun grunted. "It's to be a massed race—heaps of flailing armor everywhere."

Roland looked disgusted. "What am I doing here?"

"Keeping me company."

"Of course!" Roland's face cleared. "I knew there had to be a reason."

They were inspected by the judges to ensure they were wearing the armor they customarily competed in. Alaun waited, his habitual patience for once mislaid. Again, he felt nerves knot about his stomach, and liked it not.

"The only way for either of us to win," Roland mused, "is to grab the lead from the start and keep it. If we go down in the scrum, twill be hard to win free, nor regain sufficient momentum."

Alaun nodded grimly. "And it all hinges on which leg comes first." The fact that he had so much at stake, all riding on the whim of old Henry, prompted him, not for the first time that day, to question his sanity.

Their inspection completed, the judges faced the line of competitors. Henry smiled benevolently. His gaze flicked Alaun's way, then he cleared his throat. "You will start mounted."

Alaun released the breath he'd been holding. Mounted on Conqueror, his black destrier, he could outride any knight born. He listened as Henry appointed the church as the turning point for the first leg.

"On returning to the river bank here, you will leave your chargers with your squires and ford between the white flags."

All turned to see two stakes flying white rags planted in the river bed, a gap of twenty paces between. Alaun grimaced and muttered to Roland, "Getting across will be one thing, getting back will be something else entirely."

Roland looked even more disgusted than before.

"On gaining the opposite bank," Henry continued, his stentorian bellow loud and clear, "you must run along the forest's edge and around the marked oak before returning through the ford. You must then mount your charger by vault, take your lance at the gallop, and cleanly strike one of the quintains on the tournament field. Rounding the furthest of the ladies' pavilions, the winner will be the first knight to stand dismounted before us."

Henry beamed upon his hapless victims. "Mount up, sirs."

Swinging up to Conqueror's back, Alaun glimpsed the green of Eloise's skirts among those of the ladies lining the back of the stands to watch the first leg thunder by. Again, the paralyzing sense of desperately needing to win laid hold. Setting his teeth, he glanced at Roland. On a horse only marginally less strong than Conqueror, his cousin might well be the man he had to beat.

"Ready?"

All eyes fixed on the red scarf in Henry's fist. He opened his hand; the scarf drifted slowly down. The instant it touched earth, they were off.

Alaun went immediately into the lead, Conqueror pulling steadily ahead. With his visor down, he couldn't afford the time to turn and gauge the field. Blinkered, he rounded the church at full gallop and headed back to the river.

He was out of the saddle and into the water in one stride, leaving Conqueror to Bilder's care. He fully expected Bilder to turn the huge black side-on to impede the riders behind him—thus were knightly contests won. The fording place was hip-deep for him; it would be waist-deep for many others. The footing was treacherous; he was too experienced not to test each footfall before trusting his full weight to it. He gained the far bank without mishap, water streaming from his mailed chausses.

Pausing, he looked back. Roland was but feet from the bank with five others not far behind. The rest were a jumbled melee, half-in and half-out of the water.

Alaun turned and ran.

Loping along beside the forest, he kept a wary eye out for rabbit holes. Setting a toe in one could put him out of contention. His stride was long, easy, and effortless. He'd been taught the knack of moving his large body by a German knight. Hans had been even bigger and heavier than he. It had taken some explaining and years of practice to master the art—gliding movements not jerky ones, always using momentum not fighting it, never hurrying in anything if moving slower would do as well.

Constant repetition, not only on the training field but in every aspect of his life, had finally borne fruit. Now, he never feared draining his strength—the supply was well-nigh inexhaustible, conserved so that when he needed it, either for endurance, as now, or in an explosive release of ferocious magnitude, it was there. Hans, more than any other, was responsible for his knightly prowess.

He wondered whether a certain de Versallet witch would appreciate Hans's teachings when he finally had her beneath him.

His foot caught in a tree root.

He tripped, broke his stride, but managed to keep his balance. Cursing, he banished the distracting images that had slunk into his mind and concentrated on the race. He could hear Roland panting behind him. As he rounded the appointed tree, he saw the field strung out behind him. After Roland came a de Versallet knight, then many others in a long row.

Alaun made straight for the nearest white flag. Reaching the bank, he plunged in, knowing Roland would follow in his tracks.

The melee he'd left on the far bank had progressed by slipping and sliding, and in some cases crawling, to the forest-side of the river. By going close to the flag, he avoided the worst of it. Twice, he had to skirt heaving armor threshing helplessly in the water. His foot slipped once, but, by dint of grim determination, he held his balance. Roland was not so lucky—another knight was swept across his legs; he remained upright, but Alaun heard him swearing as he struggled to disentangle the importunate knight.

Gaining the bank, Alaun slogged up it, his waterlogged armor dragging on his limbs. He was breathing hard, his chest rising and falling dramatically. He paused for a moment, taking stock.

Bilder had reversed Conqueror, holding him steady, black rump to the river. The destrier was superbly trained; the mighty stallion would take the impact of Alaun's weight without shifting. Breathing deeply, Alaun drew himself in, then, taking three quick strides, he vaulted into the saddle.

He made it—just. To the hurrahs of the crowd, he spurred forward. Ten paces ahead, his youngest squire stood proudly holding his lance. He grabbed it up at a gallop and hefted it easily. Conqueror thundered toward the tournament ground; Alaun checked him at the edge, lining up the quintain before spurring forward.

His lance struck cleanly; the board turned and reset. Almost immediately came the telltale thud and creak of a second of the five quintains. Some other knight was close. There was a cheer from the ladies as Alaun flung his lance aside and wheeled Conqueror to round the last of the red-striped tents.

He had no idea how close the second rider was—all he knew was how much he wanted to win. Conqueror thundered down the dusty road, taking the curve to the river at full speed.

Alaun looked ahead. By all the saints!—*where* was de Versallet? He couldn't see the old man anywhere.

Panic threatened.

He was almost on top of the judges before he saw them, his visor restricting his vision so badly it was only d'Albron's habit of wearing red-and-green checks that saved Alaun from overshooting.

Conqueror pawed the air as he hauled him to a halt. He came out of the saddle at a run—only to find a gaggle of village children directly in his path. They'd been crowding behind the judges, distracted by the spectacles being enacted in the river; neither children nor judges had expected him back so soon.

The children scurried, milling and re-crossing in front of him. Exasperated, not knowing how close his nearest rival was, Alaun didn't stop. He avoided most of the brats, but was forced to scoop two small bundles up out of harm's way as he strode through the mass. They clung to him like monkeys, shrieking with excitement.

Halting before Henry, Alaun bent down and set his two burdens free, then straightened and removed his helm.

"Good work, m'boy!" Henry clapped him on the shoulder. "Excellent! Frankly, I didn't imagine you would enter this farce, not with what you've got to face tomorrow."

Chest heaving, his lungs laboring, Alaun accepted the congratulations of the other judges in a daze.

Pushing through to his side, Bilder took his helm. "Best get the rest of that gear off."

Just then, the next competitor, a young knight only recently spurred, came thundering up. He flung himself from his saddle; his legs all but buckled beneath him. Weaving, he staggered to the judges and saluted them, then he crumpled in a clattering heap at their feet.

Bilder sniffed. "All I can say is I'm surprised you ain't the same. Silly nonsense, this is."

Suddenly lightheaded, Alaun decided he agreed. Turning, he saw William de Versallet, unarmored, having clearly stood out of the race. Alaun groaned.

"Aye—I'll be surprised if you've not pulled a muscle or two after all that. And you with four jousts on the morrow." Bilder loosened the straps of Alaun's breastplate, then lifted the pauldrons from his shoulders. "Dashed if I know why you had to compete in this 'ere tomfoolery."

Alaun didn't enlighten him. Instead, he scanned the crowd of ladies clustered in the distance. As far as he could tell, Eloise wasn't among them. Had she seen him win?

Smiling a touch grimly, he watched Bilder unbuckle the plates from his left arm. It didn't matter if she'd seen or not. He'd won. And he was going to enjoy collecting his prize.

* * *

Eloise had seen him sweep to victory. She'd also seen the other knights straggling along in his wake. Being of a practical bent, she'd realized hot water would be at a premium that evening. Deciding that those of the sixteen knights who were to joust tomorrow who had also been brave enough to enter the race should, by rights, have their needs met first, she hastened back to the castle to give orders to that effect.

That done, her duties claimed her. Giving instructions for supper and supervising the preparations for the following night's banquet filled the hours. The sun was setting by the time Sir John finally left her alone in the solar.

Standing before the windows looking out at the pink sky, she frowned.

Montisfryn disturbed her.

Her feelings when his scarlet-surcoted figure had been the first to approach the quintains were difficult to justify, as was the totally illogical, utterly irrepressible urge to cheer him on that gripped her every time he took the field. It was ridiculous. He was her *opponent*. For some mystical reason known only to the saints, her brain refused to assimilate that fact.

Somehow or other, he'd warped her mind.

That was the only explanation possible for the ludicrously protective feeling that had assailed her when, from the castle gates, she'd watched him move away from the judges after claiming victory in the race. He'd moved so slowly, even slower than usual, as if the effort of shifting his enormous frame was almost beyond him.

William's explanation of why he hadn't competed had done nothing to ease her conscience. The idea that Montisfryn might have jeopardized his chances of winning the tournament—and the prize her father had promised him—by entering a race just so he could win her garter should have pleased her no end. Instead, she felt peculiarly at fault. The knowledge that such a feeling was irrational did not diminish it in the least.

She hoped he didn't think her the sort of scheming woman who would purposely suggest a wager in order to damage his chances in the tournament.

Frowning, she turned and left the solar, heading for her chamber. Supper would commence in half an hour.

"Are you sure this enterprise will pay all that well?"

The lisping tones of Sir Percival Mortyn were instantly recognizable; halfway down the steps from the solar, Eloise halted, glancing around.

"Indeed," a second voice replied, its tone gravelly and harsh. "I've put a great deal of effort into ensuring our returns will be maximized."

The corridor before Eloise, running alongside the hall, was empty, yet the voices rose, disembodied, very clearly to her ears.

"Still," Sir Percy replied, "it's not as if payment is guaranteed, is it?" His inane laugh echoed hollowly.

Eloise grimaced. Sir Percy and his friend were standing in the alcove beneath the stairs. Their conversation clearly was private—should she go forward and disturb them, or retreat to the solar and take a roundabout route to her chamber?

"Believe me, sir, the returns are as good as guaranteed. And with them in your hands, your father need never know about that little matter at Dover, need he?"

Eloise shivered. She'd never heard the second voice before, which was clearly her good fortune. The grating purr held a distinctly sinister note. She turned around.

"I'll expect to see you and your men in the Savernake next week, then, shall I?"

"Oh, aye." Sir Percy tried to counter the incipient menace with a jovial air. "I'll be there, never fear."

Sir Percy was a weakling, but, as she slipped back into the solar, Eloise almost felt sorry for him. Wriggling her shoulders, she crossed the chamber and left by the other door.

To get to her tower, she had to circle the keep. Finally gaining the stair, she rounded the first bend. Before her lay the door to Montisfryn's chamber. It was shut, but she could hear quick footsteps inside. Then, quite unheralded, came a long moan.

Her hand rising to her throat, she stared at the door. By the sainted

Virgin, was he injured?

The urge to open the door and find out was almost overpowering, but how could she explain her interest? She couldn't explain that to herself. But there were numerous salves and potions in her stillroom to ease aching muscles and soothe chafed skin.

She stared at the door for a full minute before deciding that, while she might have the courage to fetch and deliver her salves, she would never have the courage to face Montisfryn afterward. He needed no encouragement, a fact she should strive to bear in mind no matter how wounded he might be.

Holding fast to that undoubtedly sane conclusion, she continued up the stairs. She donned her black velvet, ignoring the pleas of both Blanche and Jenni, garrulous and silent respectively. Entering the hall beside Blanche, resplendent in peacock blue, she couldn't resist looking to the place beside Emma.

It was empty.

"I wonder," Blanche whispered tartly as they headed for their places, "what color the devil will favor tonight?"

It was a point on which Blanche and all the other ladies were destined to remain ignorant. Montisfryn, together with the fifteen other knights as yet undefeated, did not attend the meal. Their absence was commented on with approval as doing honor to their host by taking their roles in the morrow's entertainment so seriously.

For once, Eloise considered that chivalry and commonsense had met. After the punishment of the race, had she been in a position to do so, she would have ordered Montisfryn to bed. The fact that he had had the sense to rest without having a lady order him to do so improved her opinion of his intelligence. Clearly the man was not all brawn.

It was after the last course, when a party of jongleurs appeared to entertain the company, that the memory of her wager, and the certainty that Montisfryn would expect her to pay her dues immediately, intruded on her mind. Once it had, she could think of nothing else.

Slipping away from the table, she headed for her tower. Hurrying up the stairs, she was nearly level with the door to his chamber before she realized it was open.

She paused, considering the sight.

"Come in, lady. I've been waiting for you."

She considered some more. The chamber was unlit, the only illumination coming from a flickering brazier. There was no doubt who bade her enter; she would recognize his deep voice anywhere. Gathering her confidence, she approached the doorway.

Goblet in hand, Alaun lounged on the canopied bed. He'd bathed and suffered the torture of Bilder's massage, then dined in blissful peace. His humor, in abeyance for most of the day, was completely restored.

He watched as Eloise appeared, his gaze taking in her black velvet gown. His lips lifted. She halted on the threshold, her hands clasped before her.

Her gaze found him. He waited.

So did she.

Taking in her stance, he inwardly frowned. "I wondered when you would remember our wager." Perhaps she couldn't see well in the dark?

Eloise could see him perfectly well, clad for the evening yet clearly waiting, as he had admitted, for her.

The sight did nothing to dispel her sudden conviction: His chamber looked awfully like a lion's den—with a lion in it. "I was on my way to fetch a garter. If you will wait, I will bring it down to you, my lord."

She stepped back.

"Wait."

She watched as he rose. Setting down his goblet, he approached. Taking her hand, he backed her onto the stairs, then shut the door. He looked down at her. "Where can we talk privately?"

They had to discuss their wagers for tomorrow; she sorted through the likely spots. "There's the herb garden. I doubt anyone will be there at this hour."

His gaze on her face, he inclined his head. "Lead on, lady."

He walked with his left shoulder directly behind her head. Whenever they came upon others clogging the narrow corridors, he swung his right shoulder forward, and she had room to pass safely.

It was the first time any man had shielded her so; she found the protection unexpectedly reassuring. By the time they reached the herb garden, wedged between the curtain wall and the keep and screened by laurel hedges, her apprehension had eased. Montisfryn's honor would ensure her safety—even with him.

With considerable reluctance, Alaun had come to the same conclusion. The alluring vision he'd entertained of spending much of the night buried inside her had dispersed like a phantom. She would yield him her garter as promised; he would get no more from her just yet. She remained elusive, just beyond his reach, still easily resisting the temptation he was endeavoring to lay before her. As Henry had warned him, her walls were unusually strong. There was, however, more than one way to take a castle.

Eloise halted beside the carp pond. Giving thanks that the moon was sufficiently full to afford them decent light, she swung to face him. "As I was saying, my lord, I will send a maid with a garter, as promised."

He looked down at her, his expression shadowed. "Nay, lady. I will have my garter from *you*, as promised."

She frowned. "I don't have one with me. If you recall, I was on my way to fetch one when you stopped me."

He continued to look down at her; she felt her nerves flicker.

"What, then, is presently holding up your stockings?"

She blinked. Then, drawing herself up, she met his gaze frostily. "I refuse to walk through the corridors with one stocking hanging down."

His slow smile surfaced. "Nay, I won't ask that much of you." Reaching through the fitchets of his houppelande, he drew forth a lacing. "I've brought a replacement."

She stared at the lacing dangling from his fingers. "But the garters match this gown."

"My sorrow, lady, yet you were wearing this gown yestereve when we made our wager. I asked for 'one of your garters'. Tis what I would have."

She had no ground left on which to make a stand. Grappling with that fact, the realization that Montisfryn was definitely *not* all brawn sank into her mind. He'd trapped her very neatly; she would have to give him her garter—now.

Exasperated, she glared at him, an action that had no discernible effect. Reaching for the lacing, she flapped her hand at him. "Turn around."

His smile gave her an instant's warning, but of what she was at a loss to guess.

"Nay, lady. You had me claim my prize yestereve. I will do so again tonight."

Before she could blink, his hands closed about her waist. He hoisted her as if she weighed nothing and set her atop the pond wall. Biting back a squeal, she clutched at his shoulders. The coping wasn't high, but the flat stones were unsteady.

He looked up at her, lazy leonine satisfaction in his face.

She let fury light her eyes. "Lord de Montisfryth, this is—"

"Will you lift your skirts—or shall I?"

The question, uttered in an even tone, stopped her in her tracks. Stunned, she stared down at him.

He was serious.

It was there in his eyes, in the uncompromising set of his jaw, in the way he held himself, broad shoulders square, hands on his hips.

There, too, in the tawny brow that slowly rose.

Abruptly, she realized she would have to answer—and that, soon. Her precarious footing rendered a physical tussle out of the question; creating a ruckus and calling attention to her predicament was an even less attractive proposition.

Her haughtiness gave way to uncertainty. If he lifted her skirts?

Eyes narrowing, her expression glacial, she put her nose in the air. Shifting her weight, she set her left leg in advance of her right. "As you are so churlish as to insist, Lord de Montisfryth, you leave me no choice."

Alaun answered the acid comment with a smile. As her small hands gathered in the thick velvet and the stiffer silk beneath, her hems slowly rose, revealing a long, shapely limb.

He watched the hems inch upward. She stopped when they reached her garter. The saints were smiling; she wore her garters above, not below, her knee. "Higher—unless you wish to have me fossicking blindly beneath your skirts."

The hiss of her indrawn breath fell on his ears.

Eloise was speechless—not just with fury. The idea of him fossicking under her skirts—and she was sure it wouldn't be blindly—had let butterflies loose in her stomach. The muscles in her right leg, the one carrying her weight, quivered. He was candidly examining her left leg, not exactly bare yet her fine hose afforded but little protection. Setting her teeth, she edged her skirts up another two inches, exposing her garter to the moonlight.

When he didn't move but just stood there, looking, she lifted her head and stared straight ahead, valiantly disregarding her erratic heartbeat and the effort it took just to breathe.

Alaun didn't move until he was sure his raging lust wouldn't slip its leash. Then he stepped forward, the lacing in one hand, and wrapped his fingers about her ankle.

He heard her stifled gasp. He glanced up; she was, apparently, absorbed with the castle behind him. Lips curving, he returned his gaze to her leg. Slowly, he trailed his fingers up the back of her calf, feeling sleek muscles quiver beneath his touch. Lightly, he stroked through the hollow behind her knee, then, cupping the back of her knee, ran his hand up to her garter.

"Lord de Montisfryth!"

Her shocked protest was almost breathless.

She grabbed his shoulder as her right leg quaked.

He grinned triumphantly, but didn't look up. Quickly tying the lacing below her garter, he deftly unpicked the knot in the velvet band.

Only years of discipline stopped him from investigating further, from slipping his fingers under the filmy edge of her chemise, just visible beneath her raised skirts, to caress the warmth he knew he would find between her silken thighs.

He even managed not to touch her bare skin, which, as it transpired, proved wise.

As soon as she felt her garter fall away, Eloise dropped her skirts; letting go of his shoulder, she smoothed them down.

The shift in her weight was too much for the coping; it started to slip forward, tipping her back.

Toward the pond.

Her eyes met Montisfryn's. Whether it was the threat of eternal damnation that he must have read in them, or simply a matter of knightly courtesy, he deigned to save her.

Instead of landing amid the carp, she landed against his chest, held tight in one strong arm, her toes a good foot from the ground.

She hadn't even seen him move.

Her hands had locked on his shoulders. Disoriented, breathless, she blinked at him.

Easing his hold, he let her slide down until her head was just below his, her feet still inches from safe earth. Then his hand rose to frame her face, and his lips came down on hers.

Had she had any choice, she would never have yielded her mouth. But her lips had been parted in surprise, and he took immediate advantage. She tried to hold back, aloof, but he was entirely too persuasive. Soon, she was clinging to him, her lips clinging to his, her tongue dueling with his as it had the night before.

And, once again, heat crept insidiously into her veins, spreading through her body with every beat of her heart, coalescing in a pool of liquid warmth deep inside her. She let her body sink against his, his muscled hardness a potent temptation to her softer flesh.

She felt like purring and arching against him.

He gave her no caresses other than through the shared kiss, but when he finally raised his head, he left her wanting.

Aching. Empty.

Gravely, she studied his face, searching his eyes for some hint, some clue to the conundrum he posed. Arms of warm steel held her trapped; even had she twice her strength she could not have broken free, yet she wasn't afraid. He was larger and stronger than Raoul had been, but where Raoul's eyes had held an icy chill, his held only warmth—did that make him any less dangerous?

That he intended to seduce her could not have been clearer, yet he did not push her. His restraint puzzled her.

Trapped in her dark, fathomless gaze, Alaun sensed her interest; she was wary, suspicious, but undeniably intrigued. She was as tentative as a mare just brought into the gentling yard, curious yet poised to bolt. But she was caught—eventually, he would tame her. Triumph washed through him; he was careful not to let it show. "We have yet to discuss our wagers for the morrow." Gently, he set her on her feet.

"I did not owe you a kiss, my lord."

Her tone made it clear her protest was perfunctory; she wasn't complaining. His control at full-stretch, he dryly replied, "Consider it payment in lieu of immediate victory."

She glanced up; her eyes widened as they met his. "Ah...yes." Straightening, she clasped her hands before her. "I fear I do not wish to wager a third time, my lord."

He frowned, eyes narrowing. "We agreed on three wagers, lady."

She lifted her chin. "Unfortunately, I find I do not appreciate the pastime."

He snorted. "You're afraid of losing." He held her gaze, then smiled patronizingly. He stepped closer, crowding her against the pond wall. "It's heartening to know you feel such confidence in my victory."

Eloise clung to hauteur. Her head couldn't get any higher and with her hair in braids and crespines, tossing it had little effect. "Such is *not* the case! I'm quite sure William will best you tomorrow—if one of the other knights doesn't beat him to it."

"Coward."

The soft sneer fell from his lips, coming ever nearer. Mesmerized, she watched, then they veered to gently caress her ear. A delicious shiver slithered down her nape; she had to fight to stop it slithering further.

"Tis only jousts tomorrow—you know I'll win."

His whisper feathered her cheek; heat unfurled in her belly. Holding fast to her resolve, she attempted a snort. "Only if pigs fly."

"Don't forget to warn the swineherd to lock them in the stables."

A gurgle of laughter shattered her concentration. "Nonsense." She pulled back to meet his eyes. They glowed golden, intent, mere inches from hers.

Her gaze dropped to his lips—abruptly she remembered the feel of them against hers, recalled the warmth, the seductive heat of him. Her heart thudded in her ears.

She veiled her eyes. Wisdom suggested she shouldn't risk a third loss; the urge to, just once, dispense with wisdom welled strong...she drew in a breath and raised her head. "Very well, my lord. I will engage in one last wager with you."

It was she who had suggested the three wagers, and she had nothing to fear. A kiss, a garter—what next? A pair of hose?

He straightened, masculine satisfaction etched in his eyes.

She narrowed hers. "Do you play chess?"

The abrupt demand surprised him. "Aye. Why do you ask?"

"Never mind." She waved the point aside. "You know what I would ask—what do you ask against it?"

For a long moment, he studied her, his expression unreadable. Then his golden gaze sharpened; she got the distinct impression he chose his words with great care. "I would ask one boon of you. One act, which, once requested, must be undertaken."

"Nay." She drew herself up, unshakeable pride in her eyes. "That I will not grant. You must ask something else."

Alaun hid a surge of satisfaction. His witch would be no man's easy conquest—not even his. The fact made her all the more desirable; she was the first woman ever to have stood against him—he was looking forward to her eventual surrender. Her implacable refusal lent weight to Henry's suggestion—and his own growing suspicion—that she was, indeed, that relative rarity, a non-cloistered yet virtuous widow. Despite the hurdles that might place in his path, he was pleased nonetheless. It seemed likely that since her husband had died, she'd lain with no other man.

Possessive lust flared within him; he had to fight to control it, to conceal it.

"Very well," he growled, his frown partly genuine; holding her gaze, he allowed it to deepen.

Her brows rose slightly; she remained coolly composed.

Hands rising to his hips, he grimaced. "If not that, then..." He looked about, as if searching for inspiration. "A ride." He brought his gaze back to her face. "I ask that you ride with me."

Eloise made no effort to hide her suspicions. "A ride?" She could feel the heat stealing into her cheeks, but forced herself to ask, "On a horse?" It was, after all, a most pertinent point.

He scowled. "You may ride your own palfrey."

Eyes narrowing, her gaze steady on his face, she carefully considered, then nodded. "I will agree to ride with you, my lord, provided that during this ride we are not alone at any time."

"Done."

She could have sworn a bell tolled. Disconcerted, she searched his face, but could find nothing untoward in his disgruntled, yet satisfied expression. Pushing aside her uneasy premonition, she regally inclined her head. "As I have now paid what I owed and our terms are set, I will leave you, my lord."

"Nay, lady." His frown returned. "I'll escort you to your chamber. Tis not meet for you to wander the keep alone while so many who are not your father's vassals are about."

She arched a brow. "There is one I could name who is not my father's vassal, who, unless I much mistake the matter, would like to be a very real threat to me."

His lips curved—for an instant the image of a lion glowed in her mind.

"Nay, lady—I make you no threats."

Alaun waited until her assured, superior, cynical smile had fully curved her lips before adding, "Only promises."

The glare she sent him would have ignited wet wood. Impervious, he held out his hand, palm upward, his gaze holding hers until, with one last, fulminating glance, she consented to lay her fingers across his.

Eloise maintained a chilly dignity as Montisfryn escorted her back through the castle. But her aloofness was a sham; she was very conscious of how relaxed she had become in his presence. The fact puzzled her, even as he did.

By the time they reached her door, her icy demeanor had thawed; she left him with a quick smile.

Wishing she'd refrained, Alaun set his teeth against the ache in his loins and turned back down the stairs. Only then did he recall the garter he carried in one fist. The black band was exquisitely embroidered in gold and silver, the design a scaled-down version of that on her black surcote.

He closed his fist about the velvet band. His plan of campaign was clear—slow and constant attrition to weaken her defenses, unexpected pressure to undermine her walls.

Soon, they would fall.

His expression one of endurance, determination, and anticipation combined, he continued down the stairs.

Chapter 5

Anticipation likewise filled Eloise when she woke with the larks the next morn. Opening her eyes, she was forced to narrow them against the sunshine lancing through the shutters. Beside her, Blanche snuffled and wriggled, then subsided once more. Cocooned in warmth, Eloise stared at the sunshine, at the promise of the new day, while her mind revisited the promises of the night.

Montisfryn had promised to seduce her.

Her smile was irrepressible—she could not, despite all her wisdom, summon any sense of threat to harden herself against him. Here, in the privacy of her bed, she could admit that she would regret denying him, bidding him adieu, never to see him again, never again to feel his arms about her and his lips on hers. Yet deny him she would—she would not cede her independence to any man, much less a powerful, predatory male like Montisfryn. He might not set off the same physical alarms that Raoul had, but he was alike in many ways.

However, provided he conceded her her right to deny him, she would grant him his ride—she was looking forward to learning how he proposed to steal one last kiss; she was sure he would make the attempt. Considering the prospect, she rolled over.

"Aarrgh!" Blanche's eyes gleamed from beneath her lids before she resolutely shut them.

"Good morning. The sun's up."

Blanche opened one eye and focused on Eloise's smile. "I'm stunned. I would have thought that you would be praying that today would never dawn."

"Nay—why so?" Eloise sat up. "Dawn has come and passed. The day is nigh—tis time I got up and faced it." She left the bed.

Blanche turned on her side and stared at her. "You do realize, don't you, that Montisfryn is very likely to win?"

"William is also very strong," Eloise dutifully replied as she headed for the ewer and basin on her chest. "There's quite a few wagers that Montisfryn may have met his match."

A snort came from the bed. "You're indulging in daydreams, my girl. There's no power on earth will stop Montisfryn from winning." Blanche watched as Eloise splashed water on her face. "Will you accept him?"

"Of course not." Eloise mopped her face. "If I ever again decide to take a husband, twill be a man I will chose—I will not have him thrust upon me. As a widow, I have all rights in bestowing my hand." Discarding the towel, she started unpicking the ribbons of her nightrail. "My status is not something I have sought to hide—neither my father nor Montisfryn can claim ignorance."

"True." Rolling onto her back, Blanche stared at the canopy. "Tis what puzzles me most. What exactly *is* their reasoning? They must know tis unlikely you'll happily yield your hand to Montisfryn as his prize. Tis an iniquitous suggestion, in truth."

"Aye, and will avail them naught. If Montisfryn wins today, I will simply inform them that they will have to rethink their wager—I will have no part in settling it." Pulling her nightrail over her head, she added, "As for their reasoning, I have long known tis wasted effort trying to comprehend the minds of knights engaged in chivalrous pursuits—they are often *unbelievably* stupid."

Blanche giggled. "You'll get no arguments from me. Richard's sometimes so brainless I despair." Blanche watched her dress; when Eloise's attention was fixed on her lacings, she asked, "Do you not feel at least a *little* tempted to take up Montisfryn's offer?"

Eloise shook her head. "Nay." She saw no reason to elaborate, to explain that Montisfryn's offer had come about more by accident than design. He'd only made it to bring her under his control, to make her subject to his will, the move driven by lust, nothing more. "You know my thoughts on that topic, and Montisfryn is precisely the sort of man I would most seek to avoid. He's powerful, predatory, arrogant, ruthless—the list is infinite. I will not marry such a man."

"Not even when he's attractive enough to make most women swoon and bold enough to satisfy the most demanding?"

"Particularly not then." Her lips twitched; ruthlessly she stilled them. Blanche's description was most apt.

"Ah…then it was not you I saw in the herb garden last night? Montisfryn was there, with a woman wrapped all about him. She wore a dark gown—I had thought twas you."

There was no hope of hiding her blush. She shot Blanche a warning glance. "Twas the payment of a wager—nothing more."

Blanche snorted. "It looked a great deal more to me."

"Tis not important." She reached for her surcote. "I do not consider Montisfryn as suitable husband-material."

"Indeed?" Blanche raised her brows. "This grows interesting. What do you look for in a husband?"

Settling her surcote, Eloise paused, for the first time in a very long while actively considering that question. "He would need to be strong, both physically and mentally. I have never had much time for dolts or weaklings."

"Aye, that is true enough."

"And he would need to be protective rather than aggressive—a lord who looks after his family and people, and defends them as he should."

"Aye." Blanche nodded sagely. "Tis what any sane woman seeks."

"He would have to be of reasonable age, and hale and whole."

"And attractive enough, with a sense of humor and no tendency to black tempers or madness—I think we can take such as a matter of course." Blanche smiled. "You are, after all, not so very different from the rest of us."

Eloise arched a brow. Stepping to the shutters, she pulled them wide, flooding the room with light. "His birth must be noble, his position in the land secure—I do not seek to marry outside my class, nor would I be comfortable knowing my worth was what underpinned my lord's standing."

Blanche frowned. "In your case, tis a valid point."

When, unraveling her braids, Eloise added nothing more, Blanche prompted, "And that's all?"

Slowly, Eloise unwound her long hair. There was one other criterion, one she hadn't thought of for years. It was present in Blanche's marriage and, she had slowly come to realize, had been present in her parents'. But she'd rarely seen it elsewhere; it was not recognized as a necessary ingredient—she had never heard its worth propounded. "Aye," she eventually answered. "Tis enough."

Blanche muted her snort. "It has occurred to you, has it not, that Montisfryn fits your prescription? Extremely well? Indeed, I cannot see how you can turn up your nose at arrogant and powerful knights, when tis precisely those qualities that support those you seek. Tis two sides of the same coin, if you ask me."

Eloise frowned, looking down, easing the tangles from her hair. Having steadfastly avoided the subject of husbands for nigh on nine years, that consideration had not, until that moment, occurred to her. However, there remained the fact that, with Raoul, satisfying all the logical criteria, even to the arrogant and powerful, had not yielded the desired result.

"Tis my belief you would do well to consider Montisfryn more carefully before you dismiss him. Mayhap you might find you've misjudged him?"

She humphed.

With a determined snort, Blanche sat up.

The latch lifted. Jenni entered. Grabbing up a comb, she hurried to assist

Eloise.

With a sigh, Blanche sank back on the bed.

Mentally blessing Jenni, Eloise closed her eyes against the tug of the comb. In one respect, Blanche was right—she had misjudged Montisfryn. He was not like other men, as easily dismissed from her mind as they were from her presence. Indeed, dismissing him on any level was an art she had yet to master. Too often he invaded her thoughts, rendering all else inconsequential; when he was near, her senses rejected the world to focus on him. Even more surprising, she enjoyed his kisses—and hungered for more, prey to a compulsion to touch him, to explore the powerful contours of his chest, to lose herself in his strength.

Abruptly, she opened her eyes—and forced her mind to her duties.

With her braids finally stowed in their crespines, a wimple tucked over the whole and draped about her throat, she turned just as Blanche threw back the covers and stood.

Only to turn a delicate shade of green. "Oh, dear."

Eloise hurried forward. "What is it?"

Sinking back on the bed, Blanche smiled weakly. "Nothing. Or rather, tis merely confirmation of what is to come."

Eloise dispatched Jenni to rouse Blanche's maid, then, turning to her friend, lifted a brow. "Again?"

"Aye." Blanche's smile gained in strength, in depth, until her face glowed. "I wasn't sure—I haven't told Richard yet."

"He would very likely not have let you come." Hands on her hips, Eloise looked at Blanche, very tempted to scold.

"Nay, he is not so silly. Tis the third, after all. He's grown used to the business."

"Humph. Should you stay in bed?"

"Nay. Tis not my way. Tis very early—twas but a woozy feeling. I'll feel better if I eat." Warily, Blanche rose again. "There," she said, her smile returning. "Tis past."

Eloise humphed again. "I'll wait and go down with you." Briskly, she helped Blanche undress. Tippet, Blanche's maid, appeared with Jenni, both with eyes shining and questions in their faces. Blanche laughed and made them free of her secret. Eloise yielded her place to the maids, waiting in silence while, in concert with Blanche, the pair discussed the impending future.

Turning to the window, Eloise tried to block out the chatter. Blanche already had two lovely little girls, one six, the other three.

"This time, you have no excuse not to visit me and my latest arrival— and stay for longer than two nights." Blanche, fully clothed and coiffed, came to slide an arm through Eloise's. "Your father can spare you—he has a wife and a new daughter-in-law to see to the chatelaine's duties. I will expect you for a sennight at least, and would urge you to come for a longer stay."

Eloise smiled. "I'll see what I can arrange." She wondered how, this time, she was to avoid the trial.

It was not that she disliked infants—more that she liked them too well.

She let Blanche's chatter wash over her while they descended to the hall. By the time they reached the threshold, she had succeeded in refocusing her mind on the day—and the many challenges it would hold.

The first of those immediately greeted her. On entering the hall, she became the absolute focus of all attention.

Calmly gliding to her place at the board, she gave no sign of having noticed. With few exceptions, the ladies eyed her with insincere pity and poorly concealed envy. As for the knights, as most had been eliminated, there were many eager to discuss the rival merits of the finalists and place wagers on the outcome. The assessing glances thrown her way informed her that other bets were also being laid, ones in which she herself figured. She was reputedly unattainable; the idea that Montisfryn might win by arms what others had failed to gain by conventional means had stimulated the salacious interest of even her father's vassals.

Her brothers, of course, were unimpressed. William, sitting at the high table, ignored it all, but her other brothers, John and Roger, who, with William, had won through to the last day, and Gregory, the youngest, who had been eliminated yesterday by one of Montisfryn's knights, were all scowling blackly, growling at anyone unwise enough to tempt them.

Eloise hid her smile behind her mug, then reached for the bread. A sudden hush had her turning her head, following the communal gaze.

Montisfryn entered. He glanced up; his features hardened. His golden eyes flicked her way; his gaze touched hers briefly. She suppressed a spontaneous smile, substituting a cool, very formal curving of her lips and a small, regal nod.

It seemed to her that he hesitated before nodding distantly in reply. He moved to his usual place, quietly greeting Emma, who was, of course, thoroughly distracted. Settling on the bench, he reached for his ale mug. As he sipped, his gaze slowly traveled the room.

The whispers died. Those who had been most garrulous in their wagering suddenly found their bread and ale fascinating. A wary silence descended on the hall.

Eloise glanced back to see William grin, then nod to Montisfryn. Montisfryn acknowledged the salutation with an inclination of his head, then returned to his ale. She followed his lead.

Only when he stood to leave did he again look her way. Having watched him through her lashes, she raised her head and met his gaze squarely. The expression in his golden eyes was unmistakable. Neither complacent nor overconfident, it was simply possessive. To him, she was already his.

With a nod which set the words, "Until later, lady," ringing in her mind, he stepped down from the dais and, with characteristically deliberate stride, left the hall.

"Oh, *my!*" Blanche turned, wide-eyed.

Drawing in a steadying breath, Eloise ignored her. St Catherine's teeth! If he could shake her now, what state would she be in when he won? When, after refusing him, she went with him on their ride?

The thought elicited a most unexpected reaction—a sort of thrilled panic. Pushing it from her, she rose and left the hall to immerse herself in her household duties. An eminently safe, reassuringly mundane occupation.

* * *

"Tis time to leave for the pavilions."

Eloise glanced up from her ledgers to see Blanche shut the door.

Her friend raised a brow. "Are you going to go—or sit it out here? It would be easy to invent some catastrophe, wouldn't it?"

Eloise smiled and laid aside her quill. "Exceedingly easy. However"— she shut her ledger—"if Montisfryn wins, twill fall to me to remind that gaggle of ill-educated males that it lies not in even my father's power to compel me to marry. My presence at the ground, with not the slightest vestige of trepidation for the outcome, is a necessary supporting tactic."

Having cited her logic, thus excusing her interest, she smiled sunnily and rose. "Come." She linked her arm in Blanche's. "Let's see what the day brings forth."

Her appearance in the stands was noted by all, along with her buoyant spirits.

"What's to happen today?" Blanche asked. "Just jousts?"

Eloise nodded. "Under formal rules." Each pair of knights, fully armored and mounted on mail-caparisoned destriers, would charge each other with lances, the tips swaddled to prevent mishap, each hoping, at the very least, to break their lance on their opponent's shield, ultimately, to unseat him. That accomplished, the victorious knight would dismount and take up arms while the fallen knight was hurriedly assisted to his feet and likewise armed with mace or blunted sword. The contest would continue on foot, until one or other knight yielded.

From the start, the bouts were grueling. The first eight matches saw every man joust. Reining in her thoroughly misplaced interest, Eloise looked on, outwardly unmoved, as Montisfryn unhorsed his opponent on the second pass, then, when they resumed on foot, forced him to his knees with a succession of mighty blows.

Clapping enthusiastically, Blanche grimaced at her.

When William dispatched his opponent with skill and vigor, Eloise clapped approvingly.

By the time the ladies withdrew for dinner, only four knights remained unbeaten—Montisfryn, William, Roland de Haverthorne and Edgar de Brasely, a local knight.

"Well," Blanche said, as they returned to the stand, "I have to admit your father's tournament has been *infinitely* more exciting than any other I've attended."

When Eloise shot her a skeptical look, Blanche grinned. "Nothing to do with his organization, but simply the quality of the contestants."

Eloise raised her eyes heavenward, then looked to where William was preparing to take the field against Roland de Haverthorne.

Blanche translated the soft sighs rising about them. "Sorry, Eloise—I'm cheering for de Haverthorne."

Eloise shook her head. "I'm truly amazed."

"You're biased—and blind as well, at least in that respect."

Eloise didn't reply.

Unfortunately for Montisfryn's cousin, the support of the ladies was insufficient to permit him to overcome William's great strength. Although he labored long and hard, the outcome was never in doubt. A blow taken high on his shoulder sheered into his helm. Laid out on the ground, Roland wearily raised a gauntlet and yielded.

Montisfryn, waiting by the side of the lists to engage with de Brasely, paused only to assure himself that his cousin had taken no serious hurt before mounting his black destrier and riding into the arena.

Eloise couldn't help but note the avid, almost voracious interest his appearance provoked. The ladies openly stared, their eyes following every movement of his huge body encased in chased steel. Mail winked and blinked in the sunlight; his armored plates gleamed. Managing the huge destrier with his knees alone, he hefted the heavy lance in one hand.

"Don't try to tell me you're impervious to *that*," came Blanche's whisper in her ear. "You would have to be dead."

Her mask firmly in place, Eloise cast Blanche a reproving glance.

De Brasely was slower coming to the mark; Montisfryn showed no impatience, sitting his destrier, preternaturally still.

"Like a statue," Blanche murmured.

Like an avenging god, Eloise thought as, the signal given, Montisfryn surged into powerful life. De Brasely went down on the first pass.

A mighty cheer rose from the knights and commoners gathered about the ropes. It was echoed by a softer exclamation from by the more delicate occupants of the stands.

De Brasely, a trifle stunned by his fall, gamely faced up to Montisfryn.

"He'll never last," was Blanche's opinion.

Within minutes she was proved correct; de Brasely's squires rushed out to collect him as, to cheers and roars of approval, Montisfryn saluted the judges.

He paused, his gaze remaining on the center stand.

"He's looking at you," Blanche, quite unnecessarily, informed Eloise.

Eloise could feel his gaze, warm as ever, yet with the definite hint of a challenge behind it. She met both gaze and challenge with polite disinterest, refusing to acknowledge the thrill that coursed through her.

With the slightest of nods, Montisfryn turned and walked away.

There was a lull before the final joust to allow Montisfryn to refresh himself and attend to his armor as William already had, and to allow even more wagers to be placed—on who would win, and on whether Montisfryn would collect his prize. Thrilled chatter swelled, lapping the arena; excitement, tangible, rose on the air.

* * *

In his tent, indifferent to it all, Alaun paced restlessly, a goblet gripped in one fist, his expression tending black. Raising the goblet, he took a hefty swallow; as he lowered it, his scowl was close to a snarl.

"What the devil's biting you?" Roland, lying on a camp bed with Bilder fussing over him, felt compelled to ask. When Alaun showed no sign of replying, Roland added, "Or should I guess?"

"Not if you wish to keep charming the ladies with your smile."

There was not the slightest hint of humor in the growl. Roland cast a glance heavenward and kept his lips shut. It had not escaped his notice that his cousin's prize showed precious little interest in being won. It was, to his certain knowledge, the first time Alaun's ego had been dealt such a blow.

Alaun drained the goblet, wishing he could thus easily dull the aggravation of a certain de Versallet witch. Her detachment came perilously close to insult, at least to his mind. Thus far he'd vanquished three men for her—what more did he have to do to drag a smile—any hint of encouragement—from her? She hadn't asked to be won, but she should by now feel *something* for him. He knew she did, but she was clearly determined to deny him to the haughty last.

With a muted snarl, he swung about. His gaze fell on his armor chest— on the black band that lay upon it. For an instant he stared at it, remembering the feel of her in his arms, the taste of her in the night.

A feral smile slowly curved his lips.

* * *

Up in the stands, Blanche shifted restlessly. "Honestly, Eloise! I don't know how you can sit there so calmly. Even if it is all for naught, don't you feel *anything* over having such a man do battle for you?"

Eloise did, indeed, but was too wise to show it; neither Montisfryn nor her father needed any encouragement. Expectation gripping her, she kept her lips firmly shut on the excitement welling within, consenting only to bestow a coolly amused glance on Blanche before lifting her gaze to where the knights' pennons atop their tents were snapping in the breeze.

Being won, even if it was all a sham, was proving unexpectedly enthralling.

Finally, a trumpet sounded, summoning the finalists to their marks. Theoretically, Eloise's hopes now rested on William, yet her gaze went first to Montisfryn. To her, he loomed even larger than before, mounted on his black destrier. He'd ridden the same horse in every joust, yet the massive beast looked as aggressively intent as he had from the first. Just like his master.

Eloise sternly suppressed a shiver. She was about to turn away, to spare a glance for her brother, when a flutter of ribbon caught her eye.

Blanche had spotted it, too. "Montisfryn's wearing a gage."

A dark ribbon, it was tied above his left elbow. Eloise frowned.

"I wonder who gave it to him," Blanche said. "And why, given the circumstances, he's worn it?"

The answer came in thrilled whispers, and avid, intent glances directed at Eloise from every corner of the ground. For one blissful moment, she was at a loss. Then she focused on the black gage.

She stiffened. Her hands clenched in her lap; she could barely credit her senses. Then her temper exploded—helplessly, for she could hardly get down and march across the lists and demand her garter back.

Impotent, yet seething with fury, she shot a sizzling glare at her tormentor. He felt it—the wretch lifted a hand and saluted her! She could imagine his smile; thankfully she was spared the sight by his lowered visor. Her father's stunned delight was hard enough to bear. Thanks to Montisfryn's calculated perfidy, her sire, along with everyone else present, now thought she wanted him to win. That she *wanted* to be his prize.

She ground her teeth. Only years of training kept her seated, unmoving, her features blank, even more unwilling now to give him the satisfaction of her true reactions. Those he would have later. In private. When there were no requirements of correct behavior to restrain her in giving vent to them.

She was going to make him rue the day he had set his sights on her.

Naturally, all those present were thoroughly thrilled. All except Blanche, too shortsighted to recognize the gage, but close enough to sense her ire. "What is it?" Blanche hissed, annoyed at being left in the dark.

Eloise pressed her lips tightly together, then let out an explosive breath. "My garter." She forced the words out through clenched teeth. The effort weakened her resolve; her temper went spiraling.

Stunned, Blanche turned to stare at her. "Your...?" She blinked. "Great heavens!" Abruptly, she faced the arena. "You're going to have to tell me all about this sometime."

Eloise barely heard. "How *dare* he—!"

Rage choked her. How dare he flaunt her loss so—using it to lay spurious claim to her favor? Beyond furious, she glanced at her gown. She'd worn neither gloves nor ribbons, but she did have a long scarf draped over her shoulders, the ends tucked between her breasts.

William, astride his great destrier, sat patiently at one end of the lists. Vibrating with suppressed rage, Eloise stared at him until he looked her way. Imperiously, she beckoned. William hesitated, then, reluctantly, walked his destrier over, coming to a halt before the stand. He raised his visor; his gaze, distinctly wary, went to the silk scarf gripped tightly between her hands. "What now, Eloise?"

"I want to give you my gage."

William's mount shifted, echoing his master's start. "But you've already given your gage to Montisfryn. You can't give your favor to both contestants."

"I didn't give Montisfryn any gage," she ground out.

"But how...?" William stared. "He *stole* it?"

"Yes—no! Never mind!" Leaning forward, she looped her scarf about her brother's arm.

William watched in increasing dismay. "Eloise, Montisfryn is getting ready to pummel me into the dust as it is. I don't think this is going to improve his temper. Do I really have to wear this?"

"*Yes!*" She hung onto her temper with a visible effort. Giving William her scarf in clear view of all would call into question Montisfryn's right to bear her "gage". With a smile that was a warning in itself, she patted the floppy bow she'd unthinkingly tied about William's arm. "There. Now go out there and pummel *him* into the ground!"

With that injunction, she sat back and glared, first at William, then, defiantly, at Montisfryn.

Almost sadly, William looked down at the floppy silk bow. He sighed gustily, then, shaking his head, closed his visor and turned back to the field.

On the other side of the lists, Montisfryn sat his great black, cloaked in a stillness so absolute it was eerie. If she'd been able to see his expression, Eloise might well have quit the stands.

Instead, she was still seated in the front row, hanging forward as eagerly as any lady, all thought of maintaining an aloof distance forgotten as the two knights thundered forward in the first pass.

Both lances shattered. Both knights rode the blows, remaining upright in their saddles.

It was a battle of the titans, a herculean endeavor as pass after pass brought no other result. Lances shattered and were replaced; both knights remained ahorse. Then, unheralded, in a clash that appeared no different from any other, Montisfryn went down.

There was a gasp; the ladies in the stands leapt to their feet, Eloise foremost among them. A hand at her throat, she stared, her heart beating wildly, her emotions in an even wilder tangle as she waited for the dust to clear.

Even before the swirling clouds had settled, she heard the roars and cheers. The knights, men-at-arms, and commoners standing about the ground had had a clearer view. As William brought his charger around and prepared to dismount, the haze lifted and Montisfryn was there, on his feet, his gauntleted hand extended for the sword his squire, already halfway to him, was carrying.

Sinking back to the bench, Eloise tried to work it out, then, defeated, she shifted along to tweak her father's sleeve.

Grinning widely, he turned to her.

"What happened?"

His grin cracked into a smile. "Montisfryn got bored. Just as well, for we would have run out of lances in a few more passes."

"But *what happened?*" She could have shaken him.

Henry chuckled. "He took a fall. He wasn't unseated—he rolled from the saddle using the momentum of William's blow. See?" He pointed at the lance William's squire was carting away. "It wasn't broken. Under the rules, the score's still even."

"Oh." She was grateful that the combatants, squaring up before the stand, distracted her father.

What ensued seemed, at first, no more conclusive than the jousting, at least not to her. Montisfryn and William traded blows, but it was obvious both were fighting well within their capabilities. Then her father sat forward, an oath on his lips.

Edging closer again, Eloise asked, "What is it?"

Henry's gaze remained fixed on the contest. "Montisfryn's up to something."

She studied the heavily-armored figures banging on each other's shields. Montisfryn had the advantage of both height and reach. He was also, she thought, fractionally stronger than William. However, against that, Montisfryn's build, with his wide shoulders and narrower hips and long, if strong, legs, was more difficult to keep balanced, top-heavy as he was with armor. William was broad everywhere; even armored, he was difficult to topple. As most bouts ended when one of the participants landed on their backs in the dust, William's build offset Montisfryn's other advantages.

They were so evenly matched the fight looked set to last for hours. Or so it seemed to her.

Her father, however, had a deeper insight. "No, William!" he roared to his heir. "Don't be tempted!"

William had as much chance of hearing him as of hearing a songbird in the forest. Her gaze locked on the combatants, Eloise tried to see what the dangerous temptation was. Hand-to-hand combat was not her forte, but after some minutes, she noticed that Montisfryn was moving rather more than he had in earlier bouts. He kept weaving back, out of William's reach, often leaving her brother waving his mace at thin air.

Intrigued, she watched intently. Montisfryn did it again; this time, William shuffled forward, determined to land his blow. Montisfryn caught it easily on his shield, returning the favor with a crunch from his broadsword. She winced. The force behind that blow was frightening.

"*Fool boy!*"

Her father's half-bellowed groan drew her attention. She was about to inquire why William was foolish to try to land blows on his opponent rather than swat the air, when her father answered unprompted in a bellow to her brother, "You'll overbalance if you chase him!"

Whipping her gaze back to the action, Eloise finally saw what was exciting her sire's ire. Montisfryn was used to his disadvantage. He guarded against the tendency to overbalance, shifting his feet easily despite the weight of his armor. William, rock-solid while he remained stationary, was not used to moving so much. Not only would the effort tire him, but he was being forced to extend more and more, subtly encouraged to overreach. If he did, slow as he was, he could be beaten into the ground by a faster and taller opponent.

That was, in fact, precisely Alaun's intention. He'd quickly realized that standing and trading blows in the time-honored fashion would, very likely, end in his defeat. He and William were well-matched, but it was he who stood on trickier ground. A little more time had shown him his opponent's weakness; he had promptly set about capitalizing on it. Nevertheless, it was a grueling fifteen minutes later before William finally made that one move too many.

Alaun pounced, raining blows on William's head which William met with his shield, his feet scrabbling as, driven by instinct, he leaned back from the stunning force of the attack. That instinct cost him the match. He overbalanced and went down, landing on his back, clouds of dust shooting out on all sides.

When the dust cleared, William found himself looking up the long length of Alaun's broadsword, from where its tip rested in the mail of his gorget to where the hilt was gripped in Alaun's gauntleted fist. Instinctively, William tested his right arm, still clutching his mace, and discovered it was immobilized under Alaun's left foot.

For a chill second, they eyed each other.

"Do you yield?"

Alaun's disembodied voice floated down.

"Aye." Signaling the judges with his left hand, William squinted up. "I'll know better than to go dancing with you again."

Alaun laughed. Switching his sword to his left hand, he reached down and trapped the trailing end of Eloise's silk scarf between his gloved fingers. Jerking the bow loose, he looped the scarf about his fist. Then he removed both sword and foot and held out a hand to William.

He did not look up at the stands.

Clasping his proffered hand, William struggled up. "Twas a good fight, right enough."

"Aye. We've given them a show they'll remember."

Together, they perfunctorily saluted the judges, then turned away. Alaun stretched, then held out his sword to Bilder, hurrying up. "Aah!—I need a hot bath. Why the devil can't you fight with a sword?" He put up a hand to massage his left shoulder.

William chuckled. "Nay, a mace is a man's weapon. My father carried one in all his campaigns—he's survived well enough."

"Amazing, if you ask me."

Trading such knightly insults, they ambled from the field to the cheers and roars of the crowd. Their squires were waiting to strip the heavy plates from their bodies; hot baths and liniments were awaiting them in their tents.

Up in the stand, Eloise sat rigid, her fury in no way abated. The actual result had been distinctly anticlimactic; far from dwelling on it, her mind was moving swiftly ahead, charting her course, organizing her strategy.

She had expected to enjoy, in a distantly superior way, correcting her father's and Montisfryn's apparent misconception; now, she was relishing the prospect. But she would deal with them individually—her father's motives were at least excusable. As for Montisfryn, she intended to deal with him as he deserved.

Her jaw was still clenched, her teeth aching; she forced herself to relax. She glanced at Blanche, who had remained, mercifully silent, by her side. "Tis time I spoke with my sire."

Unfortunately, her father was surrounded by knights and the other judges, all exclaiming over and reliving the last joust. With a mental curse against the childish exploits of men, her icy demeanor intact, Eloise rose and turned toward the castle. "Come—I have duties to attend to. I will deal with this matter later."

Chapter 6

"Later" proved to be much later.

As the time for the banquet—the magnificent feast she'd spent days organizing—drew near, Eloise's mood turned black. She paced her chamber, shooting dagger glances at the door. She'd yet to speak with her father. Despite numerous attempts since returning from the lists, she hadn't been able to locate him. She'd finally dispatched a page carrying a carefully worded request for an interview to search the castle for his lord.

The page had returned, conveying her father's intention to wait on her in her chamber. When, he hadn't said.

Her temper simmering, she swung about. Her skirts swirled, gold silk beneath scarlet velvet. With her black velvet denied her, for she could hardly wear that, a reminder to all of Montisfryn's "gage," she'd opted for his colors. Given his penchant for wearing anything but, she felt confident he and she would clash hideously were he fool enough to come near her.

Close by the hearth, little Jenni, slim, brown-eyed, brown-haired with rosy cheeks—she'd ever reminded Eloise of a robin—was bent over a piece of darning.

Eloise frowned. "Tis time for the banquet, Jenni. I needs must wait for my sire, but you do not. Hurry down and take your place."

Jenni looked uncertain. "Be you sure you won't need me, lady?"

"Nay. I'll join the table once I've spoken with my father."

Laying aside her work, Jenni quietly left; the latch had only just fallen behind her when it lifted again.

Eloise swung about; her father entered.

From under heavy brows, he eyed her frowningly. "Well, daughter?" Closing the door, he advanced toward the fire, to his accustomed place before the hearth.

Hands clasped before her, Eloise raised her chin. "I would discuss with you, Father, this wager you have lost to the Earl of Montisfryn. With due respect, as I was not a party to the proposal, and as my hand is my own to bestow as I please, I do not feel obliged to consent to marry Montisfryn regardless of his victory."

"Naturally not, girl. I did not wager your hand—tis not mine to bestow."

"You didn't?" The chamber whirled. Eloise stared. A sudden sinking feeling assailed her. "Then what did you promise him?"

"You heard as well as anyone. I promised him that when he leaves this castle, you will be '*in his care*'."

She frowned. "What mean you by that?"

"By all the saints, girl!—you know the laws about females better than I. You're a wealthy, well-born widow—you must reside under some lord's protection. Neither king nor courts will have it otherwise. When you left your convent, you returned to my care. You've lived here five years as my responsibility. I'm proposing to pass that charge, the responsibility for your safety, to Montisfryn."

She literally doubted her ears. "Twas the...the *responsibility for protecting me* that you offered as prize?"

"Aye."

"Did he know what you intended from the outset?"

"Of course—we discussed the matter before he accepted the wager."

A scream welled in her throat; she set her teeth against it. The idea that Montisfryn had known all along just what her father intended, while she, so well-versed in women's law, had missed the vital point, was enough to drive her to the brink of hysterical rage. She swung away. "Tis *infamous!*"

"Nay—tis a simple enough matter in law."

She knew it. It was also not a matter in which she had any rights; she'd cast her lot five years ago, when she'd left Claerwhen in her father's charge. "I wish to return to Claerwhen."

Henry shook his head. "I cannot grant that wish. I've yet to complete the formalities, but my word binds me to pass you into Montisfryn's hands." After a moment, he added, "If you truly wish it, you may petition him to release you into the convent's care."

She humphed—derisively. Pacing aggressively, she systematically evaluated her escape routes. She would allow herself the luxury of being furious—with her sire as well as Montisfryn—later; first she had to secure her way out of the future they'd devised for her. As for her irrational, senseless disappointment that Montisfryn had not, at any time, been fighting for her hand—*that* she would keep entirely to herself. "Even if I am *legally* in his care, there's no reason I cannot reside here."

"Nay, daughter. Once you are in his care, tis his responsibility to protect you. He cannot do so if you're not of his household, or, at the very least, in one of his vassal's keeps—one he can trust to protect you from importunate knights."

Importunate knights? And who was to protect her from Montisfryn? She glanced at her father. "You seem very ready to hand my honor into Montisfryn's hands."

Henry shrugged. "Who better? His honor is beyond question. He's a companion of Edward's, a Marcher lord, well able to see to your safety."

"I seem to recall," she retorted, frowning as she dredged up the dim past, "that you and Montisfryn's father were not exactly close friends. I remember you coming into the hall one day swearing the de Montisfryths were the spawn of the devil."

"Ah, yes." Henry smiled. "A grand day's fighting."

"What?"

He blinked, then scowled at her. "The differences between Montisfryn's father and myself were never serious. You may rest assured of that."

She glared back; she could feel their net closing about her. Fury again threatened; ruthlessly, she quelled it. She faced her father. "You could petition Montisfryn to transfer me back to your care." Her face cleared. "You're his host—he would be honor-bound to at least consider it."

Henry drew himself up. "Nay. That I will not do."

She stared at him. "Why are you so ready to see me leave—to get rid of me? To throw me out?"

"Tis not like that!" He frowned. "You're everything any father could wish for in a daughter. You're obedient—your talents are manifold. You've managed this castle in your mother's stead exactly as she would have wished."

Eloise humphed and turned away.

"But now there's Emma," Henry continued. "Aye, and Julia, too. They're mice, right enough—the saints only know why. But tis their right and their duty to manage, and they'll never do that while you're by. Tis one reason I'll not urge Montisfryn to return you to my care."

Not even in her present mood would Eloise argue that point. "There are other reasons?"

"Aye. Tis in my mind you've your own life yet before you. You were not raised to grow old and molder in your father's castle. You are but four and twenty—not so old you couldn't bear a lord a brood of children."

"Huh!" She folded her arms tightly beneath her breasts and tapped a furious toe. How typically male! Her father hoped she'd marry Montisfryn, regardless of his talk of "protection" and "care." A vision of herself swollen large with Montisfryn's babe distracted her. His babes would be large, of that she felt sure. Abruptly realizing the direction of her thoughts, horrified, she hauled them back. "You know nothing of my...my aspirations."

"Nay," Henry admitted.

"You have no right to...to try to *force* such a thing on me in this way."

"Nay." Henry's voice gained in strength. "You will not be forced into anything. Tis little more than a change of scenery. Montisfryn's step-mother lives at his stronghold—you'll like Lanella." He snorted. "She and your mother always got on well. But Lanella's been ill these a-many years— Montisfryn has spoken of making you chatelaine in her stead."

"I do not wish to leave here." Even as Eloise made the statement, she knew it for a lie. If even her father realized that Emma and Julia were hiding behind her skirts, then it was past time she left. "And I most certainly do not wish to join Montisfryn's household." That statement rang with far greater conviction. The prospect of constantly being under Montisfryn's nose, subject to his lazy lion's stare, let alone his smiles, was not one she could view with equanimity. A short ride she was sure she could survive intact—days without number was another matter. "I do not wish to be in the power of any lord other than you."

"Do not be difficult, daughter." Henry's tone verged on the peevish. "It matters not in whose care you are—your rights are not altered."

She threw him a cynical glance. Did powerful men—men like Montisfryn, like Raoul—worry about women's rights? "Tis not my rights..." She paused, then waved the point aside; she doubted any man would understand.

"Nay, daughter." Henry straightened and regarded her sternly. "Tis time you took another husband. You've wasted five years here, on top of the four years before that—consider your sojourn under Montisfryn's care in the light of viewing fresh fields." He paused, then added, "Your mother would have wished it."

She whirled, scorn in her eyes. "How do you know what Mother would have wished now?"

There was an instant's silence, then Henry drew himself up. "The matter is settled. There's no benefit to be had from further discussion."

Eloise drew breath and met his eye. Her father would not assist her out of Montisfryn's trap; he would aid and abet the devil, hoping to hear wedding bells in the future. Curtly, she nodded. "Very well." It was Montisfryn with whom she had to contend. "What is to happen next?"

Henry eyed her frowningly. "The presentation of the tournament prize will be made after the third course. I must make the transfer of your person into Montisfryn's protection before witnesses."

She could imagine the scene. "Will I need to be present?"

"Nay. Tis not necessary." He hesitated. "I've already discussed the matter with Alaun."

Alaun? She gritted her teeth and forced her temper down.

"With so many strangers in the keep, he felt twould be wise to keep close the exact nature of his prize until his party is ready to leave." Henry paused. "You needn't fear that he does not fully comprehend your legal position."

She humphed. Her legal position had never been in danger—it was she, herself, the woman, who was under siege.

Just as she had been with Raoul.

Henry studied her set face; his eyes narrowed. "I would have you remember, daughter, that you will owe Montisfryn obedience in the same way you do me."

She swallowed a snort. Filial obedience—even feudal obedience—would not be sufficient to deliver what Montisfryn sought.

Encouraged by her silence, Henry turned to the door. "I must start the banquet. It would be best if you remain here until Montisfryn comes for you. He has a baggage train in the vicinity—he wishes to leave immediately the transfer is made. A small chest will be all it'll be possible to carry. I'll get Emma and Julia to pack the rest of your things and send them on. He's stationed four men at your door—just a precaution—I can't say I blame him." He paused by the door. "I'll send your maid up, shall I?"

Deep in plans, Eloise stared blankly, then nodded.

Henry hesitated, then strode back and gruffly embraced her. "Fare you well, Eloise." Abruptly, he released her and strode for the door; hand on the latch, he paused. "Incidentally, how did Montisfryn come by your garter? William said you had not given it to him."

Eloise's eyes flashed. Straightening, she lifted her chin. "Nay, Father. If I am already in Montisfryn's care, then that, I believe, is a matter that rests between him and me."

Henry chuckled; to Eloise's relief, he opened the door, went out, and pulled it shut behind him, cutting off the sound.

She relieved her temper with a frustrated growl, then, kicking her skirts about, she resumed her pacing—and her planning.

* * *

From the dais in the hall, at his place on Emma's left, Alaun graciously accepted the tributes and accolades with unruffled patience. He had already dispatched his three wagons to join with his main column, encamped near Marlborough. Three of his knights with their squires and men-at-arms had accompanied the wagons; if any brigands were watching the castle, they would follow the wagons, hoping for mishap. None would occur, not with such an escort.

Behind his lazy, satisfied façade, he carefully rechecked his plans. He and his remaining men had eaten earlier; dressed to ride, they picked at the dishes before them—and waited. Not even Roland knew the full story. Relying on accounts passed on from those at the high table, his cousin, in company with most others present, expected to witness a highly romantic betrothal, something sensationally unexpected—or both.

He was almost sorry he wouldn't be present to witness the deflation when the truth—so mundane—was revealed.

The third course was removed; Henry rose and gave a short speech, declaring the Earl of Montisfryn official victor of the tournament. Clapping and cheering greeted the pronouncement, followed immediately by a keenly anticipatory hush. People leaned forward to peer at the high table; the prize's absence had been noted by all.

Henry scanned the hall. "And now, Lord de Montisfryth and I, together with my fellow judges, will retire to complete the prize-giving. I bid you all enjoy yourselves." He gestured to the dishes arriving from the kitchens.

A stunned silence stretched, then was drowned beneath a wave of frenzied speculation, swelling dramatically as imaginations overheated. Rising, Alaun struggled to keep his smile within bounds; Henry was extracting every last ounce of drama from the situation. With his eyes, Alaun signaled to Roland, summoning him to his side.

Roland shot to his feet and rapidly made his way up the hall. William de Versallet, too, lumbered up. Joining with the judges, they left the dais and repaired to the solar, immediately behind and above the hall.

Through a squint set in the wall high above the lord's table, Henry looked down on his guests. "Twittering like a flock of starlings." Turning, he waved Albert d'Albron and the sheriff, Sir Geoffrey, to the two chairs in the chamber.

Alaun lounged against the mantel; Roland stood, much more tense, beside him. William propped against a chest.

Planting himself before the hearth, Henry rubbed his hands. "Right then! You two are the official witnesses"—he indicated d'Albron and Sir Geoffrey—"William is my next of kin and de Haverthorne here is Montisfryn's. So—you are here, gentlemen, to witness the transfer of my daughter Eloise from my care, under which she has resided for the past five years since quitting the convent to which she had retired on the death of her husband, Raoul de Cannar, to the care and protection of Alaun de Montisfryth, Earl of Montisfryn. Any questions?"

Albert raised his brows, pursed his lips, then shook his head. "It seems plain enough."

Henry glared at him. "You *knew*?"

"Well," put in Sir Geoffrey, "seemed obvious to me."

"The reality doesn't seem to have impinged on many other minds, however," Albert mused. "But then, there are few others present who have served as justices."

"Humph!" Henry was clearly relieved he was not to be cheated of his anticipated entertainment. "So—it's done!"

"Provided Montisfryn accepts the charge?" Albert glanced up inquiringly.

"Aye." Alaun met his gaze. "I accept the charge of Eloise de Versallet, widow."

Albert regarded him thoughtfully, then turned to Henry. "I think that settles it. Shall we drink to it?"

That suggestion met with approval all around. Accepting a cup, Alaun sipped the fine wine and waited, keen to have one last, private word with his host.

Roland, clearly glad to have a drink in his hands, came to stand beside him. "What in the name of all the saints in creation are you about? That woman is worth a fortune. Not a small one—a large one. From all I hear, she's the equivalent of Edward's treasury on legs."

Alaun merely nodded.

After a moment's thought, Roland asked, "And that's why we're due to leave rather abruptly?"

Again, Alaun nodded.

Roland sighed. "Am I allowed to inquire as to *why* you've suddenly been visited by this urge to take on hordes of rapacious hedge-knights?"

"I'm under edict to marry, remember?"

"I thought you'd forgotten." Roland frowned and sipped his wine. "So why haven't you asked for her hand?"

"In case it's escaped your notice, the lady's a widow. Her hand is *hers* to give."

Roland opened his mouth, met Alaun's eye—and promptly shut his lips. After a moment, he asked, "Why her?"

Alaun's jaw felt as tense as a unsprung trap. "Because she's the perfect candidate. Wealthy, well-born, and an experienced and effective chatelaine." He took a long sip of wine.

Roland waited; when no more was forthcoming, he glibly suggested, "And getting heirs on her will be no hardship?"

Alaun narrowed his eyes, but forced himself to shrug. "Aye. But in my case, as you know, while lust might wax strong, it never lasts long."

"You've already had her?"

Roland's stunned surprise grated. "The damned woman's resistance is legendary," Alaun growled. "Twill take time to overcome it."

Roland remained seriously confused. "But if you're going to marry her, why bother?"

"Nay—she knows that not." Alaun fixed Roland with a hard stare. "Neither will you inform her of it."

"Nay, she'll hear nothing from me," Roland hurriedly assured him.

Viewing Roland's startled, somewhat concerned expression, Alaun grimaced. "Tis just that she's too willful—prideful—too used to being her own mistress to settle easily under a man's hand. Tis too long since she's lain beneath a man—I plan to remind her of the pleasure before I mention marriage."

"And after that she'll meekly agree?"

He answered in a low growl. "Meekly or otherwise, she'll agree."

Roland grimaced, murmured, "An interesting hypothesis."

Alaun heard, but didn't react. Seeing Henry alone by the window, he pushed away from the mantel and strolled over. "I've been meaning to ask—what, exactly, was the substance of our families' dispute?"

Henry eyed him shrewdly. "Your father died suddenly, did he?"

"He did. A hunting accident. I was with Gloucester at the time."

"That explains it. I didn't think you knew."

"Knew what?"

"It's a little involved. It was your father's duty to explain it, but as William was yet too young for you to fight, Edmund presumably saw no point in explaining what you might not, at that age, have understood."

"Am I old enough to understand it now?"

Henry grinned. "The tradition was started by your great-grandfather, back in old Henry's time. That particular sovereign wasn't at all keen on his barons indulging in wasteful activities like tournaments. The saints only know what he thought they should get up to. Both our families have long been warrior breeds—we've been a match for each other through the ages. We could, it seemed, keep each other in training easily enough, but—and here's the rub—we've a most unhealthy habit of marrying strong-minded, strong-willed ladies. After the first illicit meeting, both your great-grandmother and William's laid down the law—the king's law, you understand. So your great-grandsires had to come up with a reason for clashing, or that would have been the end of it."

"I take it they found a reason?"

"Not easily. In the end, your great-grandfather suggested the bloodlines insult—you must have heard something of that? Ours is pure Norman while yours is mongrel?"

"That much I'd heard."

"All rubbish, but it proved good enough for the ladies at the time. As the years went on, we didn't need an excuse—it became tradition for the men of our families to fight whenever we happened on each other. Twas easy enough to arrange to meet by accident somewhere in the forests."

Much that Alaun had not previously understood was now explained.

"When your father died, 'twas the end of it. You were too young for me to fight, and William was but a boy. And with Edward on the throne now and tournaments every second week, you don't need the old excuse anymore."

Alaun frowned. "Why did you inveigle me into challenging you nine years ago?"

"The horse." Henry's smile grew distant. "I'd always wanted that brute, but Edmund wouldn't put him up. Twas his favorite, so I never pushed him over it, but once he was gone, I reasoned you would have other horses and I should have at least one Montisfryn stallion to my herd."

Alaun studied the rim of his goblet. "Did you ever get any real champions from him?"

"Nay." Henry frowned. "I could never understand it."

Alaun didn't try to suppress his chuckle.

"What?" Henry demanded.

Grinning, Alaun set down his goblet. "Tis the mares that hold the strain. We've bred for generations and never got a stallion to give the full characteristics into another mare. You need the right seed, true enough, but the right vessel as well."

Henry looked disgusted.

"Tis time I departed." Sobering, Alaun met Henry's eyes. "I'll take all care of your daughter—you have my word on it."

"You'd better," Henry growled, "or, old or not, you'll meet me in the forest."

Smiling confidently, Alaun grasped Henry's out-thrust hand. "She's in her chamber?"

"Aye, with your men without. She didn't seem overly bothered about that, but she's unlikely to leave meekly."

"She'll leave with me nonetheless." Alaun caught Roland's eye and signaled to the door.

"Hmm." Henry eyed Alaun measuringly. "I feel I ought to warn you, but…" He shrugged. "You've made your bed…" In mock commiseration, he shook his head.

Raising a brow, Alaun caught Henry's gaze. "Fear not. She'll lie in it."

Disconcerted, Henry frowned.

Smiling lazily, Alaun nodded and headed for the door.

* * *

He wasn't smiling when, ten minutes later, he paused in the passage outside Eloise's chamber. Four of his men were stationed on the stairs below; Rovogatti lounged in the alcove nearby, dark features impassive, his gaze directed down the stair. Satisfied, Alaun gripped the latch.

Eloise was pacing before the fire. She whirled as he entered, then drew herself up, the chilly cloak of her dignity wrapping about her. He took in her silks, noting their colors, then met her gaze, unsurprised to find it haughty, challenging, as defiant as ever. Deliberately, he held it, then, equally deliberately, scanned the room.

No chest. No evidence she'd even considered packing.

He spied her maid on a stool in the corner. "Leave us."

The girl started, then glanced at Eloise.

"You may wait in the passage—your mistress will have need of you shortly."

That, of course, refocused Eloise's glare on him. With a curt nod, she authorized his command; the little maid scurried out—gratefully, he suspected. He waited until the latch fell before, gripping the twin reins of his temper and his lust, he walked slowly forward.

Ignoring the frizzling sensation that had chosen that moment to afflict her nerves, Eloise waited, outwardly unmoved, for him to come to her. She'd been looking forward to this confrontation for hours—nothing, but *nothing* was going to interfere with the retribution she had vowed to exact. By the time she'd finished wringing an apology from him—likely a difficult task, but one she knew she would enjoy—he would be in no state to gainsay her in delaying his departure long enough for her to organize her escape.

Regally erect, she watched him approach. He was dressed for traveling in a brown houppelande which reached to mid-thigh, and high boots of soft leather. A cloak trimmed with fox-fur was slung back from his shoulders and fastened with a heavy gold pin. Unbidden, her mind conjured the image of his heraldic arms—of the lion that stalked, rather than slept.

He halted a foot from her, forcing her to look up to meet his gaze.

She narrowed her eyes; she was in no mood for subtleties. "I'm truly amazed, my lord, that even you possess sufficient gall to face me thus."

One tawny brow rose, but distantly, as if her tart comment was of no more than passing interest. She struggled not to grind her teeth. "Your use of my garter this day—"

"Why have you not packed, lady?"

The low, grumbling growl startled her. Then the turmoil in his eyes registered, and wariness bloomed.

Impassively, he looked down at her. "Your father informed me he told you to pack a small chest."

Nothing, but nothing. She tilted her chin higher, cursing the fact that he was so very tall. It was utterly impossible to look down her nose at him. "We will discuss the details associated with my joining your household momentarily, my lord. First, however—"

"Nay, lady—we will not discuss the matter at all. I have men waiting—our departure is imminent."

Her temper surged. Ruthlessly, she harnessed it, but allowed it to infuse her eyes and stiffen her stance. She met his gaze—and saw the same emotion swirling in the golden depths, clouding their brilliance. His muscles were tense, his jaw clenched. She frowned. "Why are *you* so angry? Tis *I* who am the injured party here."

His eyes flew wide. "You? *Injured*? With that tongue you deploy like a sword and your hauteur for a wall, twould be a wonder indeed could any get close enough to manage it!"

For an instant, his golden eyes blazed. She needed no intuition to follow his battle to regain control—it was there in the thinning of his lips, in the hardening of his face.

It was a battle he lost.

"But if we are to talk of injury, what of *me*, lady?" The words came out explosively, clearly against his will. "Doubtless it passed beneath your notice, yet today alone I defeated four men—four warriors—to win you. And what was my reward? Did I get so much as a smile from you?" His eyes burned— with accusation and something else besides. "Nay—all I have got is a chilly reception and a taste of your temper to boot. And you say *you* are injured!"

Taken aback, she held her position. "You did not do battle for a smile."

The quiet statement gave him pause; the fires in his eyes died. "Nay," he agreed, through clenched teeth, "and *that* is a matter we *will* discuss later. For now, I am concerned with leaving forthwith."

She opened her mouth to argue—then remembered that she had yet to hear anything remotely resembling the apology she'd promised herself. She eyed him straitly. "Be that as it may, my lord, I consider your use of my garter—purposely misleading people to believe that I was enamored of you— to be beneath contempt. I will hear an apology—else I will not stir one step."

The lion's jaw dropped. "Leading people to believe..." He stared, then shook off his surprise. "Lady—I have news for you. I care not a *fig* what people think—the wearing of your garter was a message for *you* and you alone. Clearly, you did not understand it!"

His fury was back, lighting his eyes, lapping about her in vibrating waves. She held firm, but couldn't resist asking, suspiciously, "What message?"

The answer came in a low growl. "I like it not, lady, that you deny what is between us. Tis there—and nothing you can say will change that."

"Nay—" She saw the flames in his eyes ignite. A muscle flickered along his jaw; a vise closed about her chest. Inclining her head, she let her lids veil her eyes. "Tis nothing more than a passing attraction."

He was silent, then said, his tones clipped, but no longer so heated, "I realize it has been some time since you were close to a man, lady, but you may believe me when I say ours is not an 'attraction' likely to simply fade away."

She considered the comment, and its inferences, for a long minute. Then she raised her head and met his gaze. "What do you think to gain by this arrangement? By having me in your care?"

His expression was unreadable; one tawny brow rose. "Did your father not mention that I am in dire need of an experienced chatelaine?"

She raised her brows. "A chatelaine? And that is to be the sum of my role whilst in your household?"

Alaun held tight to his emotions, no longer sure which held the upper hand. "Nay, lady—you know the truth of that."

"I will not be your mistress."

He looked down at her, at the defiantly proud tilt of her head and the warning flashing in her dark eyes. "Aye," he said, "you have that right—you lack the first qualification."

"*What?*"

Her tone—startled incredulity with a hint of pique—did wonders for his temper. "A soft and soothing tongue."

It was no effort to summon her dignity; Eloise fixed him with a cool, not to say icy, glance. "I would have all clear between us, my lord. Regardless of any fantasies with which you may delude yourself, I will *not* lie with you."

"Nay, lady, the wise never promise what they cannot ensure." He held her gaze steadily. "You feel the flames as well as I. Henceforth, you will be part of my household—tis not a situation conducive to our fires dying of neglect. The embers will smolder, constantly scorching—eventually you will be forced to let them burn. Then the flames will flare for however long they are destined to. Tis the nature of such things—you cannot deny it however hard you try."

She read the truth in his eyes—felt it stir within her. She might not be able to deny it, but she could certainly do something to avoid it entirely. "We shall see."

His eyes narrowed; when she met his gaze steadily, lips firmly closed, he reached into his houppelande. "Allow me to return to you something you mislaid."

Her gaze fixed on the wad of pale ice blue that he drew forth from the neck of his houppelande. Her scarf. The scarf she'd forced on William, along with her favor, rather than allow Montisfryn's claim to it to stand. Without looking up, she took it.

And felt his heat, trapped in the silk. He'd been carrying it against his skin. Abruptly, she dropped it on the stool beside her. She glanced up at him. His expression was graven, impassive. Raising her head, she met his gaze. "And my garter?"

"Nay. That I have won. You have lost all claim to it." Just as she was shortly to lose all claim to her black gown—Alaun managed to keep the words from his tongue. Abruptly, he turned and headed for the door, growling as he went, "Now hurry and pack, lady—we must leave within the hour."

"Nay, lord—tis a point we must discuss. Tis not possible for me to leave with you this night."

With an even deeper growl, he swung back; hands rising to his hips, he halted directly before her, trapping her gaze. "I understand your father has informed you of the substance of the wager I won of him."

She inclined her head. "Aye. But—"

"Do you understand you are, now and henceforth, under my protection?"

"Aye—yet—"

"And that you thus owe me the same obedience you did your sire?"

Eloise glared at him. Was this how his opponents on the tournament ground felt when he started raining blows about their heads? "Aye."

"Then I am come to collect the wager you owe me." With obvious relish, he watched her eyes grow wide. "You hadn't forgotten, I trust?"

She had—completely. "No," she said, as she saw the net snap tight. Then, as the full sum of his careful planning burst upon her, "Tis not *fair!*"

"Fair?" He opened his eyes wide. "To my mind, tis justice indeed. You thought me foolish enough to accept a wager of your hand when twas not something your father could promise. You then thought to trap me into relinquishing all hold on you with our private wagers—and what else besides?" He arched a brow. "Should I hazard a guess as to what next you would have asked had you won free of your father's wager?"

Lips tightly shut, she glared at him.

"Nay, lady—throw not your daggers at me. Tis by your own cleverness that you are trapped—tis fair, indeed."

Eloise relinquished all thought of avoiding her forfeit, yet she was far from vanquished. He might have defeated four warriors that day—he had yet to defeat her. Gathering her calm, she clasped her hands before her. "Be that as it may, I cannot leave here at such short notice."

"Lady—you'll discover you're mistaken."

The threat implicit in the words was emphasized by his tone; she raised a haughty brow. "Nay, my lord. Tis you who have not thought enough this time."

"I have your promise to do as I ask; your honor will not permit you to renege. I will hold you to our wager—you will ride with me to Marlborough this night."

"Marlborough?"

"Aye—I've been with the king in France, and was on my way home when I heard of your father's tournament. I sent my baggage train to await me on the downs. We will ride with my men about us—you'll have no cause to complain."

She very nearly stamped her foot. "I will *not* become your lover—I'll make your life miserable instead."

"Very likely," came the terse reply. "You are already trying my temper sorely. But we must leave within the hour, lady—the sooner the better."

"Nay, my lord, you cannot have considered. I am chatelaine here. Before I leave, I must hand my duties into other hands. There's the accounts to explain to Emma—you will have noticed her hesitant disposition—twill take hours to guide her through them. And then there's the keys—without direction even Sir John wouldn't know which doors they open. As a commander you'll understand how essential it is to know which keys open the storerooms."

She continued calmly enumerating her duties, ticking them off on her fingers. "And then there's the still-room. I have potions half-completed—I'll have to instruct my assistants in how to finish them. Why," she concluded, looking up, "it might be a week before I can leave."

He reached for her, so swiftly she had no chance to escape. One large hand firmed about her jaw; slowly, he drew her to him.

Struggling would have been undignified; she quelled her leaping heart and strove to appear unaffected as, her chin cupped in his warm palm, he looked into her eyes.

"I have heard tell you are the epitome of efficiency, lady." He spoke softly, gently, but steel rang beneath his words. "You may make what arrangements you must, delegate as you deem best. But you will pack a small chest as your father instructed, and I will return for you in one half-hour. The only decision you needs must make in regard to your departure is whether you wish to make it by my side—or over my shoulder."

His "do you understand?" was clear enough without words.

Trapped in his implacable gaze, her pulse racing, she felt herself nod. Inwardly, she cursed; haughtily, she lifted her chin from his hand.

"Very well, lord. I will accede to your wishes and ride this night with your company to Marlborough." She had, it seemed, little choice. But he was a Marcher lord—his lands lay on the Welsh border; his "way home" would take him close to, or through, Hereford—close to Claerwhen.

Lifting her head, she met his gaze with her own brand of implacability. "Once that is done, while I continue in your care, I will give to you the same loyalty I previously reserved for my father, and the same obedience. Beyond that, ask me not, for I will not yield."

For a long moment, their gazes held, then he gravely inclined his head. "I ask only what we agreed. As for the future, we will treat as lord and lady, day to day."

It was her turn to regally agree. As he was so determined to take her, she would go—and make use of his escort as far as Claerwhen.

"I'll leave you to your packing, lady." He turned and headed for the door. "I will send in your maid and your step-mother and sister-in-law. You will doubtless wish to take your leave of them."

"Aye. And Blanche d'Albron."

"As you wish." He paused by the door. "I will return for you in half an hour, lady." His eyes met hers. "Do not think to delay me."

Eloise put her nose in the air. "I will be ready and waiting, lord."

His lips twitched. "Your father held you were obedient, lady. Tis reassuring to have the fact confirmed."

The sizzling glare she hurled across the room bounced harmlessly off the door as he pulled it shut behind him. With commendable rectitude, she refrained from gnashing her teeth. His time would come. That was one thing she would see to—before she left him.

He was, however, as good as his word; Jenni popped through the door, eyes wide, almost immediately. They hurriedly crammed a selection of clothes and Eloise's most treasured possessions into a small chest.

"What of this, lady?"

Eloise glanced up; Jenni held up her pale blue scarf. For a moment, she simply looked at it, her thoughts disengaged. Then she held out a hand. "Give it here." She crammed the silk into a corner of the chest, then, pressing the contents down, quickly shut the lid and secured the straining clasp. Dusting her hands, she nodded at Jenni. "Now hurry and pack a bundle for yourself."

Jenni darted out, eyes shining.

Hands on her hips, Eloise cast a careful glance around the chamber. Nothing vital remained. Except her herb-box. Lifting the special box she'd had made for traveling from its shelf, she crossed to the old linen chest containing her private stock of herbs and specifics. She was busy making her choices when the door creaked open.

Emma slipped in. "Oh, dear." Her father's tiny second wife just stood, eyes filling, in the middle of the room, wringing her hands.

Stifling a sigh, Eloise laid aside her packets and went to hug Emma. "Don't. You'll make yourself ill." Bethinking herself of Emma's monthly troubles, she asked, "Have you enough raspberry leaves for the next few months?"

"Oh, yes," Emma gulped. "But tis *I* who should be comforting *you*. Oh, Eloise! How *could* he do this to you?"

"Now, Emma." She spoke firmly. "Tis nothing so sensational you need have hysterics."

"But it *is*! It's barbaric!"

Realizing that Emma was still laboring under the misapprehension to which she herself had fallen victim, Eloise succinctly informed her of the facts, painting the outcome in the mildest of lights.

"Oh." Emma blinked. After a moment, she darted a shy glance at her. "You don't mind going?"

Turning back to her herbs, Eloise shrugged. "I would rather stay here, but, as Montisfryn wishes otherwise, I will go with him."

She was forced to repeat her story to Julia, her next visitor. After drying their tears, she struggled to impress on both Julia and Emma the importance of the accounts, the barest understanding of her keys, and sundry last commands to be conveyed to her assistants in the still-room and elsewhere.

Wide-eyed, thoroughly apprehensive over the duties that were now theirs, they finally departed.

To be replaced by Blanche, agog, unable for the life of her to credit it. "It's like one of those extravagant tales the minstrels tell—too utterly unbelievable to be true! I can't believe my papa is lending countenance to such a scheme!"

So Blanche, too, had to be favored with the facts.

"Oh."

Setting her restocked herb-box atop her chest, Eloise turned to find Blanche eyeing her keenly. Brows rising, Blanche slanted a suggestive look her way. "You know, that might just be...well, *interesting*."

Eloise frowned. "You, Blanche d'Albron, are in sore need of having your husband take you in hand."

"Saints, does it show that much?"

"Aye." Eloise hesitated, then said, "You will understand, will you not, if I cannot visit after your next confinement?" If she sought refuge in Claerwhen against Montisfryn's wishes, it might well be years before it would be safe to emerge.

"Aye," Blanche grudgingly conceded. "But you will *ask* for leave to visit, won't you?"

Eloise nodded, tempted to reveal her plans. But she recalled that Montisfryn had men without; she knew not how close to the door they stood.

"Will you do me one favor—for our years of friendship?" Blanche asked.

Eloise arched her brows. "What?"

"*Think* about Montisfryn. I know you're only being taken into his household, but tis plain as the day that he wants you."

Eloise snorted.

"Nay, do not be so dismissive. If you will but consider marriage, I'm certain he'll be only too happy to oblige."

Eloise glanced at the door, then moved closer to Blanche. "You are only part right. He wants me, but tis only my skills as chatelaine he is interested in retaining on a permanent basis." The waspishness in her tone shocked her; resolutely, she shut her lips on any further revelations.

Not that Blanche waited for more. Missing her subtle admission of Montisfryn's lustful designs, Blanche's "No?" was disillusioned, but she rapidly came about. "I don't think you can be right, Eloise. Why—just remember how he..."

While Blanche relived every glance Montisfryn had bestowed on her, Eloise shut her ears and pondered a more pertinent point. Montisfryn was, indeed, utterly unlike other men—he was not, nor had he ever been, interested in marrying her. It was her body he sought—he had made that abundantly clear from the first; he was the first man to approach her with no interest in her hand and the fortune that went with it. It was a novel situation—she wasn't sure what she thought of it.

Before she reached any decision, the door opened again. This time, it was Montisfryn.

Blanche rose and shook out her skirts. "I'll bid you adieu, then, Eloise. And God speed."

Eloise returned Blanche's embrace, then watched her friend exchange polite nods with Montisfryn before leaving the chamber.

Closing the door, Alaun turned to view his prize. There was, he noted, no hint of intransigence in her stance. She appeared her usual, calmly assured self—and was still wearing his colors.

As he started toward her, he wondered if she knew how desirable she appeared, standing before the flames, slender and straight, her head regally high, innate pride in every line. He was beginning to wonder if she actually understood the challenge she posed to men such as he. Lifting his gaze from her gown, he raised a brow. "You did not change?"

She hesitated, then her chin rose defiantly. "I thought this attire most appropriate. No doubt you'll wish to flaunt your prize before the jackals in the hall."

"Nay." He picked up the cloak laid out upon the bed. Henry had, indeed, suggested such a triumphant procession, but Alaun's sense of self-preservation had prevailed over his ego—much to Henry's delight. "Tis not my intent."

He held up the cloak, a hooded pelisson lined with ermine.

Eloise threw him an uncertain glance, then turned to accept the cloak. He draped it about her, then his hands settled on her shoulders, not gripping, but holding her still. Her heartbeat accelerated, her breathing seized. She felt his gaze on the side of her face.

"Lady, if my wearing of your garter caused you distress, then I apologize. Twas not what I intended."

Stunned, she looked up. He stood by her shoulder, blocking out the room, his face lit by the fire, his eyes gilded by the flames.

He was serious. Sincere.

She let her lids veil her eyes; her mother's voice rang in her head. *It takes a very strong man to admit he's wrong—an apology from one should be treated with respect.*

Slowly, she inclined her head. "Best we consider the matter forgotten, lord."

His hands lifted from her shoulders; abruptly, driven by she knew not what, she faced him. "But if we are speaking of apologies, I would explain that tis not my way to give the masses food for talk." Level, her gaze fell on the tanned column of his throat. Dragging in a quick breath, she lifted her eyes until her gaze met his. "Tis why I would not smile at you. If I had, twould have been said..." She held his gaze for a moment, then blinked; her gaze, beyond her control, fixed on his lips.

Alaun saw. Drawing in a deep breath, he raised his head and looked across the room. "Tis no great matter, lady. The day is past." The urge to take her in his arms, to set his lips to hers, to taste her warm sweetness roared through him. But they had to leave. Now.

Within minutes, Henry would make his announcement—she would not be safe thereafter. And a castle not his own, with the risk of confusion between his men and Henry's, was not the site he would chose to defend her.

He forced himself to step back and look around; he saw her traveling chest. "We must hurry."

Softly, Eloise let out the breath that had stuck in her throat. "Aye." She frowned. "My maid should have returned by now."

Crossing to her chest, Montisfryn shot her a glance. "A little brown robin?"

"Aye."

Picking up the wooden herb-box, he pushed the chest into the room's center. "She's with my men in the corridor. You may say your farewells as we leave."

"Farewells?" She stared at him. "You don't imagine I'm leaving without my maid?"

The shock in her eyes was unfeigned; Alaun bit back an assurance that, should she need help with her lacings or in brushing out her long hair, he was eminently qualified to supply it. Her "ask me not, for I will not yield" still rang in his ears. "Very well. But she'll have to ride behind one of my men until we rejoin the wagons."

She accepted the grudging offer with a nod.

"What's this?" He held up the wooden case. It was an odd size and of a wood he didn't recognize; a subtle odor, not quite spice and not quite perfume, rose from it.

"A selection of herbs." She read the protest in his eyes and quickly added, "I go nowhere without it."

Exasperated, he dumped the box on her chest. Striding forward, he took her arm. "We are riding, lady. Hard. Do not tell me of any more things you 'go nowhere without'."

But Eloise knew of one more thing she couldn't leave behind. She pulled back against his hold, her gaze lifting to his.

He read the question in her eyes. With a groan, he raised his eyes heavenward. "What?"

"My groom." She struggled to straighten her lips. Schooling her features, she assumed her most placating tone. "Matt has no one to look out for him but me. He's but fourteen. I bought him from the manor court."

Montisfryn looked down at her. "What was his crime?"

"Stealing food." She sensed his hesitation. "He has no one to care for him, you see."

"If I agree, there's to be no one else—nothing else—not animal, mineral, or vegetable—agreed?"

"What about my horse?"

The glare she got warned her he was nearing the end of his patience. "You will be riding your horse. Beside me."

She ignored the unsubtle warning. Reassured she would have the minimum of comforts, she allowed him to lead her to the door.

A small contingent of his men was waiting without. Alaun sent two inside to fetch the chest and case. He turned to Jenni, hanging back by the wall, a bundle in her arms. Beside her stood Rovogatti.

Alaun nodded at him. "Take the girl up with you. See to her safety."

"Aye, lord." Rovogatti straightened, a smile curving his lips.

Seeing it, Eloise twisted about to stare behind her as Alaun drew her down the stairs. "Who is that man?"

"His name is Rovogatti. He's a Genoese."

"Is he trustworthy?"

"I suspect that depends on what you entrust to him."

Her eyes flashed. "Perhaps you should inform him that I rescued Jenni from her bully of a father. He's the castle blacksmith."

Brows rising, Alaun digested that fact. Taking a daughter from a freeman was not particularly easy—rescuing one from the most important freeman in a military establishment was a feat. Gaining her father's support, which she must have had, could not have been easy. "You needn't worry about Rovogatti. He'll do nothing to frighten the girl."

"How can you be sure?" Eloise grumbled as they reached the bottom of the stair.

"Because if he did, you would be displeased."

"So? Why should that deter him?"

"Because then, *I* would be displeased."

"Oh." Eloise felt curiously flattered. It was irrational, she told herself, but the idea that he did not wish to see her displeased was unquestionably reassuring.

Montisfryn stopped in the main corridor leading to the great hall. "Is there another way out? Besides through the hall?"

"Aye. Through the chapel."

He nodded. "We'll go that way."

She glanced up at him. "Don't you wish to take your leave of the company?"

"I've taken leave of your father and the other judges, as well as your family. The rest do not concern me." After a moment, he added, "I wish to be far from here when your father reveals the truth of our wager."

"Why?" She led the way into a maze of secondary passages.

"So that none will have time to dwell on the fact that you're riding tonight with only seven knights as escort."

She still didn't understand, but they'd reached the chapel door.

Setting Eloise back, Alaun went through. Satisfied there was no danger awaiting, he reached back and drew her over the threshold. The others followed; they filed quickly and quietly through the empty chapel. Before they stepped into the entrance hall, his knights and men-at-arms paused to draw up their hoods and settle their cloaks about them.

Alaun drew Eloise to face him, then lifted her hood over her braided hair.

She looked up, into his shadowed eyes.

He held her gaze, sensed her sudden uncertainty. He reached for her hand and closed his fingers about hers. "Come, lady. Tis time we were away."

Chapter 7

Their ride was unlike any Eloise had ever experienced. Montisfryn, on a massive silver-gray, set a punishing pace. Alongside him on her long-tailed roan, it was all she could do to keep up; his occasional glances made sure she did. They followed the line of the forests northward, leaving the Chute, then the mighty Savernake in their wake. Thin clouds drifted over the moon, alternately veiling, then revealing the landscape. The effect might have been quite pretty had she had time to appreciate it.

Not even when Raoul had died and she had fled Cannar Castle had she ridden so far so fast; she shifted in her saddle, minute by minute more painfully aware of the unwisdom of riding in fine silks. Their speed whipped her grumbles from her lips. She peered ahead. Denser shadows took shape—a walled town. Marlborough. The gates were shut, the town slumbering.

"We'll skirt around," Montisfryn called. "No need to panic the watch."

Predictably, he didn't slow; she gritted her teeth as the troop veered to the west.

She had wondered how he would locate his camp in the rolling dips of the downs. When she saw winking lights spread like fallen stars a league further on, she couldn't, at first, imagine what it was she was seeing.

By the time they passed the pickets, the staggering truth had dawned. As they walked their mounts past row after row of tents and wagons, she gave up all attempt at estimation. "How many men do you have?"

Halting in a clearing at the center of the camp, Montisfryn dismounted. "Over a hundred knights and men-at-arms. And the Shropshire levies march in my train."

She swiveled in her saddle. "I thought I saw a woman back there."

"There are laundresses, sempstresses, and others."

"Oh." The feel of his hands about her waist distracted her. He lifted her down, set her on her feet, and paused, his gaze on her face, his fingers firm about her. His body, warm, hard, was but inches from hers.

"Ah—I've never been in a soldiers' camp before, let alone one as large as this." She heard the breathlessness in her voice and inwardly cursed.

Matt removed her mare, and Montisfryn released her. "Until a week ago, this was part of Edward's army. We've been away for over a year—on such lengthy campaigns we carry all needful with us. All the trades for living as well as fighting."

She looked around again. "So tis like a small town—or a very big castle?"

"Aye." Alaun turned to the tents on the small hill behind them. His great scarlet-and-gold striped pavilion stood in pride of place, with Roland's and those of his household knights close by. A stand of trees gave protection from the wind; with his men surrounding the hill, protection from more mortal elements was assured. "My cousin will give up his pavilion for your use."

Roland, ambling up in time to hear his property and privacy thus disposed of, raised a resigned brow, then swept Eloise a courtly bow. "I am honored, lady."

Eloise had taken Roland de Haverthorne's measure days before. Montisfryn's cousin was almost as handsome as he was, and, despite a liking for jests and a purposely charming manner, almost equally predatory. She rewarded his gesture with a regal nod, then, with a coolly distant nod to Montisfryn and a haughty, "I will bid you goodnight, sirs," she swept her skirts about her and headed, stiffly, for Roland's blue-and-white tent.

The cousins stood side by side and watched her slow progress up the hill. When she paused for a moment, then resumed her careful gait, Roland winced. "She's not going to thank you tonight, you know. Nor yet tomorrow, when you toss her to her saddle."

Alaun grunted and turned away. "Twas necessary."

"Ah, but will she see it so?"

Staring at the campfire some yards away, Alaun made no reply.

Roland grinned and started toward the fire. "I'll get one of my squires to hunt up another pallet and place it in your tent."

Alaun looked up. "*My* tent?"

"Well, you've just given mine away. Tis the least you can do to provide a roof over my head."

Roland continued on his way, cheerily whistling; Alaun grunted again, then headed for his pavilion.

Despite the hour, the knights he'd left in charge turned out to make their reports. They'd been encamped on the downs for two uneventful days; the trip up from Amesbury had been equally without incident. He bestowed his approbation and they left, pleased.

Following them out into the crisp night, Alaun heard a distant bell peal the call for matins. The summons drifted eerily over the downs and on toward the town. Roland approached, the central fire a glow at his back.

"Twelve o'clock and all's well." Roland halted beside him.

A soft rustling of leaves had them both turning. Two curvaceous figures detached themselves from the shadows; with sinuous grace, they climbed the slope.

"Ah—all's definitely well now." No hint of weariness remained in Roland's voice.

Alaun watched as Roseanne and Marie, two of the more enterprising whores in his train, neared, hips swaying provocatively, full breasts thrusting against thin bodices cut low to reveal their lush bounty. Eyes agleam, the women paused a few paces away to silently gauge their reception.

Such women, ripe and lustful, were an essential element in any well-run camp; Alaun insisted that in his, they were treated with appropriate courtesy. A small contingent had accompanied his force into France; others, appreciative of the order preserved in his camp, had joined along the way.

Deciding the signs were propitious, the women exchanged a casual glance and came swaying forward. Roseanne, a lustful English rose, twined herself about Roland. After a whispered exchange, Roland turned her about and, one large hand caressing her generous derriere, hustled her into the trees.

Alaun heard them go, his gaze on Marie, now beside him. Catlike, she rubbed herself against him, eyes glinting wickedly. A highly-skilled practitioner, she'd joined his force after Caen; as she ran her hands over his chest, she murmured, in French, a string of explicit suggestions. His lips quirked; he wasn't sure all were possible. The temptation to find out was there, yet remained strangely dormant.

The truth was he desired another, one who had, with the quiver of awareness that had streaked through her when he'd held her, supple and slender, between his hands, raised him, then, the gentle sway of her silk-clad hips reinforcing the condition, left him standing. It was a habit of hers he was determined to break—just as soon as she let him between her sleek thighs.

He was hard at the thought. Marie, quick to notice, reached for him; he caught her hands. "Nay, Marie."

The look she sent him was distinctly surprised; her hand had made contact well enough to gauge his state. She pouted, hoping to melt his resolve. But when he stood firm and simply looked down at her, she sighed and turned away; hips still swaying, she headed for the wagons.

Alaun cast one long look at Roland's pavilion, then turned and entered his.

* * *

Inside Roland's tent, Eloise was not yet abed. As sitting was out of the question, she paced slowly in the gloom. She'd allowed Jenni to help her from her velvet surcote, then had shooed the little maid to a pallet in the corner. Eloise's cote, in fine silk the color of old gold, laced up the front; she wouldn't need Jenni's aid to rid herself of it later, once she'd settled enough for sleep.

Grimacing, she frowned into the darkness. Suddenly finding herself in a tent surrounded by untold hundreds all owing their allegiance to Montisfryn had dramatically focused her mind. Not only on her predicament, but also on the events leading to it.

There was no point ignoring facts. Ever since Montisfryn had appeared in her life, her normally reliable plans had developed a tendency to unravel. First, her calm expectation that she could dismiss her father's wager had proved unfounded; at the time, her fury, fuelled by Montisfryn, had caused her to miss the exact form of their words. Then he'd overturned her plan to delay long enough to escape him by holding her to their private wager—she had not the slightest doubt he'd foreseen her resistance and actively plotted to negate it.

Which suggested that, improbable though it seemed, in him she'd met a knight who could think as fast, if not faster, than she. Not a reassuring thought, but one she would strive to bear in mind until she won free of him.

She swung about. Even now, hemmed in on all sides, she did not doubt her ability to escape him. Opportunities would arise—she would choose the most likely while keeping close her connection with Claerwhen. *That* was not the cause of her unsettled state.

The air inside the tent was stuffy. On impulse, she groped for her cloak, left on her chest in the corner. Swinging the fur-lined pelisson about her, she drew its folds close. A sliver of starlight guided her to the tent's entrance.

Outside, the air was fresh and still. Breathing deeply, she glanced around. The camp was asleep; accustomed to life in cloister and castle, she found the soft snorts, snores, and distant, muffled conversations reassuring. The rustle of her skirts as she wandered along the tree line added another note to the crooning.

It was Montisfryn's words that haunted her. His claim that she would be unable to resist the attraction that flared between them—that her body would push her to satisfy its cravings by accepting him as her lover. Up to the moment of setting eyes on him, she would have laughed the idea to scorn. Now…

Pacing through the shadows, she decided it wasn't his prediction alone that so unnerved her, but his certainty it was true. His conviction was so absolute, he didn't bother to press her as so many others had. Given his undoubted experience, *that* was disturbing.

She frowned at the gold-striped tent perched on the crown of the hill. Then, almost reluctantly, she smiled. No matter how convinced he was, she was not likely to succumb—at least, not in the few days it would take to reach Hereford and the safety of Claerwhen.

A soft whicker floated through the trees. Straining her ears, she detected the breathy snorts of horses beneath the background chorus; they were tethered somewhere near. Remembering the majestic gray that had carried Montisfryn so effortlessly, she picked her way through the trees.

* * *

In the dimness of his tent, Alaun lay moodily gazing upward. It seemed he'd been lying thus for hours, yet he knew it wasn't so. Roland and Roseanne had returned but minutes before. Alaun had heard their muffled goodbyes, then Roseanne had giggled and left. A moment later, Roland had entered. With his eyes adjusted to the dark, Alaun had been able to make out his cousin, points all undone, hair wildly tousled, features slack with sated pleasure; he had frowned at the ceiling while Roland had stripped and found his pallet.

Now Roland was snoring. Contentedly.

Beneath his breath, Alaun swore. Abruptly, he sat up and reached for his clothes. Minutes later, he emerged from the tent, wrapping his cloak about him. Unbidden, his feet took him to Roland's pavilion. Halting before it, he stared at the flap, then grimaced and swung about.

Dragging in a deep breath, he surveyed the camp, stretched out on the downs below him. Yet his eyes did not focus on the shadowy tents and the fires, slowly dying.

Abruptly, he turned and paced back toward his pavilion.

He'd almost reached it when a glimmer of gold flickered in the trees beyond. Tales of elves who tempted mortals into bondage sprang to mind, only to be ousted by commonsense. Eyes narrowing, he waited, silent and still, a denser shadow in the gloom.

* * *

Her mind on the magnificent beast whose presence she'd just quit, Eloise emerged from the trees; eyes on the ground, she walked slowly toward her tent. She felt calm, at peace—with luck, she would get a few hours sleep.

"What in the devil's own name are you about, lady?"

She gasped and jumped back. Her heart thudding wildly, she looked up at the man she'd all but walked into. Immediately, she straightened; lowering her hand from her throat, she assumed a distantly haughty mien. "Walking."

His expression hardened. "Alone?"

"Tis a habit I've developed when I wish for privacy."

"Tis a habit you will not again indulge whilst in my care."

Incredulous, she stared. "By all the saints!—*why*? I'm hardly in any danger here, surrounded by your slumbering millions."

"You are no longer in your father's keep, lady."

She narrowed her eyes. "Unfortunately not." Briskly, she took a step sideways; even quicker, he blocked the move. Drawing herself up, she met his gaze challengingly.

His eyes held hers; one brow slowly rose. "I take it you found the bed you've been given less than to your liking?"

The softer, deeper tone sent a shiver down her spine. Ignoring it, she shrugged. "I daresay tis well enough." When he gave no sign of moving from her path, she waspishly snapped, "As comfortable as any other in this camp, I make no doubt."

The rumbling sound she heard could have been a reluctant chuckle.

"As to that, you'll discover your mistake soon enough."

"Nay—tis you who are in error, my lord. But tell me, how soon do you think to reach your castle? Is it far?"

For a moment, he was silent; she could feel his gaze on her face. Then his shoulders lifted lightly. "Tis a half-day's ride north of Leominster. But the column crawls—twill take a week and more to reach Hereford alone."

"A week?" Her eyes widened.

"At least."

When she remained silent, he asked, "What were you doing at the horses?"

She shook off her abstraction. "Admiring your stallion."

"Gabriel?" He arched a brow. "Did he meet with your approval?"

"He's a very fine beast." She stepped around him; this time he let her, turning to pace beside her. "My father has a horse just like him."

"Your father has his sire."

Surprised, she looked up. "How did *that* come about?"

"Twas at the tournament held on your marriage. I challenged your father—after considerable encouragement from him. The stake was my late father's stallion."

"Oh." A light glowed in her mind. "Is that why my father was so keen to have you fight this time? As a...a rematch of that last encounter?"

"Aye. Partly."

From there, it was a very short step to, "And you suggested *I* stand as prize in place of *a stallion?*"

Frowning, he halted.

Eyes flashing, she swung to face him. "You equated me with a *horse?*" Her rising tones carried clearly through the night. Vibrating with fury, she planted herself in his path and opened her lips to flay him. "*You*—"

Her tirade was cut off by an attack so devastating it stole her breath. She hadn't seen him move, had had no time to react. His hands had framed her face, fingers sliding under her plaits and holding her still so that his lips could settle on hers. And settle they had. Not with the punishing onslaught she'd instinctively braced against, but with a commanding persuasiveness that was far more potent.

Striving to retain her wits and her purpose, she clutched at his hands, intending to pry them from her face and break from him. Instead, when her palms made contact with the warmth of his large hands, her fingers stilled, then, slowly, gradually, her grip eased, her palms curving about the hair-dusted backs of his hands, before feathering down to his wrists.

Alaun was achingly aware of her gentle touch and the tentative acquiescence behind it. Desire soared; he held tight to the reins. When she softened against him, he released her face; instead of pulling away, she let her hands fall to his chest. He caught her wrists and urged her hands higher; she obliged, sliding them up and over his shoulders, her fingers spreading, shifting restlessly over the heavy muscles.

The feel of him beneath her hands held Eloise spellbound. He deepened the kiss, parting her lips boldly to confidently claim her mouth. She sighed and yielded, then the air about her stirred. He'd parted her cloak. His hands fastened about her waist and he drew her against him. Fitted her to him, molding her slender body to the hard length of his. A wave of longing swept her. She shivered, then felt his cloak fall about her, cocooning her against his warmth.

And, all the while, his tongue laced fire over hers. He tasted her again and again, teasing her, tempting her with his heat until her lips clung to his and her fingers sank into his shoulders. A driving need consumed her—to feel more of his heat, to drink more of the fire he offered with every kiss, with every shared breath.

Her burgeoning desire urged Alaun on. He caressed her slender body, yet her gown shielded her too well from his touch. He shifted, slanting his head over hers. She had, once again, gifted him with her mouth. He probed deeply; she drew him deeper still. His own fires were burning steadily when his experienced fingers drew her laces free at her waist. Her chemise, tied with ribbons, was even easier dealt with. Slowly, he slipped his hand, palm flat, across the soft skin above her waist.

Eloise felt the caress keenly; the sensation of his hard hand on her skin sent slow rivers of liquid warmth sliding through her veins. Her senses hung on each movement of his fingers as he touched her, explored her. With his lips on hers and his hand on her body, she was beyond coherent thought.

Her skin felt like rose petals blessed by the sun, warm, soft, yet resilient—satin with the texture of fine velvet. Alaun wanted to touch all of her. His hand rose, slowly, deliberately, to brush the sensitive underside of her breast. He savored her response, the quiver that rippled through her, the leaping of her pulse as her body turned to his. The movement, anticipated, pressed her breast fully into his palm even as her tongue boldly tangled with his.

Caution had no foothold in Eloise's mind as she stood, pressed and pressing against him. She didn't draw back from his caresses, but reveled in the knowledge that he wanted her. The intoxicating taste of him, the feel of him, so hard, so strong, muscles locked and quivering with restraint, set her alight.

When he released her lips, her only thought was that she supposed she had to breathe. Then even that fragment of lucidity was lost as her senses flooded her mind, and delight and desire filled her. His lips grazed her temple; he drew back and looked down. Suppressing a shudder, she opened her eyes, and followed his gaze to where, in the shadows between them, her breast lay cupped in his palm. Her skin glowed ivory in the weak light; his tanned hand showed dark in contrast. Mesmerized, she watched his thumb gently circle her nipple; she felt it tighten, then throb. He caressed it tenderly, as if it was the most delicate bud in the world, and the most precious.

Her breath shuddered and caught; his fingers gently stroked. She sank against him. Eyes closing, she felt her body awaken, a bloom she'd thought withered and long dead slowly blossoming.

It took an enormous effort to open her eyes, to see his fingers so gentle on her flesh, to realize all that it meant.

She looked up. His attention was fixed on her breast, his concentration complete as he pleasured her, drawing whorls of fire beneath her skin. She could feel them spreading, swelling, as, patiently, with infinite tenderness, he coaxed her to full-flowering life.

It was his tenderness that held her. Her breath tangled in her throat; her heart ached with an impossible, indescribable yearning.

"No." The word was weak, barely a whisper. But he heard; his hand stilled.

"Eloise?"

Disbelief, incredulous, utter, and complete, filled the word. His tone, deep, gravelly, and as achingly empty as she suddenly felt, almost shattered her resolve. She took a step back; his hands fell from her. Jerking the sides of her cote closed, she shook her head. "I can't…"

What she couldn't do was explain.

She looked up. Letting go of her cote, she reached up and drew his head to hers. She kissed him—deeply, passionately, with all the pent-up longing in her soul.

Then she whirled and fled.

He let her go; she had known he would. He would never use his strength to hold her—it was not that that would bind her if she stayed.

Dazed, stunned, unable to think, Alaun stood stock-still and watched, until his cousin's tent swallowed her up.

* * *

When Alaun emerged from his tent in the soft light of dawn, the camp was already a-bustle. From his vantage point, he scanned the activity, then glanced at Roland's pavilion. The flap had yet to be rolled up. He studied it, then grimaced and headed for the fire.

Half an hour later, his mind was drawn back to his prize. Her robin flitted past, eyes darting this way and that. She stopped to speak to Rovogatti, seated by the fire; the Genoese shook his head and put a question. The girl answered distractedly, then continued her search. A chill trickled down Alaun's spine. Even as his mind registered the maid's concern, he was starting toward her.

"Alaun!"

He swung about at Roland's hail.

His cousin came pounding up. "Your bird has flown."

"*What?*" The thundered question had all about them scurrying—to pack up their things and be elsewhere.

"I've just checked the horses—her mare's not there. Neither's her saddle."

Alaun swore. "Fetch me her groom." Men ran to obey. He lifted his head. The maid was standing staring, mouth agape. "You, girl! Come here!"

For an instant, he thought she would bolt. Then Rovogatti pushed her forward, whispering something in her ear. She halted yards away, trembling like a leaf. Alaun reined in his impatience. With his emotions riding him, fury the foremost, he was probably an intimidating sight.

The robin's eyes, raised trepidatiously to his, told him there was no probably about it.

"When last did you see your mistress?"

"Last night. She sent me to bed."

Eloise's state when she'd run from him remained vivid in Alaun's mind. "Has her bed been slept in?"

"Aye." Swallowing her fear, the robin looked around. "I'm sure she's here somewhere—she's changed into the cote I put out for her, but her riding cloak's still in the tent."

He frowned, then recalled the touch of fur on the backs of his hands in the night. "Her pelisson?"

The robin's eyes grew round; she glanced at Roland's tent.

"Go and see."

She flew across the camp, but Alaun felt sure the pelisson wouldn't be there.

Two of his men-at-arms approached, escorting the lanky groom. At fourteen, the boy had much growing yet to do, his appearance not improved by unprepossessing features. Alaun waited as the lad was pushed before him; the boy tried to stand straight, but clearly expected to be clouted.

"Did you saddle your mistress's horse this morn?"

"Aye, lord."

"When?"

"Before dawn a little time."

More than an hour ago. Alaun closed his eyes; beyond his control, his fists, on his hips, tightened ominously. Opening his eyes, he fixed them on the hapless groom. "Did it not seem *odd* that she should go riding alone at dawn?"

"Nay." The boy blinked. "She often does."

Roland, Rovogatti—even the two men-at-arms—simply stared. Alaun's jaw nearly broke with the effort to hold back his roar. He glanced at Roland. "Mount a troop on the fastest horses. Well-armed." Roland was off before he'd finished. Alaun turned back to the boy. "Which way did she head?"

"That way." The lad pointed south.

Alaun nodded at one of the men-at-arms. "Get me the sergeant in charge of the south pickets."

"Aye, lord." The man set off at a run.

The robin came skidding to a halt a few yards away. Alaun glanced at her—she shook her head. It was on the tip of his tongue to forbid both maid and groom to obey any more of their mistress's commands, yet she'd earned their loyalty. And the robin's eyes were overflowing with worry; the same emotion showed in the boy's pale face.

Alaun looked at the girl. "Pack your mistress's belongings and ask where to stow them. As for you"—he turned to the groom—"tell my head-groom you're to have one of the fastest horses. You're coming with me."

To see what danger your mistress has got herself into.

Alaun hoped his premonition would prove false; experience warned otherwise. The boy hurried off.

The troop was mounted by the time Alaun reached the lines. Pulling on his mail gloves, he swung up to Gabriel's back; he paused only to check that his great broadsword rested in the saddle scabbard before wheeling the gray south. They'd gone only a few yards when the sergeant in charge of the south pickets lumbered up.

Alaun drew rein. "Did the lady I brought into camp yestereve pass by you this morn?"

"Aye, lord. Near on an hour ago."

Presumably she was making for Versallet Castle. Surely she knew Henry would simply hold her, and hand her back when Alaun arrived? What did she hope to gain, beyond a taste of his temper? Deciding she must be overwrought, he grunted, then asked the sergeant, an experienced campaigner, "Did you not think of questioning her?"

"Aye, lord. Naturally. But…" The man squirmed. "Twas her eyes, if you take my meaning."

Alaun set his jaw. "Aye." His de Versallet witch could command a king with her eyes; dismissing a sergeant would have been child's play. "Stand clear."

Gabriel, sensing his impatience, surged. They'd cantered through half the camp, heading south, when a shout went up behind them.

Swearing furiously, Alaun reined in. "What now?"

The sergeant in charge of the north pickets came panting up. "Lord—

the lady you brought in with you yestereve? She's out a-riding the downs. Alone."

Alaun stared. The downs. *North?*

As the realization that his prize had deliberately laid a false trail, that she was not fleeing in senseless panic but with her usual calm deliberation, seeped into his mind, Alaun clenched his teeth. His eyes narrowed. *Lady-witch, when I catch up with you...* He left the threat unfinished—it would take hours to enumerate the ways in which he was going to ease his temper.

At his terse command, the troop wheeled. Retracing their route, they left the encampment, taking the heading the sharp-eyed picket pointed out. Spurring Gabriel forward, Alaun coldly turned his mind to the one remaining mystery. Where was Eloise going?

As if in answer, the clear tones of a bell came floating over the downs.

Alaun swore. Cricklade Priory. Once behind religious walls, Eloise would be beyond his reach, at least temporarily. As an excessively wealthy widow, she had only to demand sanctuary to be welcomed with open arms. The church, very fond of the wealth of widows, would oppose any move he made to retrieve her.

His curses turned vitriolic. He had to catch her before she reached the Priory—or face the possibility of losing her.

* * *

Eloise also heard the prime bell. She'd gained the crest of the downs bare minutes before to find an ancient track crossing her path. Reining in Jacquenta, her palfrey, she had sat in indecision, uncertain whether to follow the track, hoping it would lead to convent or monastery, or follow her instincts and head north. Now, she swung Jacquenta to the northwest and followed the sweet sound of the bell.

Some way ahead, the dark shadow of a forest lined the edge of the downs, directly in her path.

Resisting the temptation to go faster, for she had no idea how far away her chosen sanctuary lay, Eloise held Jacquenta to a steady pace. Going far enough south to convince any watchful pickets that she had, indeed, taken that direction had slowed her, but the deception had been necessary. She couldn't outrun Montisfryn.

Blinking, she straightened in her saddle, easing the muscles in her back. She had had no sleep, too consumed by the need to flee. When she'd left the horses in the middle of the night, her plans had been simple and clear. After meeting with Montisfryn in the moonlight, they'd been in chaos. Bringing an immediate end to their association had become imperative, overriding all other concerns.

After stripping off her cote and refastening her chemise with shaking fingers, she'd taken to her bed—not to sleep, but to search for a route to safety. Eventually, exhausted, she'd prayed to St Catherine for aid. And the bell for lauds had sounded, its deep tones rolling over the camp, coming over the downs from the north.

She'd left as early as she'd dared, sorry to have to leave Jenni without a word. After due consideration, she'd left Matt as well; he did not have a horse, and she couldn't order him to steal one. She trusted Montisfryn to either take care of the pair, or send them after her. She knew well enough that *he* would follow, but once behind religious walls, it would be foolish to meet with him again.

The thought depressed her, a fact she recognized and stoically accepted. It didn't deter her. Safety, she had long ago learned, was not found in the arms of powerful men.

Forest, dark and dense, loomed before her. A bridle path continued, much in the direction she wished to go. Eloise halted, misliking the stillness beneath the trees and her inability to see ahead. But the bridle path was her route; on either side, the forest stretched, apparently unending. Looking back, she scanned the gently rolling landscape. And saw no one. With a sigh, she turned Jacquenta toward the path.

She'd escaped.

The sudden rumbling of the ground, shuddering beneath the impact of many horses' hooves, gave that assumption the lie. Startled, Eloise glanced back. Previously hidden by a dip in the downs, a body of horsemen exploded into sight, thundering toward her, only minutes away.

She had no difficulty recognizing the figure at their head.

With a breathless curse, she swung Jacquenta onto the path and clapped her heels to the mare's sides. Half-spooked, the mare flew down the narrow trail.

Eloise leaned low over Jacquenta's neck, urging the mare on. The trees blurred as the path twisted—there were no junctions, no minor paths, nowhere she could hide. Then she heard a shout, not from behind but from the side. A minute later, the path abruptly opened into a clearing.

She was in difficulties from the first, her headlong flight impeded by men and baggage; she had to fight to keep Jacquenta from stumbling. Momentum carried them on; Jacquenta pranced, tossing her head, tugging at the reins.

Wrestling the panicky animal to a snorting, quivering halt, Eloise dragged in a quick breath and looked around. Fifty or more unkempt men in padded jerkins and crude, rusty mail surrounded her. Some stood rubbing sleep from their eyes; others, their faces alight, advanced on her.

Inwardly, she recoiled. Before she could react, one of the men, a beefy, brawny ape, lunged and caught Jacquenta's bridle. Eloise gasped and fought to jerk the mare free; Jacquenta tried to rear, but the man held her easily.

To Eloise's amazement, he grinned insolently up at her, his close-set eyes taking liberties no knight would dare.

"Welcome, lady. And tis truly most welcome you are."

Sniggers greeted this pronouncement; ignoring them, and her welling fear, Eloise drew herself up. "Loose my horse, knave!"

The man roared with laughter. Piggy eyes leered at her. "He said you wert a likely enough lass, but with some right starchy ways. I'm a-thinking you won't be a-feeling *quite* so starchy after you've laid those long legs *wide* for me 'n' the boys." One ham-like hand rose to her thigh.

Eloise slashed down hard with her riding crop and fought to regain the reins.

The man's lecherous grin turned into a vicious snarl. "Like it rough, do you? Only too happy to oblige."

He reached for her; she slashed again, this time at his face. He weaved—too late; the quirt cut into a fleshy jowl. The man roared; he grabbed her hand and yanked hard. She swayed, almost falling from her saddle. Panic seared her; she gripped tight with her knees, using her full weight to resist. At the edge of her vision, she saw men closing in.

There was a shout; the men halted, looking around.

The thunder of hoof beats rolled across the clearing—the outlaws raced for their weapons.

An explosion of sound—shouts, howls, and curses—nearly deafened Eloise. Then a savage war-cry rent the air, immediately followed by the clash of steel on steel.

Eloise all but wilted with relief. Montisfryn was there.

Both she and her attacker stilled. Outlaws streamed past, running to support their fellows. The brute holding Jacquenta's bridle, apparently their leader, urged them on.

Squinting through the dust engulfing the melee, Eloise spotted Montisfryn's tawny mane. Roland was beside him, both raining blows on the outlaws surrounding them. Their troop had drawn close, packed tightly together; although mounted they were heavily outnumbered.

She was not yet safe. The entire outlaw band stood between her and Montisfryn.

The outlaw leader saw that, too. With a savage snarl, he tugged hard at her hand.

She hung on, grimly resisting. Muscles straining, she clamped her thighs to the saddle skirts. Jacquenta backed and sidled, tossing her head against the brute's hold. With one hand on the mare's bridle and the other locked about Eloise's hand, he couldn't focus his strength to pull her down.

He realized as much and bellowed to a lanky youth skulking about the rear of the fight. "Here! Help me pull the bitch off."

The youth hesitated.

"Fool! To me! We can use her as hostage to make them surrender."

Surrender? And then what? Eloise shoved the thought aside. The youth came up on her other side; she lashed out with her free hand, catching him a sharp blow. He cursed foully. Ducking and weaving, he eventually caught her hand. She tugged—he tugged back. As did the brute who held her other hand. After a moment of crazed see-sawing, the outlaw leader cursed.

"*No*, you fool! *Push* her!"

Comprehension dawned in the youth's pale eyes. Still gripping her hand, mercilessly squeezing her fingers, he reached for her knee.

Eloise gasped; as the youth wrenched her thigh away from the saddle, the leader seized the opportunity to shift his hold and savagely twist her quirt from her grasp.

From the corner of her eye, she saw him raise it. Grabbing the front of her saddle, hips and thighs burning, she fought to deny the youth the leverage to tip her off.

Her quirt whistled through the air, slicing down on her fingers, gripped white on the saddlebow. She choked back a cry.

The youth bent, setting his shoulder below her knee; any moment he would dislodge her.

Desperate, she glanced up—Montisfryn wheeled in, his face contorted in a ferocious snarl. His sword descended with unforgiving force, shearing the youth's shoulder from his body.

Blood flew—Eloise felt the youth's fingers lose their grip, then slip away.

Before she could think, Montisfryn's left arm came around her, dragging her hard against him, locking Jacquenta against his stallion. He half-stood, twisting in his stirrups, his bloody sword whistling in a wide arc.

Clutching at the arm wrapped protectively about her, Eloise turned her head in time to see the outlaw leader, a long knife in his raised hand, die.

With a shake, Montisfryn freed his sword. He sank back into his saddle, easing his hold on her.

Eloise turned; she met his eyes.

He blinked, and she saw the blankness behind the savage mask. As if he'd suppressed all his emotions and was now lost without them.

"I'm all right." She ignored her burning hand.

The golden gaze focused, then he nodded. "Stay here. *Don't move.*"

He released her as he spoke and immediately wheeled his horse, his face resuming the ruthless, merciless, deadly mask of battle.

Only then did she see the danger that still faced them.

How he'd managed to reach her at all she couldn't comprehend. The fighting still raged, with his force bottled in tight where the bridle path opened into the clearing, while he and she were hard by the far side of the space, dense trees a wall at their backs.

Now the outlaws had two fronts on which to fight; like their dead leader, many chose the easier option. In increasing numbers, they left the battle with Montisfryn's men to concentrate on likelier prey—a single knight defending the woman whose life would buy their freedom.

Jacquenta was quivering. Tightening her reins, Eloise watched as outlaws, slinking like jackals, closed about them in a half-circle, wary of Montisfryn's long sword. Abruptly, he drew another blade, a short-sword, from his saddle.

Startled by the sudden hiss, the outlaws wavered. Then, as if embarrassed by their childish start, they brandished their weapons, and with blood-curdling cries, charged.

Three fell to the first sweep of Montisfryn's sword, but then they closed. His deadly blades kept them before him, but for how long he could successfully defend against all the blows aimed at him Eloise didn't know. Forgotten, she watched, her heart in her mouth, hands tight on the reins. Jacquenta snorted and sidled. Instinct prodded Eloise to ease along the clearing's edge, but Montisfryn's orders rang in her head; she held Jacquenta steady where he'd left her, a bare foot to the rear of his stallion's rump.

A heavy club was swung, then released—it struck Montisfryn on his shoulder. Eloise winced, but he barely seemed to notice. His mail saved him again and again as he caught the outlaws' wild slashes on his arms. The hordes about him howled in fury—more came running.

Then a battle cry sounded over a mighty crash, followed by cries of anguish. Peering past Montisfryn, Eloise saw Roland literally ride through the press, charging through the human wall. He slewed his black around to come up on Montisfryn's left, then another knight followed Roland's lead.

The outlaws wavered. Shifty eyes darted, searching for ways out.

But there was to be no escape.

Trapped behind Montisfryn and Roland, Eloise saw little of what followed. She did see Rovogatti, sitting his horse at the clearing's edge, a crossbow in his hands. After an incredulous instant, she recognized Matt on the horse alongside, handing over the bolts Rovogatti fired.

When the fury eventually died, she was stunned to see that Montisfryn's men numbered only ten. Yet more than fifty outlaws lay dead in the clearing.

Montisfryn looked about; she saw his shoulders lift as he drew in a deep breath. Then he handed his dripping sword to one of his knights. "Have we any survivors?"

Rovogatti was checking the bodies as he retrieved his bolts. He pointed to a bundle of rags under a tree. "Only him." Then, as if to excuse this lapse, he added, "He didn't fight."

"Bring him here."

Alaun didn't move, nor did Roland, leaving Eloise trapped behind them, shielded from the carnage.

The rags proved to be one of the mercenaries too fevered to do more than weave on his feet. Alaun waited until the man was hauled before him. "Who sent you?"

The mercenary spat. "Sir Roger Barnabas. Down Cholderton way."

Alaun heard the hiss of Eloise's indrawn breath. "One of your father's vassals?" His tone made it clear it was not to the cowering man that he spoke.

"Nay." She exhaled. "But I have met the man. He's a local knight."

Alaun looked again at the mercenary. "Say on. What was your purpose here?"

"We was to grab the lady."

Eloise couldn't bear it; she leaned forward in her saddle and peered around Montisfryn. After one glance at the human litter in the clearing, she confined her gaze to the man standing before the gray stallion.

The mercenary saw her and nodded. "Her. Seems tis common knowledge about Sir Roger's parts that she sometimes rides alone, but never far from her father's keep. Sir Roger heard as how she was headed along with your train and sent us to keep watch. Twas thought likely the wench would wander off. Then we was to grab her and take her to Sir Roger."

His words sent a chill through Eloise; Montisfryn didn't move. Staring at the ragged mercenary, standing gazing up at Montisfryn's face, she saw the man's eyes glaze.

"Hang him."

Closing her eyes, she drew back. The man was dragged away. Within seconds, she was being led out of the clearing, Jacquenta's reins in Montisfryn's mailed fist. Matt gazed reprovingly at her as she passed.

Without a word, Montisfryn handed her her reins when they gained the path. The rest of his men fell in behind.

As they broke from the cover of the trees and into the open air, Eloise dragged in a deep breath. Faintness threatened. She quelled it—it was over; she was safe. She held herself proudly, Jacquenta pacing neatly beside Montisfryn's gray. One glance at Montisfryn's face confirmed that further trials awaited her, but he said not a word, his silence so vibrant with suppressed fury that she dared not broach it. They reached the old track on the crest of the downs and, crossing it, started down the long slope.

Beside her, wracked with rage, Alaun didn't trust himself to speak. There was a storm of emotions roiling inside him and *she* was responsible for putting it there. Never in his life had he felt such fury, but it was fear that had brought him to the edge of his control—fear for her. It had yet to recede, despite the fact she was safe beside him.

Angrily, he glanced at her. Her composure had held throughout her self-inflicted ordeal; her expression remained serene, but her cheeks were unnaturally pale. His gaze fell to the red welt marring the backs of her fingers. Concern welled; ruthlessly, he squelched it. She would not escape his ire. But he could not yet speak. Instead, he rode on, mentally rehearsing the words he would heap on her head once his temper was safely tethered.

The column was already moving by the time they reached it. He cast an expert eye along the train, then led the way forward. Once in position at the column's head, he rode on through the morning.

In silence.

Eloise knew well enough to keep her place beside him. Roland remained on her other side, but slightly behind, doubtless holding himself ready to drop back should his cousin decide to have private converse with her. Awaiting that eventuality, she grew increasingly tense.

By the time they stopped for the midday halt, Montisfryn's tension had infected her.

He lifted her down. "Wait here."

He waited for no acknowledgment, turning instead to his sergeants. Eloise folded her arms and looked at the sky, keenly aware of the anticipation riding, not just her nerves, but those of all in the train behind her. Born in a castle, she'd never known real privacy; she was not the least bothered that by now everyone would know their lord was overdue to berate the lady traveling with him.

What did bother her was that he'd yet to show any signs of getting to it. How could she apologize if he didn't give her the chance?

Increasingly irritated, she studied their surroundings. The dusty road led onward, bordered by fields. Just ahead on one side stood a small copse.

Hard fingers closed about her elbow.

"I would have words with you, lady."

The deep growl required no answer. She acquiesced with what meekness she could muster. He marched her into the copse, not stopping until they reached a small clearing well away from, and out of sight of, the road.

His insistence on such absolute privacy puzzled her—until she recalled that most would consider him perfectly justified in beating her. Not harshly, but in chastisement. There was no question, even in her mind, that she'd done more than enough to deserve it—a good spanking was often recommended as greatly benefitting ladies who showed themselves too willful.

An unnervingly primitive sensation swept through her.

Stopping by a log, he released her. Head high, spine stiff, she quivered.

He scowled. "Sit, lady."

Swiftly, she obeyed, silently exhaling.

He paced the few steps across the clearing, then halted. His back to her, fists on his hips, he gazed at the trees. "Your actions this morn, lady, were inexcusable." His tone was harsh; he made no effort to hide his anger. "You were made into my care—placed under my protection—you had no right to seek thus to remove yourself."

"Nay, lord." Hands clasped in her lap, head meekly bowed, she tried for a placating tone.

"The Prior of Cricklade would have been none too pleased to find an army before his gates."

She glanced at his rigid back. "Is that what you would have done?"

"Until you came to your senses. Twas senseless to run so." Alaun forced his fists to unclench. "I would have you think long on the danger you placed yourself in—and what would have befallen had I not been close behind."

The image of her struggling with the outlaw leader rose unbidden to his mind; with a muttered curse, he banished it, wishing he could thus easily rid himself of the helpless fear it evoked. He scowled. "You willfully laid a false trail—you did not flee in panic, lady."

She made no attempt to deny it.

"I know not what maggot got into your head to push you to such a foolish start." He considered demanding an explanation, then abruptly thrust all memory of the previous night aside. "But I tell you now, your actions were *culpable*! I have three men injured because of your crazed flight."

He swung about—and read the question writ large in her eyes. "Nay." He waved a hand dismissively. "Their wounds are none of them serious, but tis no thanks to you. You know better than to ride alone, yet it seems you have done so before. Was that knave right in claiming twas so?"

His gaze glittered, saber-sharp. Eloise bowed her head. "Aye."

His chest swelled. "*By all the saints, woman!*" The air between them vibrated, incredulity fanning his anger. "You're intelligent and capable, yet in this respect you have behaved like the veriest widgeon! Apparently on a regular basis!"

She bit her lip and fixed her gaze on her hands.

"Your station alone makes you a target; your wealth makes you a rich prize. Think you there are not men aplenty who would risk their lives to gain such treasure?"

"I had not previously realized..." She frowned. "Such as this morn has never before occurred. I did not imagine men—knights—were of such ilk."

"Aye, some are so. Twill be well for you do you remember it." He paused, eyes narrowing. "But your ignorance suggests your father guarded you well—I would not have expected otherwise. Do you tell me you willfully disobeyed his orders to ride unescorted?"

"Nay." She raised her head. "There were no orders to disobey."

He narrowed his eyes even more. "He never knew?"

She focused on the trees behind him. "I rode in the early morning—tis rare to meet others about. And that knave said rightly—twas never far from the castle."

"That fact does not excuse you." Grimly, Alaun hung onto his temper. "Think you you could not have been grabbed by ruffians in the forest?"

"I never rode in the forest alone."

Jaw clenched, he snarled, "Nor carried off by some knight?"

His tone gave her pause. Fleetingly, she met his gaze, then lifted her chin. "It has been my experience that knights are rarely found abroad before dawn."

"Lady..." He let the word trail off in a warning growl. He took a turn about the clearing, then halted, hands on hips, before her. "Understand me,

Eloise. While you remain in my care, you will not go abroad alone. You will keep to my side and ask permission to quit it. And you will accept with good grace whatever escort I deem fit."

Briefly, she met his gaze, then bowed her head. "Aye, lord."

Her meek response did nothing to appease his fury; he caught her chin and forced her head up until her gaze locked with his. A deep calmness stared back at him; he longed, just once, to shake it. She had caused him anguish unlike any he'd previously known—his nature demanded retribution.

He narrowed his eyes. "You are a burden, lady." Her dark gaze flickered, then became, if anything, even more impenetrable. Savage satisfaction beckoned. "As things stand, I am responsible for you—legally, morally, and by my vow to your father. I am bound by my honor to protect you—a widow wealthy enough to attract half the hedge-knights in England! Should harm come to you whilst in my care, twould be a stain on my honor I could never hope to expunge. Tis a bad enough position to find myself in, but to top it all, I now discover you are witless enough to go riding alone and plot to forsake my protection."

Her demeanor had changed; it was colder—haughty distance had crept in. He told himself he was glad. He released her. "Now that I have explained to you, lady, what a very great weight on my shoulders you are, can I hope that, in future, you will behave with greater sense?"

For a moment, silence reigned, then, slowly, she rose, wrapping dignity like a cloak about her. Slim, slender, she faced him. "Aye, lord. I crave pardon for any inconvenience I have, through my unthoughtful actions, caused you. I pray you also to accept my humble thanks for your timely rescue of me this morn."

He blinked.

"As for the rest," she continued, "I sorrow that you find my care such an onerous weight, but would respectfully remind you twas not by my wish that you claimed such a prize—our relationship is no doing of mine. Should you wish to relieve yourself of a burden you clearly find irksome, you have only to give me escort to the nearest convent."

Frowning, he searched for the right words with which to correct her mistake.

She looked down; her lids veiled her eyes. "I will hold myself ready to depart at any time, lord. I will not inflict my foolish presence on you any longer. Pray excuse me." With a decorous nod, she started back to the road.

His hands on his hips, Alaun watched her go. His fury was largely dissipated; the rest of his emotions were tied in knots and writhing.

Narrowing his eyes, he uttered one, comprehensive, distinctly savage oath—then followed his prize back to the road.

Chapter 8

The afternoon saw no easing in the oppressive silence engulfing the head of the column. Eloise rode on, her attention fixed in the distance; the set of her head and the rigidity of her spine succinctly conveyed her mood. Her face was as pale as marble; her expression had taken on a correspondingly stony chill. Alaun remained grumpily silent, irritatingly aware of the absence of the quick, sideways glances she'd cast him throughout the morn.

They reached their campsite, nestled in the curve of a river, in late afternoon. The next hour went in the usual chaos as the wagons were positioned, tents erected, and cook fires started. Alaun withdrew with his sergeants to set the picket lines, leaving his prize under Roland's watchful eye.

Seated on a log, Eloise watched the noisy performance, unwillingly fascinated by the organization displayed by Montisfryn's men. Horses were tethered in lines; grooms and squires scurried everywhere, ferrying weapons, chests, and pallets. The tents of Montisfryn's household knights and men-at-arms clustered around his and Roland's pavilions, close by the river.

When the dust settled, she retired to Roland's blue-and-white pavilion. There she remained as the sun slowly sank.

Lying on the pallet, stubbornly ignoring the claustrophobic atmosphere, she idly picked at the supper she'd had Jenni fetch; she was determined to avoid Montisfryn come what may.

She was only remaining with him until Hereford, anyway.

The tent flap stirred; Jenni slipped in. Eloise raised a brow. "Well?"

She'd noticed a deep pool in the river behind the pavilions. After due consideration, she'd sent Jenni to ask permission to use it; the saints only knew when next she would get a chance to bathe.

"The lord said the pickets were stationed well beyond the other side, so the pool is safe to use."

"Good." Eloise sat up, swung her feet to the grass and stood. "Bring a towel. We'll go now—it's already dark."

Swirling her cloak about her, she went to the tent flap. Pushing it aside, she looked out.

A large fire blazed in the clearing before the tent. Men were gathered about it, eating and chatting, telling tales and bawdy jokes. Across the flames stood Montisfryn's pavilion, the gold stripes dull in the firelight. The flap was only partially lifted; she couldn't see inside.

Between the two pavilions lay the track to the river. There were no men in that direction. She slipped out.

* * *

From his seat at the board in his pavilion, Alaun saw Eloise's shadow, along with that of her maid, thrown against Roland's tent. He hesitated, then lifted one hand. Bilder hurried up. A few words sent Bilder out to the fire; he paused by Rovogatti, then the Genoese stood, nodded, and set out in the shadows' wake.

Seated opposite, Roland grinned. "Think a good soak will soften her up?"

Alaun grunted.

Roland wagged a chicken leg at him. "Your conversation has taken a decided turn for the worse. I wonder why?"

The narrow-eyed glare Alaun directed across the table should have ended the conversation altogether.

Roland's grin only broadened. "I hesitate to mention it, given your mood, but has it occurred to you that it's the devil's own work to seduce a woman in a snit?"

Alaun's jaw nearly cracked. "Shut up."

Roland shrugged. "Just thought I should point that out." His grin still in evidence, he attacked his chicken.

Sunk in silence, Alaun toyed with his meal.

After a suitable interlude, Roland asked, "So, are we heading home at speed?"

Alaun shook his head. He'd been wrestling with the question for hours; with a select detachment of knights, he could have his prize safe in his stronghold within a few days. The column would take ten or more days to cover the same distance; staying with it was a risk, one he felt compelled to take.

He drained his goblet. "There'll be a list of duties as long as my sword awaiting my return. I'll be busy for weeks." By remaining with the train, he could devote the next ten days to securing his prize.

Roland's eyes flew wide. "By St. George and all the saints—this grows serious! I've never known you rate a woman so high."

Alaun scowled. "Given the position I wish her to fill, a little time seems a worthwhile investment."

"Ah—so the lion hasn't grown spots?"

"Nay, tis merely temporary. Once I have her safely wed, life will be normal once more." He certainly hoped so. He shifted restlessly, vainly trying to ease the tightness in his groin.

The thought of yet another night of enforced abstinence had him gritting his teeth. His wandering gaze met Roland's—and suddenly it was all too much. With a growl, he stood. "I'm going for a walk."

"Don't get your feet wet."

Alaun pretended he hadn't heard. He circled the campfire, pausing long enough to share a jest with his men. Drifting into the shadows, he found the track leading to the river.

He was almost upon Rovogatti, quietly chatting with the maid, before the Genoese knew he was there. The fact did not perturb him; few men moved as silently as he. He dismissed both maid and guard, irritated by the robin's scandalized face. He only wanted to *talk* to the woman—in private, without others looking on. While Rovogatti and the robin retreated to the campfire, Alaun followed the track on to the water's edge.

The pool was bathed in shadow and moonlight, patches of silver rippling into dim darkness. He found Eloise's clothes in a neat pile on the lush grass by the bank, a linen towel set ready beside it. Across the top of the pile was draped a delicate chemise.

For a long moment, he stared at it, trying to keep his mind from consciously acknowledging what the sight meant.

He failed. Completely.

Drawing a slow, deep breath, he fought to contain the compulsive, impatient beat in his blood. His eyes searched the pool; she was there, cavorting in deep water. Silver gilded her arms as she lifted them to smooth back her hair. Her face, uptilted, was serene and mysterious.

Then she smiled and dove beneath the surface; smooth feminine curves flashed, shimmered briefly, then disappeared. Mesmerized, he stood, still and silent, held captive in the dimness.

Calm, freed of restraint, Eloise twirled in the cool, clear water. The gentle current drew her troubles from her, leaving her refreshed; the ageless murmur of the river comforted her, easing her mind of its cares, reminding her of how short life was and how essentially earthy its pleasures. Floating into a patch of moonlight, she stretched up one arm, smiling delightedly at the silver droplets that hung from her fingertips, moonlight trapped for an instant in their quivering hearts before they fell to join the river once more.

Still smiling, she turned and languidly stroked to shore. The river had stolen her inhibitions, a fact the chill invading her limbs called to mind. She should have kept on her chemise, for modesty's sake if nothing else, though what defense she would gain from drenched linen she'd never understood. And she would still have had to strip off the wet garment and dry herself; it was one of those social decrees that made no practical sense.

The river bottom sloped upward to the bank; she came to her feet and waded the last yards, the water at her knees. Five feet from the bank, she stopped to squeeze the water from her hair, still in braids about her ears.

In the shadows fifteen feet away, Alaun stood transfixed. A vise had closed about his chest; every breath was an effort. Not realizing the water was so shallow, he had waited, intending to speak once she had swum to the bank—before she'd left the cover of the night dark water. Now, she stood before him, bathed in moonlight, her skin pearlescent in the soft glow. She was a goddess risen from the river, a being of exquisite beauty and timeless fascination.

She was the embodiment of his most primitive dreams. His eyes devoured her, feasting on the ripe curves of full breasts above a neat waist, on the generous lines of hips and sleek thighs outlining the cradle in which he ached to lie.

She looked up—straight at him.

It wasn't her eyes that warned Eloise he was there; by sight, he was no more than a shadow among many, so perfectly still she would never have seen him if he hadn't seen her. His gaze gave him away, touching her with fingers of flame.

She didn't react as she, or he, expected.

Instead, she returned his gaze calmly, and shook the last drops from her braids. With neither sight nor sound to guide her, she nevertheless sensed she held him enthralled, trapped in a web she'd unwittingly spun.

And he was burning. For her.

She could feel his heat reaching for her, the dragon's fire in his eyes as enticing as any caress. There was no sense in any foolish show of modesty, in trying to hide from his gaze. He knew her by now; she was imprinted on his mind, on his senses.

He wanted her. Badly.

Power flowed through her, potent, undeniable, an age-old sensation that had never before been hers. It filled her, completed her, strengthened her— and compelled her. A long shiver—of need, of anticipation—rippled through her.

"Lady, come out. Or you'll freeze." The words were strained, his voice deep and grating. His body was tensed, muscles locked, all but quivering.

She wasn't cold—could not be cold, not while she basked in his golden gaze. "I'll come out if you turn around."

The flames she'd seen before in his eyes had to be blazing fiercely; she wanted to see them again, even though she suspected only one thing could reduce such a blaze to embers.

Another long shiver shook her.

Dragging in a breath, Alaun held it, and turned, the most difficult maneuver of his life. He was shaking—with need, with lust, with burning desire—all balanced on the knife-edge of control. He had never felt so in thrall to a woman, so completely at her mercy. He'd intended to conquer, but found himself the conquered. His mind was not coping with the reversal at all well.

"You have my back, lady. Now get dry and get dressed." Given the current uncertainties in their relationship, that was unquestionably the safest course.

Eloise grinned at the growled command. Wading to the bank, she stepped onto the grass. She should have swooned, or, at the very least, been thrown into totally flustered disarray, but she wasn't the swooning or flustering sort. And being viewed by Montisfryn had been a great deal more pleasant than standing naked before her husband, as she'd been forced so often to do.

Scooping up the towel, she applied it to her dripping braids, squeezing to drain enough water to stop them constantly wetting her. Then she shook out the towel—and realized her mistake. The towel was saturated. Grimacing, she rubbed at her skin, removing the drops, but leaving it damp.

Then she struggled into her chemise. "Why are you here?"

Hands on his hips, he was staring at the trees. "Twould be well, lady, if you would remember you will never again be entirely out of my sight."

It was just as well, she decided, that he couldn't see her smirk. Tying the ribbons of her chemise, she glanced down to see it dampening, already clinging to her skin. She reached for her cote. "Aye, but why did you come to find me? You knew what I was about."

"I wish to speak with you."

"About what?" She hauled her cote over her head, then freed the skirts from her damp shoulders.

"You know well what matter lies between us."

"Nay." She struggled to force her damp arms into the tight sleeves. "You will have to explain it to me. I am, after all, only a witless woman who is so foolish I am naught but a burden to my lord."

His fists, at his sides, clenched tightly. "Lady…"

"Aye, lord?" Looking down, she started lacing her gown. Her fingers were cold; the laces kept slipping from her grasp.

A muttered expletive fell on her ears.

"You, lady, are no more witless than I—and you know well you are a burden I will yield to no man."

Those words, she decided, were amongst the sweetest she'd ever heard. His tone, of course, left much to be desired. "Indeed, lord?"

Glaring at the trees, Alaun refused to reply. "Have you not finished yet, woman? I like not talking to the trees."

"Nay. My fingers are too cold."

He glanced over his shoulder. She'd only managed the first two crosses of her lacings; her cote gaped open from her waist upward. Given all he'd seen, all he'd touched the previous night... "Here. Let me."

Eloise blinked as his hands appeared at her waist and took the laces from her chilled fingers. She glanced up and met his gaze. She smiled briefly, then looked down.

The flames were still burning, not blazing but still strong; even though she wasn't looking at him, she could feel his heat. It reached for her, enfolding her in its warmth, slowly seeping into her cool flesh.

Tempting her.

His long fingers were managing her laces with dexterity. She tried to focus on that fact, tried to hold back the tide of yearning that swept through her. Her heart swelled, the beat compelling; breathing was suddenly difficult—she felt faint, yet exhilarated. Her skin was slowly heating. As she watched, his hands slowed, then stopped.

She saw them tremble.

"Eloise...?"

The whispered word was loaded with such aching desire, it rendered all else irrelevant.

Slowly, she raised her head. Her gaze locked with his; golden, burning bright, it stole her breath. His body was a mass of locked muscle, quivering as he held firm, denying the primitive urge that stared at her through his eyes. She sucked in a quick breath. Desire lanced through her, sharp and sweet; flames danced down her veins. A shiver shook her.

He saw it, but held still—the decision was hers.

She had no choice, or so it seemed; St Catherine herself could not have kept her from his arms. Her heart thudded, her pulse an insistent tattoo. She stepped closer, putting aside all resistance; with him and only him could she challenge her fate. Only he possessed the strength to reassure her. Lust, desire, and need were all there in his eyes, yet he mastered them, holding them at her command.

She placed her palms on his chest, then ran them slowly upward; locking her hands about his neck, she stretched up and set her lips to his. She felt him quiver, then one arm closed gently about her. His lips moved, covering hers. She felt him touch her hair, then his fingers slipped beneath one braid, framing her jaw.

A deep sigh escaped him, then his lips closed possessively over hers.

Desire blazed; flame upon flame, it rose quickly within them.

His lips firmed, demanding, commanding. She melted against him, flowing into his heat, eager to share it. She parted her lips; he swiftly laid claim, plundering, ruthlessly wasting all resistance.

Not that she resisted.

She wanted him—after Raoul, after the years of empty loneliness, despite all her nebulous fears.

And he wanted her.

His ardent lips, his all too evocative plundering of her mouth spoke clearly of his need; the hard, hot column pressed to her belly left the matter in no doubt. She exulted, her desire freed by his. Need burgeoned, passion grew. Hard muscle surrounded her, engulfed her, tempted her. Her fingers, twined in his thick locks, clutched tight as she arched against him.

The flames within her roared as she kissed him back, urgent and urging.

After the traumas of the day, the danger, the fears, her temper and his, Alaun needed little urging. Molten desire flowed in his veins; he could no more control it than hold back the sun—his last rational thought was a fervently grateful prayer that tonight, he wouldn't need to.

Her response, her incitement to claim her, was far more than he'd expected. Her unbridled passion shredded his control; his blew the tattered remnants away.

Within minutes their blaze had become an inferno.

She was pressed tightly against him, her hips shifting needfully. He swept the back of her skirts, the back of her chemise, up to her waist, trapping them in one hand. The other sought the smooth globes of her bottom, caressing the satin skin, expertly tracing their contours. A feverish dew sprang up at his touch; he reached further, slipping his fingers between her thighs. Her secret place lay waiting, soft and swollen, heated and damp. He caressed the sumptuous flesh, feeling it flower, unfurling to reveal still further delights. Her honey flowed, slick on his fingers; he parted her petals and slid into her warm wetness.

She moaned and pressed closer still, undulating against him, shifting his fingers within her.

Eloise dragged her lips from his and buried her face in the hollow of his throat. Gasping, barely rational, barely able to stand, she clung as his fingers probed, shafting fire through her. He was hot enough to ignite cold steel, yet the heat building within her seemed empty, incomplete. A strange impatience rode her. She moved against his hand; he muttered something, his lips by her temple. Then his fingers probed deeply.

Intense pleasure streaked through her. She gasped and arched against him, hips thrusting against his hard thighs. Her fingers, on his shoulders, sank deep; she felt her body tighten. The heated emptiness within her pulsed, ached; she pressed against him, trying to assuage it, then heard herself moan.

Alaun needed no further encouragement. She was hot and very wet; her hands found his face and brought his lips back to hers, urgently entreating. He dropped the back of her skirt and dragged up the front, crushing it, tucking it under her tight-fitting bodice. Her hands came to help, tangling with his. His clothes were easier dealt with, his houppelande slashed from waist to hem leaving only the folds of his braies to push aside.

He pressed against her, letting her feel his strength, then edged back enough to splay one hand across her bare belly. She melted against him. He supported her with one arm, teasing her lips with his as he threaded his fingers through her springy curls. Her softness lay waiting, slick and very swollen, wet and desperately wanting. He found the nub of her desire and swirled his fingertip about it. She gasped and shuddered; he withdrew his hand. Gripping her hips, he pulled her hard against him.

Eloise moaned as her legs gave way. His lips held hers as his hands slipped around, closing firmly about the backs of her thighs. His tongue delved deep in a shatteringly possessive kiss, then he lifted her, hoisting her against him. Unwilling to relinquish the intensity of their kiss, she caught his face between her hands. Her thighs parted; instinctively, she wrapped her legs about his hips. He took her mouth again, in a deep, devastating conquest that melted her very bones.

Then she felt him touch her there, where her heated flesh throbbed. Her aching emptiness swelled.

His muscles locked, Alaun slowly lowered her, letting the broad head of his staff part her soft flesh, sliding past her slick lips to lie throbbing at her portal. He paused fleetingly, gathering his will for a gentle invasion—

Her tongue thrust boldly against his.

His control snapped.

Chest swelling, he struggled for breath. The wet heat of her body beckoned; his wouldn't wait—with one powerful thrust, he sheathed himself in her softness.

She screamed.

The sound, trapped between them, resonated through his head, stunning him completely. She went rigid in his arms, every muscle in her body clenching hard.

Every one.

For one crazed instant, he teetered on the brink of madness. Not only had the impossible occurred, not only was his entire body locked in a battle to hold back his raging lust, a battle so fraught it was reducing muscles hardened by campaign and tournament to quivering lumps of jelly, but she was holding him on the brink of pleasure and pain; her inner muscles had clamped so tight he couldn't even think.

He had to pull out of her—at least long enough to understand what had happened. But he didn't have the strength to lift her from him, not while holding his rabid impulses in check. She was clinging tightly, her body taut, quivering in his arms.

"Eloise?"

Slowly, her lids rose. She was breathing raggedly, shallowly; so was he. A frown puckered her brows; her eyes, finally revealed, were wide, dark, impossibly lustrous. "I forgot," she breathed, then her lids fell.

For a moment, he was *sure* he was mad. "Forgot?" He licked his lips, set his teeth. "That you were a virgin?"

She nodded. "I wasn't...thinking." She shifted against him—and winced.

He held her still. "Gently, lady-witch."

She blinked at him. He brushed a kiss across her bruised lips then, very carefully, he sank onto one knee. Moving with extreme caution, he eased her down onto her back in the long grass.

He followed her down—she gave him no choice. He eased his body over hers, taking his weight on his elbows. Then he lowered his head and kissed her, softly, gently, long and deeply. Then he tried to ease out of her.

It was impossible.

Close to defeat, his muscles shivering with the effort of holding back, he shut his eyes and dropped his forehead to hers. The long sleek muscles of her thighs that he'd admired earlier were as nothing to the muscles lining her velvet sheath. They'd never been stretched, had never become accustomed to letting a man inside her—and now wouldn't let him out. Sheer surprise had got him in in the first place; he was so large and presently so engorged, he couldn't withdraw without hurting her even more. Let alone him. He was hurting as it was. "Eloise—you're going to have to relax."

Eloise didn't think she could. She seemed wound very tight around something. The pain of his entry had receded, but the shock of his invasion went deeper; she could feel him throbbing inside her, impossibly large, impossibly hard. He filled her completely...

The sensation was not unpleasant.

From beneath her lashes, she glanced at his face, saw the strain, the taut tendons in his neck, the evidence of the effort he was expending on her behalf—so that he didn't, wouldn't, hurt her.

If she was ever to know more, learn more, experience more, it was here, now, with him.

Alaun felt her muscles relax fractionally. He tightened his own, dragged in a tortured breath and, very gradually, drew back.

He'd retreated no more than halfway when, without warning, she tilted her hips, arching under him.

"*Lady!*"

He glared helplessly down at her as his body reacted, surging powerfully back to rock her womb. The flare of satisfaction in her eyes made him groan. Deep within her once more, her scalding sleekness engulfing him, he shut his eyes. "Eloise—I *cannot* be gentle. Tis not wise—believe me."

His body was hard, immensely powerful; even now, his weight pinned her to the ground.

Eloise recognized the danger, but the heat was still there, deep within her, no longer empty but swelling, beckoning. She let her lips curve, touched them to his. "Nay—you will not hurt me. I have ever been told I was bred to lie thus."

The stunned look on his face had her lips twitching. Twining her fingers in his hair, she shifted suggestively. "Let us have done. Tis what I wish."

What she wished. No other words could have more effectively defeated him. With a stifled curse, Alaun gathered her to him and slowly eased his reins. He attempted to keep them in his hands, but, as he'd feared, after the third delicious thrust, they snapped. After that, nothing, not even the saints, could have stopped him from taking her—deeply, almost savagely. She was his to claim, conquered, lying supine beneath him, her thighs spread wide, cradling his hips, her long legs clasping his flanks. His body rode hers in a pagan celebration of lust fueled by deep desire.

The abrupt introduction to rampant congress shook Eloise, stealing her breath, leaving her gasping mentally as well as physically. For an instant, her confidence wavered. The powerful repetitive invasions rocked her, demanding some response. She lifted her hips, meeting his; the action absorbed some of the impact. With each deep, forceful penetration, an odd quiver of delight rippled through her. Her inner muscles had surrendered, forced to yield to his repeated assaults; when next he thrust inward, burying himself inside her, she tightened about him, holding him for an instant before allowing him to resume his driving rhythm.

A deep shuddering groan was her reward.

Alaun couldn't believe what she was doing, or what she was reducing him to. The tempo swelled; completion drew near. He sought her lips in a kiss as savage as their joining.

She met him—accepting, giving, surrendering, challenging.

His release swept over him, explosive, profound, and prolonged. With an agonized groan, he spilled himself into her, then collapsed, senseless, in her arms.

Eloise held him, marveling at the sudden dying of his tension, like a spring abruptly released. Her body hummed, still heated, but oddly content. Deep inside, she felt the warmth of his seed. She lay quietly beneath him, savoring the sensations, amazed at how good his weight upon her felt.

His head lay beside hers; she could feel his breath against her ear. Lips curving, she reached up and, very gently, stroked his hair. When he didn't stir, she let her hands explore, caressing the broad muscles of his shoulders and back through the soft folds of his houppelande.

He still didn't move; she wondered if he'd fallen asleep. There was a twig poking into her ribs, but he was so heavy, she couldn't even wriggle.

Resigned, she lay back and looked up at the stars. Drawing a short, shallow breath, all she could manage with him crushing her chest, she reviewed their recent endeavors. Overall, the only complaint she had was of their brevity. Perhaps, next time, she could persuade him to slow down?

Next time?

She frowned.

Alaun returned from the dead with painful slowness. As soon as he regained sufficient wit to realize the danger, he withdrew from her. Rolling onto his back, he rested for a minute, then sat up. Draping his arms over his knees, he slanted a glance at Eloise.

She was frowning.

His heart sank. His gaze shifted to her thighs, still uncovered, and the darker streaks marking her ivory skin. Hauling in a gigantic breath, he stood, grateful that his muscles obeyed him.

Eloise frowned even more as he walked away. Why, she wondered, did she feel so bereft? Disappointed—and peculiarly hurt? Her body, which had thrummed contentedly while he'd rested within her, now felt all at odds with itself, as if her nerves were tangled. She tried to rise, but discovered her limbs were too weak to risk it, so she tugged her skirts loose and flipped them over her legs.

If this was the way he usually behaved, simply walking away after it was done, then she would have to change his ways. She didn't know what she'd expected, but she would have liked to have held him for longer; she had liked the sense of closeness that had engulfed her while they'd been locked together.

Her frown darkened.

He reappeared beside her. She looked up in surprise as her cloak settled over her. Then he crouched; his hands slipped beneath her and he hoisted her into his arms.

She clutched at his houppelande. "What are you doing?"

His expression was grim. "If you try to walk now, your legs won't hold you."

She knew that—very little of her felt normal, particularly not her thighs. Still frowning, she curled into his chest, swaying as he negotiated the track up to the pavilions.

When the glow of the campfires appeared before them, she struggled slightly; his grip merely tightened.

She thumped his chest. "You may put me down, lord. I can walk from here."

"Nay, lady. Be still."

She glared. "What will your people think?" she hissed, wishing he wasn't quite so strong. Now, she couldn't even wriggle her toes.

"No more than what they've been thinking already."

Her breasts swelling, she redoubled her glare—to no avail; he refused to look at her. He was suddenly very recognizably male; she couldn't imagine why, but minutes before, she had thought him any different.

She was even less pleased when he carried her straight to his tent. Very conscious of the eyes, surreptitiously but definitely upon them, she held her tongue. She might brawl with him, but she would prefer to brawl in private. With awful patience, she waited for him to set her down.

He did.

In the center of his very large bed.

Suddenly no longer quite sure of her standing, she frowned warily up at him.

He straightened, met her gaze. "Are you sore?"

She returned his look frostily.

He narrowed his eyes, then swore and turned away.

Tentatively, she shifted her hips and stretched her legs. Nothing seemed broken, which, given his lustiness, doubtless qualified as a minor miracle. There was an odd ache at the tops of her thighs, and a few twinges elsewhere. And a degree of heat between her legs, as if from something rubbing. Other than that, she seemed remarkably whole.

He reappeared at the bedside, a pewter bowl in his hands. Placing it on the ground by the bed, he sat on the pallet, fished a cloth out of the water and carefully squeezed it out.

She watched, a pitying light in her eyes. Why he thought a cloth for her forehead would help—

He flipped up her skirts and applied the wet cloth to the junction of her thighs.

Choking down her shriek, she struggled to sit up; a muscular forearm held her down. She tried to twist her hips, pressing her feet into the pallet— her thighs parted.

He slipped the cold pad more fully into place and held it there, his palm immovable between her thighs.

Muscles quivering, she glared her indignation.

His golden eyes, sober and serious, held hers. "And now, lady, you may tell me how a widow comes to be virgin."

Chapter 9

For a long moment, Eloise stared at him. Then she fell back against the pillows, shifting her gaze to the gold-striped ceiling. "Nay." She'd acted on impulse; she hadn't thought this far. "Tis not an edifying tale."

"Nevertheless, I will have it."

She continued to stare at the tent roof.

"You were married to Raoul de Cannar nine years ago. You were put into your marriage bed. I was in the hall; I saw you leave, then he was carried up."

"Aye." The gold stripes wavered and dimmed, and she was there, in her marriage bed, watching as her husband stripped and stalked toward her. But she was no longer the girl in the bed; now, she viewed the scene and her younger self from a remote and safe distance.

"De Cannar was brought in to you. What happened next?"

The commanding, authoritarian tones drifted across her mind, distant but insistent. "He locked everyone else out of the room. Then he undressed."

"He joined you in the bed?"

"Nay. He ordered me out of it."

"And then?"

The story fell from her, neither haltingly nor nervously; she responded to Montisfryn's judgelike questions, recalling each moment clearly, vividly, yet, for all that, without emotion.

"We left early the next morn for Cannar—Raoul saw to it that I had no private words with my mother." She paused, deep in the past, then shrugged. "Truth to tell, I was too confused to know if I should speak—some would have considered me lucky."

"The journey to Cannar?"

"My father sent an escort. Raoul kissed me, touched me—I had always to lie naked in his bed. He started teaching me how to touch him, but did not seek my direct assistance in gaining his release. That came later, after my father's men left us at Cannar."

She paused; after a moment, Montisfryn prompted her. And so she told it all—the campaign her husband had devised and ruthlessly waged to break her will, to break her pride and turn her into a mindless, sniveling wretch who went in fear, day to day, hour by hour, of her sexual duties. Her marriage had not been the partnership she had been raised to expect, but a relationship of conquest and subjugation—total subjection and subjugation on her part, and a twisted kind of victory on his.

"He didn't like women, not of any station. To him, women were an enemy to be cowed, conquered, and degraded. Victory in that sphere was as important to him as victory on the field—he practiced the necessary skills religiously. Fear was his most potent weapon, and if that didn't work, then there was always public humiliation, or the threat thereof."

She paused, then sighed. "And in my case, he had the added weapon of my own self-pride. He realized from the first that I took my vows seriously, so he ordered me to do whatever I would not do willingly."

Detached, unaffected by the horrors she recounted, she described all the skills and arts she'd been forced to learn. "The more degrading, demeaning, the more mentally hurtful, the better, but he was always careful to leave no marks, no physical evidence. He was cunning and clever—and perceptive. Outside our chamber, he always treated me with due courtesy, a mockery in itself. But he ensured there was nothing of which I could complain. And I could send no word to my mother—I could not send a messenger without his permission. To all outward appearances, he was a kind and generous lord—only I must always attend him in our chamber whenever he summoned me."

"Yet he did not bed you."

"Nay, that was to be his moment of ultimate victory—all else was designed to lead to that." Distantly, she heard a savage oath, but her memories held her fast. "He made only one miscalculation—he forgot my monthly flux. It interrupted his program. But he was an experienced campaigner—he sought to turn even that delay to his advantage."

Her voice grew colder; her breasts rose more rapidly as she recalled the rest. "He was obsessed—I do not believe he was entirely sane, not when it came to me. He arranged to have a villein's daughter brought to him—a girl my age who looked like me. He tied me to the bedpost—and tied her to the bed. He told me it was to be a lesson for me and I had to watch everything, and if I so much as turned my head away, he would consider the lesson aborted and repeat the exercise the next night, using the girl's ten-year-old sister."

"He raped the girl." For the first time in her recital, emotion shivered through her voice. Her eyes, wide, filled with tears; her gaze was fixed in the past. "First naturally, then...as men use boys. He was...merciless. She screamed and sobbed—eventually, she fainted. He didn't stop, but used her until he had done."

She paused, swallowing to free her voice of her tears. "Later, he put her out of the door, then made me recount, in detail, all I had seen—he embellished the account, then, satisfied I would not forget, he released me and had me lie beside him. The very last thing he said, after he'd doused the candles, was 'Tomorrow, twill be you.'"

Seated, frozen, on the bed, Alaun closed his eyes. Muscles locked, he waged an inner battle to suppress the impotent rage that demanded he rend de Cannar limb from limb. Breathing deeply, he opened his eyes. "The next night?" His mouth was dry; his fists, clenched tight, ached.

To his surprise, a ghost of a smile touched Eloise's lips. "He wasn't there. Warwick called him to assist with some outlaws. He went, but warned me he would return immediately the battle was over, with the battle lust raging through him."

"And?"

"He and his men dispatched the outlaws efficiently. Raoul was so focused on my conquest—on his ultimate victory—that he left the battleground immediately to return and complete his campaign. The castle wasn't far—he didn't wait to disarm. A summer storm swept in, and he was hit by lightning."

"He died?"

"Aye. His squire, the only one riding with him, brought the news late that night. I was waiting, watching, expecting Raoul—I was the only one in the keep awake. As luck would have it, I saw the squire ride in—I reached him before he told anyone. He hadn't been able to lift Raoul's body, so all the guards on the walls saw was the squire returning, apparently with a message for me. I realized immediately in what danger I stood. My father had explained the marriage settlements—if Raoul died, I would be paid half the profits of all the de Cannar estates every year. His family would never have stood for it—at the very least, I would never have left Cannar keep alive, and, of course, I knew I wasn't with child. So I gave the squire a sleeping draft, and fled."

"For Versallet Castle?"

"Nay." Her voice was regaining its normal tone. "I left Cannar Castle swearing that no other would ever take Raoul's place—the last place I would go was home. Twas my father arranged the alliance with the de Cannars—as a wealthy young widow, I would be naught but a pawn to be traded in marriage again. Nay—I wasn't so foolish, even then. And my month with Raoul had given me opportunity and incentive enough to dwell long on the rights of women. I knew well that, as a widow, I was free—freer than I could otherwise be. So I went to Claerwhen."

"Your convent?"

She nodded.

"You reached there safely?"

"Aye. The saints watched over me."

Rendering heartfelt thanks to the Holy Virgin, Alaun bent and lifted the basin from the ground. His muscles were stiff. Rising slowly, he carried the basin across the tent. While she'd recounted the horrors of her marriage, he'd washed the last traces of her virginity from her; she hadn't noticed, so deeply sunk in the past had she been.

Moving like one aged, he set the basin on his chest. Then he gripped the edge and, head bowed, breathed deeply. He felt stunned, disoriented, his gut knotted as if he'd just survived a battle in which his side, though victorious, had paid a heavy toll. Emotions warred within him, many unfamiliar. Rage was there, impotent and ineffective; the pain was hard to define. As for his pity—he had no outlet for it; the woman in his bed would not welcome it. And it was not her at whom it was directed, but a thin, prideful girl of fifteen. She was no longer that girl.

She'd spent a month married to a fiend. De Cannar had done everything possible to ensure her degradation, to make her fear and loathe her sexual nature.

But tonight, she'd given herself to Alaun.

The memory glowed bright; he clung to it.

It was some minutes before, blinking up at the silk above her, Eloise realized the questions had ceased. She returned to the world; a sense of relief washed through her, as if speaking had released her from some invisible restraint. She'd never spoken of it before, not to any living soul, not even in the confessional; she'd buried the memories deep, and had never let them out.

Now that she had…while time had not made those memories less awful, it had, she discovered, made them less relevant. She was not her younger self; she had come a long way since then.

Drawing a deep breath, she lowered her gaze—and discovered her skirts modestly drawn down to her ankles.

She squinted across the tent. Montisfryn was washing his hands. His expression was grim. Her recollection of exactly what she had told him was already hazing, but, experienced knight that he was, she doubted her tale would have shaken him. How he now viewed her, however, was beyond her ability to guess. Calmly curious, she watched as he returned to the bed.

His face was an uninformative mask. He bent and took her hands, drawing her to her feet. She acquiesced, wondering what came next. Without meeting her eyes, he reached for her laces.

Stunned, she watched his hands busily undoing what he'd earlier done up. "What are you doing?"

He met her eyes briefly. "Your clothes are damp. Tis past time we retired."

She blinked. Then she clutched the gaping sides of her bodice and stepped back. "Nay! I'll not stay here."

With one tug, he wrenched the laces from her gown; eyes of dulled gold captured hers. "Lady—of one thing in this world you may be sure. *That*"— one finger jabbed at his bed—"is henceforth your couch. And I will be sharing it with you."

Faced with those eyes and what she could see behind them, Eloise realized she'd misjudged him again. Her story *had* seriously troubled him. She hesitated. After the riverbank, it could hardly hurt to share his bed. And the idea that he wanted her there, that her presence would comfort him, held a seduction all its own. "Very well. I can sleep in my chemise."

"Nay. Tis too damp."

He was already helping her from her cote.

Straightening as her skirts, helped by his large hands, slid to the grass, she planted her hands on her hips and fixed him with a narrow-eyed glare. "I will *not* lie naked in your bed."

He met her gaze, eyes narrowing, his jaw clenching as he wisely held back the words she could imagine forming in his mind. Just because she'd stood naked before him on the riverbank, he had better not imagine she was about to make a habit of it.

Alaun's thoughts were, indeed, of that incident, and others that had suddenly been explained. Her peculiar wantonness, the actions that had convinced him he was dealing with an experienced woman rather than the virgin she had so amazingly proved to be, were now revealed for what they were. De Cannar's legacies.

He drew a deep breath. Her defiant gaze didn't waver. With a low growl, he swung around and stalked across the room. Throwing back the lid of his chest, he rummaged, then marched back, a shirt clenched in one fist. "You may wear this."

Recognizing a most grudgingly granted boon when she saw one, Eloise took the proffered garment. Then she held it before her and calmly looked at him.

He returned her stare, his expression growing more goaded with every second. Then, with a disgusted sound midway between a growl and a grunt, he swung on his heel. "Quickly, lady. I want my bed this night."

She grinned. Stripping off the clinging chemise, she struggled into the shirt. As fine as her chemise but more than twice as large, it enveloped her in voluminous folds; the hems brushed her knees. Satisfied, she climbed beneath the furs. "I am done, lord."

He glanced back, as if to check that she was, indeed, in his bed, then strode across the tent.

Alaun hurriedly undressed, doffing houppelande, hose, and shirt. With one hand on his braies, he glanced at the bed. She was lying straight under the covers, eyes on the roof, like a sainted effigy. But if she looked down…

He pinched out the candle, plunging the tent into darkness. Quickly, he stripped, then, eyes adjusted to the dark, crossed to the bed. Time enough for her to see what she was accommodating after she'd grown more accustomed to doing so.

The bed bowed as he slid in beside her; she clutched the side to stop herself from rolling into him. He settled; the tilting eased. Exhaling softly, she eased her grip; when no further upheaval ensued, she relaxed.

He lay beside her, hands clasped on his chest, and tried to do the same. To no avail; the turmoil inside was too great. He tried to think through the anger, the frustration, but the more he battled his emotions, the more they writhed, snarling his thoughts. He gritted his teeth. The scent of rosemary drifted hauntingly past. He sniffed, and detected lavender, too. From her drying hair.

A soft huff focused his attention, and hauled him back from the abyss.

She was there, beside him. On the riverbank, she'd welcomed him into her arms, had accepted him as her lover. Her past *was* past; her future lay with him.

Slowly, he exhaled. His tension drained; he sank more deeply into the pallet. Shutting his eyes, he sought his rest.

Only then did he notice his bed-partner was having difficulty finding hers. She tossed fretfully. He lay silent, listening to her twist and turn.

The penny dropped.

Mentally cursing, he excused himself on the score that it had been years since he'd left a woman wanting.

She was facing him; he eased onto his side. With neither fillet nor crespine, her thick braids hung down, one on each shoulder. Her eyes were open; he didn't need to see to know they were filled with suspicion. Moving with his habitual deliberation, he lifted one hand and cupped her cheek; drawing closer, he set his lips to hers.

He kissed her until she was breathless, soft and pliant against him. When he raised his head, her eyes, lustrous in the dark, blinked up at him.

"A thousand pardons, lady-witch. Lie back and I'll bring you release."

She frowned. He saw her puzzled look—a sudden premonition seized him.

"What mean you, lord? What release do I need?"

He closed his eyes. What more trials had the night in store for him? Opening his eyes, he said, "You are still wanting, lady."

Her frown deepened; she opened her mouth—

"On the riverbank, before I took you, I touched you here." He trailed his fingers between her thighs, brushing her curls through the fabric of his shirt. "You were hot and wet."

"Aye. " Eloise struggled to subdue the shivery sensations evoked by his touch. "Twas strange."

"Nay—tis not strange. Tis what happens when you are aroused, when your body is ready to mate. The dampness is needed to ease your flesh against a man's passage."

"Oh." Eloise wished he would touch her again. "But what has *that* to do with this release that I want?"

"We were both aroused on the riverbank. I gained my release, but you did not."

For a long moment, she simply stared at him. "Nay. Tis not possible."

He frowned sternly. "Do you not still feel a certain tenseness, lady?"

She knew she did; it had been there since they'd first kissed on the riverbank. "Aye. But twill ease soon."

"Not tonight."

"Nay—twill be gone shortly." She was suddenly quite certain she didn't need to know more about release. The thought of completely surrendering herself to passion, as he had when he'd lost himself in her, the memory of how vulnerable he'd been when he'd collapsed in her arms, convinced her that release was an experience she was not yet ready for. "Lie back and sleep, lord. Do not concern yourself—I will not disturb you more."

With an exasperated growl, Alaun dropped back to the pillows. She was the one needing release—why, then, did *he* feel so frustrated?

The fact that he hadn't pleasured her sat like a blot on his record. Furthermore, he didn't approve of having his expertise so lightly declined. Grappling with her problem, he stared at the roof. After a moment, he sighed. "So you'll let the bastard win after all?"

She glanced at him. "To which bastard do you refer, lord?"

"Your late husband, of course. How many other bastards have there been in your life?"

"One was quite enough." She frowned. "But what mean you, 'win'?"

He didn't have to fabricate his disapproval. "It suited de Cannar's purpose that you shouldn't learn of a woman's pleasure. Twould not have aided his campaign had you done so—he sought to frighten you from the subject. While you remained but half a woman, you were no match for him."

Half a woman? Eloise had a sneaking suspicion this was one of those times she would do well not to underestimate Montisfryn. Nevertheless… "This release you speak of—will you need to come inside me to give it me?"

Half a minute passed before he answered. "Nay, lady." He shifted, coming up on one elbow beside her. "My hands, lips, and tongue are more than adequate to the task."

She wasn't sure whether she was thankful or disappointed. He'd hurt her before, but she'd heard tell it would not be so again. Indeed, the sensations she'd felt later enticed, yet perhaps she shouldn't tempt fate and suggest he try that way again. "Show me."

He needed no further urging—he framed her face and kissed her, long and deep. She responded ardently; before long their fires were well-lit and burning brightly. Only then did he draw her into his arms, lying back and urging her atop him.

Eagerly, she accepted the invitation to explore. She spread her hands

wide, tracing the contours that had always fascinated her. Her fingers twined
in the springy gold hairs; she discovered a flat nipple hidden beneath them.
Boldly, she caressed it, delighted when it hardened to a button and he shifted
restlessly beneath her.

His movement drew her attention to other tactile possibilities. As he
drew her lips back to his, she undulated against him, letting her legs tangle
with his, her satin-soft skin teasingly abraded by his hair-roughened limbs.
His tongue surged against hers, passionate, yet controlled. She responded
with a slow, snake-like wriggle, rubbing her breasts against his chest, shifting
her hips against his. She felt rather than heard his low groan. Then one hand
left her face to sweep down her back, boldly slipping beneath the hem of her
improvised nightrail. His warm palm slowly caressed the backs of her thighs,
before rising to bestow the same attention on the globes of her bottom and,
finally, the smooth planes of her back.

Warmth flooded her. She sighed her approval.

Alaun heard. He continued to kiss her, repeating his gently arousing
caresses, slowly progressing to greater intimacy, relentlessly stoking her fire.
Only when she was thoroughly and mindlessly heated did he turn her on her
side.

Again, his hand sought the hem of the shirt, this time in front. Her
thighs were warm silk, sleek muscles quivering. He let his fingers play in the
crisp curls at their apex, and listened to her breathing fragment before lazily
trailing his fingers upward. By the time he reached her breasts, her fingers
were flexing on his shoulders.

Breathless, Eloise let her head fall back. Eyes closed, she savored the
feel of his palm against her breast, felt her body swell and burgeon, ripening
beneath his touch. Then his fingers found her nipple. She gasped; sharp
sensation speared her. Desire surged; an unfamiliar urgency gripped her.
Every caress, some gentle, others less so, wound her tauter, tighter. She
quivered like a spring wound to its limit. Waiting for the final turn.

She heard him murmur, his voice deep and gravelly. Then she realized
he was urging her arms up to draw the shirt from her. She hesitated, eyes
shut, sure she should resist. Yet she didn't, the now familiar feel of his hair-
dusted skin too achingly tempting to forgo. Then the barrier was gone, and he
moved against her.

Hard muscle, hot and solid, surrounded her. His hands stroked, feeding
flames into her already fevered flesh. Dazed, she wondered how much tighter,
how much hotter she could get. He urged her onto her back; she obliged,
conscious of the growing ache deep inside, the sense of emptiness he
conjured so easily. As his lips returned to hers, confidently possessive,
increasingly demanding, she hoped he would soon fill her.

She speared her fingers through his hair, then dropped her hands to his
shoulders, urging him against her. He held back, his shoulders above her, one
hand on her breast. His tongue thrust boldly against hers. His hand moved

down to splay possessively over her belly, then moved lower, fingers trailing through her curls to lay a tracery of fire up and down her inner thighs. Mindlessly, she parted them. Ripples of sensation streaked upward to where she was again hot and wet, even though he had yet to touch her there.

When he did, one long finger sliding effortlessly into her, she came off the pallet, arching in his arms. Held fast, she shivered, shafts of delight lancing through her.

She was alive to her fingertips, every nerve-ending quiveringly sensitive. The tension within expanded, swelled, more urgent with every breath she dragged in—short, almost-gasps that filled the darkness. His finger moved within her. She arched again, fire spreading, flames licking hungrily along every vein. Her heart pulsed strongly, the urgent cadence echoing through her. Close to her heated core, his finger languidly stroked, heavy, foreign, immeasurably welcome.

She wanted to see his eyes. His head was lowered, his face turned to watch as he caressed her. She raised one hand to his cheek; he was reluctant. Only when she brought both hands to his face did he yield, allowing her her way. His lids were heavy, veiling his eyes. Then, as if understanding her need, he raised his lids, and met her gaze.

His eyes were blazing, heat layered on heat, flame on flame.

Alaun stifled a groan and dropped his head to her shoulder. He was in pain—deep, wracking agony. It was barely an hour since he'd had her, yet he was rigid with need again. Throbbing with an overwhelming urge to bury himself in the soft, sweet flesh his fingers were stroking. She was so hot—her honey-slick flesh scorched him. The heady, musky scent of her rose to tease, to tantalize.

"Lord?"

He couldn't ask it of her—not so soon. The saints knew twas not what he'd intended. He shouldn't—he'd said— "By the Holy Virgin, lady, I want you." The words were a hoarse plea. "Take me inside you, Eloise."

Eloise couldn't think. Luckily, she didn't need to. She knew he wanted her mightily, the evidence there in his fiery eyes, in his locked muscles, in the heavy throbbing reality pressed against her thigh. And she knew that, whatever was to come, she would enjoy it far more if he was with her, inside her again.

"Aye, lord," she murmured. Then memory intruded. "Will it hurt?"

"Nay." Teeth gritted, he swung over her, spreading her thighs and sinking between. He didn't need to adjust himself to her; the head of his staff found her portal as if guided by some higher authority.

She felt the broad tip part her swollen flesh, pressing inexorably inwards. Breathless, she arched, nails sinking into his arms. "Lord!" He stopped. She found his eyes. "Can we not take it...slower?"

Poised above her, muscles straining, Alaun stared down at her. She wanted it slow? By St George and all the saints, she'd have her wish—even if it killed him.

It nearly did. He sank into her so gradually, he felt every little ripple in her heated sheath as it stretched fully to accommodate him.

Eyes shut, Eloise savored every rigid inch of him as he filled her, his penetration so achingly slow, so deep, that for one breathless instant, she thought it would never end. Prayed it would never end. Instinctively, she tilted her hips, greedily wanting more.

Her movement nearly finished Alaun. Grimly, he hung on. "Aye, lady-witch. Take me all."

With one last surge, he filled her completely, the head of his staff abutting her womb. He held still, muscles bunched and quivering, giving her time to adjust to his invasion.

She looked up from under her lashes; he saw the dark gleam of her glance.

"Am I hurting you?"

She shifted slightly, experimentally; he gritted his teeth.

"Nay." More confident, she wriggled. "But it feels...somewhat strange to have you inside me. Tis different from before."

Testing her stretched muscles, she inadvertently pulsed around him; he jerked. Biting back a groan, he fought to keep still. A peculiar little smile swept her face. She undulated beneath him, her slender body lifting, twisting, instinctively seeking fulfillment.

"Will you ride me now, lord?"

He caught his breath. "Aye, but tis a ride for two."

She blinked up at him. "I know not the way of this riding, lord."

Saints in heaven!—he had to end this conversation. "Nay—your body knows the way of it well enough." Slowly, determined not to permit a repetition of his earlier unbridled performance, he slackened his reins. He drew back, then surged inward, gently rocking her. The passion in her dark eyes smoldered, but was not yet ablaze. "Come, lady-witch—ride with me."

Lady-witch. He kept calling her that. But Eloise let the odd name pass as more urgent matters claimed her. Heat welled as he moved within her. To her surprise, she discovered he was right; without conscious direction, her body met his, mirroring his movements. And this time *was* different, her body more in tune, their desires more evenly matched.

Then all thought was submerged beneath waves of pleasure, surging through her with every slow thrust. The pace he set was a rolling canter, a steady deliberate rhythm that pushed her ever upward, through foothills of pleasure into mountains of ecstasy. As they rode together, their bodies in effortless concert, her tension returned, then heightened dramatically, gripping her tighter and tighter.

She couldn't breathe.

Gasping, she strained against him, gripping his arms, rising toward something, faster and faster. He thrust deeply; she met him. Flames coalesced, engulfing them, searing them. Abruptly, she focused on where their bodies joined, hand in glove, his staff gliding effortlessly within her slick channel.

Stretching her, filling her, possessing her.

She gasped, and tightened about him.

Release took her by surprise. Like a sun bursting through the thick haze of pleasure, it caught her up. Fire and flame exploded, and ecstasy seized her, crashing through her in wave after wave of rippling delight.

The sensation peaked, then, slowly, receded. Heat remained, cocooning her; relaxing, she pulsed with the glow.

Distantly, she heard a muffled shout and a deeper warmth flooded her. Montisfryn collapsed upon her, pressing her into the pallet, his breathing labored. Barely aware, she held him, running her hands down the great muscles of his back. His heart thudded heavily, the beat echoing inside her.

Much later, she felt him lift from her. She frowned and clung, mumbling a sleepy protest.

He chuckled. "Nay, lady-witch." His lips touched her forehead. "Sleep. There will be plenty of time, now, for us."

Later still, on the threshold of sleep, her lips lifted. His tournament motto was wrong. He was not "fearsome when aroused." Making a mental note to mention the matter when next the point arose, she surrendered to her dreams.

Chapter 10

The point arose much earlier than she'd expected, a little before the dawn. From a deep and dreamless sleep, Eloise jerked into wide-eyed, heart-pounding panic. With a strangled shriek, she leapt from the bed, grabbing up the shirt she found beside it. She was halfway to the flap before the unexpected touch of grass beneath her feet opened her eyes to reality.

She slowed, then halted, blinking at the scarlet and gold tenting. Dragging in a shuddering breath, she turned.

Montisfryn had surged to his knees in the bed, his sword, unsheathed, in his hand. "What is it? Outlaws?"

She stared. Her heart thudded in her ears, in her throat. She couldn't speak; she could barely hear.

A succession of shivers shook her.

Her face stopped Alaun in his tracks. She was deathly pale, her eyes huge. Dark pools filled with an unnamable fear, they watched him with no hint of recognition.

He froze.

The silence outside the tent assured him there was no enemy without. Moving slowly, deliberately, his eyes locked on hers, he laid his sword down. She stood poised for flight, his shirt clutched to her breasts, her fingers clenched hard on the linen folds. Shivers continued to rack her, spasm after spasm. "Come back to bed, Eloise."

She blinked.

"Tis freezing, lady-witch."

It was, their breaths misting in the pre-dawn chill.

He watched her carefully; he kept his tone light. He couldn't rise and fetch her; he was fully aroused; she might well flee from him. He would catch her within yards of the tent, but he didn't want to have to subdue her, to carry her, struggling, back to his bed. "Come and let me warm you."

He saw uncertainty in her eyes; a more intense shiver racked her. "You know I will not harm you. Now come and be warmed, or you'll catch a chill."

The patient reasonableness in his tone pulled Eloise over the last threshold, back into the real world. Her vision cleared; blind panic receded.

Slowly, she returned to the bed, frowning, bewildered, perplexed. Montisfryn slid down among the covers; he lifted them for her. As she put one knee on the pallet, he reached for the shirt she still clutched. She tightened her grip.

"Nay, lady—twill not aid in warming you. Tis as cold as you are."

He was right. She let him take it from her; he threw it to the end of the bed. Shivering, she slipped beneath the covers and lay on her back. "Your pardon, lord. I know not what so frighted me."

Alaun knew, but all he said was, "Twas doubtless just a night-fear, lady. Tis gone once you awake." Long shivers still racked her. He turned toward her—

She tensed. Immediately, quite definitely. From beneath her long lashes, she shot him a wary glance.

Hiding his dismay, he disguised his movement as if he was simply settling himself. With a deep sigh, he lay on his back and let his body fall slack. He waited until she shivered again. "You are very cold, lady. Come and warm yourself by me. I would not have you take a chill whilst in my care."

He felt another of her suspicious looks linger on his face. Then, like a small chilled animal, she crept closer.

It was another trial he had to endure, her slow, inching progress, but, eventually, she settled her head in the hollow of his shoulder, one arm across his chest, her body fitted snugly along the length of his. With slow deliberation, he moved the arm on which she lay and placed his palm in the small of her back. She tensed, then relaxed again. Relieved, with his other hand, he found hers where it lay on his chest, and raised it to his lips; she watched as he placed a gentle kiss in her palm.

Laying her hand back on his chest, he kissed her forehead. "Rest, lady-witch. You're safe with me."

A smile tugged at Eloise's lips. She snuggled down, her cheek pillowed on the broad muscle of his chest. His heat stole into her bones, driving out the lingering chill. With a sigh, she relaxed completely, feeling her body cleave to his. Silly man—after the last twenty-four hours, did he think he had to tell her? She knew she was safe in his arms. Entirely confident of that fact, she fell asleep.

Alaun did not.

He mentally cursed himself for not guessing that she would react badly to being approached from behind; he was shaken by how deep her fear went—her mind seemed to blot out the cause. Her gentle breathing reassured him; he hadn't lost her. With the soft sound in his ears, he considered their situation. No matter how he viewed it, one conclusion stood firm.

His simple, straightforward campaign to win Eloise de Versallet to wife had encountered a major obstacle.

He brooded on that fact as, about them, the camp came to life.

Eventually, disturbed by the din, Eloise sleepily stretched—then froze.

"Good morning, lady. Tis time we were about."

Half-sprawled across his chest, Eloise felt every word as well as heard them. They sounded disgruntled. She glanced up; he met her gaze, his expression resigned.

"If you will let me up, I will fetch you your clothes."

She blinked, then, despite a very real reluctance to leave his warmth, she carefully disentangled her limbs from his.

Alaun bore the moment stoically, manfully resisting the urge to roll over, trap her beneath him, and remind her of the night's pleasures. When he was finally free of her soft body, he rose and pulled on his braies, then retrieved her cote and chemise. They were dry, but chilly. She accepted them with a polite word, her lids veiling her eyes.

Bilder appeared with warm water for washing, the robin wide-eyed behind him. Alaun washed and dressed quickly, then left the tent to his prize.

He did not set eyes on her again until she trotted forward on her mare to take her position alongside him as the column got underway. None would have guessed that the siren of the riverbank lay behind her distant mien, much less that she'd lain all night in his arms. He greeted her with a grunt, and returned to his calculations.

The miles slid by unnoticed, the scenery unremarked.

Beside him, Eloise tried to appear unconscious; with each league that passed, her distraction grew. The happenings of the night demanded consideration, yet objectively analyzing them proved impossible, at least while riding beside their perpetrator, one eye constantly on him. Her nervousness communicated itself to Jacquenta; the mare jibbed, then sidled.

Her struggle to settle the mare cut through Montisfryn's absorption. He glanced at her, hesitated, then said, "Tell me, lady—do you need to send a message to your man-of-business? Your father told me you engage in commerce of sorts."

She inclined her head. "Aye. Some part of my fortune is vested in cloth manufacture."

He raised a brow. "I know Edward thinks tis the way of the future, but do you find it profitable?"

To her considerable surprise, Eloise found herself explaining the intricacies of the fledgling cloth trade. For his part, Montisfryn knew the wool trade forward and back, his lands contributing the major part of the local clip.

"My broker tells me there have recently been serious disruptions to the supply," she said. "The master-weavers are not happy."

Alaun frowned. "Have you heard what has caused these disruptions?"

"Nay. My man was not specific—we do not deal directly with the wool merchants, only the weavers and their guilds."

They continued to exchange views and predictions; the time to the midday halt flew.

"My broker is in London." Eloise returned to his original query as they drew rein. "But I have no need to send any message to him presently."

Alaun's lips tightened—it was on the tip of his tongue to remind her of her new direction. Instead, he dismounted. "When you have the need, you have only to ask."

The hour allotted to the midday meal passed quickly. Montisfryn was called back along the train; Eloise found herself strolling a nearby wood, accompanied by Jenni and escorted by Roland, Rovogatti, and a full company of men-at-arms.

When Roland, in whose care Montisfryn had left her, had agreed to her suggestion, she hadn't expected such a crowd. "Surely, sir, tis a trifle excessive?"

"Lady." Roland placed his hand over his heart. "Much as I might agree, believe me, tis not worth the lion's roar to dismiss them."

Inferring that it was Montisfryn's orders and not Roland's that had furnished her guard, she accepted her fate with a dismissive shrug, delighting Roland.

Montisfryn was waiting when they got back; he lifted her to her saddle without a word, the dark mood of the morning again upon him.

Unsettled all over again, she took the lion by the mane. "An' it please you, lord, I would ride back to view the column. I've seen but little of the host that travels with you."

His expression impassive, Alaun watched as she drew her mare, prancing skittishly, about. He met her dark gaze; a touch of haughty challenge had crept in—she was as skittish as her horse. For the first time in hours, he felt like smiling. "Your escort will accompany you."

Appalled, she glanced at the score of men-at-arms who rode at her back. "Nay, lord. Tis not necessary."

"How say you that, lady, when you ran so easily from me yesterday?"

Elevating her chin, she met his sharp gaze. "I did not, yesterday, fully comprehend the dangers."

"But now you do, you will understand that, while I stand your lord, I will continue to protect you adequately, as I see fit."

Eloise swallowed her snort. How ludicrous!—to ride down a military column with twenty men-at-arms at her back. Her eyes clashed with his, implacable gold. "If I give you my word, lord, that I will not run from you again, will you permit me to ride down your column without such an unnecessary escort?"

His eyes narrowed. For a long moment, he held her gaze, then grudgingly conceded, "I will accept your word on condition that, for any excursions about column or camp, you will take Rovogatti with you. And that at no time will you stray beyond the line of outriders or pickets."

Eloise considered, then inclined her head. "Tis reasonable."

Alaun bit back an acid rejoinder. He watched as, with a gracious nod, she wheeled away, summoning Rovogatti with an imperious gesture. Grunting to himself, he returned to his musings.

His disaffected mood was not improved when, on retiring to his pavilion after settling the dispositions, he discovered his prize absent. Not only absent, but very definitely not in residence. There was no sign of her chest, nor her cloak—not even her maid. He paused to check his memory, then, assured of the solid foundation of his complaint, he stalked out and across to Roland's pavilion. The robin was chatting to Rovogatti close by the lowered flap. She started up at Alaun's approach; he waved her away. Without pausing to announce himself, he marched in.

Warned by the sudden turbulence that a body rather larger than Jenni's had entered, Eloise glanced around, then quickly edged around the open chest over which she'd been bending. "Lord?" The lion looked ready to roar.

Stopping before the chest, he trapped her gaze. "You seem to have lost your way, lady."

Straightening to her full height, she returned his gaze steadily. "Nay, lord. This is the tent you yourself assigned me."

The golden eyes narrowed. "Do you or do you not recall me telling you, quite clearly I believe, that henceforth my couch will be yours?"

She did, quite clearly; she was not, however, about to admit to willful disobedience. "Naturally, I assumed you made that statement in the...er, heat of the moment. You cannot expect me to share your pavilion on a permanent basis."

One tawny brow slowly rose. "Can I not?"

She blushed, but refused to lower her eyes. Her normal assurance was tied in knots, as it had been all day. She was not at all sure what she wanted. She did, however, know what should be. "Tis not suitable, lord."

"*Suitable?*"

"Aye." With feigned calmness, she folded the cote she'd been packing. "I'm a widow—a virtuous widow"—her quick glance dared him to contradict her—"presently traveling in your train. Tis not suitable for me to share your pavilion."

Bending over the chest, she laid the cote within. She straightened—and found him beside her.

"Do you tell me twas not you who left half-moons scored in my arms? That twas not you who lay arching beneath me last night?" His eyes flared. "My suitability did not seem in question then, lady."

He stepped closer; instinctively, she backed, then abruptly halted, forcing him to stop, a bare inch away. Head up, hands rising to her hips, she narrowed her eyes at him. "Nay—you will not catch me with that." With one finger, she prodded his chest. "You know well twas not *your* suitability I referred to."

Scowling, Alaun rapidly redeployed. "Tis just as well, for there is no question of suitability here. Tis more a matter of your willfulness. Henceforth, you will occupy my pavilion. I will not consider it *suitable* for you to be elsewhere."

She opened her eyes wide. "You plan to move out?"

He narrowed his. "Allow me to make the matter plain. You will *share* my pavilion—with me."

"Nay. I will not be your mistress—I told you before."

"And as *I* told *you* before, tis not a position for which I would consider you!" He glowered. "I do not wish to argue this matter further, lady." If he did, there was every possibility that he would lose. He had no real right to insist she share his tent, yet after the revelations of the night, followed by those of the morn, he had no intention of letting her slip from his grasp. At the moment, desire was the only real hold he had over her—and he wasn't even sure of that. "You will repair to my tent forthwith—the only choice you need make is your mode of travel."

She lifted an unrepentant brow. "What choices do I have?"

"You may walk by my side—or I'll carry you."

She actually considered calling his bluff; he saw it in her eyes. "Do not tempt me, lady." He pointed a finger at her nose. "I wish you in my tent—tis an end to the matter."

Abruptly, Eloise shrugged. "As you wish, lord." At the moment, her dignity was more important than whether the tent about her was blue or red. She dropped the lid on her chest as she rounded it. "But allow me to comment that your invitation lacks charm."

"Allow me to comment that your tongue has a sharp edge." He followed her around the chest.

"Nay, lord." She tossed her head. "Tis merely that you have little experience in dealing with ladies."

Catching her arm, Alaun swung her to face him. "You are in error, lady. I have *considerable* experience in dealing with ladies—just none as hoity as *you.*"

Her eyes darted fire; she opened her lips—he lost the last of his patience.

He silenced her with a kiss—a hard, possessive, thoroughly stirring kiss, a kiss he'd been waiting for all day.

His hands rose to trap her face, then gentled, framing her smooth cheeks as his tongue systematically plundered. Her hands came up, but, as had happened before, only softened about his. He kissed her deeply, demanding her surrender, commanding her senses until she gave way. Only when she sighed and softened against him did he raise his head.

Slowly, her lids rose to reveal lustrous eyes, dark and wide, brimming with disgruntled confusion. The sight pleased him greatly. "Get you to my tent, lady." His voice was a low growl. "Rovogatti will bring your baggage."

Her lips throbbing, her hands still on his as he released her face, Eloise blinked. Her senses were reeling; her wits were in similar case.

"Come." His hand closed about hers; he lifted the flap and handed her through.

Outside, one of his sergeants hung back, clearly wanting a word. She looked up. Montisfryn's gaze was on her, a clear question in the gold. Haughtily, she inclined her head, then glided across the clearing.

She swept into the scarlet-and-gold pavilion, the light of battle in her eyes. Her first victim was his squire; the man met her narrow-eyed stare with a bland, somewhat vacuous expression.

With a humph, she swung about, her gaze raking the furnishings. Despite having spent the previous night within the scarlet-and-gold walls, she had precious little memory of much beyond the huge, well-stuffed pallet. Supported by a plain wooden frame, it took up most of one side of the tent. On the opposite side of the central pole stood a long oak board atop a pair of trestles. A tall-backed chair sat behind it; a stool was pushed beneath the board's edge. Nearer the wall stood a campaign chest and a flat-topped armor chest, a pewter basin and ewer gracing the lid. A collection of weapons, sheathed swords and lances, lay beside the chests.

With a disdainful sniff, she turned as Rovogatti lumbered up, her chest in his arms, Jenni close behind. "Place it there." She pointed to the side, a little way from the bed. "Leave my herb-box beside it." Tapping her toe, she watched, then said to Jenni, "I will have my psalter."

Directing the squire to retrieve the stool, she had him place it by the entrance. Settling herself, she took her psalter on her lap—and devoted herself to her psalms.

Alaun found her thus, the very image of a virtuous widow. He cast her a darkling glance, then, suppressing a growl, passed on into the tent. He unbuckled his short sword and dropped it on his armor chest. The clatter elicited no response from his guest. He pulled his chair from the board—then changed his mind and prowled across to stand, hands on his hips, behind her. The tome in her hands was a handsome volume, beautifully lettered on fine vellum with rich illuminations surrounding the text.

He watched as she calmly turned a page.

With a disgusted snort, he swung inside, forcing his feet to carry him away—battling the temptation to pick her up, drop the tent flap, and have her instead of supper.

The arrival of Bilder and the robin with their meal proved fortuitous.

Once he and his guest were settled at the oak board, the dishes before them and wine in their goblets, Bilder twitched the robin's sleeve; the pair withdrew.

Eloise devoted her attention to the savory stew and crisp brown bread.

She'd come across Montisfryn's commissariat, under the care of one of his vassals, a Sir Eward Steele, in her brief foray down the column. The logistics of feeding eight hundred mouths while traveling had fascinated her; it was certainly more complex than castle management.

As the silence stretched, she shot a glance at Montisfryn. His expression grim, his eyes on his plate, he was applying himself to his food with methodical thoroughness. She looked down at her plate—and kept her lips firmly shut.

To his considerable chagrin, having achieved his immediate objective, Alaun had no idea how to capitalize on the situation. How—where—should he start his explanations? Was it even wise to begin?

The revelations of the night, and even more those of the morn, suggested she would flee in panic if he so much as mentioned the word "husband"; how to persuade her otherwise was a point he'd spent hours debating.

All he had to cling to was the promise implicit in her surrender, both on the riverbank and later, the sure knowledge that she found pleasure in his arms. Without that, he would be no closer to gaining her hand than all the others who had wooed her.

Yet she seemed set on denying him even that much victory.

Glancing sideways, and finding her expression still serenely remote, he grimaced and looked at his plate. His reputation in the field was for wringing victory from adversity—he had never imagined he would need the same talents to win his chosen wife.

The meal ended without a word spoken.

Bilder and Jenni returned and cleared the table. At Eloise's instruction, Jenni carefully replaced the psalter in her chest. Then the little maid hovered; Bilder had already left.

Finding herself the object of a lowering, very pointed golden glance, Eloise lifted her chin. "You may go, Jenni." She hesitated, then added, "I will not need you again tonight."

With a studiously blank expression, the robin flitted out.

Alaun humphed and drained his goblet. Saints!—what was the matter with him? He was rarely grumpy, let alone surly. Tonight, he felt thoroughly churlish.

The object of his ire sat calmly staring out of the open tent flap.

His pavilion was tonight sited on a small knoll, the tents of his followers spread around on the plain. They were still heading north; Gloucester lay ahead, Hereford beyond. The light slowly faded; the evening calm descended.

When Eloise remained stoically distant, he set down his goblet with a decisive click. He rose, stalked to the entrance, and let down the flap. Bilder had left a candle burning on the board. Returning to the table, he studied her face, unshakably serene in the flickering light. By St. George and all the saints! Did she want him tonight—or not?

As if in answer, she stood and stretched sinuously, then looked about. Her gaze settled on his lance, lying in the shadows. Then she turned to survey the bed.

For one incredulous instant, he watched her glance back and forth, measuring...he calmed himself with a deep breath. The lance was too heavy for her to lift. And if she thought he would help, she would need to think again. "Lady..."

It was the first word he'd uttered since entering the tent.

She turned, brows politely rising. "Aye, lord?"

Having opened the discussion, he couldn't think how to proceed; for the first time in years, his imagination failed him. He'd rarely needed to persuade a woman to his bed, and certainly never after she'd occupied it.

He met Eloise's gaze—a glimmer of triumph glowed in the dark depths. He narrowed his eyes. "Lady, did I not pleasure you well last night?"

The dark eyes blinked wide. A tinge of color crept into her cheeks. "Aye."

"And was it not at your decision that our intimacy came about?"

She eyed him warily. "Aye."

"Then what, by all the saints, have I done that you seek to deny me this eve—to discard me as your lover?"

"Nay—tis not that." She frowned. "Tis that it is not proper for me to be with you thus."

"*Proper?* In whose eyes?" He gestured to the sky. "The saints? Tis my belief that after all you suffered at your husband's hands, and through his memory thereafter, they'll hardly begrudge you your time with me. I have ever heard they are caring and understanding of mortals, merciful, not harsh and unyielding—do not your psalms tell you so?"

She frowned harder. "There are still your people—"

"Who will hardly think ill of you for sharing my bed." He paused, then added, his tone more gentle, "And there is no one else to know, to censure you, rightly or otherwise."

She looked down at the table; he tilted his head to study her face. Even more gently, he said, "If tis the danger of getting with child that worries you, there are ways—"

"Nay." She cut him off with a quick gesture. "That is not an issue here." She glanced up and saw his puzzled frown. "Tis the way in my family. William was born three years after my parents wed; there are three or more years between the rest of us. My mother was healthy and strong; she suffered no miscarriages." She shrugged. "And Emma is the same. Tis doubtless a characteristic as common as the other."

Alaun blinked—and swallowed the words that had risen to his tongue. He'd grown up with horse-breeders and horse-breeding; he could think of at least one other reason why her mother had not quickened sooner. And

Emma's condition simply made it more likely. But he was, first and last, a strategist; he kept his thoughts to himself.

A fleeting vision of Eloise swollen large with his babe sent a surge of unadulterated desire straight to his loins. He stiffened.

Uncertain, Eloise met his gaze—and felt her resistance waver. She frowned at him. "During the day, I did not know if you wanted me more."

He stared at her. "Did not know…?" Abruptly, he ran a hand through his hair. "I've wanted you from the moment I saw you."

Her lips twitched. "In the forest with the pigs?"

"Aye." His expression warned against flippancy. "If you'd shown willing, I would have taken you then."

The thought sent a fresh surge of blood to Alaun's groin. In increasing discomfort, he stalked around her, then returned to stand beside her, fingers lightly trailing the board.

"The concept seems a mite precipitous, lord." She slanted him a considering glance.

Inwardly, he groaned. "With you, lady, my wanting is frequently precipitous. Such as now." He grasped the hand furthest from him and drew it to the bulge in his braies.

Panic gripped him. He'd just done what her husband had, forcing her to touch him.

Aghast, he released her, only to feel her slim fingers curl knowingly about his erection. Her face was half-turned toward him; she was smiling. Quietly exhaling, he studied the ageless, thoroughly feminine, witchy little smile that curved the ends of her lips; it softened her whole expression. Her lids were lowered, her gaze mysterious.

She looked as if she was thinking of how he would feel inside her.

The thought sent another powerful surge through his loins; he swelled beneath her hand. His jaw clenched against the impulses battering him, he reached for her, and slowly drew her closer.

His restraint was not lost on Eloise, any more than the fact that the night still hung on her decision. To be thus in control of such a strong and powerful man was a deeply attractive, compulsively seductive, irresistibly potent temptation. She let her hand fall as, still smiling, she raised her eyes to his. "Nay—you cannot expect me to know that. I cannot tell by looking."

His eyes were brightly golden, his expression that of a man goaded to his limit. "Lady—know this. I want you—often. Frequently. Morning, noon, and night. I can no longer, saints preserve me, imagine a time when I will *not* want you."

It took a moment for his words to filter through the haze clouding Alaun's brain. When they did, he was shocked. Saints preserve him, indeed! Any hope she hadn't heard, had not fully comprehended, was laid to rest by her widening smile.

He groaned. And swept her into his arms.

For long minutes, he simply kissed her, tasting her with relief, letting his inflamed passions settle once more under his control, soothed by the clear promise of what was to come.

Eloise settled willingly in his arms, content to be there, content to allow him to lead her where he would. He was right—the saints would forgive her; twas justice that she have at least a few nights—however long it took to reach Hereford—in which to enjoy being a woman whole.

Gradually, the kiss deepened; her hands wandered, roaming the vast acres of muscle and heavy bone, searching out ribs and shoulders amid the hard contours.

When he finally disengaged and raised his head, looking sleepily down like a lion surveying his next meal, she yielded to her most wanton desire. She smiled. "Allow me to be your handmaid this night, lord. Let me disrobe you."

Brows rising, Alaun hung on to his raging lust, and wondered if he'd ever become inured to her prattle. Probably only when he was dead. She could raise a statue with her words. He couldn't deny her request, even though, tonight, compliance would cost him dear. It was a clear sign she wanted him—that she was embarking on their play with her usual calm deliberation. The thought rattled him. He might have the advantage of experience, but she would have the advantage of surprise. "Aye, lady." His voice was gravelly and low. "You will serve me well tonight."

Her lips twitched, but she gave no other sign of having caught his meaning.

Calmly, Eloise set about unlacing his houppelande, exulting in the sense of being in control. His eyes were already glowing, although the flames had yet to appear. She knew she could light them. After loosening all his ties and points, she had to stand on the stool to draw the voluminous garment off. That done, she quickly dispensed with his shirt, marveling at the wide expanse of golden flesh revealed to her sight. She let her fingers trail over the backs of his shoulders, hiding her smile at his indrawn breath.

Pushing the stool under the table, she folded both houppelande and shirt, and laid them on his chest.

Alaun gritted his teeth and willed himself not to break.

Returning to stand before him, she glanced into his face, then raised both hands to the heavy muscles that crossed his chest. Placing her palms against the warm skin, she let them slide, slowly, down over his ridged stomach to where his hose were fastened by buttoned tabs to his braier. His stomach contracted at her touch. Delighted, she unbuttoned his hose, quickly rolling them down his thighs. They slipped off easily, along with his soft leather boots.

She set boots and hose aside. Her eager fingers reached for the twined ends of his braier, for the last knot she would have to undo; he closed his hands over hers. "Nay, lady. Not yet."

Surprised, Eloise glanced up.

His smile was that of a lion hunting. "Tis my turn now, maid."

Understanding that being a maid gave her no right to argue, she acquiesced with a nod. Her breath caught in her throat. Her hand quivered when he took it in his. Reaching back, he shifted his chair, so that he could sink down upon it, his thighs widespread. Looking up, his smile slowly widened; as he drew her down to sit on one knee, she wondered what it would feel like to be devoured.

He reached around her to unlace her gown. She kept her head up, her gaze fixed beyond him. When the laces where free, he brought his hands to her shoulders and gently drew the soft material down. It caught above her breasts.

She looked down as he reached for her hand, holding it while he undid the small buttons that closed her sleeve from wrist to elbow. First one, then the other, sleeve was laid open. Then, his hands rose again. She could barely breathe, her lungs tight, parched. Slowly, he drew one arm, then the other, free of the tight sleeves. The soft fabric collapsed in folds about her waist.

Glancing up, she saw his eyes, glittering, fixed on her breasts, outlined beneath her chemise. As the fact registered, her breasts swelled.

Alaun's fingers shook as he reached for the bow at the neckline of her chemise. One tug, and it was undone. Dragging in a breath, he tightened his grip on his surging passions. Maintaining the steady deliberation that he knew was heating her, he slipped his fingers beneath the gathered neckline of the chemise and spread it wide, then guided it down, off her smooth shoulders and down her arms. The edge caught on the peaks of her breasts. He lifted her arms free before running his fingers along the inside of the neckline, unhooking it from her nipples. Without allowing his hands to touch her skin, he pushed the soft folds of cote and chemise down, revealing her waist and the smooth flare of her hips.

She sat on his knee, bared to the hips, the most delectable handmaid he'd ever had.

And definitely the proudest. There was a calmness about her, a quality in her heavy-lidded, mysterious eyes that counteracted the quivering tension he could feel laying siege to her flesh. Her prideful assurance aroused him— he would get no meek submission from her.

He raised a gentle hand to her face and turned her lips to his. Hers were soft, parted, very ready to be kissed. He spent long moments inciting her to kiss him. When one small hand fastened on his shoulder and she took the reins, he lowered his hand from her face.

For one timeless moment, Eloise found herself poised, quivering, on some invisible threshold. His hands had disappeared, but his lips demanded her attention. Then the hand behind her rose to press in the small of her naked back; slowly, it stroked upward to her shoulder blades, long fingers caressing her nape as she gasped. Her body arched. The hand stroked back down to the base of her spine as his other hand closed, warm and firm, about her out-thrust breast.

She shivered; liquid fire danced through her veins. As his fingers stroked and caressed, teased and taunted, she felt the flames heat her. The glow inside her grew, swelling with every pounding beat of her heart. His hand moved to her other breast, now eager for his attention.

As he continued his unhurried play, the subtle pressure in the small of her back keeping her upright, she floated just short of heaven.

She was firmly on some pleasured plateau when he finally released her lips. From under heavy lids, she studied the flames in his eyes, the intent expression on his face as he caressed and cajoled, coaxing her nipples into even tighter buds.

She shivered again.

He glanced at her, and smiled, slowly, sleepily. Then he looked down. His hands left her; he lifted her skirts. His fingers found her garters; he quickly dispensed with her stockings and soft shoes, then flipped her skirts down.

His lips returned to hers for a long, slow kiss; the hand at her back moved, closing about her hip, while his other palm eased around her, pushing her clothes down. He gripped and lifted her slightly, his hand passing under her as he swept her gown and chemise down her legs. They puddled on the grass at her feet. He released her lips and drew back.

A deep shudder shook her as the knowledge that she was naked, held on his knee where he could touch her at will, sank into her mind. She wondered if he treated all handmaidens so. The thought curved her lips; lifting her heavy lids, she glanced at him.

He was looking at her, studying her, as if she was his next battlefield.

Alaun wished he could shut his eyes, but they no longer obeyed his injunctions. They devoured her soft, indescribably sleek body—she was perfect; she was his. Tonight he would enjoy her fully, as she would enjoy him. Only the promise of the pleasure to come allowed him to harness the lust rampaging through him. Leashed, it waited, obedient but quivering.

Another long shiver shook her. He smiled. The tent was too warm for her to be cold. In the morning, it would be freezing, but after the day's sunshine, the air trapped beneath the silk was pleasant on the skin. And she would soon be so heated she wouldn't feel the air's touch. He lowered his head, finding her lips as he drew her closer, into the curve of his arm.

Eloise relaxed, warm and secure, comfortable against him. One muscular arm was draped around her, holding her firmly, his large palm flattened over her waist; his other hand gently fondled her breasts, effortlessly reestablishing the haze of pleasure in her mind. His lips played on hers, drawing her from herself. Eagerly, she followed him into realms of delight.

Only when he was sure she was totally enthralled did Alaun allow his fingers to leave her satin breasts, trailing down over the slight curve of her belly to tease the dark curls at its base. He touched her very gently, the lightest of lovers' caresses, then let his fingers trail, tantalizingly light, over her ivory thighs, still closed against him. He repeated the actions, again and again, until he felt her shift, her body arching lightly in his hold.

He drew back from their kiss and repeated the delicate torture. Her eyes were closed; a slight frown played between her brows. She shifted again. He caught his breath.

"Open for me, Eloise."

Almost on the words, she parted her thighs. Victory pounded in his veins; he ignored it. He lowered his lips to hers; her hands rose to his face. Slowly, keeping his touch deliberate, he stroked her curls, then reached further. He parted her soft folds, damp and slightly swollen. At his touch, they swelled more; probing further, he found her slick heat. She shivered in his arms, but did not pull away. His jaw clenched, ignoring the ache in his groin, he gave himself over to caressing her.

At first, the struggle to breathe consumed Eloise, then, discovering that her body seemed to cope despite the heated tension gripping it, she let the pleasure he was lavishing on her sweep her up, and carry her on to an even higher plateau of earthly bliss. Every stroke of his broad fingers evoked exquisite sensations. With each tender touch, she felt herself softening, blossoming, offering herself more fully for the next.

When she was hot and slick, her honey scorching his fingers, Alaun drew back from their kiss. She lifted her heavy lids, her gaze darkly langorous. He met it, then he looked down.

Eloise followed his gaze. The sight of his large hand between her thighs, of his fingers rhythmically stroking her, sent a shaft of erotic need shivering through her.

He felt it and glanced up. His eyes, afire with golden flames, met hers. "Look down, lady-witch. Watch as I love you."

Driven by a compulsion even stronger than her will, she did.

His fingers repeatedly caressing her heated flesh, Alaun watched her face. "Your lips are open for me, lady-witch, pouting and swollen and so soft." He gently stroked them. "And here lies the nub of your pleasure."

He slid his thumb between the soft folds to where the tight button, aroused by his caresses, throbbed in the shadow of its hood. Slowly, he circled it; her thighs quivered.

"And here lies the portal to your sheath, sweet lady-witch." With one fingertip, he slowly circled the tight band then, deliberately, slowly, inexorably, he slid that finger into her.

Eloise felt the invasion keenly. She arched, then shivered and spasmed, her muscles instinctively clamping about his finger.

"Aye, lady-witch." He rested his head against hers. "You are hot and slick, tight and strong." His hand moved rhythmically between her thighs, his finger gliding easily in and out of her body.

She gasped. Wild-eyed, she looked at him, and saw the flames leaping, gold in gold. She reached for his face, drawing his lips to hers, needing his kiss to anchor her as her body strained against its earthly bonds.

Her unrestrained ardor sent fire surging through Alaun; grimly, he held on. He had a plan of campaign he was unwilling to surrender.

As her flames rose higher, he continued his stroking, pausing only to slide another finger in alongside the first. She was alive in his arms, arching, straining against his hold, wild in her passion.

Breathing was suddenly far too hard. Eloise let her head fall back, arching against his supporting arm. She gasped as she felt his fingers part slightly, stretching her gently. Then he probed more deeply; her fingers sank into his arm. "Will you mount me now, lord?"

Alaun heard her breathless question. He gritted his teeth, only just finding the strength to say, "Nay, lady-witch. Not yet. Tonight, I would have you fly first alone."

Fly? Eloise thought she was already in heaven. Then she felt the soft touch of his hair on her shoulder.

Carefully, Alaun caught one puckered nipple with his lips. He circled it with his tongue, and heard her shocked gasp. He suckled, drawing the sensitive nub into his mouth, then he laved it.

Her body bowed, her head tipping back. The sound she uttered was a cross between a cry and a moan. It was the first true sound of passion he'd drawn from her. He tried the same trick on her other breast; the result was even more pleasing—a soft, almost sobbing cry. It was the sweetest music he had ever heard.

"Sing for me, lady-witch."

It was a siren's song that fell from her lips as he skillfully pushed her ever onward. As he felt her tightening, rising towards the final starburst, he moved hands and mouth in concert, orchestrating her sensitized nerves to give her the ultimate joy.

When she gave one last cry and convulsed in his arms, it was the most deeply erotic sight he'd ever seen.

As her muscles spasmed about his fingers, pressed deep within her, Eloise forced her eyes open. Struggling to find enough air, she whispered, "Will you come inside me now, lord?"

She wanted to feel him inside her, to share the glory with him. It was beautiful, but it would be more beautiful yet if he was with her.

A surge of anticipation flooded her as she heard his gravelly reply. "Aye, lady-witch. Tis time."

Drawing his fingers from her, Alaun stripped off his braies, lifting her slightly and rising an inch to slip the soft linen off. Then, juggling her, he swung her about so she straddled him.

He'd intended to kiss her, then her lift her onto him without giving her a chance to look down; she defeated him, bracing her hands against his chest and leaning back to view him.

He swallowed a groan. He didn't have sufficient strength left to reassure her. But she ignored the urging of his hands and continued to stare.

Resignedly watching her face, fully expecting to see fear, horror, shock, or any combination of the three, he was not at all prepared for the wonder that lit her eyes, nor the very feminine smile that curved her lips.

She reached for him, her small hand closing about him with a knowing touch.

He groaned and closed his eyes as she clasped and unclasped her fingers, then set them a-wandering.

"Tis beautiful," Eloise breathed, utterly captivated. She'd seen more than two in her lifetime, inevitable in a castle full of men—this one was a prize. A prize she wanted inside her.

Her smile deepened. Feeling more consciously feminine than ever in her life, she glanced at him. "Will you mount me now, lord?"

It was a delight to be able to surprise her. "Nay, lady. This time, you will mount me."

She looked down, then up at his face, brows lifting, the conjecture in her eyes more than he could bear. With a groan, wanting no more of words, his or hers, he lifted her, then lowered her. Slowly, easily, he sank into her.

Eloise let her head fall back; the sensation of him slowly filling her claimed her mind. He supported her as he eased her down. And then he was there, high inside her, deeply embedded in her body. She tightened about him and heard him groan.

Her thighs gripped his hips; his hands gripped her bottom. He raised her, then let her sink onto him again.

They set the tempo between them, he lifting, she slowing her downward slide.

The end was a holocaust of feeling, sensation after sensation shuddering through them both. Head back, she strained against his hold as the final, all-consuming spasm shook her. Boneless, she collapsed against him, her arms limp on his shoulders, her thighs spread wide over his, with him buried to the hilt inside her.

Alaun paused only long enough to savor the strong ripples of her release, then he raised her slightly, his body coiling to plunge once, twice, deeply into her, and he, too, reached the bright pinnacle. The shudders that racked him flowed away, even as his warmth flooded her.

His breathing hoarse and labored, he bowed his head and pressed a kiss to her temple.

The last thing Eloise remembered was his arms locking about her; she clung to his warmth and strength.

Chapter 11

On leaving his pavilion the next morning, Alaun paused to look out over the countryside. Soft mists veiled the surrounding plains, obscuring the horizon. The air was crisp, the sky clear. He drew in a deep breath, then slowly exhaled.

Hoping he did not look as smug as he felt, he headed for the campfire. He'd left his prize with her maid, the robin busy brushing out Eloise's long hair. He hadn't seen the dark tresses free before; the sight had given him ideas, which in turn had driven him from the tent. Now was not the time to rush her, precipitous reactions or not.

Roland appeared as Alaun was breaking his fast. His cousin looked refreshed and pleasantly disheveled, a fact he immediately explained.

"I've reclaimed my tent. From your smug look, I take it tis unlikely the lady will be needing it more?"

Alaun managed a frown. "Nay, she will not. But there's her robin to house—we'll need to find her some place to perch."

Roland waved expansively. "Rovogatti's already got the robin in hand. Seems she's found his tent to her liking."

Alaun grunted. "Just as long as I hear no complaints. The girl's little more than a child, and under my lady's protection."

"Nay, I doubt you'll get any complaints. From all I've seen, tis wedding plans you're more likely to hear."

"Already?"

Roland turned to stare. "You're one to talk."

"Tis not the same," he mumbled, draining his ale. He lowered the mug, and encountered Roland's amused glance. He scowled, "Tis time the wagons were loading."

The next hour went in chaos as the camp broke up and the column reformed.

As before, Eloise found herself on her mare, ambling alongside Montisfryn's gray at the head of the long column. She was blissfully free of yesterday's uncertainties, convinced beyond doubt that Montisfryn still wanted her.

It was, she'd discovered, very nice to feel wanted.

In the chill gray of early dawn, he'd shaken her awake, his hand warm and heavy on her shoulder. His soft, "Lady-witch, lady-witch," had opened her sleepy eyes. She was sure she should take exception to being so addressed, yet his tone made it clear he meant the term as an endearment—a reluctant endearment which, to her mind, made it all the more endearing. By the time she'd decided that, he'd settled her on her back. Looming over her, he'd parted her thighs with his, his fingers finding her softness and coaxing a welcome from her. Then he'd lowered his powerful body to hers and possessed her. Utterly.

Sternly quelling a shiver, she glanced at him. He was riding easily, the reins held loosely in one gloved fist. As usual, his powerful frame combined with the tawniness of his mane and his golden eyes left the distinct impression of a lion. Today, his clothes of ochre and brown further enhanced the image.

He felt her gaze and looked sleepily down at her. "Pensive, lady? Of what are you thinking?"

She couldn't resist. "Why, that you remind me of a lion, lord."

The tawny brows rose.

"A sleeping lion," she quickly qualified. "As on your tournament shield." Reminded of an earlier thought, she added, "Incidentally, to my mind, your motto is less than apt."

He eyed her impassively. "How so?"

Seriously, as if debating a Latin declension, she offered, "'Fearsome' is not as accurate a descriptor as might be. To my thinking, 'awesome' is more fitting."

His eyes gleamed, embers glowing in the gold; his jaw firmed. "Twould be well for you, lady, an' you let the lion sleep."

The comment, uttered in a low growl, proved too tempting. "Lack-a-day," she sighed. "And here was I thinking it might be diverting to stroke him and make him purr for me."

The sudden turbulence beside her resolved itself as, cursing beneath his breath, Montisfryn brought his stallion back under control. That done, he leveled a narrow-eyed glare on her. "Lady, unless you wish to divert as far as that copse on yonder hill, to discuss the precipitousness of my reactions to your sharp tongue, I suggest you tease this lion no more. Perhaps you should seek entertainment back along the train?"

She smiled placatingly, feeling slightly guilty. "Aye, lord. Perhaps twould be best. There is much I would learn from Sir Eward."

Finding balm not only in her mysterious eyes but in the fact that she had teased him at all, Alaun curtly nodded. He watched her draw away, then turn back down the column, Rovogatti close behind.

His lips slowly curving, he faced forward once more. More than once, he had been on the verge of commanding her to dispense with her 'lords' and, instead, use his name in private, yet she had a wealth of ways in which she uttered the simple title, infusing it with nuances both evocative and, quite often, erotic. Deciding he had yet to hear her full repertoire, he fell to considering how best to coax it from her. It was certainly one way to pass the miles.

Deep in thought, he merely grunted when Roland spurred forward to fall in by his side.

Eloise had an ulterior motive in riding down the column that morn. Despite her comments about Sir Eward, she did not stop by Montisfryn's commissary, but rode further along, eventually slowing to an ambling walk so that her keeper could come up with her.

When he did, keeping his horse a little behind hers, she turned to throw him a smile. "Tell me, Rovogatti. How do you come to be with Montisfryn?"

"Twas after Crecy, lady."

She turned in her saddle so she could speak directly to him. "He hired you then?"

"Nay." A quick grin lit the Genoese's dark features. "I was a prisoner."

There was nothing remotely prisonerlike in Rovogatti's present status. "How did that come about?"

With an eloquent shrug, Rovogatti grimaced. "I was one of the many Genoese hired by the French king to meet the English Edward at Crecy. We are arbalesters—crossbowmen, lady."

"What happened?"

"With my men—I was a captain, you understand—we advanced on the English right. I even recall seeing the dragon and lion banner—twas beside the Prince of Wales' standard, which we were ordered to attack." The Genoese made a disgusted sound. "Twas calamity, lady. The goose-feathers rained thick and I—we—went down. I was shot many times and left for dead on the field. I know not how I survived, for the charges must have rolled over us. And I've been told the night was chill, as it is in those parts."

"But you were found and made prisoner?"

"I was found by sheer luck. Twas the lord himself—he was assisting those who took the tally of the dead the next day. He told me he stooped to check my captain's badge—it used to be here." The Genoese pointed to a blank patch on the breast of his padded leather jerkin. Then he crossed himself. "Praise be to the Holy Mother, he realized I still lived. His squires carried me from the field and I was given into the care of the women in the train."

Eloise frowned. "If you were his prisoner, how is it you weren't ransomed?"

"Me?" Rovogatti's amusement was plain. "Nay, lady. There's little ransom to be gained from a poor captain of mercenaries, particularly not one from the losing side."

She raised her brows. That was a fact of which Montisfryn must have been aware, yet he'd given orders for the man, an unknown mercenary, to be cared for. "What, then, is your relationship to Montisfryn? Are you in his pay?"

Rovogatti grimaced. "I would follow him without coin, you understand. Twould be fitting, for he saved my life. Yet he insists I take an archer's pay, even to the point of my rank, though he has no arbalesters I could command."

Eloise nodded; facing forward, she resettled in her saddle. If Montisfryn had deemed the Genoese worthy of his payroll, and as he obviously considered Rovogatti trustworthy and able enough to act as guard to herself, then presumably there was no reason for her to disapprove of Jenni's liking for the man.

Nor his liking for Jenni. Eloise pursed her lips, still not entirely sure she approved. Jenni was yet very young to be lying with a man.

When the little maid had come to her that morning, Eloise had initially assumed Jenni's frequent blushes were due to Eloise's own state—in sympathy, as it were. There had certainly been reason enough to suppose so, with her clothes in a heap by the table and the bedclothes wildly a-tangle. Only when it had dawned that Jenni was blushing at nothing, or rather at her own thoughts, had Eloise seen the light. Released from attendance on her, her robin had spent the night much as she had.

Her shock had been ameliorated by the pleasure she herself had found in the night's long watches. Deciding that her only quibble was over what manner of man Jenni had given herself to, Eloise now deemed her questions satisfied. If Montisfryn trusted Rovogatti, then presumably she and Jenni could, too.

They had rounded the end of the column, dutifully wheeling ahead of the rearguard to ride forward along the column's other side, when a thin, high-pitched wail reached Eloise's ears. When the plaintive cry continued, she spurred forward to come up alongside the wagon from which the pitiful sound emanated.

It was an unremarkable conveyance indistinguishable from most others, with narrow boards covering the wagon's spine and rude vertical planks for sides. Drawing in beside it, Eloise looped Jacquenta's reins around one plank. "That child is ill. Show it to me."

Only as she looked up did she realize that she'd joined the whores of the train. Bright eyes and pale faces regarded her with an astonishment far greater than her own. Most of the women in the wagon were young—younger than Eloise. Subduing her momentary fluster, she allowed impatient command to creep into her tone. "Come—I have many herbs with me that might help the babe, but I cannot tell until I see it."

"'Deed, and I have many herbs, too, but I know not so much of babes. Know you more, lady?"

Eloise stared at the peculiar apparition that rose before her eyes. After a second's sheer astonishment, she realized the old woman, kneeling on the cart floor, had been bending over her patient.

A faded, but clean linen cap was perched over wispy, iron-gray curls. Remarkably bright hazel eyes regarded Eloise shrewdly. The woman's face was heavily-lined and tanned, but her gap-toothed smile and birdlike gaze suggested a still sprightly mind.

Eloise blinked, then calmly replied, "I have no babes of my own, but I've treated a whole castle for five years. There's little of children's ailments I have not seen."

"Five years?" The old woman looked her down and up, even as she lifted and held out a swaddled bundle. "In truth, lady, you seem older than that."

Reaching for the child, Eloise absentmindedly replied, "I spent many years in a convent."

The old dame snorted. "Waste!"

Nervous giggles came from the other occupants of the cart.

Eloise studied the babe, who blinked weakly up at her from the old wraps wound tightly about it. "Is it boy or girl?"

"Boy," came a weak voice.

Eloise looked up. A fair girl struggled up from her previously supine position, anxiously watching the babe. The girl's face was wan, but flushed. Eloise reached over the wagon's side and laid a hand on her brow.

The movement was greeted with startled surprise.

"You're burning with fever." Eloise sat back. "How long have you been so?"

The girl glanced worriedly at the old dame.

"Three days she's admitted to me." The old woman's expression was reproving. "But I wouldn't swear twasn't more."

Under the combined stare of dark and hazel eyes, the girl hung her head. "Perhaps twas five. I've lost count."

"Humph!" The old dame pressed the girl back to her makeshift bed. "Whichever it be, rest you there while the lady sees if there's anything she can do for your littley. Twill be a load off your mind and help you heal quicker."

In complete agreement, Eloise beckoned Rovogatti forward. "Here— hold him."

The Genoese looked stunned, but she gave him no chance to argue. Placing the half-unwrapped, weakly squirming bundle in his large hands, she bent over the small body, noting the slackness of the babe's soft skin, the dullness filming his pale blue eyes, and the weakness of his suck when she placed a fingertip in his tiny mouth. Gently, she palpated his belly, but could find no constriction.

With a sigh of relief, she straightened and relieved Rovogatti of his burden. Turning back to the wagon, she found all its occupants watching her anxiously.

"Tis not serious." She handed the child back to the old dame, who promptly rewrapped it and returned it to its mother.

Standing in her stirrups to peer over the wagon's side, Eloise addressed the girl. "Tis just that, with your fever, your milk is too thin for him—his body is trying to grow lustily and there's not enough going in to let him thrive. Twill be as well to start him on gruel and cow's milk. And mashed turnip, if there is. But he's weak, and will not feed well yet—if you will bring him to me when we make camp, I'll give him a dose that will let his body take nourishment more readily."

The girl's smile was weak, but full of relief. "My thanks, lady."

"Aye, but you need treatment, too." A question in her eyes, Eloise glanced at the old dame.

The old woman understood. "Nay. She's not got that, that I do know. My girls are clean and stay that way if they know what's good for 'em." The edict was uttered in a growl, but elicited quick smiles from the other women in the wagon, even the patient. The old woman humphed. "I've been treating her with chamomile thrice daily. Tis generally effective."

"Tis sound," Eloise acknowledged. "But I have feverfew and yarrow with me. Together with your chamomile, they should act more quickly."

She glanced down at the sick girl. "Think you you can come to the fire by Montisfryn's pavilion once we make camp? I will not have my herb-box until then, and we'll need boiling water."

There was an instant's hesitation; the girl looked at the old dame.

Who nodded. "I'll bring her, lady. And the child. Yet"—the old woman's lips pursed—"tis in my mind that the lord might not like to see you with us."

Eloise waved dismissively. "If tis in my power to help child and mother, then clearly tis my Christian duty so to do. Montisfryn will agree. As you are part of his train, you are also his responsibility. Tis not in question—I will expect you once we make camp."

She twitched her reins free of the wagon, but paused to ask, "I would have your name, good dame, in case I need send for you."

The old woman's face creased into a wide smile. "Tis Old Meg, lady. Even the lord knows it."

Eloise nodded. With a regal wave, she rode off.

Stopping on her way forward to ask certain, highly specific questions of Sir Eward, absorbed with considering the best diet for weakened babes, she rejoined Montisfryn at the head of the column.

The afternoon passed swiftly. They made camp early in the lee of a wood with the wind rising about them. It brought with it the first autumn leaves and the smell of rain.

As soon as Bilder appeared with her herb-box, Eloise laid it on the oak board and sent Jenni for a wooden bowl. Opening the camphorwood box, she selected a stoppered vial and a small metal spoon, then quickly sorted through her packets. When Jenni returned with the bowl, Eloise sent her to set a kettle on the fire just leaping into life in the dip below the big pavilion. Crumbling feverfew and yarrow into the bowl, Eloise wrapped a scarf over it, picked up the wrapped bowl, the vial, and the spoon, and carefully carried all to the fire.

As she reached the welcoming blaze, Old Meg appeared with the baby in her arms. The sick girl came behind, supported by two other women. Eloise nodded in welcome, then tipped water from the steaming kettle onto the herbs in the bowl; leaving the brew to steep, she turned to the babe.

The infant was crotchety, but lacked the energy to cry. Eloise held up her vial. "Tis a strengthening mixture in honey, and twill also ease his stomach." She poured a small amount into the spoon.

Meg, anticipating her, slipped her thumb into the babe's mouth, opening it. Deftly, Eloise tipped the mixture down, letting the babe suck on the spoon.

"There." She extracted the spoon, stroking the downy cheek with one finger. "That should deal with your problems for tonight."

Gently, she tucked the tiny hand that had come to grip hers weakly back into the wrap. Lifting her gaze, she spoke to Meg, "Sir Eward says he has honey, and some powdered oats and barley for gruel. Twill have to be with water tonight, but I've heard we'll be hard by Gloucester tomorrow evening—it should be simple enough to get milk for him there. I will see to it."

"Thank you, lady," came from the slight figure huddled by the fire.

"Nay." Eloise returned to her bowl. "Tis nothing more than what should be." She checked her infusion, then set the bowl in the girl's hands. "Sip slowly, and try not to drink the leaves."

On the hill above, Alaun stood in the entrance to his pavilion, watching the scene below through narrowed eyes. It was easy enough to guess what was passing; he would wager his witch was lecturing Old Meg on what to feed the girl and how to care for her. Amazingly, Meg, cantankerous old biddy that she was, was accepting the advice peaceably, nodding as she rocked a bundled baby in her arms.

The toast of the castle whores in his father's day, now long past the age of active service, Meg played the role of abbess, keeping a shrewd eye on the flock of girls who made their way by accommodating Alaun's knights. As Meg was more than a match for any over-lustful knight, Alaun tacitly encouraged her. Despite the size of his following, he was rarely called on to settle disputes over wenches, nor wrestle with charges brought by whores against abusive men. A man abused one of Meg's girls at his peril; in many ways, he regarded her as his lieutenant in such affairs.

That did not, however, mean that he approved of his wife-to-be's acquaintance with the old biddy.

Satisfied she'd done all she could, Eloise turned toward the pavilion, then stopped to ask, "How many other young children are in the train—ones who should be getting milk?"

Meg's brows rose. "Bella!" One of the women by the fire looked up. "How many young'uns have we now?"

The woman began to enumerate, using the names of mothers to define the children. Eloise kept count on her fingers, astounded to find the tally filling hand after hand. When Bella and her friend stopped naming names, the count had reached thirty-three.

"By all the saints! And you've had no milk for those off the breast?"

"Nay, lady. But most girls keep their young to the teat for as long as maybe."

Eloise knew why. "Aye, but they'll be needing more. I will speak to Montisfryn and see what can be done."

With a nod, she left them, quickly climbing the hill in the gathering gloom.

She entered the pavilion to find Montisfryn at the table. Bilder had already fetched their bowls and bread. With a nod for Montisfryn, she washed her hands in the basin on the chest, then took her seat. After pouring their wine, Bilder left. Engrossed with her discoveries, she opened her mouth—

"I would prefer it, lady, did you not associate with the women with whom you were recently speaking."

She glanced at Montisfryn, mildly surprised. "Nay, lord—tis not my intention." She picked up her spoon. "However, while there's sickness in your train, you must expect to see me use the skills the saints have granted me. Tis my duty as a Christian so to do—and you, of course, must be sorely grateful for my assistance."

Alaun choked.

Eloise watched him, her gaze wide and innocent.

Coughing, he grumbled, "I can imagine being sorely *tried* by you, lady, but grateful?"

She shrugged. "Tis your train and your people—twill not aid your enterprise if they sicken."

Frowning, he took up his spoon. "Is it serious?"

"Nay. The girl will recover well enough, but the child needs better nourishment. And its fellows, too."

He foresaw what was coming, but could not stop his, "Oh?"

"Did you know you have thirty-three babes in your train, lord?"

"That many?"

"Aye. And you have no source of milk for them."

"Tis common knowledge—" He stopped.

She waved her spoon dismissively. "Oh, aye. There is that. But the majority of these babes are many months old and need more than the women have to give. Would you not rather have thirty-three strong and healthy villeins than thirty-three sickly and poor-grown? Even once we reach Gloucester, I hear twill be at least six days' more marching to your castle."

For a pregnant moment, he held her limpid gaze, then he raised a hand. "Enough, lady. Clearly the brats have a savior in you. Just tell me shortly what's required."

Pushing her plate away, she gifted him with a glorious smile. "Tis simple. If you will be so good as to give Sir Eward orders to get a milch cow—or if one is not available, a goat—and some ground cereal and turnips from Gloucester market, the matter will take care of itself."

He stared at her while trying to imagine Sir Eward's face if he approached that long-serving vassal with orders about milch-cows, goats, and turnips. Then he thought of Roland's face should he hear of it. "Nay, lady. I know not enough of your requirements should Sir Eward have questions. Twill be best do you see him directly. You may say you have my authority in the matter." As a wife would.

The smile she bent on him was full of feminine triumph. He hid his own, allowing her a moment to savor her victory before adding, "Of course, in return for this boon, I would ask a boon of you."

Suspicion replaced her smile so quickly he was hard-pressed to keep a straight face.

Eyes narrowed, Eloise considered him. "What boon?"

"In a moment."

She turned as Bilder and Jenni came in to clear the board. She sat with scant patience until they withdrew, dropping the tent flap behind them. Outside, it was already dark, the wind howling mournfully through the trees. It was a night for retiring early, to the warmth of the covers and the comfort of sleep.

Meeting Montisfryn's eyes, she arched a brow. "Your boon, lord?"

He smiled slowly, sleepily. "I would have you let out your hair for me."

She blinked. Women of her age and station did not wear their hair down, not even for sleep; long tresses were the mark of a maiden. Still, it would hardly harm her to acquiesce. "If you wish, lord. I will summon Jenni—"

"Nay, Eloise. You need not your maid when I am with you."

She watched as he rose and came to stand beside her. Gently, he lifted the fillet from her head, freeing her twin braids from the confining crespines; they fell, heavy and darkly lustrous, one on each shoulder.

Laying the fillet aside, he moved his chair closer; taking her hands, he drew her to face him with no table between. She watched as he picked up the end of one long braid; his fingers loosened the tie, then started to unravel the tresses. The moment was hypnotic, relaxing.

Alaun also found it so, the silky strands sliding easily between his fingers, softly *shushing* as he drew them apart. As he progressed up the braid, the night closed around them, the camp settling, the calls of the sentries distant and faint on the wind. The candle flickered, casting a soft glow, a circle of light enclosing them, private and alone.

He was halfway up the second braid when, fascinated by his intent expression, Eloise asked, "Of what are you thinking, lord?"

He did not look up, his attention on his fingers. "Of how beautiful you will look when you stand before me clothed only in this silken shawl."

Her breath caught; her eyes widened as he raised his head and she saw the flames in his. He smiled, plainly satisfied with what he saw in her face, then looked down at her braid once more.

Holding back a shiver—of anticipation, she knew—she closed her eyes.

When her braids were all undone and her tresses rippled over her shoulders and arms, he rose and fetched her ivory comb. For the next ten minutes, he combed the long strands, teasing out the tangles, smoothing and laying the tresses to form the silken shawl he'd envisaged. She closed her eyes, savoring the rhythmic tug on her scalp, the relaxing effect of the exercise.

His eyes occasionally lifting to her face, gauging her state, Alaun, too, was very conscious of the moment. Her hair was warm, alive, sheened by the candle's glow; with the tresses down, her face appeared younger, more vulnerable. The knowledge of what he was doing, and why, was strong in his mind, making him tread warily, sensitive to her needs even more than his own.

When the last shining strand was in place, he laid the comb aside and took her hands. "Come, lady."

Eloise lifted her heavy lids only enough to see where they were going. He led her to the side of the bed and turned her to face him. The green cote she had on laced up the front. He parted the shimmering veil of her hair and, unhurriedly, efficiently, undid the laces. Without disturbing her mood, nor the fine veil he'd laid over her shoulders to hang in a dark curtain to her hips, he eased cote, stockings, and chemise from her, laying them neatly on her chest.

When he turned back, she tensed, instinctively straightening her spine. His eyes glowed golden, the flames banked, controlled.

Alaun hesitated. When de Cannar had done this, he'd remained fully clothed. It was more intimidating that way, reinforcing the image of master and slave.

With a fleeting, slightly strained smile, he touched his fingers to his lips, then to hers. "Wait, lady-witch."

Held, quivering, in the web of heightened anticipation he'd induced, Eloise watched as he rapidly undressed, flinging his clothes on his chest, his jerky movements in stark contrast to the smooth deliberation with which he'd undressed her.

Flickering candlelight gilded his back, all smooth muscles and golden skin. Naked, he turned. He glanced at the candle, close to guttering, then, fully aroused, he returned to her, his stride swift and sure. He slowed as he closed the last yard between them, coming to stand by her side.

Moving with deliberate slowness, Alaun slipped one hand behind her, under the lower edge of her silk veil. Gliding his palm over the satin skin at the small of her back, he curved his hand possessively about her hip, drawing her close, locking her nearer hip against his thigh.

She looked up at him; there was no trace of fear in her eyes. She was awaiting his pleasure and hers, a small, utterly feminine smile curving her lips.

The temptation to taste those lips was strong, yet if he gave into it, they would end very quickly in a wild tangle on the bed. Dragging in a deep breath, he girded his loins, then threaded his other hand through the front of her silk mantle and closed it possessively about one firm breast.

Warmth rushed through Eloise. Her breast swelled at his touch, the nipple puckering as his fingers found it, then teased it to aching hardness. Her lids fell; resisting the impulse to soften against him, she concentrated on holding herself erect.

He continued to touch her unhurriedly, savoring her curves, his hand roaming at will, from one breast to the other, splaying over her taut belly, trailing tantalizingly over her hips and thighs, exploring the contours of her waist while the hand at her back glided over the hemispheres of her bottom. Again and again he returned to her breasts, keeping them swollen and peaked. Then, with the same purposeful deliberation, he parted the curtain of her hair, pushing it over her shoulders to fully reveal her charms.

Eyes still shut, she heard his breath catch. She wasn't cold, could not be cold, not with him so close beside her. His warmth enfolded her, keeping the chill of the night, and of long forgotten fears, at bay.

"Lady-witch, you are beauty personified."

The low, fervent words deepened her smile. She lifted her lids and raised her free arm, needing to turn into him, to press herself against him. But she halted as he bent his head to her breast. His lips found her nipple; he drew it deep.

A low moan filled the tent. She laced her fingers into his hair, holding him to her. The sound came again as he suckled harder; she wondered if it was the wind. Only when he transferred his attentions to her other breast, and she heard the sound again, did she realize from where it came. And by then she was too deeply in thrall to care.

Alaun was hungry, ravenous; she turned and stretched against him, arms twining around his neck. Wantonly, she pressed herself to him. Their lips met, held, tongues telling of their need. His hands on her hips, he urged her to move against him; she gave herself up to the exercise, swiftly reducing him to a quivering state even more urgent than her own.

He lifted his head and gazed down at her, at the dark, mysterious eyes that gave him back his own flame, not reflecting it but taking it in, the dark drinking the gold until it glowed with a bewitching light. A light he longed to lose himself in.

Pressing a hand between them, he reached for the curls at the apex of her thighs. Gently, he caressed, then eased one finger into the soft hollow beyond. "Are you ready for me, lady-witch?"

She smiled. Her hand slipped down to lingeringly caress the throbbing rod of his erection. "Aye, lord. I would take you now." She drew back.

In a state bordering on pain, he let her go. She knelt on the bed, her eyes glowing as she turned to him, her smile filled with a thousand promises.

Holding one of his hands, she pushed back the covers, then sat, tugging him to her. He placed one knee on the pallet's edge and she lay back, spreading her bent legs wide. "Come to me, lord."

He groaned, and did, wondering who was tampering with whose mind now. She had possessed his, just as she possessed his body, her own arching as he pushed slowly, deeply, inside her.

His arms extended and braced, he held himself high above her, and let his hips meet hers fully. She writhed as he rode her, faster and deeper, taking them quickly toward the paradise that beckoned.

Eloise raised her legs and locked them about his hips, wanting to lock him to her forever. She reached a peak; with a cry, she tumbled over, only to discover another rising before her. And then there was nothing but suns and stars, and heat and warmth, and a thousand slivers of pleasure shattering her. And him. He collapsed on top of her; she held him, cradled him.

Later, he rolled, taking her with him to their sides.

They fell asleep, locked in each other's embrace, the beat of their hearts united, their bodies still joined.

Chapter 12

Rising excitement pervaded the long column as it got underway the next morn. As they marched through the day, the spires of Gloucester materialized through the haze.

Leaving Montisfryn to his lieutenants, Eloise spent the hours ambling along the column, scanning the wagons, noting the children, some ragged, others less so. Their mothers looked harried, tired; even the craftsmen looked worn down. As Montisfryn had said, the train was composed not just of fighting men able to take care of themselves; it was a community very like that of a castle.

The midday meal was a scrambled affair taken while the train slowly forded the river Frome. On the far bank, Eloise sat her mare and watched, increasingly critical. Time and again, she opened her mouth, sage advice on her tongue; time and again, she closed her lips, the words unsaid. She had no right to order, to interfere. Yet the temptation positively itched. Finally reformed, the column lumbered on toward the commons east of the town.

Excusing herself, she rode back to check on her patients. She'd already spoken with Sir Eward; the commissary had blinked, twice, but when she'd asked if anything was amiss, he had quickly denied it and had agreed to find her a milch-cow, cereal, and turnips when he went to market the next morn.

Reining in by the first of the four wagons carrying the unwed women and their offspring, Eloise was pleased to see the sick girl, Jill, upright, with a little healthy color in her cheeks.

"Thanks be to you, lady, I do feel much better today."

Checking her forehead, Eloise nodded. "You should be free of it by tomorrow. How is the babe?"

The little boy was handed over; gently, she cradled him. His eyes were wide; he batted playfully at her fingers when she touched his cheek.

Her expression blank, she carefully handed him back. "He'll grow well once you have milk and mash to feed him. Sir Eward has promised to get all necessary, and will give the milk and allot the provisions to each babe from tomorrow night. You and the others should go and see him then."

They all stared at her.

"You have done that, lady?" Even Old Meg seemed taken aback.

Eloise frowned. "I did naught but ask Montisfryn to provide what was needed. Tis his service you are in, after all."

Slowly, Meg digested that. "Aye. You're right." Then she grinned. "You'll have to excuse our surprise, lady—tis a long while since we've had any to take an interest. Her as is at the castle now is good-hearted, but she's sickly and comes not down from her tower, nor has done for years. And the lord might be as fair and as generous as any knight born, but yet he's a man." Her shrug was eloquent. "No more, n'less."

Meg's gaze sharpened. "I saw him standing by that great tent of his, a-watching us last night. Did he get at ye afterward?"

Eloise raised a brow. "He mentioned the matter, but when I pointed out the facts, he gave permission to have the necessary items bought."

"Didn't like you talking to us, did he?"

"He now knows tis not a point that should concern him." Eloise hoped her chilly accents were hint enough.

"Stood up to him, did ye?"

Eloise drew in a breath and fixed Meg with a strait look. "I have been my father's chatelaine for five years, as my mother was before me. I know well what duties you and your girls perform in a castle, as you do in this train. You have your duties; I have mine. *Both* are necessary to ensure a castle runs smoothly—or so I have always believed."

Stunned silence greeted her pronouncement, then Meg cackled richly; her girls grinned. "Heh, lady-mine—I've never heard it put so, but to my mind, you've the right of it. You take on him at the head of the column, while the rest of us takes care of those behind."

Eloise colored; she stopped herself from nodding and drew Jacquenta back. "Don't forget to look to Sir Eward tomorrow."

A chorus of 'ayes' answered her.

"A moment, lady." Meg leaned over the side of the wagon and lowered her voice. "As I said, I know something of herbs, though my lore is not the same as yours. If there comes a time when you need the sort of help I can give, or if there's aught else in which we can aid you, you have only to ask. We remember our debts, we do."

Eloise held the old woman's gaze. "Nay, Meg. You owe me no debt. Twas my duty to help."

She was about to wheel Jacquenta away when Jill, the babe at her breast, leaned to the wagonside to say, "You're a saint, lady. Twould have been on my conscience for the rest of my days had my littley died." Smiling, she looked down, smoothing the soft puffs of brown hair as the babe suckled steadily. "Purgatory shouldn't be for such little ones."

"Purgatory?" Eloise froze. "Do you mean to tell me that child is *unbaptized*?"

Even Meg sat up at her tone. "Twould have been done, lady, but there is no priest."

"*No priest*?" A column of this size marching with no priest? *What* was Montisfryn thinking of?

"There was a priest as left England with us, lady," Meg hurriedly explained. "But he was a right sickly little stick, and died of fever just after Caen. As I heard it, the lord decided the knights could use the king's chaplains until we were back to Montisfryn. Our old priest will doubtless still be there."

As she took this in, and all the reasons it should not be rose in her mind, Eloise knew she couldn't let the matter rest. "Tis not right or proper. I will see to it."

She nodded curtly and wheeled Jacquenta.

As Eloise galloped up the column, Meg and her girls exchanged glances, then Meg shrugged. "You never do know—miracles sometimes do happen. And there's no denying she's a powerful one with her tongue."

That was, no more and no less, precisely what Alaun was thinking when, some fifteen minutes later, having successfully commandeered his attention, Eloise poured her feelings, complaints, and instructions, in that order, into his unwilling ear.

She'd found him deep in discussion with his lieutenants over how best to quarter his force. Instead of dropping back and leaving him to the difficult business, she'd brought her mare alongside his stallion and, without the least effort, simply by riding along with her spine stiff and her nose in the air, had intimidated his most senior knights until they couldn't keep their minds on his words. Concerned, they'd constantly stolen wary glances at her, until, thoroughly disgusted by their susceptibility, he'd dismissed them to consider their suggestions. While he dealt with their distraction.

When she finally reached the end of her eloquence, he looked at her sternly. "Lady, this matter is not urgent."

"*Not urgent*?" She stared at him. "A babe might have died unbaptized, and you say the matter is not *urgent*? There are thirty-three such babes, I believe, lord, and each should weigh *heavily* on your conscience!"

Outrage poured from her, investing her gestures with sufficient force to be clearly comprehended by all watching them. Exasperated, he growled, "Lady, I have six hundred men under my command. Gloucester is the first town of note we have camped this close to since landing in England. If they run amok through the streets this night, I will have the burghesses down on Edward's head by the drove. Deciding how to apportion the watch while allowing time for all to visit the town is no easy task. I need not further distractions at this moment."

Their gazes locked; Eloise noted that his eyes were not bright but cloudy, agatelike, aswirl with irritation. She narrowed her gaze; he remained impassive, his jaw squared. She felt his will lock with hers, two very tangible forces…

Abruptly letting her features ease, she sat back in her saddle. "My pardon, lord. I had not realized you were so beset."

She gave him time to deny it, but he was too wily to fall into that hole. There was, however, more than one way to skin a cat—presumably, the same held true for lions. "Nevertheless," she smoothly went on, "the situation with these children, as you must acknowledge, cannot be allowed to continue." He shifted; she quickly added, "However, as you are so hard-pressed, and tis not until tomorrow that we pass through Gloucester, perhaps we can postpone discussing the details of the baptisms until this eve?"

The look he gave her warned her that her plot was transparent.

Slowly, he exhaled through clenched teeth. "Can it not wait until Montisfryn, lady?"

She shook her head decisively. "Nay, lord." She paused, then added, "But we can discuss the details anon."

His gaze trapped hers; what emotions now clouded the depths she could not guess. But he nodded. "Aye. Twill be as well if we do."

Magnanimous in triumph, she reined Jacquenta back. "I will leave you to your affairs, lord."

With a sound very close to a grunt, Alaun let her go.

Only when he was sure she was safely to his rear did he allow his lips to curve.

The dispositions that evening were complex in the extreme; by the time he approached his pavilion, night had started to fall. He was famished. And his witch had had time to polish her arguments, and her solution to what she quickly informed him was a grave stain on his religious conscience.

Relieved that she had, at least, waited until Bilder and the robin had withdrawn before opening fire on him, he allowed her to rattle on, grunting noncommittally every time she paused for a response, but otherwise applying himself to his plate.

She wound to a conclusion as he pushed the empty plate away. He stretched mightily, easing muscles that had grown stiff during the long day, then turned to eye her speculatively.

Engrossed in her closing arguments, she didn't notice. "The matter, lord, is quite clear. Tis your bounden duty to correct the oversight, and, as it happens, tis no difficulty to rectify the omission."

He leaned back, crossed his arms behind his head, and studied the roof. He knew she was right, but it was pleasant to hear her behaving as his wife. "Lady, thirty-three baptisms will take all day. My men will not wish to dally—not unless I make them free of the town, which I will not."

"Nay—tis one ceremony only. Tis perfectly acceptable they be done all together."

Bilder and the robin entered. While they cleared the board, Alaun considered how best to wring victory from the adversity currently besetting him.

"So"—he lowered his gaze to Bilder who, correctly interpreting it, secured the tent flap behind him—"you would have me stand sponsor to all these children, none of whom are mine, I might add."

Her fractional pause told him that she had wondered. "Tis not such a great burden," she returned. "Your wagons are heavy with plunder, and these children, after all, are the outcome of the campaign."

Deciding he would definitely have to share that gem with Roland—and Edward, when the king next commented on Alaun's haul—he sleepily eyed the canopy. "And how think you this mass ceremony would be accomplished?"

"Why, tis straightforward, lord. The priests at the cathedral would be more than happy to perform the ceremony."

"For thirty-three times the usual tithe? I make no doubt."

"Nay, twould be a matter to be agreed. Twould be more than one baptism, but not, to my thinking, more than two."

"And I would have to bestir myself tomorrow morn to see the priests and arrange this matter?"

Eloise raised her brows. "Tis difficult to see how it might be done otherwise. They are your villeins." Frowning, she added, "But you are always up betimes, and the train will not be moving on awhiles, for Sir Eward has to go to market, if you recall."

"I recall well enough the boons I have granted you, lady, but for your information, the column moves out as usual tomorrow. The crossing over the Severn will take hours. My lieutenants will have it in hand through the morn."

She quickly adjusted her plans. "But that is no impediment. The baptism could be performed in the morning, and the women and babes could rejoin the column before it quitted the town. I, too, would ask permission to visit the market with Sir Eward. There are herbs I would restock, if I can."

"Lady, if I am to be standing sponsor to thirty-three babes, you may rest assured you will be by my side throughout."

She grimaced, then glanced at him. "Perhaps there'll be time to visit the market after the service?"

Alaun heaved a heavy, artistically disgruntled sigh. "Why, lady, do I see my whole morning going in pursuit of your plans?"

There was no viable answer to that. She kept mum.

"If I grant you this boon—these boons—thirty-three baptisms plus a visit to the market"—he lowered his gaze until it met hers—"what will you grant me in return?"

Eloise blinked, dazzled by his golden eyes. "You wish a boon, lord?"

"Aye." He nodded. "One boon in compensation for thirty-four. Tis not too much to ask, I think."

He looked sleepy, lazy, a golden lion just waiting to purr. She wasn't deceived—he wasn't sleepy at all. He was hungry, and she was the prey his golden gaze had fastened on.

Subduing the shiver that rippled through her, she calmly arched a brow. "What is this boon?"

He smiled. "Tis a fantasy I have."

"Oh?" A delicious wariness tickled her spine. He rose and held out his hand; she hesitated, then placed her hand in his. As he drew her to her feet, she quickly asked, "This fantasy—what does it involve?"

"Tis purely imaginary." He drew her around the table, then closer still, until she stood pressed breast to chest with him, firmly locked within one muscled arm. He smiled down at her. Then he lowered his head; his lips found hers in a slow, easy caress, a caress that left her hanging, waiting, hungry for more.

"Tis a simple enough situation."

The words drifted featherlike past her ear. His lips traced the arch of her brow from forehead to temple, then swooped to brush her parted lips once more.

"Tis me, in my castle, but in my fantasy I have a wife."

"A wife?" She turned her head and trapped his lips with hers.

"Aye," he breathed as he drew away again. "A wife who is haughty and imperious—just like you."

Alaun kissed her before she could think too much on that. Disengaging, he continued, "She has been at me to correct some oversight—she's been nagging me for days, like an burr trapped under my shirt. Her tongue is sharp-edged and her complaint is valid—tis a situation many men find both aggravating and arousing."

"Arousing?" She blinked large, lustrous eyes at him, as if she couldn't focus.

He smiled. "Aye, tis a fact few women realize."

Eloise certainly hadn't, but before she could come to grips with the concept, he was speaking again.

"In my fantasy, I have finally done her bidding—rectified whatever omission I have made—and am on my way to claim my reward."

"Reward?"

"Aye." Bending his head, he trailed kisses from her collarbone to her jaw. His hand settled at her waist, gripping but not tight enough. "Tis afternoon. She's in the solar with her women. When I enter, she's standing by the table." Raising his head, he glanced at the oak board beside them. Then his golden eyes, flame-etched, returned to hers. "I order her women out, and they close the door behind them."

His lips found hers; still held firmly in his arm, she strained upward to meet him, but he held back, keeping the contact light, tantalizing—two steps short of satisfying. As their lips parted again, she sighed. "And then?"

"Then I tell her I've done her bidding."

His hand left her waist; fingertips trailed from her brow to her ear, dipped into the hollow behind, then lazily traced her throat, stopping on the spot where her pulse beat wildly.

"I acknowledge her right to correct me in such matters, as a good wife should."

Languidly, his lips followed the path his fingertips had traced. She shivered.

"She's pleased—she preens."

She laced her fingers through his hair, sucking in a quick breath as his tongue stroked the pulsing vein at her throat. "What happens next?"

"I smile, and tell her she must now pay the price—the price of being my wife."

Silence ensued; slowly straightening, he broke it, his voice softly challenging. "Will you pay the price tonight, lady-witch?"

Breathless, her lashes screening her eyes, she looked into his, and found them burning. "I'm not your wife."

His lips curved; she licked hers.

His smile broke; he bent and feathered a kiss across her hungry lips. "Lady, you have *nagged* me this day—who else but my wife has that right?"

She caught his face between her hands and kissed him. Still he held back, denying her the satisfaction she craved. "What price do you speak of— that your wife must pay?"

"Nay, tis simple enough. Nothing more than a wife's duty."

"*What?*"

He chuckled. "Tis merely that she should provide me with my just deserts."

She tried to draw back; she wished she could frown. Instead, her body thrummed with a need she couldn't deny. She met his gaze; his expression was mild, yet distinctly challenging. "What happens in your fantasy?"

His chest swelled. "I take her in my arms—thus." He drew her about so her back was to the table.

She went readily, twining her arms about his neck, pressing herself to him as his arms tightened about her.

"And then I taste her—thus." He did, long and deep.

She welcomed his invasion. She melted against him; as the kiss went on, she felt her body awaken, stirring against his. He retreated to nibble tantalizingly at her lips.

"I taste her lips." He took them in a swooping kiss. "And her tongue." He demonstrated with a slow, shatteringly possessive kiss, his tongue gliding over hers, twining and inciting her passion. "And her breasts."

His voice had dropped to a husky growl. She glanced down to find her laces all undone and her chemise yielding to his quick fingers. He laid her breasts bare, then cupped a firm mound in one palm, caressing the soft peak with his fingers before bending to take it into his mouth.

As his tongue swirled about the sensitive bud, she let her head fall back, her body arching, offering herself more fully to him. Her fingers twined in his hair, holding him to her; she gasped as he suckled deeply. Then she felt his hands at her waist, pushing her clothing down. Her skirts fell with a soft *whoosh* to the ground.

Alaun released her breast and lifted her to sit on the table. His hands on her back, stroking her silken skin, he brushed his lips across hers until she was ravenous for his kiss—then kissed her deeply, slanting his head over hers as he lowered her to the polished board.

He raised his head. She lay before him, naked and delectable. He smiled into her wide, dark eyes, then let his gaze wander slowly down, over her slender limbs and womanly curves. She was breathing rapidly, her breasts rising and falling, her belly taut with anticipation. His smile deepening, he returned his gaze to her face. Leaning forward, he touched his lips to hers. "And I taste her sweet honey, my lady-witch."

Eloise heard, but did not, immediately, grasp his intent. Even when his lips trailed down her body and the first inklings trickled through the rapturous haze, she could not, even then, credit her imaginings. He couldn't—wouldn't. Not there.

But he could—and did—with paralyzing slowness, having first reduced her to a quivering, barely sentient being, her mind flooded with fire as his mouth moved from aching peaks to equally aching hollows, the touch of his lips laying flames beneath her skin. He tasted her—all of her—his tongue following each contour of throat and shoulder, tracing the smooth curves of her swollen breasts, pausing to lave the tight buds of her nipples before exploring further, outlining her waist with long rasping sweeps before thrusting provocatively into the hollow of her navel.

By then, she was writhing between his hands, trapped by the sweet pleasure of his loving. When his hands parted her thighs, she sighed, sure he was going to possess her. She opened herself eagerly, anticipating that delight. Instead, she felt the soft caress of his fine hair against her sensitive skin, then feathery butterfly caresses as his lips trailed light kisses along her inner thighs.

It was too late to close them. She moaned and arched, insensibly sure she wouldn't be able to bear it if he touched her there. She would go wild, explode, disintegrate.

She did all three when his lips settled firmly over her soft flesh, sucking lightly as she gasped and squirmed helplessly between his hands.

Alaun hurt, ached, throbbed with desire, yet it was the sweetest ache he'd ever known. He shifted his hold, placing one forearm across her waist. With his tongue, he parted her, the flushed, swollen flesh apple-sweet. Her nails sank into his arm. Smiling, he caressed her, allowing his expertise full rein, tasting her softness, teasing the little nubbin hiding in its hood, luring it out so he could roll it between his lips.

He took her from peak to peak, never quite letting her rush over the edge and into sweet oblivion.

Adrift in unchartered seas, Eloise panted, gasped, sobbed, and sighed—again and again. With his free hand, he guided her legs up and over his shoulders, then slipped his hand beneath her, long fingers stroking her bottom before caressing her sensitive cleft. Beyond thought, she locked her legs about his head, holding him to her as he drove her ever on, over the troughs and peaks of some wildly sensuous sea toward some dimly perceived harbor.

And then, all at once, she was clinging to the edge of the world, poised above a drop so high she would surely shatter when she fell. For one long instant, she hung there, quivering, knowing beyond all understanding that she wanted him within her—now.

Then he was there, but not as she was used to. She fractured as his tongue thrust boldly into her, taking her, ravishing her, sending her not plummeting but soaring, higher and higher until the sun rushed to meet her, a golden, very familiar blaze. She melted, pulsing about him.

As consciousness slowly returned, she felt the gentle lap of his tongue as he savored her.

She gasped; he raised his head, his expression elementally, triumphantly male, one tawny brow rising as if inviting her comment.

"I want you." She could barely get the words out. "Inside me. Now."

His eyes flamed; his heat reached for her even as his hands did, firming about her hips, drawing her closer to the table's edge. Her thighs parted wide.

Alaun looked down, then bent and placed a kiss on her triangle of curls. A single movement of one hand released his staff, throbbing and urgent, hungry for her. He lifted his eyes, locking them on hers, wide, wild, darkly glowing. Gripping her hips, he pressed slowly into her.

Eloise gasped. She breathed in, arching as he entered—then couldn't breathe out. Her eyes flared, her lips parted, but no sound came forth. Stunned, captured, she watched, held immobile as he forged relentlessly, slowly and inexorably, into her. Her already heightened senses sizzled. She could feel him stretching her; his hands on her hips anchored her, permitting his steady, intensely powerful, absolutely controlled invasion. Such deliberate penetration coming so soon after her wild release was intensely erotic.

Alaun didn't blink as he sank deep into her body. Her flesh scalded him, indescribably slick, her tight passage yielding to his steady advance.

Her body surrendered, melting about him as he came to rest, hard and rigid within her.

Eloise slowly let out the breath she'd been holding. Eyes wide, her gaze trapped in the blaze of his, she lay quivering, her breasts rising and falling. Slow ripples of pleasure radiated from where he held so still within her.

Palms flat against the board, her heart thundering in her ears, she waited, her mind caught in his web, focused on him.

Dragging air into his lungs, Alaun released her hips. Gently, he closed his hands about her breasts, already swollen to firm fullness. He kneaded slowly, possessively. She pulsed hotly about him, her body thrumming anew.

His touch on her breasts was exquisite; Eloise shuddered and closed her eyes. Pleasure rippled outward from where they joined as he started to move within her. Each solid stroke pushed her higher, into spiraling pleasure; each demanding caress wound the spiral tighter.

Soon she was lost, trapped in the vortex, surrounded by pulsing pleasure and keenly rapturous delight.

She arched strongly; Alaun locked his hands about her hips, holding her steady as he plumbed her depths. She went wild, her hands gripping his, slim fingers curling like talons about his wrists. The short, sharp, desperate cries that fell from her lips urged him on, her body straining against his hold.

Then she convulsed, a long shuddering wave spreading through her. For one timeless instant, her tension held, then it dissolved, the steady pulsing of her release calling on his own.

With a soft tremulous sigh, she eased back to the table.

Head thrown back, he lost himself in her.

* * *

His witch was yet abed when, a thoroughly satisfied smile on his lips, Alaun left his pavilion the next morn. He visited the sheriff, and the priests, then repaired to the bridge to supervise the start of the Severn crossing.

Eloise joined him there, neat and elegant on her roan mare. Their eyes met—she smiled, slowly, then glanced away.

Satisfaction swelled, a warm glow in his chest.

Even the fact that she'd come to fetch him to the cathedral was insufficient to dim his mood. He went with her readily, the time spent standing beside her by the font given over to consideration of another church ceremony. As it happened, the how, where, and who would be there were questions requiring some thought.

He roused himself as the last child was wetted and duly squalled. The priest offered a benediction, and Alaun's people, some, certainly, unwed girls, but many others couples, tradesmen in his train whose wives had accompanied them as laundresses and semptresses, turned away, smiling and nodding gratefully to him. And to the lady by his side.

Sir Eward waited at the door of the chapel to present each family with their lord's baptismal gift. It was little enough, five silver pennies, yet each family was delighted to receive the vail, acknowledging their bond to him and his acceptance of their child into his overall care.

Noting the commissary and the small crowd about him, Eloise gifted

Alaun with a brilliant smile. "Tis very good of you, lord."

He shrugged. "Nay. Tis no more than our custom."

"But tis good of you to remember it at a time when you're so hard-pressed."

Brows rising, he caught her gaze. "Am I to take it you wish to further reward me, lady?"

To his delight, she blushed. "We are in a cathedral, lord."

"Aye—tis hard to imagine a more challenging venue."

The shocked look she sent him had him swallowing a laugh. "I must see the priest a moment, lady."

Serenely, if a little stiffly, she inclined her head. "I will await you here, lord."

Rovogatti stood by the wall mere yards away; four men-at-arms shadowed the door. Alaun nodded and turned away. The priest was waiting; he gestured to the vestry beyond. Alaun followed him up the worn steps.

Left to herself, Eloise strolled to the arched windows. Mid-morning sunshine poured in, pooling in warm puddles on the floor. The bottom of the recessed window was at chin height; only by rising to her toes could she see what lay beyond the thick walls. A small, well-tended graveyard with many finely carved gravestones met her gaze. The clergy's graveyard, she surmised, reserved for those who served in the cathedral.

"Sir Cedric. I am glad to see you, sir."

At the tortured, peculiarly strangled tones, Eloise blinked her eyes wide. She'd heard that voice before. She strained to look out, keen to set eyes on its mysterious owner.

"And I you."

The second voice, deep and heavy, came from directly below the window. The ground outside was several feet lower than the chapel floor; Eloise could see nothing beyond a feather, which she assumed was in one of the men's hats.

"We must settle this matter, my dear sir. A quick agreement would serve us both best."

The strangled voice again. Eloise was certain it belonged to an older man, one nearer her father's generation.

Her supposition was proved correct as, to her curiosity's satisfaction, the men moved away from the wall. They continued their discussion while strolling the paths between the graves. Their voices grew indistinct, then inaudible, yet she heard enough to identify the owner of the strangled voice as the older of the pair, a man of medium height and build, slightly stooped, clearly a gentleman although his station could not be discerned from his clothes—a long garnache reaching to his feet and a soft, folded cap. From his stoop, she decided he was either scholar or clerk. His clothes were of good quality, but held no touches of richness; the lappets of the garnache were, she judged, squinting against the glare, of rabbit fur, not the more costly vair or ermine.

The man was definitely not one of the knights or nobles who had attended her father's tournament. What, then, had he been doing at Versallet Castle? Frowning, she decided he must have been acting as a courier on church or king's business, and thus had been of insufficient station to warrant the personal attention of her family. Sir John would not have seen any need to bother her about one such.

Satisfied with that explanation of the man's presence, both at Versallet Castle and, no doubt, here, she turned her gaze on his companion.

Sir Cedric was definitely a warrior-knight, not as tall or as broad-shouldered as Montisfryn, or even William, yet a heavy, deep-chested ox of a man. His face, under a soft cap sporting a pheasant's feather, was heavy-jowled, dark-browed, and showed no hint it had softened in years. A deep-voiced, dark-tempered ogre of a knight. Eloise wrinkled her nose and turned away.

To see Montisfryn coming down the vestry steps, his eyes on her. Without conscious thought, she flashed him her most brilliant smile.

As he came to join her, she drew on her gloves and turned toward the door. "If it please you, lord, I would go to the market now. Tis only till noon, they say."

"Aye." As they strolled to the door, Alaun glanced at her, wondering, as he had all morning, what she had thought of last night. "I will escort you, lady."

Looking up at him, she opened her eyes wide. "But you're needed at the bridge, are you not, lord? I would not disrupt your affairs."

He struggled not to smile. "Lady, one day your tongue will be your downfall."

She laughed, a light, carefree sound he realized he had not heard before. "Nay, lord, say you so? I have ever heard that a lady needs sharp wits to claim her due."

As they emerged into the bright sunshine, he grunted. "I have no argument with your wits, lady. Tis your knife-edged tongue I would see sheathed."

The odd little smile she shot him, a mixture of feminine triumph and comprehension calculated to bring a saint undone, sent a possessive surge through him. Naturally, it terminated in his groin.

Stifling a curse, he forced himself to pace by her side, rather than a half-step behind from where her gently rounded hips, swaying provocatively under her tight cote, were all too distractingly evident.

The market sprawled over a square in the shadow of the cathedral. Vendors of every description displayed their wares in booths or on the cobbles. Eloise wandered between the stalls, making purchases from various old dames offering herbs and potions. Alaun remained beside her. At his signal, two of his men-at-arms moved ahead, clearing their path. Behind came

Rovogatti and Jenni, followed in turn by two more men-at-arms.

Alaun anticipated no danger; his brief visit to the sheriff had revealed no undesirable elements in the town. Nevertheless, he kept a close watch on his prize; she was too precious to contemplate losing.

Finding a soft parcel wrapped in hessian and tied with string pushed into his arms, he blinked. "What's this?"

"A cloth for your table, lord." Her purchases apparently complete, she headed toward the stables. From under her lashes, she cast him a quick glance. "Tis uncivilized to eat off bare board."

His gut clenched. He glanced at her, but could make nothing of her serene expression. He hesitated, then said, "Twould have got in the way last night."

Head high, her gaze fixed forward, she shook her head. "Nay. I will have Jenni remove it with our plates."

For a very long moment, he couldn't breathe. Then, as the constriction that had gripped his chest eased, he drew in a deep breath. The stables lay just ahead. "Lady." His voice was gravelly. He moved closer so his words fell by her ear. "Tis going to be a very long day. The inn yonder has comfortable chambers—perhaps we should fantasize awhile before heading on?"

Eloise let her smile deepen. With no hint of coyness, she met his eyes. Sparks flared in the golden depths. Had they been flames she might have yielded, but sparks could be quenched—temporarily.

"Nay, lord." She looked ahead to where the ostlers were scurrying. "Your train awaits and we should not dally." She glanced at him from beneath her lashes, a slow smile curving her lips. "Perhaps later?"

Later. By later, he was going to be...

With a poorly stifled groan, Alaun followed her into the stables.

Chapter 13

The next day found Eloise in pensive mood. The incident of the baptisms had raised a warren of hares in her mind.

Dropping back along the train, she joined Sir Eward. After thanking him for his efforts of the day before, she asked, "Tis a large host returning to the castle for winter—what think you will be the state of the castle stores?"

Sir Eward looked grave. "I live not at the castle, lady—my manor lies to the west. Tis Sir Edmund, the lord's steward, who has that matter in hand. Edmund does his best, but tis not the same when there's no chatelaine to oversee the stocks. In days not long hence, the castle could supply both stronghold and town, and yet have enough left to carry the near holdings at need, but ever since the lady's illness took her from us, tas never been so."

He sighed and shook his head. "I doubt not we'll find the storehouses half-empty, or worse. Twill be a priority to get them filled, what with winter ahead and all of us back." He glanced at her and smiled. "Tis many thanks you'll be getting, lady, for coming to the castle's relief."

Eloise met his look blankly, then colored and inclined her head. Forcing a half-smile, she dropped back.

Only to notice the rough weave of the material in the hands of a woman toward the back of the train. The woman was stitching a rent in a man's cote, timing her needle to the wagon's roll. Eloise drew nearer, leaning from her saddle to examine the slubs that marred the weave.

The woman glanced up, then shyly smiled—a smile that turned to a grimace as she looked back at her work. "Aye, lady—tis doubtless not the quality you're used to seeing."

Eloise frowned. "Tis from the castle looms?"

"From three years back. They needed repair then—I like not to think what state they'll be in now. But as you can see, tis the spinners need more instruction than us weavers—tis not possible to make fine out of coarse. Not that it's their fault neither—ever since the poor lady's affliction came on her, there's been none to set standards."

"But surely there are other ladies—at least girls in training—to oversee such work?"

The woman shook her head. "Nay—she sent all away. She's rarely from her bed, and never out of her rooms—seems she felt twas unfair to keep them when she couldn't instruct them. Now there's only her lady-companion, and she, poor soul, has enough to do just to keep the lady's spirits up.

"There!" The woman shook out the cote and folded it, then she flashed a smile at Eloise. "But that's all in the past, praise be, now that you're coming to be chatelaine. You'll find us willing to work, lady, and right grateful to have you to guide us."

Eloise smiled weakly.

The last straw was provided by Old Meg.

When Eloise drew in beside her wagon to check on their patients, Meg greeted her with a grin. After assuring her Jill and the babe were thriving, the old woman chuckled. "Heh, lady-mine, you'll be an asset to his household, no doubt of that. We've been a-wondering these a-many years how much longer he'd leave it, and who he'd pick for the job. But, as usual, he's done right well for himself, even if, as they tell it, twas unexpected."

Hazel eyes glittered cheekily, then Meg sobered. "Aye, and there's no doubt but what the castle's going to need a strong woman at the helm once this lot gets back." She indicated the troops with her chin. "And you're a healer, too—those we had are gone, now. Taint no one knows rightly of herbs and such. Tis not wise, with all the children and winter coming on. I did my best the last winter we was there—the saints only know how they fared while we've been gone. Winter's a bad time, for the snows come in hard, and there'll be no stocks or specifics laid up." Meg turned, her old eyes steady and serious as she met Eloise's gaze. "Praise be to the saints you'll be with us this time."

Eloise looked ahead. She drew in a long breath, then slowly let it out— and forced her lips to curve reassuringly.

For what remained of that day, and all of the next, she rode in relative privacy parallel to the train, just within the line of outriders.

And wrestled with her dilemma.

Then, on the morning of the day that would see them to Hereford, her increasingly tangled arguments were shattered—scattered—by a startling revelation from a most unexpected source.

She was sitting on the stool in Montisfryn's pavilion, alone except for Jenni, who was industriously brushing Eloise's hair. There were tangles aplenty to be coaxed from the long strands; Montisfryn had insisted it be out again the previous night. Resisting the tug of her distracting memories, Eloise was treading the mill of her thoughts to the steady rhythm of Jenni's prattle, when Jenni's words jarred her to full attention.

"Him and me"—Jenni was speaking, as ever, of Rovogatti—"have decided we'll wed, lady. Tis better so, be there any children. I was hoping to ask the priests at Hereford, but Guilio said as how'd be best—more proper, if you take my meaning, him being in the lord's service an' me being in yours— to wait till after your wedding, lady. So that's what we'll do."

Only by the exercise of considerable restraint did Eloise remain seated. After a long moment, she asked, "How did you hear of it—our wedding? Nothing has been said." Her voice sounded odd to her ears.

"Nay, lady, but you know how tis. All the lord's people know he's under edict from the king to marry as soon as maybe, and tis plain as the smile on his face who he's chosen."

Recalling precisely what had caused that smile—this morn and the past seven—Eloise clenched her hands in her lap. But a royal edict? She forced herself to remain seated, outwardly calm, while Jenni braided her hair.

"They say we'll be hard by Hereford tonight."

"Aye." As soon as Jenni had settled her fillet in place and tucked her braids under the crespines, Eloise stood. She shook out her green skirts and nodded to Jenni. "Hurry and pack."

When her mistress walked out of the tent without another word, Jenni blinked. Then she snatched up gloves, quirt, and cloak and hurried after her.

Throughout the morning, Eloise rode back in the column, alongside the men-at-arms. And tried to think. In vain. If before her thoughts had been tangled, they were now inextricably knotted. They went round and around with no apparent beginning, much less an end. Again and again, one observation resurfaced: Montisfryn played chess—very well. Just how well she had discovered over the last two evenings.

On spying a chess board tucked in his armor chest, she had challenged him to a match, confident of at least holding her own. Up until then, she'd considered herself an adept.

He'd trounced her. With an ease that bespoke a mind not only trained to strategy and tactics, but immersed in those disciplines. What disturbed her most was the recollection of how often he had maneuvered to block a move she hadn't thought of making until two turns later.

In the early afternoon, she discarded all attempt at rational analysis and decided to beard the lion direct. He had, to her considerable relief, been absorbed with his lieutenants all morning, and through the brief midday halt; she'd felt his glance more than once, but he hadn't questioned her wish for solitude. Riding forward, she came up alongside him.

He turned immediately, his golden eyes unreadable, one tawny brow rising.

"I would a moment of your time, lord." She met his gaze, then regally conceded, "When you are free."

He nodded. "In a moment, lady." He turned back to his lieutenants.

Harnessing her impatience, Eloise held Jacquenta to a walk beside his gray. Her temper was unstable, stirred by her speculations; her temples ached.

Fifteen minutes later, Montisfryn dismissed his lieutenants and turned to her. "You have my ear, lady."

"There is a matter I wish to discuss in private, lord."

Alaun eyed her set face. "Now?"

"Now."

His expression impassive, he scanned their surroundings. "There's an old orchard a league or so ahead. We could ride on and speak there."

With a curt nod, she assented and loosened her reins. Leaving Roland in charge, Alaun quickly overhauled her, settling to a steady canter beside her. The train was soon left behind; ten minutes later, a splash of brighter green to their left marked the orchard.

It was cool and peaceful under the gnarled branches. The harvest had been gathered in; only a few late fruit remained. Lifted down from her saddle, Eloise paced to where an old drystone wall marked the boundary of the holding. Montisfryn tethered their mounts, then followed. Her arms tightly folded beneath her breasts, she glanced sharply at him as he sat on the wall close by. Seated thus, his eyes were level with hers; to her irritation, she could read nothing in the golden depths.

"You told me, lord, that I was to be your chatelaine. Now I have heard that you are under royal edict to marry. Might I inquire *who* you have chosen to be your bride?"

The question hung in the stillness beneath the trees. In the distance, robins chattered; the breeze ruffled the thickly growing canopies and rippled through the long meadow grasses. Montisfryn blinked, then refocused on her face. "Nay, Eloise—let us not fence. You know the answer to that."

He held her gaze steadily; she looked long into his golden eyes. Her emotions surged; their intensity shook her.

Abruptly, she swung away. "And just when did you decide I was to be your wife?"

Frowning, Alaun studied her rigid back and the defiant set of her head. "On that first night at the banquet."

She turned her head to stare at him. "Before or after the wager?"

"Before."

For an instant, incredulity held her still. Then she kicked her skirts about and, arms crossed, faced him. "Why?"

He frowned harder. "That much should be obvious." He shifted on the stone, then, when she continued to wait, grudgingly offered, "You are suitable in every way—your birth, your family's standing, your fortune as your dowry. You're an experienced chatelaine of whose skill I am in dire need. And your mother bore your father four strong sons—tis likely you'll have no difficulty providing me with heirs."

Eloise humphed. She wasn't sure what answer she'd hoped for, but that certainly wasn't it. She narrowed her eyes. "What *exactly* was the wager you agreed to?"

"Nay—the wager was as you were told. The understanding I had with your father was that once you were in my care, I would use every endeavor to win your agreement to our marriage."

Every endeavor. Like seduction. Like gentle tenderness. Like warm strength in the dark of the night. Her breath threatened to choke her; she swung around and started to pace. "So! You both set about organizing my life—and assumed I'd meekly agree?"

"Meekly, lady, is not a word either of us made the mistake of associating with you." Alaun watched as she paced back and forth, her agitation, despite her control, very clear. Inwardly, he sighed. "Nay, Eloise—neither your father nor I ever imagined the decision would be other than yours."

"You deliberately deceived me."

He set his teeth. "Twas clear from the first you had no liking for the idea of another husband."

She shot him a glance. "You now know my reasons."

"Aye, but then twas our belief you needed time to grow accustomed to the idea. That with time your resistance would decrease. Mentioning our intention would only have served to set you against it needlessly, before you had a chance to…consider the benefits of such a union."

Tracking her, he frowned. "We both had reason to believe you would not be entirely averse to such an outcome."

Eloise made no attempt to argue the point. "And if I refuse to accept you, what then?" She met his gaze. "Will you pressure me to agree?"

Irritation flashed in the gold. "Nay, there will be no coercion. I want no unwilling bride."

"Good! Then I will trouble you to return me to my convent." Not for a moment did she imagine he would agree.

"Nay, Eloise—your future lies not at Claerwhen."

The name stopped her in her tracks. She lifted her head, then whirled to confront him. "You *knew*?"

He smiled grimly. "Your father mentioned it. I know of it by repute, and I know it lies close by Hereford." He held her gaze. "You would not have escaped me, lady."

That she believed. With a snort of disgust, she resumed her pacing. Yet another move he had blocked before she'd had a chance to make it. Not, of course, that it mattered; she knew there was nothing for her there anymore. Her future, whatever it might be, lay north—with him. "What, then, is to be my fate an' I do not agree to marry you?"

He met her gaze, his own unwavering. "I accept tis your decision to agree to marry me. Until you make that decision, I will keep you by me, much as at present."

She stopped, stared. "You mean it's my decision as long as I agree?"

"There *is* no other reasonable decision. In time, you'll see that that is so."

She narrowed her eyes. He sat there, rocklike, unshakeable leonine certainty in every lean line. "So time will mend all?"

"Time, and trust."

"Trust?" She arched her brows.

"Aye—tis what you lost in your first marriage. You had every right to expect that you could place your full trust in your husband. By treating you as he did, he destroyed it. Twill take time to grow again—tis why I have not mentioned the matter before this."

His strategies had gone to his head. She studied him for a long moment, then ventured, "You think I need to learn to trust you, and then I'll agree?"

"Aye." He hesitated, then went on, "Trust is important in a marriage such as ours. Tis necessary that you place your trust in me to protect you and care for you—and that I place mine in you to bear and raise my children, and to unfailingly support my position, both when I am in residence and as regent in my absence. Without trust, such a partnership as our marriage must be cannot succeed. Tis the lack of it that has made you wary of marriage for so long—twill not return overnight."

His golden gaze sharpened; the implacability behind it had never been clearer. "And to my mind, twill only return if you are close by me, living the life you would live as my wife. Once you have learned to trust again, you will agree to call me husband."

He believed that. His conviction was there in his steady gaze, in the concerted determination that held him so still.

Inwardly, Eloise shook her head, amazed. What did he think it took to lie beneath him every night, every morn, to surrender herself to him knowing that with one hand he could snap her neck, or with one blow crush her face? She had never feared him—she had trusted him from the first. As for the rest, he was preaching to the converted.

And didn't know it.

Slowly, she drew in a deep breath; inwardly, she trembled, as if on the brink of some momentous step. Ever since Gloucester, she'd been considering Blanche's advice, at first unconsciously, then very consciously. Somewhere in the confusion of today, she had made up her mind.

He could resurrect her dreams—if she let him. He would be her husband, strong and protective by her side, and his castle would be hers to run. And, in time, he would give her the babes she craved.

But there was one thing missing—one part of her dream she had never put into words nor crystallized in her thoughts. But she knew what it was. If she took the time he offered—the time he thought she needed to learn to trust him—she could use that time to try to gain what she sought.

It was the ultimate security for ladies such as she. If there was any chance of winning that prize, she had to take it.

Holding his gaze steadily, she narrowed her eyes. "If I remain in your care, how do you imagine we'll continue?"

Relief washed through Alaun with the force of a tidal wave. He rose, shrugged. "Tis no great matter to go on as we have been until you decide otherwise."

"Nay—what will your people think?"

He opened his eyes at her. "As you've already discovered, they believe we are to wed."

"And when the wedding does not shortly take place?"

"They'll simply imagine, as will all of my knights, that there's some legal impediment yet to be settled—perhaps something to do with the settlements themselves, given you're a widow. There are any number of possible reasons for delay." She was going to agree to go on—that was all that mattered. Time would see to the rest.

Slowly, she nodded. "Be that as it may, I do not believe it wise for me to continue sharing your tent."

Relief fled. Hands rising to his hips, he closed the distance between them. "Lady, your concern for your reputation comes a little late."

Her dark eyes widened in spurious innocence. "How can you speak so of the lady you would wed, lord?"

He swallowed a growl. "You were ready enough to put aside your reputation when you thought twas merely until we reached Claerwhen."

"Aye—twas to be an affair, nothing more."

"Yet you were a *virtuous* widow, as I recall."

Eloise blushed. She met his eyes; after a moment's silent tussle, she lifted a shoulder. "So put another notch on your sword hilt."

"Lady—"

"Nay, lord. I will concede that I should remain in your care and continue to your castle, there to become your chatelaine. But all else between us must cease."

"Nay—such behavior will cause talk. And, unlike you, I have been taking great care of your reputation. We have not stopped at any castles or manors where I could demand hospitality—none but my people know you are sharing my bed. However, they *do* know, and would think it very odd were you to cease doing so."

She grimaced and rapidly rejigged her plan. "Very well. I will continue to share your tent."

"And my bed."

She pressed her lips together, then reluctantly conceded, "And your bed. But there it must stop."

His eyes narrowed. His golden gaze boring into her, he stood over her, all but vibrating with frustration. Just when she was sure he was going to roar, his lips tightened and he nodded.

"If that is your wish, so be it."

Graciously, somewhat warily, she inclined her head. Raising it, she saw the dust of the column rolling down the road.

Montisfryn followed her gaze, then glanced at her. "Come. Tis time we rejoined the train."

They made camp a bare mile down the road. Consequently, when she again found herself alone with her prospective lord, she had had no time to reflect on their discussion, or to polish her plans.

As soon as the flap dropped behind Bilder, Montisfryn rose and stretched. "Tis time to retire, lady."

She blinked, and slowly rose. "No chess?"

"Nay—I am not in the mood."

He was already unlacing his cote. She glanced at the bed. Then she looked to the corner, to where his lance lay concealed in the shadows.

"Don't even *think* it."

The deep growl vibrated through her; startled, she glanced at him.

He gritted his teeth. "The bed is wide. Rest assured I will not touch you."

Stiffly, she inclined her head, and glided to her side of the bed.

That, however, was only the beginning of her troubles. Her cote laced at the back. After struggling for five minutes to no avail, she glanced over her shoulder—and saw him watching her, hands on his hips, stark naked. She swallowed. "Ah...can you help?"

Without a word, he came toward her. She quickly faced forward, quite sure she didn't need to see the expression in his eyes. Deftly, he undid her gown, then left her to slide out of it. Determined on her path, she kept on her chemise. Without raising her eyes, she slipped under the covers.

He immediately snuffed the candle.

She heard him cross to the other side of the bed, then the mattress bowed. She waited until he'd settled, then carefully turned on her side. With her back to him, her fingers clinging to the side of the pallet as if it were a cliff edge, she closed her eyes and searched for sleep.

To her surprise, she found it.

It was deep night when she awoke. Moonlight speared through the chinks about the tent flap, dispersing a weak, shimmery glow. Warm and secure, she let her heavy lids droop and resettled her cheek on the resilient expanse of hair-dusted muscle beneath it.

She froze.

Slowly, she opened her eyes. The moonlight confirmed she was on Montisfryn's side of the bed; her senses informed her that he was not touching her—she was touching him. She was sprawled across his chest, one hand tucked beneath his side, her hips angled over his, her legs tangled with his. Her chemise had ridden up to her waist. Smothering a groan, she carefully raised her head and peered at his face.

He was awake, watching her; she saw the moonlight glint in his eyes. He made no move to touch her, yet the familiar warmth still flooded her, leaving her heated, but empty.

Realization flooded her. In her brilliant plan to use his lust as a prod to make him woo her anew, she had overlooked one vital point. She wanted him—needed him—as much as he did her.

A deep quiver shook her. A flush spread over the backs of her thighs and the globes of her bared bottom. Her skin prickled; pressed to his chest, her nipples tightened to painful crests.

He lay immobile, apparently oblivious of her state. Clearly, if, after her insistence otherwise, she now wanted him, she would have to issue an invitation.

She held his shrouded gaze, then, deliberately, lowered her head and, with the tip of her tongue, licked the nipple her fingers had found beneath the crisp mat of his hair. The flat disc tightened, hardened. Glancing up at his face, she spread her fingers over his chest, flexing the tips deep into the thick muscle. Beneath her, his body tensed. Curling her hands about his shoulders, she drew herself up, sinuous and slow, until she could frame his face with her hands. She looked down at him for a moment, then she set her lips to his.

His body felt like iron beneath her soft curves, his staff a scalding, throbbing rod cradled between her thighs. He let her kiss him; her lips curved as she teased and taunted, feeling him quiver with the effort of holding back. His will was strong; slowly, she undulated her body against his and felt his lips firm against hers.

Boldly, she angled her shoulders back and reached down. Her fingers found him, hot and hard. Gently, she stroked, her thumb caressing the broad velvet head while her fingers curled about the shaft, then, with her nails, she lightly scored his length.

A deep, guttural groan vibrated through them both. His resistance broke. His hands came up to frame her face; his tongue thrust into her welcoming softness and he shifted, turning them to their sides.

She continued to stroke him as his tongue stroked hers. Then he lifted his head and caught her hand, drawing it from him and raising it as he rolled her to her back. With a sigh, she sank into the pallet, reaching up to draw his head down, drawing his lips back to hers. His hands found her waist, then slipped around and beneath her hips, positioning her against him. They kissed long and deeply, tongues twining, inciting, as their bodies shifted, adjusted.

Then he raised his head; his eyes on hers, with one slow, powerful thrust, he joined them.

Her long sigh hung in the dark above them. He held still; she could feel the hardness of him buried inside her. "This doesn't mean I've agreed."

"Nay." His voice was dark, raspy. "You will tell me when you do."

Her lids fell as he moved within her, swiftly taking them to where they longed to be. As her fingers tightened, sinking deep into his arms, her lips curved.

At last, she'd gained the initiative.

She would tell him what he wanted to hear—after he had revealed what she needed to know.

* * *

Of necessity, their cavalcade had to pass through Hereford, entering by the south gate and exiting by the north. At Montisfryn's side, Eloise crossed the bridge over the Wye and rode through the narrow streets, entering the cobbled cathedral square before the town's burghesses had left their beds. The market, however, was already in full spate, the noise rolling down the Broad to where they drew rein by the cathedral steps.

Montisfryn glanced at her. "I needs must call on the sheriff. Montisfryn is just over the border, so I keep in touch with Sir Neville. His house is by the eastern gate."

Eloise met his gaze. "I have met Sir Neville before. Perhaps twould be as well if I awaited you here. I would stop by the market, and spend some time in the chapel."

He frowned. "Lady—"

"Nay, lord." She arched a brow. She had little trouble guessing what was behind his frown. Hereford was, after all, where she had planned to leave him. "You will do better with the sheriff without me."

A moment passed, then his lips tightened. "Very well. But you will keep Rovogatti beside you, and you will take an escort."

A single gesture had eight men drawing up behind her.

She resisted an impulse to appeal to the saints. With a serene, "As you wish, lord," she nodded and wheeled Jacquenta up the Broad.

Alaun watched the group wind its way up the street, then, reluctantly, headed for the eastern gate.

The market was much as Eloise remembered it. She idly wandered the rows of stalls, pausing to chat to the old women selling herbs in the sun by the wall. She made a few purchases—some medicinal wine, honey, and a stoppered flagon of cider vinegar. Piling her purchases into Matt's arms, she sent him with Jenni to deliver the goods to their wagon.

As Eloise reemerged into the Broad, the bells of the cathedral pealed. She had Rovogatti lift her to her saddle, then, at the head of her party, she rode down the Broad; the pink sandstone cathedral squatted at the southern end.

Leaving their horses with two of the men outside, Eloise led the way in. Gliding down the nave, she paused to genuflect to the altar before sweeping forward to the front pews reserved for the nobility. Rovogatti, unable to follow her, found a position halfway down the nave among the burghesses' servants. The rest of her escort remained outside the door.

The cathedral was crowded, as it always was on market day. The mass was short, tailored to the needs of the flock, most of whom had commitments at the market. The benediction said, the congregation rose to leave. Eloise rose, too, only to feel her sleeve twitched.

Looking around, her eyes widened. "Father David—how good to see you again!"

The white-haired priest, who had once held the cure of the ladies of Claerwhen, smiled serenely. "Indeed, lady. Long years have passed since last my old eyes beheld your face. How have you been keeping?" Gently, he drew her free of the bustle. Answering his questions, asking her own, Eloise strolled beside him into the vestry.

* * *

In the sheriff's house hard by the eastern gate, Alaun shifted restlessly, trying to concentrate on Sir Neville Grayson's words.

"I spent last week doing the rounds so I could inform the king that we've no major band of outlaws presently about Hereford." Sir Neville, a thin, ascetic personage with a long, pointy nose, pulled at his chin. "I can't understand why he imagined there would be."

Alaun shrugged. "With Edward, one never knows. I take it he's back?" He rose from his chair, setting down his goblet.

"As to that, I cannot say." Blinking, Sir Neville got to his feet. "But surely you'll stay longer?"

"Nay." Alaun dropped a hand on Sir Neville's shoulder. "I must not tarry. My train will soon be clear of the town."

Startled, Roland hurriedly swallowed the last of his wine.

"Ah, well." Sir Neville nodded. "Daresay I should get on to the barracks. Give my regards to Lady de Montisfryth."

Parting from the disappointed, but forever courteous knight, Alaun rode quickly back to the cathedral, Roland beside him.

The first thing they saw when they entered the square was Rovogatti standing before the cathedral door, his hands on his hips, a look of utter bewilderment on his face. The Genoese looked up as they drew near. And paled.

"Lord—she is gone." Rovogatti started down the steps as Alaun swung out of his saddle.

"*How?*" His face black as thunder, a fist closing about his heart, Alaun mounted the steps to meet the Genoese. "I left her *under your eye.*"

"Aye, lord. And she was there—at the front of the church. Then, when the crowds left, she was…not." Rovogatti's gesture suggested that Eloise had vanished into thin air.

Alaun ground his teeth; a chill sank to his bones. Despite their talk, despite her words, the damned woman had run from him. He should have known better than to believe in her surrender, in her easy acquiescence.

"Should we search the church, lord?" Rovogatti asked. "I know not what the priests will think."

"Nay—she knows the building of old. She will no longer be there." Alaun paused, trying to marshal some coherency from his whirling thoughts. She had gone; she had left him—his mind wouldn't focus on anything else. Blindly, he shook his head. "You!" he snarled at one of his men-at-arms. "To the west gate—I want it shut!"

Roland, standing below him on the steps, blinked. "Ah—Alaun—"

"And you." Alaun singled out another man. "To the barracks—I want Sir Neville here at once!"

"Alaun." Roland's tone had grown insistent.

"The rest of you—pull a company each from the column. I want this town quartered, every stone turned. I want her *found*—and brought to me here." His voice sounded savage, even to his own ears. His men glanced at him nervously, and backed down the steps.

Roland tried again. "Alaun—"

"And *you*." Alaun's gaze fell on Rovogatti. "Take a troop and head out on the road west, just in case she's got clear of the gate." He pointed a warning finger at the Genoese. "If you find her, *bring her back*! Don't listen to any of her tales."

Rovogatti swallowed and nodded. "Aye, lord."

Alaun waited—but none of them left. "*Well?*" His temper spiraled. "What the devil's the matter with you? I want that damned woman back here—"

"*By all the saints!*" Roland stepped up and caught Alaun's shoulders, shaking him—or trying to.

Stunned, Alaun stared at him.

Then he gathered his strength to throw Roland off—

Roland enunciated clearly, "For God's sake, look behind you."

Alaun blinked. As Roland released him, he turned.

Eloise stood behind him, two steps back, her arms folded, one toe tapping. Her eyes, dark pools of accusation, told him she'd heard every word.

He scowled. "Where the devil have you been, lady?"

He heard Roland choke down his laughter and order the men-at-arms away.

Her gaze growing frostier by the minute, Eloise raised one brow. "Talking to the priests in the vestry." Unfolding her arms, she picked up her skirts and descended the steps. "You knew I was familiar with the house."

He followed her down the steps, his expression even blacker than before. "You had no business disappearing."

Reaching Jacquenta's side, she swung about. "You"—she emphasized her point with a sharp jab at his chest—"had no business doubting me." Nose in the air, she met his gaze. "Trust, so I have heard, cuts both ways."

He clenched his jaw so hard it nearly cracked. For a long moment, he held her gaze. Then, swallowing a growl, he reached for her and tossed her up to her saddle.

He did growl as he swung up to his.

They exchanged barely a word throughout the rest of the day. By the time he repaired to his pavilion, it was late. Eloise was waiting at the linen-draped board; Bilder hovered nearby. With a distant nod, Alaun passed Eloise and went to wash his hands. Their meal was placed before them immediately he took his seat.

Treading on eggshells, Bilder and the robin withdrew, leaving Alaun and Eloise in silence. A silence that stretched, apparently without end. After one swift glance at Eloise's serene, totally uninformative expression, Alaun kept his eyes on his plate.

But when the plates were cleared and Bilder withdrew, closing the flap behind him, Alaun had had enough. He turned—only to discover that Eloise had slipped from her stool. Glancing quickly about, he found her in the shadows, bending over her chest. As he watched, she straightened and dropped the lid, clutching something in her arms. As she returned to the table, he saw it was her psalter.

Dumbfounded, he watched as she laid it on the table and carefully positioned the candle before opening the book. She turned through the pages, then settled to read.

He lasted five minutes.

When she turned the third page, he reached for her hand. Lifting it clear of the tome, he shut the book. Then, still holding her hand, he rose and drew her to her feet. "Lady, I apologize."

Her eyes met his; coolly, she raised her brows.

He set his teeth, then had to force his words through them. "For thinking you foolish enough to run from my care."

Her serene expression dissolved into a frown. "Nay—that is not right. You did not think me foolish—you thought I had deliberately left you." She folded her arms and lifted her chin. "You did not trust me, lord."

He could feel his brows lowering, his eyes darkening. "Nay, lady—I trust you well enough."

"By which you mean barely at all?"

"*Nay!*" He closed his eyes as he heard his own tone. For an instant, he relived those minutes before the cathedral—the cold terror that had claimed him, a chill emptiness he could find no words to describe. Abruptly, he opened his eyes and locked them on hers. "Lady—I trust you. Twas the surprise of the moment—if I had stopped to think, I would have known you were within."

Her eyes opened wide. "Nay—you cannot expect me to swallow that. Tis my experience you think all too quickly—you are ever three steps ahead of me."

His hands rose to his hips without conscious direction. "Lady, I trust you well enough to want you for my wife. Let us leave it at that."

"Nay, tis a moot point." Eloise stood her ground. "You would have me learn to trust you, yet I find it difficult to believe that you trust me."

"Lady—"

"Perhaps, *if* tis as you say and your trust is real, you should let me put it to the test?" She tilted her head, raised her brows.

The wariness that spread through him, from his eyes to his tensing muscles, strained her control.

"What test?"

"Nothing too convoluted." Airily, she gestured. "A simple test— something...unequivocal." She considered him. "For instance, if you *truly* trusted me, twould be no great thing for you to agree to do as I wish, exactly as I wish, just for an hour."

Suspicion supplanted his wariness. "An hour?"

"Aye—tis not too much to ask, I think."

"And if I do as you ask for the next hour, you will accept that I trust you?"

"Aye."

"I will hear no more of your sharp comments on the matter?"

She smiled. "Nay. If you do as I ask for one hour, I will be satisfied."

Alaun studied her smile. It hinted at mischief; there was an expectant glow in her eyes. Too many of his muscles had tensed; his nod was distinctly stiff. "Very well. You have one hour. What is it you wish me to do?"

Her smile deepened. She moved around him and pointed to his chair. "Move that—there." She indicated the clear space by the central pole.

Puzzled, he did as she asked.

"Now sit." Hands on her hips, Eloise watched as he did, setting his shoulders square against the back, placing his fists, loosely clenched, on his thighs. Like most men, he sat with his thighs widespread. Muting her smile, she lifted her eyes to his. "You are to remain seated. You must not get up unless I give you leave. And you must obey any command I give."

His eyes narrowed. "Eloise—"

"Nay—I would have you be silent." She glanced down at her gown, and grimaced. Walking forward, she came between his thighs, then swung about. "Unlace my gown."

She waited, breath bated, to see if he would obey...then felt him tug at her laces. She smiled, triumphant, anticipation rising. He reached the end of the lacings in the small of her back; she felt his lips nuzzle her spine. His hands curved about her hips.

"Eloise..."

"Nay!" Abruptly, she whirled out of his hold. "You must do as I say." She frowned—disgruntled, he subsided.

She paused, then, positioning herself a step beyond his reach, she faced him—and slowly peeled the bodice of her gown down, letting it pull tight beneath her breasts as she freed her arms, thus outlining the bounty of her breasts and their peaked crests beneath the fine, taut silk of her chemise. Slowly, she inched the tight-fitting gown down over her hips, then let it fall to the floor; stepping free of the folds, she stooped, picked the gown up, shook it, then set it on the table.

Spying the stool beneath the table's edge, she drew it forward; placing one foot upon it, very slowly she lifted her chemise to reveal her garter. She unpicked the knot, then rolled her stocking down, lovingly smoothing the fine knit over her knee and calf. She did the same with the other leg, then dropped hose and garters on top of her gown.

Clad in nothing more than her chemise, she turned to face him; stretching both arms over her head; she glanced at him from beneath her lashes. His face was expressionless, his eyes far less so. As for his body, every muscle was locked. Lowering her arms, she smiled.

Her gaze fell on her psalter. Picking it up, she carried it to her chest. Opening the chest, she bent over it, ignoring the cool breeze that caressed the backs of her thighs. Replacing the psalter, she rummaged for a moment, then strolled back to the tent's center, her pale blue silk scarf in her hands.

Alaun watched her approach. He'd taken the opportunity of her visit to the chest to shift on the chair, to do what he could to ease the fullness in his groin that was shortly going to be an urgent ache. With an effort, he dragged his gaze from the hem of her chemise and focused on the strip of silk she was running back and forth through her hands.

His mouth was dry. "Eloise, what are you about?"

"It occurred to me, lord, that we have played out one of your fantasies." She smiled. "Tis my turn, now."

He closed his eyes—then quickly opened them as she drew near. "You have a fantasy?"

"Aye." She came to his side and reached around him, draping the scarf about his waist. She circled him, drawing the scarf about him and the chair's back, then securing it—he thought with a bow.

He frowned. "Eloise—"

"Nay, lord." Eloise stepped back to admire her handiwork. It would hardly hold him if he chose to move, but it would slow him—long enough for her to call him to order. Besides, the sight of him bound with her scarf—the scarf he had won in winning her—was definitely satisfying.

Lips curving, she circled to stand before him. "Tis my thought, lord, that you would not have previously been thus, in the power of another."

His frown grew baleful, but his eyes had lost the dull sheen of aggravation; he narrowed them, but couldn't hide the brightness now gilding them. "Lady, I like not these mind games."

Narrowing her own eyes, she held his golden gaze. "Nay—what you mean is that you do not like having such games played on you...but you're adept at playing them on others, are you not?"

The last was uttered softly; the surprise that flashed through his eyes made her smile. She arched a brow and moved closer. "Did you think I did not know?" She stopped between his knees. "That I did not realize you've been carefully revisiting my memories, overlaying the distasteful with the pleasurable?"

Slowly, she lifted a hand to the tiny buttons that closed her chemise. She held his gaze as she undid them, aware of his muscles rippling as his tension grew. When the chemise was open to her waist, she leaned forward and placed her hands on his thighs, bringing her eyes level with his. "Yet there are some of my memories you have skirted, perhaps fearing to do me harm. But this is my fantasy—tonight, tis you who must submit." Her lips curved irrepressibly. "And *I* who will dispense the pleasure."

He understood then. His eyes widened; the muscles beneath her palms went granite-hard. He drew in a breath—she cut off his protest with a swift, sure kiss. His hands rose, but before he could hold her, she whispered, "Nay! Be still. You must do as I ask," even as her quick fingers found him.

Her eyes met his; she watched desire claim him as her fingers wrapped about his staff, then she sank to her knees before him.

"Nay—Eloise…"

"Hush!" He was already well-risen; as she took him between her palms, he swelled even more. She had touched him often, yet she had not before had a chance to examine him. She did so now, boldly viewing him, then gently caressing the broad dome as she pushed the soft folds of his braies aside.

"Eloise…you do not have to do this."

His words were weak, breathless. Helpless.

She smiled. "I know. Tis my wish."

It was. She had never before imagined that she might enjoy pleasuring a man so; she'd hated, deeply loathed and abhorred, every minute Raoul had forced her to spend thus. But Raoul was long dead, and the idea of lavishing such pleasure on her lion was too deeply tempting to resist.

She glanced up through her lashes; he was watching her from beneath heavy lids, lips parted, his chest rising and falling rapidly. His fists were clenched hard on his thighs. Deliberately, while he watched, she ran her tongue over her lips, then blew, gently, softly, upon his broad head.

He bit back a groan and closed his eyes. His muscles locked tight. In his face, the angular harshness of grim endurance warred with the slackness of passion. Currently, grim endurance was winning.

She grinned—and tipped the scales. Slowly, savoring the salty taste of him, she ran the tip of her tongue around the rim of his shaft. An involuntary shudder racked him; muscles flexed, then were stilled. She smiled. And, with great deliberation, took him into her mouth.

For an instant, Alaun thought he had died—his eyes flew open but he couldn't see. He closed them again; his faculties had disintegrated, overwhelmed, overthrown. He could sense nothing, knew nothing beyond the warm wetness that engulfed him. She drew him deep, then deeper still. He heard a groan and knew it was his. Against his will, he felt his body shift, not pulling away but to give her better access.

But there was worse to come. Within minutes, he was cursing de Cannar. The blackguard had obviously been a connoisseur—he'd taught her well. Never, not even from Marie, had he received such exquisite service. With each luscious lick, each soft yet powerful suck, she drew him deeper into her web.

He groaned again. Beyond his control, one hand reached for her; his fingers stroked up her nape, then tangled in her braids. She took him deeply again; he felt his body tighten. His fingers firmed about her head.

His next groan was one of abject surrender.

Eloise chuckled, the sound trapped deep in her throat. Slowly, she pulled back and released him, more to get her breath than anything else.

Alaun's brain was reeling, worse than if someone had taken a mace to his head. Despite his orders, his body wouldn't move. He looked down. "Nay, lady." His voice was hoarse. Her fingers, curled around the base of his staff, were gently stroking. "Tis enough."

"Nay, lord." She looked up at him and smiled. "Tis just the beginning." Her dark, infinitely mysterious eyes, sirenlike, more dangerously feminine than any he'd ever seen, held his steadily. "You have most of an hour yet to go."

Before he could stop her, she drew her tongue upward in a long, slow lick. He shuddered.

"Your pleasure is mine to bestow, lord."

Another witchy smile was followed by another long lick. He could hardly find breath enough to groan. "Eloise...?"

"Nay, lord. Be still."

There was a hint of reproof in her tone. Dazed, he looked down at her bent head. His fingers, tangled in her braids, firmed involuntarily as she again drew him into the warm cavern of her mouth.

He had thought she was jesting—that there could not be anything she could do that could better what she'd already done. Nor that she could draw out the process for anything more than ten minutes.

On both counts, he'd underestimated her skill.

His head tipped back, his other hand joining the first, his fingers tangling in her hair, he was forced to yield to her will. She took him deep into her hot wetness and he lost touch with reality. He struggled for breath and lost that fight, too. His mind wandered, disengaged, cut free by the pleasure she so skillfully pressed on him.

One remnant of lucidity reminded him that ladies did not behave thus. Lady-witches, apparently, were another matter.

He knew that was true when a deep moan was ripped from him. Any doubt that her heart was not in this had flown; she was enjoying it, enjoying having him at her mercy, totally in her control. Again and again, she exercised her power, driving him mindless.

To the very edge of existence.

He hauled in a desperate breath as she artfully toyed with the sacks beneath his painfully rigid staff. He felt them tighten, his whole body slowly coiling.

Calling on his last remaining shred of will, he abruptly leaned forward; grabbing her about her waist, he hefted her up.

Eloise barely had time to release him before she was suspended above him. His lips found hers in a kiss so intense, her fingers were curling even as she reached for his shoulders.

Alaun brought his thighs between her knees, then spread them wide as he lowered her. For an instant, he held her poised just above him, searching for her entrance before, her heat and welcoming warmth pouring over him, he let her slowly down.

As his throbbing staff sank into her, he let out a long, slow breath.

Wrung out, but, by the saints' grace, once more in control, he slumped back, eyes closed, jaw clenched. Without conscious direction, his hands pressed aside her chemise and cupped her full breasts.

Stunned—by her change in position, by the feel of his hot strength unexpectedly buried inside her, by the sudden swelling of her breasts as his hands firmed about them—Eloise gasped. "Lord?" Instinctively, her hands rose to his.

He cracked open his lids; his lips curved as he took in her expression. He rotated his thumbs over her nipples, and winced when she reflexively tightened about him. "You know how to ride." His voice was hoarse. Briefly, he undulated beneath her. "Pretend I'm your stallion."

She looked down. His chair was not high; although her legs were spread on either side of his hips, her feet still reached the grass. Laying her palms on his chest, she eased upward—and smiled.

Sinking back, she widened her eyes at the resulting sensations. She rose and sank down again, closing her eyes as delight coursed through her.

She wasn't, she decided, going to protest. She would start at a trot, then progress to a canter. The gallop would be most interesting.

It was.

When she finally collapsed against his chest and felt him climax deep inside her, she made an exhausted mental note to pleasure him more often. It was delicious beyond anything she'd dreamed.

That was Alaun's conclusion, too, when, many minutes later, his mind returned, and with it some degree of awareness. It was late; the candle was guttering. And his lady-witch was sunk in deep oblivion on his chest.

Her hour was over.

Holding her to him, he reached back, tugged the silk scarf loose, and stood. She didn't stir. He brushed a kiss across her temple, then, his smile triumphant, he carried her to his bed.

Chapter 14

H er father had called Montisfryn Castle a stronghold. When, two days later, Eloise set eyes on the massive sandstone pile, she realized her sire had, as usual, been indulging in understatement.

Built on a rocky outcrop overlooking a briskly racing river, the castle towered over valley and town, shadowing the fields. The morning sun gilded the staggered battlements of curtain walls and keep. As she watched, Montisfryn's personal banner was hoisted aloft, the wind catching and unfurling it to snap in joyous welcome.

She glanced to her right; he rode beside her, alert and intent, his eyes scanning, assessing.

The castle stood on the opposite side of the river; they half-circled it to cross by a bridge, the clattering of hooves thrown back by the soaring walls.

The town nestled snugly between river and walls. They cantered up a broad street toward the barbican beyond. Everywhere she looked, people tumbled from doorways and leaned from windows to call greetings. Montisfryn acknowledged the salutations with waves, as did his men. Children ran whooping beside the column; townsfolk pressed close. They slowed. Names and questions rang all about them.

Montisfryn leaned close. "The two men ahead in caps?"

"Aye."

"The reeve and bailiff."

She smiled and nodded graciously as he acknowledged them by name.

The barbican loomed ahead. As they clattered across the drawbridge, the guards snapped to attention, weathered faces lit by broad grins, then the shadows of the entry arch descended. They passed beneath two portcullises before emerging into the sunlight to cross a last drawbridge spanning a spike-lined dry ditch.

A great shout went up from the battlements as they approached the gigantic wood and iron gates; cheering welled and swelled as those in the bailey caught sight of them. They passed beneath another pair of portcullises set below the gatehouse, emerging into the bailey to a tumultuous reception.

People thronged, milling close; a cacophony of names, greetings, and questions buffeted them. Montisfryn, still beside her and likewise hemmed in, raised a fist skyward. A huge cheer rose from the assembled multitude; it reverberated between the curtain walls, the inner as massive as the outer.

A proud smile on his lips, Montisfryn lowered his fist to indicate a pair of towers in the inner curtain wall. Between them stood the gateway to the courtyard beyond. He nudged his gray into a stately walk; the crowd parted, forming a corridor to the gate, still eagerly calling and questioning the men who rode behind.

Keeping her position beside Montisfryn, Eloise took stock of her surroundings. The outer curtain wall was segmented by towers jutting into the bailey, each large enough to house a small garrison. Between them stood storehouses and smithies, armorers' forges and the like, all leaning against the outer wall. There were animal pens and stables galore, an alehouse, and a huge granary. As the cool dimness of the courtyard gate engulfed her, she turned and looked ahead.

Only to find Montisfryn's gaze upon her. She smiled; he lifted a brow, then looked forward as they clattered onto the courtyard cobbles.

The welcome here was less rowdy, but nonetheless heartfelt. Pages, maids, cooks, grooms, scullions, serving men, washerwomen—all came running, waving, bobbing curtsies or nodding respectfully as Montisfryn's gaze touched them.

Eloise raised her gaze to the keep. As custom dictated, the chief members of Montisfryn's household were gathered at the top of the steps. She barely noticed them. Instead, she felt her eyes widen, then widen again as she took in the massive scale of her new home.

It was not merely huge, it was *monstrous*! From the outer gate, the ground rose steadily; the solid rectangular keep was built on the crest of the rocky outcrop, abutting the curtain wall, beyond which would lie a sheer drop hundreds of feet to the river flats below. Six stories, Eloise counted, and there would be dungeons as well; it was a formidable edifice.

To its right, a hall had been added more recently, built on the same massive scale with three levels of arched windows. Further yet to the right lay more buildings, also of three levels, the lowest taken up by storerooms. Beyond lay the kitchens and outhouses. Swiveling, she looked left. A chapel stood beside the keep; in its shadow, she spied a covered well. In the lee of the west wall lay gardens and dovecotes.

Montisfryn halted his gray before the broad steps leading up to the keep door. Jacquenta halted alongside. As Montisfryn swung down, his steward descended to greet him.

"Welcome, lord! Tis indeed a great day that sees you return to us." Of medium height, thin and gray-haired, the old knight yet stood straight as a pikesman; joy and relief lit his face.

"Thank you, Edmund." Stripping off his gloves, Montisfryn gripped the steward's hand. "How goes things here?"

"All is well with the estate, lord."

Eloise pricked up her ears. She cast a quick glance at Montisfryn; he was looking about him, an expression of satisfaction on his face.

"And Lady de Montisfryth?"

"As well as maybe, lord. She is eager to see you."

As Montisfryn came to lift her down, Eloise saw an odd gleam in his eye.

"Aye, I warrant she is." He set her down on the cobbles, then, taking her hand, led her forward. "I would make you known to Sir Edmund, lady. He is my steward here. Edmund, this is Lady de Cannar. She will be residing here henceforth, and will act as chatelaine."

His blue eyes intensely curious, his smile delighted, Sir Edmund bowed low. "Tis an honor, lady."

As he straightened, Eloise saw sudden consternation sweep the elderly knight's face. It vanished immediately, yet his smile had waned.

"Come, lady." Montisfryn drew her up the steps; Sir Edmund slowly turned, then followed. Roland and Montisfryn's senior lieutenants joined them as he introduced her to his chamberlain and wardrober.

Both men bowed low; to Eloise's sharp eyes both seemed strangely unnerved. Inwardly, she frowned.

Montisfryn turned her to face the excited crowd congregated about the keep steps. "Look you well, lady." With one arm, he gestured broadly, encompassing the courtyard and all it contained. "Henceforth, this is your domain."

His words, strong and clear, carried easily over the sea of heads. There was a hush, then an explosion of excited chatter.

Eloise looked, but found no animosity. There were plenty of shy, speculative glances, yet his people seemed merely curious—and genuinely relieved. Given all she'd heard, she found nothing surprising in that.

She glanced at Montisfryn, and encountered a proud, intensely satisfied smile. She arched a brow at him; he gazed at her for a moment, then turned her to the door. His smile, if anything, deepened.

They passed ceremonially through the huge oak doors and into the entrance hall.

And encountered their first surprise.

That the cobwebs festooning the ornate carving decorating the arched doorway to the hall were as much of a surprise to Montisfryn as they were to her, Eloise could not doubt. He stopped and stared, all expression leaching from his face. Then, his hand tightening about hers, he slowly led her beneath the hanging tendrils and on into the great hall.

It was certainly great and it was undoubtedly a hall. Beyond that, she had never seen its like. The place was filthy. Dust hung heavy in the air; the rushes simply stank. The banners hanging from the walls were themselves hung—with great swaths of cobwebs trailing down to catch at unwary heads.

The floor was a sea of moldy rushes scattered with bones that not even dogs would touch. The raised dais, set along one end of the wide, vaulted chamber, fared but little better. The lord's table sat, a massive edifice in oak, in its customary position. Its surface was clear, but that, and the benches and stacked boards lining the walls, were the only sign that anyone still used the place. Even the fireplace, a wide hearth in the center of the floor, seemed to hold the cold ashes of centuries.

Releasing her, Montisfryn slowly walked on, eventually stopping by the hearth. His hands had risen to his hips; the tension in his shoulders testified to his shock.

"Edmund?"

The question was quiet, dazed, not the horrendous bellow she—and Sir Edmund—had anticipated.

Gamely, the steward stepped forward. "Tis by the lady's orders, lord." He bowed his head as he made the admission; realizing, he raised it and squared his shoulders. "I was permitted to order only that which fell within the steward's jurisdiction, and most especially forbidden to undertake, or in any way see to, matters which fell to the chatelaine's role."

Alaun dropped his head back, closed his eyes, and groaned. Feelingly. "How *long*? Since I *left*, saints preserve us?"

"Nay—twas after we heard of the victory at Crecy. Tis my belief she expected you home after that."

Alaun emitted a low growl. Slowly, he turned to his new chatelaine. She regarded him calmly, no hint of her thoughts in her face. Inwardly, he grimaced. "This is now your affair, lady. I would not have had you face such a task"—grimly, he surveyed the horror—"but the matter lies before us, nonetheless. Give what orders you will to Sir Edmund; he will convey them on."

His fists tightened as his gaze swept his once-proud hall. Jaw clenched against the urge to roar, he cast a narrowed-eyed glare at his servitors. "Hear me well. I wish to dine in this chamber—and that in no more than two hours."

Sir Edmund paled.

Eloise sent a raking glance about her, then, coolly composed, turned to Sir Edmund. "I would have all the women in, regardless of their normal duties—all except the kitchen staff. The women are to start with the walls— mops on sticks will reach. I would have the grooms and any other likely men—you will know who—in first of all, to sweep the cobwebs down and remove the banners. The laundresses can take charge of those. I want them beaten and brushed and their poles oiled before rehanging." She continued, calmly reciting order after order, decision after directive.

Reassured that she was not about to run screaming from his hall, Alaun turned toward the dais.

Three minutes later, Eloise concluded her orders.

Sir Edmund regarded her gravely. "Tis indeed what is needed, lady." His gaze flicked warily to his lord's broad back. "But we'll never accomplish all that in two hours."

She raised her brows. "Naturally not. But tis senseless attacking jobs like this in halves. Have the squires remove the lord's table and the boards, trestles, and benches, and set them up in the gardens. In honor of the lord's triumphant return, we will naturally have a celebratory dinner for the entire household. The day is fair—I believe we should hold it outside."

Edmund blinked, then smiled, slowly at first, then more broadly.

She met his eye. "Can I leave it to you to instruct the cooks?"

"Aye." Edmund nodded. Straightening his shoulders, he shifted his gaze to Montisfryn's back.

"Nay, Edmund. Leave the lion to me." Smiling at the surprise in the old knight's eyes, she laid a reassuring hand on his arm. "Tis my scheme. He'll not eat me."

Edmund frowned. "Lady…"

"Nay, sir. Enough." She drew herself up. "Do you away and start this business—to my mind there will be *no* excuse can we not eat supper in this hall." She arched a haughty brow. "And I have it on good authority that my tongue is a lethal weapon."

Despite the warning, Sir Edmund's smile was more grateful than wary. With a low bow, he left her.

Lips curving, Eloise turned. Montisfryn stood behind the high table staring up at his family crest carved into the back wall. The others had taken advantage of her discussion with Sir Edmund to escape the unwholesome atmosphere. Lifting her skirts, Eloise picked her way across the floor. Stepping up to the dais, she calmly clasped her hands before her and waited, the image of a dutiful chatelaine.

Montisfryn glanced at her. His lips quirked as he took in her stance, then he sobered. For a moment, his gaze held hers, then he grimaced and held out his hand. "Come. If this welcome has not prostrated you, we'd best go and visit its perpetrator."

Eloise preceded him up the stairs that led from the dais. Even though she wasn't touching him, she could feel the anger radiating from him. It was as well she was with him; hopefully her presence would restrain his ire. Perhaps the poor old dear had simply lost her wits?

Minutes later, brought face to face with Lanella, Lady de Montisfryth, Eloise rapidly revised her assessment of Montisfryn's stepmother. Lanella was not that old, she was certainly not poor, and if this bright-eyed lady had lost her wits, then so, too, had Eloise.

"*Alaun!*"

Lanella greeted her stepson with unaffected joy. Propped in a large chair and swaddled in scarves and wraps, she held out crabbed hands, her face wreathed in smiles. She remained seated; she clearly could not rise.

"*Maman.*" Montisfryn took her hands, dwarfing her as he bent to place a filial kiss on her cheek. Straightening, he fixed his errant parent with a stern and distinctly irate glare. "I am not pleased with you, *maman*. Particularly not when I've brought a new chatelaine to relieve you of your duties—as you've requested for so long."

Eloise could not doubt the eager surprise that lit Lanella's countenance.

"You have?" Lanella looked for all the world like a child about to receive a long-dreamt-of treat. "But..." Her expression clouded.

Montisfryn shifted, standing directly between them. From her position by the door, Eloise saw Lanella try unsuccessfully to peep around his large frame. "How did you know...?" "I didn't." Montisfryn's tone was clipped.

Lanella blinked up at him, her expression blanking. "Oh."

Eloise felt for the lady. She glided forward and sank into a curtsy. "I'm pleased to make your acquaintance, Lady de Montisfryth."

Lanella beamed at her.

Then they both looked at Montisfryn.

Suddenly finding himself the focus of a pair of polite, but pointed glances, Alaun growled, "Allow me to present Eloise de Versallet, lady of the late Raoul de Cannar. She is under my protection, and will henceforth reside here and assume the duties of chatelaine." Hands on his hips, he had no difficulty summoning a resigned scowl. "I will leave you to get acquainted."

With a curt nod, he headed for the door, pausing at the last to acidly comment, "Perhaps, *maman*, as it will be Eloise's duty to rectify them, you might warn her of what other horrors you have laid up for me."

Under his glare, Lanella squirmed.

Immediately the heavy arras over the doorway settled behind him, Eloise found Lanella's bright and remarkably shrewd gaze on her.

"My dear—I'm *so glad* to welcome you." Lanella held out both hands, her smile inviting Eloise to take them. "And I must apologize for whatever state the hall was in. I cannot easily go down. Was it truly horrendous?"

"Worse." Eloise gave up the struggle to hide her grin. Lanella had the most expressive face, her features moving fluidly to keep pace with her thoughts—delighted one moment, a trifle worried the next. "But I've already given orders to put all right." She studied the older woman for a moment, then asked, "Are you truly not upset at being put aside as chatelaine?"

"*Upset?*" Lanella's blue eyes flew wide. "My dear, if you only knew! I've been at him for at least the last three years to replace me!"

Eloise let her brows rise. "You've been ill for three years?"

Lanella grimaced. "Nearer four. I cannot get about. My companion,

Maud, takes care of me, and I've learned to be content here in my chamber. But as you know, to fulfill the duties of chatelaine, one needs to take one's eyes on tour. I've done the best I could these last years, but when I heard of Crecy—I assumed Alaun would shortly be back, you see—I thought to make plain to him how much this great house needs an active chatelaine."

"I think you succeeded." Eloise smiled at the memory of Montisfryn's face when he'd first seen his hall.

"But come—pull up that stool and sit beside me here." Lanella waved to a stool with a beautifully embroidered cushion. "You must tell me how you come to be in my stepson's care."

As she shifted the stool, Eloise wondered how much to reveal. From Roland, she'd learned that Montisfryn was as close, if not closer, to Lanella than one might expect had she been his real mother, that Lanella had never sought to promote her two sons ahead of their stepbrother, but had staunchly supported Montisfryn throughout his career. Her own daughters were married, well-established, yet she'd chosen to remain in her rooms in Montisfryn's castle, far from her grandchildren, and await his return.

Glancing at Lanella, Eloise encountered a limpid, transparently hopeful gaze. With a swish of her skirts, she sat. And smiled. "It started with a pig."

* * *

On leaving Lanella's apartments, Alaun slowly paced the corridors, and wished he was a fly on Lanella's chamber wall. His new chatelaine had been as impressed as he could have wished with his castle and his keep—until they'd entered his hall.

With a low growl, he shook aside the memory. Just when he thought his problems were over, that he'd finally reached the end of his difficult trail and had Eloise safe in his castle, to act as his wife until she trusted him enough to acknowledge him as her husband, fate had tempted Lanella to one of her tricks.

Suppressing another growl, he forced himself to stop by a dust-strewn arch. The familiar view could not hold him; he snorted, then sneezed.

His feet had taken him toward his own apartments on the second level of the new block next to the hall. Not sure what he would find there, or that he wanted to know, he hesitated. His antechamber lay at the end of the long, tapestry-lined corridor; warily, he poked the hanging beside him.

A cloud of dust billowed forth. Choking, he fell back, then, muttering dire imprecations against manipulative stepmothers, he turned and headed for the top of the keep.

The bracing breeze blew the cobwebs from his mind.

Summoning his lieutenants, he paced the battlements while they made their reports. By the time they were done, the autumn sun was high and his stomach insisted the dinner hour was nigh. But the gong had yet to be struck;

he was determined not to set foot in his hall until it was fit to receive him.

Eschewing the sight of the ant-like creatures scurrying about the courtyards far below, he lifted his gaze to the surrounding lands—his lands, under his law, his rule, his hand. Like a dark ribbon, forests swathed the northern and eastern horizons, trailing away to the southeast. The Long Forest covered the northwest, the Shirlet next it, with the Wrekin beyond. To the northeast lay Morfe; from there, a dark green streak took in Kinver, directly east, and Feckenham, stretching southeastward.

Pivoting, he looked south to the river flats, good grazing land interspersed with fertile fields and lightly wooded terrain. To the west lay the foothills of the Welsh mountains, rough hills hiding small, rock-strewn valleys, gradually rising to the craggy, mist-shrouded sentinels lowering on the horizon.

Home.

Closing his eyes, he dragged in a breath, sweet with the tang of the forests. A sense of peace came with it, seeping through him, sinking into his bones.

She was there. In time, she would be as much a part of his home as the hills and fields before him. She was there—there was nothing more he needed to do. Time would soothe her, would persuade her that calling him husband posed no threat.

As for himself, it was time he took up the reins once more, and reestablished his life, much as it had been before. Little had changed. There was, after all, only one significant difference having a wife made—he wouldn't have to bother choosing a leman to warm his bed.

Smiling, he heard footsteps, light, hurrying, tapping up the stairs. Opening his eyes, he turned, acutely aware of his anticipation, the speeding of his heart, the impatience that gripped him.

His smile deepened; he went forward to greet her.

But it was not Eloise who emerged in an impulsive rush from the stairs.

He froze, shock and spontaneous revulsion dousing his inner flame. His expression hardened. "Elspeth." He nodded to the apparition before him.

Wide eyes so washed out that they were neither blue nor gray fastened on him with an avidity that, had he not been so used to her, would have caused him some alarm.

"Lord? *Saints be praised!* You have returned to us!"

A wild mane of tangled red tresses surrounded a pale, sharp-featured face. Elspeth's slight, girlish body vibrated with a peculiar tension, a warning that his mother's best friend's daughter was in the grip of one of her more highly-charged flights.

Alaun frowned, holding her at bay with his look. "Behave, Elspeth."

He noted her blue velvet surcote and the dark blotches marring it. His gaze hardened; his expression grew grimmer. "Hunting again?"

Her pale eyes gleamed. "Aye. We had very good sport. My merlin—"

"Elspeth, we will be dining soon and I have other guests. I suggest you change your gown." With a curt nod, he moved past her, cutting short what he knew would be a disturbing tale. From the stains on her gloves, he surmised Elspeth still indulged her habit of holding the prey her hawks had killed, exulting as the warm blood flowed out of breasts and necks ripped apart by the birds' talons and beaks. She had been thus warped ever since he had known her—which was to say all of her life. "I will see you at table."

Hiding his disgust, he left her, quickly descending to the lower levels of the keep, and thence turning into the corridor leading to his stepmother's sanctum.

"What the devil's Elspeth doing here?" he growled, the instant the arras fell behind him.

Jerked from contemplation, Lanella frowned. "Oh, dear. Is she having one of her fits?"

Alaun snorted. "As far as I can tell, these days, Elspeth's life is one long fit. Why, by all the saints, can't Davarost see it?"

Lanella sighed. "I had hoped she might improve while she was here, away from the excitement of her brothers and sisters."

"*Maman*—Elspeth will *never* improve." His voice was hard, his verdict final.

"I know." Lanella closed her eyes, then opened them, a slight frown in the blue. "Even I know that, and Maud takes great care to hide Elspeth's worst from me. Lucilla knows it, too, but she's a trifle indisposed at the moment."

"Oh?" Lucilla Davarost was Elspeth's mother, and Lanella's oldest friend. They'd been girls together; Lanella was Elspeth's godmother, as Lucilla was Alaun's. He waited for the explanation he hadn't requested, but which his stepmother knew he was owed.

"Lucilla's just been brought to bed of her latest."

He opened his eyes wide. "*Another* one?"

Aware of his opinion of Howell Davarost, Lucilla's meek husband, Lanella pressed her lips together firmly, then airily waved. "I daresay this will be her last. She's almost as old as I am, after all."

Alaun sent Lanella a sharp glance. "You aren't that old."

Lanella smiled. "Anyway, Lucilla had to get rid of Elspeth—you know the trouble they've had with her before. Confinements, for some reason, send her into a frenzy."

"So you volunteered to take her." It wasn't a question. Lanella, forever openhearted, once appealed to, would have offered the hospitality of Montisfryn most readily. And, despite his disgust, Alaun couldn't fault her. Everyone in the castle was used to Elspeth's oddities, having seen ample evidence of them during her innumerable visits through the years; no one would be surprised by her peculiar flights.

"Davarost is here, too," Lanella confessed, then hurried on, "And he's brought a female to keep an eye on Elspeth—a Mistress Martin. She's a quiet, but watchful soul—I don't think you need worry overmuch about Elspeth."

Alaun grunted and turned away. He didn't really care whether Elspeth or her father was here or not, but a household full of distractions was not what he had been expecting. A wistful longing for the privacy of his camp, surrounded by a veritable army, stole over him. He shook it off, yet his disgruntlement lingered.

Lanella eyed him speculatively, no doubt wondering how best to interrogate him. Before she could find the right words, the gong clanged.

The brassy note resounded about the castle, bouncing and echoing from the many stone walls. Frowning, Alaun lifted his head. The sound had come from outside. He headed for the window. "By St George and his dragon—"

The arras shifted; he halted. Eloise calmly entered. A smile touched her lips when she saw him.

"Ah—there you are, lord." If she'd heard his exclamation, she gave no sign. Nodding to Lanella, she continued, "Dinner is ready to be served. In celebration of your return, lord, a feast has been prepared and the tables laid ready in the gardens."

"The gardens?" He remained before the window, his gaze on her face. Slowly, he arched a brow. "I thought I gave orders for the hall to be prepared?"

His question was quiet, but Eloise did not mistake the look in his eye. She raised her chin, drawing righteous dignity about her. "Perhaps, lord, before you give such orders in future, you might care to consult with your chatelaine? All the saints in heaven—acting in concert—could not have cleaned your hall in two hours."

Their gazes locked; she felt the shafts of gold lancing into her. At the edge of her vision, she could see Lanella watching; his stepmother grinned delightedly when, after what seemed like an age, Montisfryn briefly inclined his head.

"If you say so, lady."

Breath suspended, she watched as, moving with prowling grace, he neared, stopping beside her, towering over her, his eyes still locked on hers.

She held his gaze defiantly, her eyes flashing a clear warning; she was not about to beg his pardon.

To her relief, he seemed to accept that. Lips easing, he held out his hand. "Allow me to escort you to this celebration, lady."

"Nay, lord." Laying her hand on his sleeve, she looked at Lanella. "It was in my mind to ask if you would carry your lady-mother to the table."

"*What?*" Lanella stared, sheer astonishment in her face, then she laughed shakily. "Oh, no—you don't understand. I haven't been down in years."

Alaun raised his brows. "Why not? Twould be simple enough to carry you downstairs, and you're well enough, these days, to sit through a meal."

"Oh, no." Lanella gathered her shawls about her. She shook her head. "I don't think so, Alaun. I should stay up here quietly—I'm sure Maud would agree."

"Maud has taken down cushions for your chair and awaits you at table," Eloise calmly announced.

Lanella shot her an exasperated glance. Turning, she discovered Alaun by her side. "No, Alaun, really!" Helpless, she found herself hefted against his chest; she glared at him from close quarters. "You don't need me down there—you've got a new chatelaine, remember?"

Ducking beneath the arras Eloise held aside, Alaun strode down the corridor, a grim smile on his lips. "Precisely. And if my new chatelaine gives orders that you should attend meals from now on"—he shrugged—"I should at least make some attempt to humor her, shouldn't I?"

Lanella looked from his face to Eloise's, equally determined. Then she humphed and settled in his arms.

They were the last to appear. The tables had been erected about the trout pond, the lord's table in pride of place before a creeper-covered wall. The entire household had turned out, all, from senior vassals to the most junior maid, eager to join the collective celebration. The most eager of all was Alardice, the harper, who, Lanella whisperingly informed Alaun, had spent the months since Crecy polishing a ballad of his own composition.

"The saints grant me strength," Alaun muttered.

Lanella's appearance was greeted by cheers; there were few who had seen her in over three years.

Noting the slight flush in Lanella's pale cheeks, Eloise hurried ahead to arrange the cushions in her chair. The two carved chairs from the hall had been lugged out and placed at the center of the lord's table. As Montisfryn gently lowered his stepmother to hers, on the left of his, Lanella shot Eloise a darkling glance, which converted to a grateful grimace. Eloise smiled back. She hesitated, then, holding her breath, turned to move down the table.

Hard fingers closed about her elbow.

"Wither away, lady?"

She glanced up, into golden eyes. "I thought that, as your chatelaine, I should sit beyond your guests, lord."

His gaze held hers. "Nay, lady. Henceforth and forever, your place is by my side."

His tone suggested he would brook no argument.

She hesitated, then inclined her head. "As you wish, lord."

He led her to the bench to the right of his chair; his knights had left a space for her there, confirming his reading of their expectations. As he sat her, another round of cheering erupted from the lower tables.

This time, it was she who blushed.

She shot a glance at Montisfryn, which he fielded with an arrogant look. Then, beyond him, her eyes met Lanella's, delighted and encouraging beneath raised brows. Inwardly, Eloise grimaced.

Warmed by Lanella's welcome, she had rashly confided that she and Montisfryn expected to wed shortly, once a minor impediment had been overcome. In describing as minor the act of bringing Montisfryn to his knees, she had clearly inherited at least one of her father's traits.

The cellarer bustled up to fill their shared goblet. She sent a supervisory glance around as the first dishes were set forth, then reached for the goblet. Cradling it in her hands, she offered it to Montisfryn. "Lord?"

His eyes met hers. He reached for the goblet, grasping it by the stem. Pushing back his chair, he stood.

"Friends!" He raised the goblet high. "We have returned victorious!" Mad cheering echoed through the courtyard. "But in so doing, we who return must give thanks to those who remained behind to hold our hearths for us while we ventured on the king's command."

Twisting on the bench to look up at him, Eloise listened as he smoothly acknowledged his principal retainers who had remained to hold Montisfryn for him. At the last, he dropped his gaze to Lanella, inciting another round of laughter. Glibly, he continued, thanking all those, knights and less exalted followers both, who had accompanied him on the campaign, pausing to list by name the few who had not returned.

Eloise glanced at the assembled throng. She had heard such speeches before; her father and brothers had all campaigned. Yet she'd rarely witnessed such a consummate performance; Montisfryn had them hanging on his every word, each convinced he was addressing them personally, and that he valued each and every contribution, no matter how small.

When, with a recommendation that they should now apply themselves to their meals in honor of the whole company, he resumed his seat, she met his glance with a serenely approving smile. Roland sprang to his feet and proposed his liege lord's health, to which everyone drank deeply, herself included, her eyes meeting Montisfryn's over the rim of the goblet.

The formalities complete, the company fell to.

"This roast kid looks very succulent, lord. Will you try some?"

When he did not immediately reply, she glanced at him. He was sitting back in his chair, his gaze on her, his expression unreadable. She raised an inquiring brow; after a moment, he nodded.

"If tis your recommendation, lady."

She smiled and served him. He sat forward to sample the meat, well-seasoned with saffron and raisins. When he reached for their goblet, anticipating him, she had it ready.

His gaze trapped hers. She could not be sure what was going on behind the gold screens, yet she sensed he was puzzled, and not a little suspicious. Smiling sunnily, she reached for another platter. "There are oatcakes, too, lord. Will you have one?"

"But what of you, lady?"

She turned back—to be offered a portion of roast kid, poised on the tip of his eating knife.

"Twould not be to my liking were you to grow any slimmer."

Her smile was perfectly genuine. "Nay, lord." She let her eyes meet his, then veiled them with her lids. "Tis not my intention to deny myself." Lifting one hand, she curled her fingers about his wrist and delicately took the meat from the knife.

She felt his instant response to her touch; her smile deepened. "An oatcake, lord?"

As the feast continued, she took great delight in playing her role to the hilt; it was pure pleasure to see him trying to fathom just what she was about. She held few illusions over how hard the task she had set herself would be; nevertheless, she was determined to prevail. That being so, making the most of any opportunity to focus his golden gaze upon her was imperative. Entrenched once more in the rounds of castle life, they would spend but little time within each other's orbit; she needed to make each minute count.

Selecting a plump fig from a bowl of sweetmeats, she turned to place it on his plate, only to feel his fingers fasten about her wrist. His eyes trapping hers, he lifted her hand and, with lips and teeth, gently plucked the fig from her fingers.

It was impossible to suppress the shiver that shook her.

His eyes held hers; he did not release her hand.

"Lady, I would apologize for your welcome." A frown played behind his eyes; he spoke softly, just for her. "Twas not as I would have had it. I'm sore vexed Lanella chose thus to make her point with me, and so marred your arrival here. I would apologize for her—tis in my mind she will not have done so."

Her smile came from her heart. She leaned closer so her words would not carry. "Nay, lord—I need no more apologies. Indeed"—she arched a brow—"I'm thinking twas a very good thing—a most fitting and helpful welcome for your new chatelaine."

His frown materialized. "How so? I cannot see that an uninhabitable hall is any great recommendation."

"Not a recommendation, lord." She smiled into his eyes. "Think you I needed one?"

Before he could answer, she continued, "But as to its usefulness, through the challenge of dealing with it, your stepmother's welcome has allowed me to establish my credentials with your people." She gestured at the company. "Those of your household I had not met before. By the end of the day, I warrant they'll be in no doubt as to the caliber of chatelaine you have brought them." She glanced at him, one brow arching. "Who knows? Even you might be impressed."

His frown evaporated. "Nay, lady—you have no call to further impress me. I was convinced of your talents the instant I laid eyes on you."

"Aye—but this time, tis your intellect I seek to impress."

He choked. When she rescued the goblet from his hand, he shot her a heavily gilded glance. Coughing, he shifted in his chair.

She waved the cellarer forward, then, the very picture of a dutiful wife, solicitously offered her lord the full cup.

Chaper 15

"Where would you have this, lady?"

On the dais, Eloise turned to see Rovogatti standing in the body of the hall, her chest clutched in his arms. Jenni hovered beside him, carrying Eloise's herb-box.

Before Eloise could answer, Bilder hurried past. "The lord's chamber be up those stairs, lady. To the right." With a nod, Bilder indicated the stairs Eloise had climbed earlier with Montisfryn, before rushing on down the hall.

Eloise grimaced. Mired in the mammoth task of rejuvenating the hall, she had had no chance to explore. However, given her objective and Montisfryn's opinions there seemed little doubt over where her chest should rest.

"Come with me." Dusting her hands, she led the way up the private stair. Warned by Lanella, she'd sent six women upstairs to deal as seemed best with whatever they discovered. Turning right, she wrinkled her nose at the dust.

"Aye, but tis much improved, believe me, lady." A middle-aged woman of generous girth nodded respectfully. She was rubbing a tapestry rod with an oiled rag. "They're beating the hangings now. We thought to scrub the walls and floors before rehanging them."

"Aye." Eloise cast a swift glance over the walls and arched windows. "I would have you do so." With a nod for the woman, she walked on.

Three women were on their hands and knees, scrubbing the antechamber floor. Two young squires Eloise had not previously seen huddled in a corner ready to move the heavy furniture at the women's behest. All turned to stare with varying degrees of curiosity; she nodded and glided on.

Lanella had recognized the wisdom in allowing Montisfryn's chambers proper to be regularly cleaned and kept ready, a boon for which Eloise had thanked the saints. The door to his bedchamber resisted her tentative push. Exerting more strength, she felt it give, the hinges groaning. Making a mental note to have the carpenter in, she set the door wide.

Sunlight poured through the unshuttered window, highlighting a low table set before the hearth. Upon the table stood a handsome chess set, marble pawns as big as her fist, the exquisitely carved nobility standing six inches high. Smiling, she glanced back. Rovogatti was still negotiating the outer doorway. Slowly, she wandered into the room, taking note of its understated beauty.

The fireplace took up a full half of one wall; it was surmounted by a heavy mantel carved with Montisfryn's arms, repeated again and again, interspersed with shields and weapons. The walls were half-paneled in oak, the rich amber complementing the mantel's pale sandstone. Above the paneling, the walls had been plastered and painted with local scenes—hunting, fishing, hawking, harvesting—lending color and interest to the room.

A single large, heavily carved chair sat before the hearth, its embroidered cushions displaying the dragon and lion crest. Lips curving, she noted the simple chests pushed back against the wall, then let her gaze wander on—to the bed.

Huge, four-postered, draped with scarlet and gold velvet curtains tied back with tasseled cords, the carved oak bed dominated the chamber. Both head and foot boards were ornately worked, with oak leaves and fruit surrounding Montisfryn's coat of arms. The four pillars supporting the canopy of scarlet and gold silk were carved to appear lagged with heavy ropes.

It was a handsome example of the woodcarver's art.

It was an unexpectedly familiar sight.

Her mouth was dry. Eloise swallowed. Beyond the bed sat more chests, a carved bench and two stools; a rare carpet splashed jewel colors across the floor. Of these, she was only dimly aware. Her senses had fixed on the bed—and there they remained.

Even the curtain cords were the same as those on the bed she had shared with Raoul.

"Lady?"

Realizing her hand had risen to her throat, she lowered it and turned. Blinking, she focused on Rovogatti. "Ah…yes. Over there, I think."

Following her gesture, the Genoese placed her chest against the wall beneath an empty shelf. Spying Jenni in the doorway, the herb-box in her arms, Eloise waved her forward. "Let Rovogatti put that on the shelf."

That done, Jenni faced her, dutifully awaiting instructions. With a respectful nod, Rovogatti made to slip away—Eloise stayed him. "Nay—a moment." She glanced again at Jenni. "Neither of you have lived here before—you will need quarters assigned to you. I have discussed the matter with Sir Edmund; there's a chamber in the keep, behind the old hall which is now the armory. Both Sir Edmund and I see no obstacle were you wishful of sharing it—if that is your inclination?"

Jenni shot a questioning glance at Rovogatti. He answered with a quick nod. Jenni turned a glowing face to Eloise. "Lady—I know not how to thank you." She flew forward; grasping Eloise's hand, she pressed it fervently.

"Nay, Jenni." Eloise struggled to keep her own smile within bounds. "Do not thank me yet—tis likely the chamber is deep in dust, and I cannot spare any to help you."

"Nay, lady—I care not for that. I will set all aright, and that most gladly." Jenni released her and stepped back. "But first I'll unpack your things, then come help you downstairs. I saw they're sore-pressed in the hall."

"True, but I believe I'll be happier do you unpack, then apply yourself to getting your own room in order. I would not have you up half the night at the task."

"But—"

"Nay, Jenni. Do as I say. I have helpers enough in the hall." Glancing at Rovogatti, Eloise smiled. "But first I suggest you both go find this room and discover whether it will suit."

"Nay, lady." Rovogatti bowed deeply. "We have no doubt on that score." He exchanged a quick glance with Jenni, then said, "We are your servants always, lady. You have our thanks."

Eloise was touched; smiling, she waved them away. They withdrew.

Leaving her with the bed at her back.

For long moments, hands clasped before her, she stood and stared at the blank wall beside the door.

"Beg pardon, lady."

Eloise blinked. A young maid stood bobbing in the doorway, round eyes fixed on her face.

"Tis that Sir Edmund's wishful to know if you want the hearth irons dipped, or if a good scrubbing will do?"

Eloise blinked again. "Ah..." With a grimace, she waved the maid back. "I will come and see."

She left the room without a backward glance.

* * *

Three hours later, Eloise hurried down the private stair, the supper gong echoing in her ears. As she set foot on the dais, she looked up—and saw Montisfryn pass under the arch from the main entrance. He stopped; hands rising to his hips, he gazed about him.

Her eyes on his face, she glided forward to stand at the right of his great chair. Slowly, he strolled up the chamber, taking in all the changes, openly noting each aspect that made up his hall. Her expression impassive, she savored the slow change in his, from amazement to relief, and, at the last, when his gaze met hers, to deep appreciation.

There was a low murmur as his senior retainers and the men-at-arms joined those already at the boards. All threw wondering glances about, grins and ready praise on their lips.

It was his praise she sought.

When he joined her by his chair, he gave it—unstintingly with his eyes, rather more circumspectly with his words. Taking her hand, he reached for the goblet the cellarer had already filled. Raising it, he lifted her hand and turned to the company.

"I bid you welcome your new chatelaine."

The answering roar echoed from the vaulted ceiling. All raised their mugs high; some called her name. Her cheeks warm, she gracefully inclined her head. When the din died, she met his gaze, then, veiling her eyes, declared in a steady voice that carried the length of the hall, "I am pleased to join your household, lord."

The statement pleased him—she read as much in his eyes. His gaze flicked to the carved chair to the left of his, presently vacant, then he raised a brow at her. Calmly, she sat on the bench to the right of his chair. With a fleeting frown, he permitted it. He took his seat beside her, before stating, his voice low, "Lanella would not mind."

"Nay, but I am not your wife." It was the most definitive gesture, the right that only his wife could claim, to sit in the carved chair, the mate of his, on his left at his table. She would yield him most of what he sought to claim, but not that. Not yet.

He shot her a severe look, but accepted her decree.

"Your stepmother begs you will excuse her." Eloise drew the first of the supper dishes closer. "She was tired by the festivities at dinner, and is resting. Twill take a little time before she's used to coming among the household again—she's been hiding away for years, I understand."

Alaun frowned. "Aye." Absentmindedly, he took a bite of the dumpling Eloise had placed on his plate. It was delicious—cheesy and well-flavored. He glanced at the other dishes; all held simple, but tempting fare—egg and cheese concoctions flavored with herbs—with slices of crisp, fresh bread. Yet another surprise his chatelaine had served him; he was beginning to wonder how many more she had in store.

The celebratory dinner had been a riotous success, the open air feeding appetites and encouraging boisterous revelry. Everyone had joined in the chorus of Alardice's new ballad, "Montisfryn" rolling in a great roar again and again across the courtyard. And Lanella, for the first time in years, had been a part of it. As the meal had wended its way through the various courses, many of his retainers had stopped by the high table to bow, or drop a curtsy, and whisper a word of greeting, then to shyly welcome his new chatelaine.

Those long golden moments spent basking in the afternoon sunshine were etched in his mind; the fact that he owed them to Eloise hadn't escaped 'him.

Just as his hall, restored to its full grandeur, the carving ornamenting both stone and wood leaping sharp to the eye, the long trailing pennants bright as the colors on an illuminator's palette, hanging free, high above on their newly polished poles, all owed their resurrection to his latest vassal.

She had slipped away from the dinner table to attend to it. Others had followed, not summoned but going when they saw their new mistress off to work.

He set down his goblet. "Lady—"

"Can I tempt you, lord?" Her eyes met his as she lifted a platter. Her lips curved lightly. "With one of these pastries?"

He narrowed his eyes, but reached for a golden pastry. "Eloise, I would thank you. For all this." With the fan-shaped pastry, he transcribed an arc encompassing the whole hall.

With a light smile, she looked away. "Nay, lord—how so? Tis merely my duty."

For some unfathomable reason, her answer irritated. Like a burr, it got under his shirt and itched. Shifting in his seat, he reluctantly gave his attention to Sir Howell Davarost, sitting in dull inconsequence beyond Lanella's empty chair.

At the conclusion of the meal, Eloise turned to Alaun. "With your permission, lord, I would withdraw. Your people have earned their rest this day. Twould be unkind in me to dally."

It was on the tip of his tongue to suggest that he might see things differently; instead, with a grunt, he assented. With her usual calm dignity, she rose and departed.

Eloise took the main stair from the hall to the solar, expecting the other ladies present—Mistress Davarost and her companion—to join her there. To her surprise, they did not. Passing the door she had deliberately left open, they disappeared down the corridor to the visitors' wing. Eloise frowned. She hadn't been introduced to either lady, an oversight due, no doubt, to the non-stop activity of the day; she had been looking forward to making their acquaintance. Deprived of all potential for social distraction, she idly wandered the room, studying the tapestries and the exquisite embroideries.

She opened a shutter and peeked out. It was dark; she could see little. Closing the shutter, she remembered the weaver's comments about the looms. She would need to organize some female companionship for both Lanella's and her own sake. Some young girls to train, too.

Glancing about, she frowned. Never before in either cloister or castle had she been without the company of other ladies. She had not before considered such companionship, the often ceaseless prattle, in any way necessary.

Tonight, she would have welcomed both Emma and Julia with open arms.

With a snort, she swung about. Crossing her arms, she stared at the floor. And dragged in a deep breath.

Prevarication was senseless—she could hardly fool herself. Eventually, Montisfryn would retire, and would expect to find her awaiting him. In his bed.

There was no point putting off the inevitable.

Dragging in another breath, she straightened her spine and lifted her head. With determined stride, she headed for the door.

Bilder was sorting weapons and armor in the anteroom. He nodded respectfully, then went on with his work. Beyond him in the shadows by the wall, Eloise glimpsed three neat pallets and three boyish faces in which a certain awe could be discerned. With a regal nod, she passed on—to wrestle with Montisfryn's door.

Entering the bedchamber, she closed the door behind her. She looked at the fireplace; a goodly blaze cast warmth and light into the room.

Gathering her courage, she turned to the bed.

The curtains had been loosened, but not drawn; the bed itself lay wreathed in shadows. One of the curtain cords lay, snakelike, across one corner, the silken tassel winking evilly in the flickering light.

Eloise stared at it. Minutes slipped by.

Then, moving slowly and deliberately, she turned and opened the door.

Bilder looked up as she emerged. Surprise and incipient consternation flooded his face. "Lady...?"

She smiled, the gesture not as reassuring as she would have liked. "I believe I'll spend a little time in the chapel." She started for the door, then paused to ask, "Where is it?"

* * *

Slumped in his great chair, Alaun scanned his hall; its transformation from moldering wreck to majestic magnificence had yet to lose its fascination.

Sprawled beside him, Roland was likewise in contemplative mood. Somewhat inebriated, he hoisted his cup. "By the saints and St. George, this place looks better than it *ever* did! Here's to the future!" He and the others at the table drank deeply.

Twirling his half-empty goblet, Alaun smiled and leaned toward his cousin. "If you don't stop drinking soon, the welcoming committee will find no future in you."

Roland blinked. "Ah." He blinked again, as if assessing the damage. "P'rhaps you're right." He placed his goblet on the table and firmly pushed it away. "Wouldn't do to disappoint them, would it?"

His smile broadening, Alaun inclined his head. "Just so. Don't forget that you carry the honor of this house in my stead."

Roland grimaced. "The saints alone know how many of 'em there'll be." He frowned at his goblet, then grinned. "Sure you don't want to help and do your share?"

His expression perfectly serious, Alaun dropped a heavy hand on Roland's shoulder. "I have complete confidence in your ability to fulfill all expectations."

The others laughed.

Roland humphed. "Speaking of the satisfaction of others, Lanella seemed just like her old self today. Looking at her face, you could almost believe she wasn't ill at all."

"Aye." Frowning, Alaun looked down.

"So!" Roland stretched mightily. "What's next to tackle?"

Alaun grimaced. "According to Edmund here"—he crooked a thumb at the knight now on his left—"I've a full list in the court. But I'm only going to sit until dinnertime." He considered, then said, "I'd have you take a company and do a round of the villages to the west—let our Welsh neighbors know we're back to full strength. Then"—he glanced around—"after dinner, perhaps we should investigate the state of the deer herds?"

The suggestion was greeted with vociferous enthusiasm.

Alaun grinned and pushed back from the table. "I suspect I should warn my chatelaine that there'll be game for the kitchens on the morrow."

Roland's brows rose. "Is that what you're going to discuss with her?" His brows couldn't get any higher.

"Among other things." With a lazy smile, Alaun headed for the stairs.

On gaining the dim corridor, he quickened his pace. Burgeoning impatience gripped him.

He went straight through the antechamber, not sparing a glance for Bilder, a shadow at the corner of his vision. Alaun pushed the door to his chamber wide; the squeal of the hinges announced his arrival. Closing the door, he advanced, anticipation lending a salacious quality to his smile.

The bed was empty—untouched.

Unoccupied.

Ten seconds sufficed for him to confirm that Eloise was not in the adjoining chambers. Then he was back at the door, hauling it open, stalking into the anteroom to where Bilder stood waiting.

One glance at his squire's face told him what his own had become.

"Where is she?" He managed to get the words out without roaring.

"In the chapel, lord."

He closed his eyes and drew a deep breath. Then he opened them, and fixed Bilder with a narrow-eyed stare. "The chapel?"

"Aye, lord. Said as she thought to spend some time there."

His breath hissed out through his clenched teeth. His gaze fell on his three youngest squires, all just fourteen; their awe-struck expressions would, in any other circumstances, have struck him as comical. "Get you abed," he growled. "I will not need any of you to assist me this night."

Only Bilder's lips twitched. "Aye, lord."

Alaun caught the words as he went through the door. He stalked down the dim corridor, his fists clenched tight. His jaw ached.

Recently—ever since Hereford, in fact—none of his carefully planned maneuvers seemed to go precisely right. *Almost* right, but never *quite* as he expected.

For instance, despite Lanella's tricks, Eloise's behavior on entering his castle had been everything he could have wished. It was *his* response that had him mystified. He had expected to be able to let the matter of their relationship rest; he was confident of the outcome—why, then, could he not get her out of his mind?

She invaded his thoughts, not just when she was present but at unpredictable moments—like when he had been on the battlements, looking over his lands. Throughout the afternoon, he'd been conscious of a desire to know what she was doing, and of a strong wish that she was by his side so he could show her the little things about his home that mattered to him. Ridiculous behavior in one such as he—he was hardly a love-smitten youth.

He could only assume his reaction was due to some deep-seated uncertainty. Hopefully the distracting sensibility would fade once she was legally his.

And now the saints only knew what was going on—he certainly didn't. Since Hereford, she'd given herself to him so completely, so consistently, he was quite sure the memory of her husband was long dead.

Why, then, was she not in his bed?

Even worse, why was she in the chapel?

With a growl, he swung into the lower corridor. The only thing he felt reasonably certain of was that he probably didn't want to know.

Gritting his teeth, he strode on.

In the chapel, close by the old hall in the body of the keep, Eloise slowly paced by the faint light of the altar candle. She had uttered countless prayers—to no avail. The saints had offered no aid. Which left her still facing the problem that had brought her there: What alternative could she suggest to sharing Montisfryn's bed?

Finding the words to tell him that she didn't like it was a mind-boggling enough task, explaining her aversion when she wasn't even sure that was what she felt. Would feel, once she lay beside him under the scarlet coverlet. Her memories had haunted her for so long, she couldn't believe they would simply disappear.

She heard his footsteps an instant before the door flew open. Whirling, she tensed, expecting it to crash. It didn't—because his hand had clenched tight on the latch. She dragged in a quick breath and drew herself up.

He met her gaze, his eyes shrouded in shadows. Then he stalked toward her. "Lady, we have been through this before."

His words were even—and very, very clipped.

She clung to her calm. "Nay, lord. Tis not what you think."

"Good."

He stopped by her side, then he swooped and lifted her.

"*Lord!*" She clutched at his shoulders. "What...?" She stared, stunned, as he carried her through the door. His intentions could not have been clearer. Breasts swelling, she fixed him with a fulminating glance. "Is this how you intend to behave once we are wed? Treating me like the veriest scullery maid?"

Keeping his gaze on the corridor ahead, he shook his head. "Nay—I never carry scullery maids. One catches them by the hand and drags them."

She glared. "As you have many times, I suppose?"

He shot her a warning glance. "Lady, as the saints can bear witness, *you* are the only woman I have ever had to drag to my bed."

"Ah...yes." She blinked. "Tis a matter I would discuss with you."

"Later."

Frowning, she looked into his face. "What mean you, 'later'?"

Fleetingly, his eyes met hers. "After."

She didn't need to ask after what. She gave vent to an exasperated hiss. "You are the most pigheaded man I know!"

Again, his eyes touched hers. "Nay—I am not pigheaded. Merely single-minded—tis different."

From the corner of her eye, Eloise saw a quick movement. Turning her head, she heard a smothered giggle. Looking forward once more, she realized his long strides were rapidly eating up her margin of safety. "Lord, I must protest the damage you are doing to my dignity." If she could get him to let her walk, it would take longer—much longer.

"Nay, if anyone's dignity is being done damage here, tis mine. Tis as well most are abed, and not about to see this sorry sight."

His tone was so disgruntled she couldn't help but ask, "Which sorry sight?"

"The sight of *me* being reduced to *fetching* my wife-to-be from the *chapel* to my bed."

She narrowed her eyes. "You would not have to fetch me at all, if you would only *listen*."

"Nay—my ears will not function ere I relieve my tension. Tas been building all day."

She certainly didn't need to ask which tension. The look she slanted him was wary. "All day?"

"Longer. In fact, since Hereford."

"Hereford?"

"Aye—when last we dabbled in fantasies."

She couldn't stop herself. "Fantasies?"

His eyes, golden flames devilishly beckoning, flicked her way. "Tis my turn, I believe." His tone turned conversational. "You might have noticed the scarlet silk cover on my bed?"

"Aye."

"I've a need to see you upon it." Again, his eyes captured hers. "Naked."

She sucked in a breath. "Nay. Lord—"

"Totally naked. Your skin is like ivory—twill look well against the scarlet."

She swallowed.

"Your body will twist and lift, flushed with desire and gilded by the firelight." His eyes locked with hers. "I would see you writhe. In ecstasy."

Her heart was thudding so wildly, she could barely breathe. "Lord," she gasped. "There is something—"

She broke off as he strode into the anteroom, affording her a fleeting glimpse of three shocked young faces before they crossed the threshold of his room.

"Your squires, lord—"

"Are not yet old enough to think about bedmates."

She waited for him to set her down. Instead, he kicked the heavy door shut—and advanced on the bed.

Frantic, she grabbed his shoulders. "*Alaun!*"

He tossed her on the bed.

She bounced once before his weight pinned her.

She dragged in what breath she could and opened her lips—he captured them in a searing kiss.

For two long minutes, she struggled to hold tight to her purpose, sure she needed to warn him that she might not behave as he expected—might not behave rationally. Then all thought was swept away as he caught her up in the tide of his loving.

He'd kissed her passionately, urgently, demandingly before, yet it had never been like this. His desire was a hot flame that scorched; for one wavering instant, she thought she might retreat before the intensity of the blaze. Instead, her own desire answered his, surging through her until she sighed into his mouth. Pulling her arms free, she twined them about his neck. Wantonly, she arched against him, explicitly inviting his conquest.

He needed no further direction. He lifted onto his elbows to finish unlacing her gown, then dealt with the ribbons of her chemise. He laid her breasts bare, then bent his head to do homage.

Tonight, he wasn't gentle; his tongue rasped her nipples to instant attention. From beneath heavy lids, he watched as he drew gasp after gasp from her. Experienced, knowing, he set his fingers and tongue to rove her body as he bared it, leaving her mind and her senses reeling.

She closed her eyes and heard herself moan. Heat flowed through her in waves. Then the comfort of his weight was removed; she felt his hands caress her hips, her bottom, as he drew her clothes down.

He left her for no more than a moment, then returned. A wave of prickling heat washed over her as his hair-dusted legs tangled with hers. He came down on his side beside her.

She lifted her lids; her gaze found his face. He was watching his hand trace her curves. His look alone dragged another moan from her. His fingers trailed down her breastbone, then splayed possessively over her taut stomach. She sucked in a breath; heated tension gripped her. She felt the telltale warmth erupt inside, felt the empty ache grow, the ache only he could assuage.

He knew. His fingers travelled down to slip through her dark curls. She parted her thighs and let her lids fall.

He was forceful, yet skillful—she saw another side of him that night. Soon, she was writhing, exactly as he must have wished. He wanted, demanded, everything she had to give; she gave gladly, awash in a sea of pure pleasure.

Propped beside her, Alaun watched her, watched her body lifting, twisting, responding freely to each ardent caress. Her ivory skin glowed with desire; the firelight gilded each smooth curve, shifting as she writhed.

There could be no sight more beautiful than a lady-witch in wanton abandon.

The thought pushed his strained control to the limit.

With a groan, he lowered his head to take her lips again. She met him eagerly, her tongue twining with his. His fingers were buried in her wet softness; he stroked, then probed deeply. She gasped; her nails sank into his shoulders, her hips lifting, searching.

Drawing away, he moved over her, positioning himself between her thighs, arms braced, holding himself above her so he could still view her.

Her eyes were closed; she shifted beneath him, arching in entreaty.

His smile was half-grimace; he lowered his head to brush her lips. "Say my name."

Her lids lifted fractionally; her dark eyes gleamed. "Alaun."

With controlled force, he thrust into her. Her eyes widened, then her lids sank; he came to rest fully embedded in her tight embrace.

Then, rising above her once more, he plunged them into the vortex that beckoned.

He didn't ask again, yet time and again, she gasped his name, arching wildly as he loved her. Together they soared; together they touched the sun. Then, as one, they slowly fell back to the mortal plane, to the tumbled sheets and the tangled furs, and the warmth of each others' arms.

It was eons later, when he'd recovered enough wit to lift his weight from her and settle them both in the warmth of the big bed, that he remembered to ask, "What was it—the so-important subject you needed to discuss?"

Eloise's eyes snapped open. She lay curled beside him, her body exhausted, her wits in similar case.

Blinking, she focused on her surroundings. The fire was mere embers, its glow barely enough to pick out their discarded clothes. Weak moonlight shone through the window, allowing her to make out the rumpled sheets and furs, the scarlet silk coverlet thrown roughly over all.

And in the deep shadows where the moonlight did not penetrate stood the carved bed post; closer, by the side of the undrawn curtains, hung a tasseled cord.

She screwed her eyes shut.

But no hideous moans came to disturb her, no piteous shrieks. Not even the maniacal chuckle of her dead husband came to challenge the quiet peace of Montisfryn's chamber.

A sigh caught in her throat. Slowly, she opened her eyes.

Somehow, somewhere, the dreadful banshees of her memories had finally been laid to rest—vanquished by her champion.

She felt him shift. His arms slipped around her and tightened possessively.

"Well?"

She rubbed her cheek against one hefty bicep. Shutting her eyes, she felt her lips curve. "I've forgotten."

Chapter 16

What staples will the demesne provide before winter?

A simple enough question, Eloise had thought, yet none within the castle could answer it. So she spent her fourth morning as chatelaine mounted on Jacquenta's back, finding out.

As Sir Eward had warned her, the storerooms were close to empty. While with the forests all around and Montisfryn and his knights in residence, the supply of meat was assured, the supply of grain was another matter.

She rode out with Rovogatti and Matt at her heels. She only had time to visit the nearer fields. Luckily, the workers knew enough of the holdings further down the valley to give her rough estimates of the yields. With careful management, twould likely be enough.

Reassured, she returned to the castle as the dinner hour drew nigh, riding through the bailey and into the courtyard. Rovogatti lifted her down before the keep steps. She was smoothing her gown when hard fingers gripped her elbow.

"I would have words with you, lady."

She glanced up. Even before her eyes reached Montisfryn's face, his tone had registered. Then she saw his eyes and the set of his jaw. Something had made him furious. "I am yours to command, lord."

He growled and swept her up the steps, striding without pause straight through the hall and up to the solar. As usual, the chamber was empty.

"What has so provoked you, lord?" she asked, the instant the door shut behind them. Hopefully, he would grasp the opportunity to vent his spleen and take the sting from his ire before he started on the poor unfortunate who had been so unwise as to vex him.

The tight grip on her elbow disappeared. She swung to face him. And realized who the poor unfortunate was.

His eyes were steely, his glance sharp as a scimitar. It pinned her as she took an involuntary step back.

"Did I not extract a promise from you, lady"—he stalked forward as she backed—"that while in my care you would never venture forth without a suitable escort?"

Eyes wide, she all but gasped, "I took Rovogatti and Matt." Her hips struck the table, forcing her to halt.

"*Suitable!*" He stopped two inches away. "By that I do not mean one man without a sword and a beardless boy!" Hands fisted on his hips, he towered over her; to look into his face she had to bend back.

"But…" He'd seen her ride in; he didn't know where she'd been. She smiled placatingly and laid a hand on his chest. "Nay—I only went to the nearer fields of the demesne."

There was no appreciable lessening in the turbulent fury that faced her. His eyes were agate-hard, the muscles in his jaw set. Beneath her palm, his chest felt like iron.

He leaned closer; mesmerized, she felt waves of raw anger lap about her.

"Lady—I care not where, nor how far, you have ridden. All I see is that you have ventured beyond my gates—without my permission, which, if memory serves, you were required to solicit—and with *no suitable protection.*"

His eyes had narrowed; she let hers do the same. "Nay, lord—I was out about my legitimate duties. And I was not for any time beyond the purview of your men on the walls."

His rage was on a tight leash; she felt it quiver.

"That is *not acceptable.* Henceforth you will take a full escort should you exit the gates." He swung away, the movement almost violent.

She grimaced. After a moment, she ventured, "Lord, I like it not having ten men at my back. Tis boredom supreme for them, and highly irritating to me to have my every breath watched over. Given I do not venture beyond the shadow of your walls—"

A snarl cut her off; he swung around, pinning her once more with his gaze. "Lady, I have told you what will be. Do you think to say me nay?"

She fought to keep her hands from her hips. "You are being unreasonable."

Alaun locked his gaze on hers; his chest rose as he drew in a steadying breath. "You are in *my* care—you are *my* responsibility."

"Aye—I have not questioned that."

"You will do as I say."

He watched as she digested that edict, prayed that she would accept it. Her solemn vow to do so was, he was quite certain, the only thing capable of calming the turmoil inside him.

Slowly, she folded her arms, her gaze narrowed, assessing. "I will do as you ask, provided you give me a sound reason for doing so."

He could give her one very good reason, but refused to even consider it. He eyed her menacingly. "You would put conditions on your obedience to your lord?"

She tilted her chin. "When my lord utters orders that appear quite ludicrous, tis merely sensible to request an explanation."

He scowled, then grunted. The unreasoning fear, the same cold terror that had gripped him twice before, was slowly receding. Each time it laid its chill talons on his soul, the effect grew worse; he was shaking inside. Abruptly, he swung away. "We are hard by the Welsh border; raiders sometimes ride close."

"Within bow-shot of your walls?"

Smothering a growl, he paced before her. "This area is no different from any other. Occasionally undesirable elements pass through."

"*Armed* undesirable elements?"

He shot her a malevolent glare. "After your encounter outside Marlborough, I would have thought you would have learned your lesson."

"Aye—I have learned not to ride unescorted through forests. But with Rovogatti and Matt with me, only an armed knight or a band of armed serfs could do me harm."

"Nay—an escort of two could be shot down easily enough by one man, then would you be defenseless."

Eloise lifted her eyes heavenward; raising her hands, palms up, she wordlessly appealed to the saints. "*On your land?*" She lowered her gaze to his. "With you and your knights constantly riding out, I would own myself surprised had you so much as a single illegally armed *serf* within three leagues, let alone a band of mercenaries. You're being ridiculous!"

He was pacing like a caged lion; now he swung to halt directly before her. Unrepentant, she met his stormy glare.

For a long moment, they waged a silent war; she could feel the tension that gripped him.

Then he closed his eyes, his lips compressing to a thin line. "Nay, Eloise—let us not argue." His voice had deepened. "I have told you what I wish. I would ask that you do this thing"—his lids rose; his eyes, still cloudy, captured hers—"for me."

Her eyes searched his; she drew in a deep breath. He hadn't given her a reason—he was playing chess again, even though the why of it defeated her.

"Very well." She frowned. "If it matters so much to you that I take a full escort when I ride outside your gates, so be it."

The relief that flooded him—his eyes, his whole frame—was so marked she could scarcely credit it.

He lifted her hand and dropped a kiss in her palm. "My thanks, lady."

She humphed. "Tis nearly time for dinner."

"Aye." He smiled winningly. "I will go fetch Lanella."

"Twould be helpful."

He turned away, then hesitated, her hand still in his. He looked down; his thumb caressed the backs of her fingers, then he lifted his eyes to hers. "I have been meaning to thank you for your help with Lanella."

"Nay—she has made me feel more than welcome. She reminds me of my own mother—tis no hardship to do what I can to ease her days."

He held her gaze. "Perhaps. Yet no other has accomplished as much—I doubt me another could."

"Nay." She waved the point aside. "You are making too much of it. I merely did what I could—I had a strong suspicion she had become reclusive through lack of encouragement otherwise." She met his gaze. "Tis not easy for a woman to suddenly find herself useless."

His lips twitched. "I can understand you would sympathize."

"Aye, tis a point another woman would see." She paused, then added, "You should not hold yourself at fault."

He met her gaze, then looked away. "I will fetch her down."

The gong clanged. He let go of her hand and strode to the door. She turned to the window; frowning, she stared at the blue-gray sky. The gong clanged again; with a quick shake of her head, she headed for the hall.

* * *

"There you be, lady. I was a-hoping I would catch you here."

At Meg's cracked tones, Eloise swung about. She was in the still-room, a chamber sealed behind thick stone walls on the ground floor of the keep, accessible only from the first floor via a steep stair. Small windows covered with thin horn set high in the walls let in narrows shafts of light. Built on bedrock, the air was evenly cool and dry, perfect for storing herbs and the elixirs and potions made from them.

The old woman stood in the doorway, struggling to catch her breath.

"Come and sit." Turning from her workbench, Eloise pulled out a stool. "Tis a fair haul up the steps and down the stairs."

She had only reclaimed the still-room three days ago; until then, there had been too much elsewhere needing her attention. The heavy beams overhead were festooned with bunches of herbs, still green for they had only been gathered yesterday. The herb-garden had run wild; the necessary pruning had yielded bunches of most of the herbs she regularly put by.

The beginnings of various extracts and potions lay scattered on the bench. Dusting her hands, she watched Meg ease her bulk onto the stool. "What brings you here, Meg?"

Folding her hands in her lap, Meg fixed her bright hazel eyes on Eloise's face. "Tis a favor I have to ask of ye, lady, and I tell ye now that I mislike how the lord might see it."

Eloise smiled. "What is this favor?" Despite the evidence of their eyes, which, as had been made abundantly clear over the past seven days, Montisfryn's people were well able to interpret, they persisted in treating his temper with an awe they couldn't seem to accept she didn't share. "If tis reasonable, then I will grant it. As our lord is a fair man, I see no reason to imagine any difficulties."

Meg shot her a skeptical glance. "Tis the matter of my successor, and her training."

Resuming stripping the feathery leaves from a branch of lad's love, Eloise raised her brows inquiringly.

Meg sighed gustily. "Eh, me, but I'm getting older, and tis in my mind that I won't be here forever. Tis Roseanne I've chosen to take over after me, lady. She's a strapping wench, well-liked, and strong enough to maintain order, yet not without a brain."

Nodding, Eloise conceded the point. Her observation of the wenches most favored by Montisfryn's senior men had brought Roseanne to her notice. The girl was far from daft, and uncommonly open and confident, untouched by any shadows despite her life.

"And, o'course, she's Montisfryn-born and bred—been here all her life."

Which, presumably, explained Roseanne's assurance. "But tis not in my sphere to supervise such arrangements." Eloise glanced at Meg. "And I doubt the lord would countenance me lending direct support."

Meg shook her head vigorously. "Nay—tis not that that I would ask. I can teach Roseanne all she needs to know, and the saints have not called on me just yet. Before they do, I'll have her firmly in charge, and teach her all 'bout drafts, and potions, and such as the girls do need for our business, if you take my meaning."

Eloise did. She nodded, and Meg went on, gazing earnestly at her, "Tis the things I don't know, lady, that I wondered if you would teach her. How to care for the little ones and treat the simple ailments. I know not much of that, but there's much need of it, and the castle's very large. If any sickness comes on us, tis the babes and girls as are the last to get treatment. If you could teach Roseanne just the simple things, and if she was to help you here preparing the specifics, I thought as how she might then be able to give care more promptly to the young'uns."

Eloise's brows had risen. She nodded. "Tis a valid point."

"And some of the girls was talking, seeing you in the garden yesterday. They say they could help keep it tidy in return. Little Marie—she's the Frenchie—'parently she started in a convent. She knows a thing or two 'bout planting, and nurturing, and such."

The offer was tempting. Eloise had had to supervise the weeding of the herb-garden most closely; the gardeners, men all, considered anything smaller than a bush totally without consequence.

"Your ideas are sound, Meg." Her fingers had stalled; Eloise set down the stripped branch. "Tis my feeling twould be wise to have someone other than myself trained in the healer's art." After a moment, she grimaced and met Meg's eye. "I would agree, yet I fear I must seek the lord's permission in this. The healer's art, even in simples, encompasses knowledge I dare not spread without his consent."

Meg's face fell. "I doubt he'll be agreeable, lady. Tis asking a lot, for Roseanne would have to work closely with you."

Eloise didn't try to brush the remark aside; Montisfryn wouldn't approve. Yet the commonsense of the suggestion was compelling. "Nay, do not give up hope. I will ask, and do everything I may to convince him."

After scrutinizing her expression, Meg humphed and hauled herself to her feet. "I'll leave you to your business then, lady." With a nod, she headed for the door, only to pause, hesitating, in the doorway.

Eloise raised her brows in mute question.

Meg shifted, then vouchsafed, "Tis a bit of advice, lady, if you'll take it. Twould be best if you saved your request until you and he are alone."

Eloise blinked.

"In your chamber," Meg added. "Tas been my experience men are more amenable at such times to persuasion."

The pointed look that accompanied those words very nearly overset Eloise. Heat seeped into her cheeks.

Meg saw it and snorted. "Pleasure him well, lady, and I'm thinking he'll agree to almost anything you ask."

Eloise's felt her cheeks burn.

Luckily, Meg didn't wait for a reply. With an unrepentant cackle that echoed eerily in the stairwell, she shuffled out.

With a belated glare at the empty doorway, Eloise relieved her feelings with an unladylike snort, then reached for a branch of verbena.

A week had passed since she'd first ridden into the castle; ever since, both she and Montisfryn had been furiously busy. After eighteen months' absence, the duties requiring his attention were manifold; he had to be everywhere—in court, in bailey and town, and riding through the countryside inspecting his vassals' holdings and his own. For her, there had been the storehouses, the gardens, and the dovecotes and beehives outside, the cooking, preserving, ale-making, spinning, weaving, and garment-making inside; all had had to be reviewed and practices up-dated. Winter loomed large; with a castle full to bursting, they would need all they could produce in the next few months.

Mixing the leaves of lad's love and verbena, she stuffed them into a linen pouch. Picking up needle and thread, she stitched the pouch's opening, squinting in the poor light.

Despite consistent effort, she had yet to make significant progress in bringing Montisfryn to his knees. A reluctant smile tugged at her lips. That he appreciated her wifely attentions she didn't doubt; he was always lustily generous in reciprocating. Nevertheless, there remained between them a certain wary reticence, as if he kept his true feelings behind a shield and, natural warrior that he was, he was reluctant to lower it.

Luckily, he seemed in no overt rush to drag her before the priest; she yet had time to convince him to trust her. In all other respects, their relationship, their partnership, albeit not yet blessed, was working.

Very well.

Tying the thread firmly, she tossed the pouch into a basket with a handful of others, each filled with a different combination of herbs. Dusting her hands on her cote, she cast a last glance around, then picked up the basket and walked to the door. Pulling the heavy oak door closed behind her, she headed for Lanella's chamber.

A late afternoon visit with Lanella had become an established part of her routine. It was a time she looked forward to, keen to glean the snippets Lanella let fall of Montisfryn's life. For her part, she'd freely confessed to most of her existence—the fact of her marriage, her years in the cloister and, later, at Versallet Castle, reserving only the details of her ill-fated marriage, details she no longer classed as relevant.

She paused before the arras barring the entrance to Lanella's chamber. Today, she would ask if Lanella knew of any female connections suitable to invite to stay—the first step in establishing her own group of ladies, something she had thought she would never do.

Smiling, she put a hand to the heavy tapestry and pushed it aside. "Good afternoon, lady. I've brought some sachets to sweeten your robes."

* * *

"Check, and mate."

Sitting forward in the chair before their bedchamber fire, Eloise stared at the destruction of her grand strategy. "I don't believe it." Her tone, a medley of disgust and incredulity, mirrored her feelings. With her eyes, she retraced their last moves, then she groaned. "Tis unfair!"

Alaun chuckled, his grin widening into a maddening smile. "Nay, lady. Tis what you earn for being both too cautious, then too impulsive."

"*Impulsive!*" Incensed at her twelfth successive loss, she glared. "I am *never* impulsive."

One brow arched; his golden eyes opened wide. "Am I to understand that your behavior last night was premeditated, lady?"

She blushed—furiously. "Twas not...I—" She broke off, her memories disrupting her defense. He'd been detained in the hall last night, discussing legal matters with Edmund. When Alaun had failed to appear for their nightly bout of chess, she'd retired, slightly miffed, to their bed. But sleep had eluded her. When he had finally parted the heavy curtains and slid beneath the furs, she had all but thrown herself at him. Needless to say, he'd been perfectly willing to catch her. Bending a look of haughty disdain on him, she retreated with, "Tis unchivalrous of you to tease me so."

He laughed and rose from the stool, stretched mightily, then extended a hand to her. "Perhaps, lady." His tone deepened. "Yet I have it in mind to tease you more this night."

She kept her eyes on his hand as heat blossomed within her. She remembered Old Meg, heard her words...Eloise looked up. "Stay a moment, lord. There's a matter I would discuss with you."

His expression clearing, he resumed his seat. "Say on, lady. You know you have my ear."

She knew that was true. He had pleased her greatly by bring his problems into their chamber and, as if he'd been doing so all his life, laying them before her. As they had debated the matters of law brought before him, she had begun to learn the ins and outs of Marcher lordship. He would listen to her views, sometimes agreeing, sometimes dismissing them, but never lightly. So she hesitated only long enough to marshal her arguments into battle-order—she held no illusions of easy victory.

"Tis the matter of an assistant to help me with the still-room, lord." Despite Meg's advice, she was determined to win the point on the field of logic, rather than in their bed. If they were partners in truth, he would listen to her arguments and weigh them on their merits. "I have been thinking much of the matter, as it's not wise to have only one person trained in healing when there's such a large community to be served."

He nodded. "There used to be an old woman and her daughter, but both are gone now." He met her gaze. "Tis hard to think of any who would suit. I would suggest Maud, but she has too much to do already with Lanella."

"Aye. And as there are presently no girls in training, there are none to act even in a temporary capacity."

Frowning, he nodded again.

Assuming her most earnest expression, she ventured, "Tis my thought, lord, that as the need is urgent what with winter coming on, we should not lightly dismiss any potential candidate."

His eyes narrowed, his golden gaze lance-sharp. "Who is it you have in mind, lady?"

There was an ominous ring to his tone. She didn't hesitate. "The girl known as Roseanne, lord."

"No."

She stared. "You've admitted the need for another to be trained. Roseanne is quick to learn—she could tend those in the outer bailey to relieve me of the load."

"No."

She assimilated that declaration of male decision. Allowing her expression to become as stony as his, she raised one brow. "Who, then, do you suggest?" She let a moment elapse before adding, "I would have you know that while there are herbs enough for the purpose, alone, I will not have time to prepare them as needed to last through winter and spring. Many might die before the thaw have I not the specifics with which to treat them."

Alaun narrowed his eyes even more. "I do not deny your need, lady, but Roseanne will not do."

"Why not?"

Suppressing the impulse to grind his teeth, he answered, his tone cutting, "I do not deny that she is quick to learn—Roland has frequently commented on the fact."

Eloise smiled—sweetly. Eyes darkly impassive, she inclined her head. "I am glad, lord, that her wit has been vouched for by one whom I know you trust."

The sting in her words slipped under his guard. He was rising, scowling, before he knew it; on his feet, he placed his hands on his hips. Discovering himself outmaneuvered, he glowered down at her. "I trust you well, lady. Thrust not that barb at me."

Eloise regarded him with calm skepticism. "How can you expect me to believe that when you will not take my advice in an area that is so peculiarly my domain?" And not yours was the inference, but she held the words back.

With a sound midway between a growl and a snarl, he spun about and paced. Then he halted, fixing her with a glance sharper than tempered steel. "Roseanne is a whore, lady. I will not have you consort with such."

"Roseanne is a woman—what she does with her nights does not concern me. Her days are her own and mostly free. She's quick-witted and has nimble fingers." She held his gaze. "I suspect Roland can vouch for that, too."

For an instant, she thought he might roar. The glance he bent on her brimmed with exasperation.

"Roseanne has all the needful traits for one handling herbs and potions." She noted how cloudy his eyes had become; well-versed in the tactics of such battles, she recognized the moment and delivered her disabling thrust. "If I do not shy from training her, why should you object?"

He eyed her grimly. "I like not the idea of you associating with whores."

She swallowed a wayward impulse to ask him why—did he imagine she might learn something too shocking even for him? "Tis my understanding the condition is not contagious."

She saw his lips twitch—and knew she'd won.

Disgruntled, not at all used to such defeat, Alaun heaved a sigh. "Nay, lady. You know tis not that that I fear."

Smoothly, she rose and came to stand before him, looking up into his face. "Yours fears are groundless. Twill not hurt me to train Roseanne as my assistant."

He held her dark gaze. "Tis not as I would have it, Eloise."

"Perhaps, yet there is much to be said for the notion, if you would have me tell you true."

"Oh?"

She told him of the other girls' offers to help with the herb-garden. Before he could object, she added, "Their help will be vital to get all in readiness."

When his scowl didn't soften, she offered, "I will undertake to train Roseanne solely within the still-room and herb-garden. There's no need for us to be together elsewhere."

He gazed into her upturned face, seeing her determination and the conviction that fueled it. He made one, last, half-hearted protest. "I like this not, lady."

The soft, disgruntled growl made Eloise smile. She laid a hand along his cheek. "Nay, lord." She looked deep into his eyes. "Trust me." Lowering her lids, she stretched up and touched her lips to his.

As she made to draw back, he growled. His arms locked her to him; his lips captured hers.

It was a storming in truth, his frustration finding an outlet in conquest. She yielded readily, clinging to him, wrapping her arms about his neck and holding tight as he ravaged her senses—a thoroughly enjoyable consequence of victory.

When he finally consented to raise his head, easing his hold on her as they turned without words to the bed, she grinned.

Trapping her before him, his fingers busy with the front lacing of her gown, Alaun glanced at her face. "Why such smugness, lady? Think you you will win all our arguments so easily?"

She flicked him a teasing glance. "Nay, tis just that I was thinking I must explain my tactics to Meg."

"Meg?"

"Aye. She suggested I approach you quite otherwise."

He snorted. Pressing the bodice of her gown wide, he unraveled the ribbons of her chemise and, slipping one hand beneath the soft materials, cupped her breast. Slowly, he brought his fingers around her nipple, smiling with satisfaction when she shuddered and closed her eyes. He lowered his head and drew the crinkling nub into his mouth, softly laving it with his tongue before suckling lightly.

Eloise gasped. Her fingers, twined in his soft locks, tightened on his skull.

"What did Meg suggest?"

Her legs gave way. She leaned against his supporting arm. "She said"—she broke off as he bared her other breast—"that if I pleasured you well"—he stroked her tightly furled nipple and her breath hitched—"you would agree to anything." She rushed the words out before his lips touched her aching flesh, then sighed deeply when they did.

After he'd rendered her witless, he dispensed with her clothes, leaving her to lean against one of the bedposts for the few moments it took him to strip. Naked, he drew her into his arms, moving suggestively against her.

The rasp of his crisp hair against her smooth skin drove her wild.

"I've been thinking."

Distracted, she blinked up at him, thoroughly dazed as one large hand curved about her bottom.

"About agreeing to your idea."

She frowned. He rarely changed his mind. "Why?"

Ignoring the question, Alaun stared at the wall. "Vacillating," he mused. "I rather think I'm suddenly unsure."

Looking down at Eloise, he arched a brow. "Perhaps you should follow Meg's advice—just to make certain of your victory?"

Her frown vanished, replaced by a wide, siren's smile. Brazenly, she rubbed her taut breasts against his chest, clearly delighting in the hiss of his indrawn breath.

"Mayhap twould be wise, lord," she purred. "Just to make sure."

With a wicked grin, she lowered her head to lay a tracery of nibbling kisses across the width of his chest. He closed his eyes the better to savor the pleasure as she moved from side to side, slowly working her way downward.

By the time he realized just what she intended, it was far too late. His jaw tightened as his fingers clenched in her braids; an unbearable tension gripped him. His heart thundered in his chest, his breathing more labored than in battle.

His last coherent thought was one of intense relief that she hadn't tried this method first.

Old Meg had had the right of it.

* * *

Two days later, Eloise solved the problem of how to determine what foodstuffs remained in the castle's capacious storehouses. The matter had been exercising her mind for days; she could ill-afford the hours necessary to sift through the odds and ends. Finally, the idea of using the castle's chaplain, along with the pages he instructed in their letters every morning, had dawned.

Standing in the shadowed mustiness of the largest storehouse in the inner bailey, she smiled as the chaplain and the undercook, summoned to pass judgment on the usability of remnants from years past, peered into a barrel of salt pork. Two pages, slate and chalk in hand, waited to take down the verdict, their faces fixed in concentration to make sure they missed nothing.

"Lady—I've been searching for you everywhere."

Eloise turned as a figure darkened the doorway. Squinting into the glare, she recognized Sir Edmund. "I'll leave you gentlemen to finish this," she announced, then made good her escape.

Emerging into the autumn sunshine, she smiled at Edmund. "You have discovered me, sir. Is anything amiss?"

"Nay, lady." The steward returned her smile. "'Tis merely that the carpenter is here. He had to look to some of the falconer's perches—I wondered if you wished to speak to him about the pigpens?"

She nodded. "Aye. The sooner that matter is in hand the better. Twill do us no good to have the beasts wandering the bailey—I doubt not our lord would disapprove."

"Indeed. The first time he backed into a sow while practicing swordplay would be the last of the sow, I make no doubt."

"Actually"—she smiled—"he's quite fond of pigs. I once saw him cradling a piglet in his arms."

When Edmund looked stunned, she laughed, but when he looked his question, she shook her head. "Nay—I'll not give away his secrets. But why not ask him yourself?"

Edmund looked intrigued enough to do so. She sincerely hoped he would. "Is the carpenter near the mews?" When Edmund assented, she laid a hand on his arm. "I can find my way there. You must have many matters awaiting your attention. I would not detain you."

"Nay, lady." Edmund smiled. "'Tis my duty to escort you. I find it no hardship."

Continuing beside him, she frowned. "How mean you 'your duty'?"

"Our lord has made it clear he would not have you unattended in the outer bailey, lady. In truth, 'tis a sensible precaution—you're yet new here, and there are townsfolk and sometimes strangers in the outer ward."

"Ah." She should, she supposed, have expected it.

They left the calm of the courtyard via the arched gateway, emerging into the merry bedlam of the outer ward. There were people everywhere, pot-boys and grooms playing an impromptu game, as well those of more sober mien bustling about their business at storehouse, forge, and armory. The stables lay to one side, with the mews beyond.

Surveying the vibrant scene, Eloise strolled towards the mews, Edmund beside her. Suddenly, Edmund made a choking sound and swung toward her, clearly protecting her from some sight passing beyond him.

"Edmund?" She was too polite to peer around him when he was so intent on sparing her sensibilities. "What is it?"

Edmund reddened, more, she thought, in anger than embarrassment. "'Tis nothing as should concern you, lady."

His next words, "And will hopefully soon be gone," reached her on a disgusted mutter. Too curious to let that pass, she waited until they were almost at the mews to glance casually back.

Elspeth Davarost was making for the inner ward, striding along in her usual, rapid and arrogant manner. From the heavily-cuffed gloves Eloise glimpsed as the girl disappeared into the shadows of the gateway, Eloise assumed Elspeth had just returned from flying her hawks. It was, apparently, a fancy she much indulged.

That, however, did not explain the wary, sidelong glances cast her by the castlefolk she encountered. Hastening to remove themselves from Elspeth's path, more than one glanced back, surreptitiously making the ancient sign of warding.

Frowning, Eloise faced forward.

The carpenter was waiting in the lee of the mews. A rough-hewn local, he reminded her of a knotty old oak, his hands twisted and scarred, yet still strong and deft.

"The pigpens? Aye—twould be all of ten years, maybe more, since I last had a look at 'em."

Nodding, he led the way to the pens, located in the corner where the inner and outer curtain walls met. Eloise waited while he and Edmund conferred on the repairs needed to reinforce the barriers against the hulking sows.

Her thoughts returned to Elspeth. A strange girl.

They had been introduced very briefly by Lanella; Eloise had been surprised to learn that Elspeth was eighteen, yet still unwed. Although they'd exchanged barely two words since, Elspeth had taken to watching Eloise, much in the manner of a cat at a mousehole, even as she visually devoured Montisfryn at every opportunity. He seemed oblivious; Eloise, however, found Elspeth's strange, colorless stare disturbing. Sternly quelling a shiver, she turned back to the matter at hand.

"I would say the end of the week, lady," the carpenter replied in response to her query. "Should not take longer."

"Good." She raised her brows. "The normal rates?"

After three minutes' brisk haggling, they agreed on a price. She and Edmund were turning away when the carpenter stopped them.

"A word in your ear, steward. For the lord. About those chairs he ordered—the one to match the one in his chamber and the dowager's chair for the hall. He's in luck—the wood can be had in the town, so I won't need to go to Worcester as I'd thought. He said he wished for them as soon as may be—you could tell him both should be ready by the end of the week after next."

"I'll do that." Edmund nodded, clearly pleased.

Behind her calmly impassive expression, Eloise wondered.

As if in answer to her thoughts, Montisfryn emerged from the inner bailey. Scanning the throng, he saw them, and made straight for them, the smile on his face making it clear he wasn't after his steward. It seemed doubtful he even saw the older man.

Edmund took his invisibility in good part. With a bow, he smilingly withdrew.

Montisfryn halted before her, his gaze caressing her face. "I am bound for the demesne, lady. I'd thought to check on the colts and fillies born since my departure. Are you busy—or can you spare an hour to accompany me?"

Her heart leapt. Rarely could they spend time together during their busy days. She returned his smile. "Aye, lord. I will make time."

His brows rose arrogantly; his eyes teased. "Even should it mean taking time from your herbs and potions, lady? You surprise me—I had thought such matters were pressing."

"Aye, they are. But I have an assistant now, lord, as you might recall, and one needs to preserve some perspective in life, think you not?"

He smiled, his gaze lingering. "Aye, lady, that I do. Hurry and find your cloak. I'll get the horses and meet you by the keep steps."

She needed no further urging. Walking briskly back to the keep—it would never do for the castlefolk to see their chatelaine running—she hurried through the hall and up the stairs.

Turning into the upper corridor, she saw a slim figure coming toward her. The rapid gait and the tangle of straggly red tresses identified Elspeth.

Eloise slowed. Without a sound, Elspeth came on. Although she had not conquered the ladylike art of gliding, her footfalls were silent. Half an accomplishment, presumably better than none.

To Eloise's surprise, Elspeth didn't slow, but continued past her. Elspeth's expression remained distant, her features registering no awareness of Eloise.

A chill sensation swept Eloise's nape. Pausing, she turned, studying the younger woman. Elspeth had changed into a fresh cote of ice-blue. The color heightened the insipidity of her slack features and emphasized her pallor.

Without a backward glance, Elspeth disappeared around the corner.

Eloise shook her head; wondering, she continued on her way. Only as she pushed open the door to the anteroom did she realize that that corridor led to Montisfryn's chamber—and nowhere else.

Frowning, she lifted her cloak from its hook on the wall and swung it about her shoulders.

But she forgot Elspeth, and the unease the girl raised in her, in the sheer exhilaration of riding out with Montisfryn. Only in their more intimate moments did she think of him by his first name; strong and impressively large, mounted on his gray alongside her, he returned the townsfolk's greetings as they rode through the cobbled streets. Glancing at him, allowing her eyes to feast, she decided he was the embodiment of the most important of the lordly virtues—strong, admittedly arrogant, but protective, too.

The very opposite of Sir Howell Davarost. The baron had moved to sit beside her at table. Despite her best efforts, she had succeeded in coaxing no more than a few colorless phrases from him. He held a wealthy manor not far from Worcester, yet he was so retiring, so very weak, he melted into the paneling in the presence of Montisfryn and his robust knights.

Patiently sitting her palfrey while Montisfryn spoke to the guards on the bridge, Eloise surveyed the mounted troop of men-at-arms behind them.

Reconciled to the inevitable, she hadn't even commented when they'd fallen in as she and Montisfryn had crossed the outer bailey.

Finally quitting the town, they rode south, then splashed across a ford a mile below the castle and climbed toward the higher pastures devoted to the most acclaimed of Montisfryn's possessions—the warhorse stud.

Shifting to a canter, they let their horses stretch their legs on a long upward slope. She drew the crisp air deep into her lungs; the scents of summer's demise rose about them, rich and earthy. Leaves piled in drifts beneath the trees; shrill birdcalls echoed through the branches. The *clump* of hooves on the lush ground thudded like a heartbeat around her.

It was the turn of the season, the fruit of summer's fecundity poised at the moment where the lifeblood would ebb; soon, it would wither.

But today, life was rich and full, and all about her.

When they drew rein at the top of the rise, she glanced back at the town and castle, then exchanged a glance with Montisfryn, delight in her eyes. He smiled, amused. As one, they set their mounts along a shady path between the trees.

They ambled, the men-at-arms hanging back to afford them greater privacy. The chill of the shadows reminded Eloise of another chill lately encountered. She glanced at Montisfryn. "Lord, is there anything amiss with Elspeth Davarost?"

Alaun blinked, and rapidly canvassed his options. "She is not, perhaps, the most conventional of young women." He glanced at Eloise, his expression impassive. "She has been much indulged, I fear."

"Aye, but Lanella has told me she is gone eighteen." Frowning, Eloise met his gaze. "'Tis very old, lord, to be unwed."

Reading the questions writ clearly in her eyes, Alaun hesitated. When it came to it, he felt no more at ease explaining Elspeth's affliction than did her sire. He might rail at Davarost's inability to face reality, but he, too, shied from stating the truth in plain words. He recognized Elspeth's illness for what it was, but given Elspeth would be leaving soon, he could see no reason to burden Eloise with the knowledge. No more than he would she be comfortable with the fact—worse, she might think to help Elspeth in some way.

That thought was unsettling; the possibility of Eloise drawing close to such strangeness was not one he would countenance. "'Tis not something I would have you concern yourself with, lady." The words came out as a brusque command, harsher than he'd intended. Seeing her surprise, he grimaced. "Nay, Eloise. She will be leaving soon, and is of no importance to us."

Eloise was puzzled, not least by his uncharacteristic abruptness. "But 'tis most unusual, lord, to find one of her station so poorly-prepared. She has no accomplishments that I've yet discerned, and seems ill-inclined to learn. Are her parents so disinterested that they seek not a marriage for her?"

She glanced up in time to see Montisfryn's expression grow stern.

"Nay, lady—leave be. You have concerns aplenty without adding Elspeth Davarost to the list." He let only a bare second elapse before commanding, "Come—let us ride."

Distracted by the need to keep pace with him, Eloise mentally consigned Elspeth Davarost to the nether regions of her mind, only too ready, when all was said and done, to fall in with his suggestion.

They broke from the trees following a well-beaten track over a broad sweep of open ground. Ahead stood a formidable wooden palisade, within which a stone tower rose high above the treetops. As they cantered toward it, Montisfryn explained, "The fields closest to the fort hold the yearlings. These enclosures"—a broad sweep of his gauntleted hand indicated the fields on either side—"hold the mares in foal. That way, if an attack is feared, the guards can get the most vulnerable animals inside the compound before any raiding party gets close. The tower is visible from the keep, so a signal to the castle will call the garrison to their relief."

Casting her eye over the terrain, Eloise recalled how well he played chess. "Do the Welsh raid this far?"

"Aye, but they rarely come close to us—our horses hold little temptation for them. Destriers are not agile, and their mountain tracks require great nimbleness. Nay, tis English, outlaws and others who should know better, who have ever been the stud's greatest threat."

"But where are the stallions? Aren't they the most valuable stock of all?" She turned to see him smile.

"Aye, but tis not advisable to approach a stallion trained for war while he is with his mares. The few who have tried..." He shrugged. "We have rarely found enough left to bury."

Eloise grimaced.

They'd reached the heavy gates of the hill-fort. The retainers who held the stud were a blend of soldier and herdsman; they knew how to fight and they knew horses. Leaving their mounts within the palisade, she accompanied Montisfryn as, together with the master-in-charge, he strolled the nearest paddocks examining the newest arrivals with a keen and critical eye.

To her, the colts and fillies appeared much as young horses everywhere, skittish, high-spirited, and gangly. The mares in foal, however, were undeniably elegant beasts, sleek and powerful, muscles rippling beneath sheening coats as they ambled about their paddocks. Nevertheless, it was only when, remounted and led to a large paddock some way from the fort, she set eyes on a prize stallion, his brood mares about him, that she fully comprehended the awesome reality.

"He's beautiful," she breathed in response to Montisfryn's raised brow. The destrier stallion stood watching them suspiciously even though they had halted well back from the fence. Montisfryn held Gabriel tight-reined, preventing the gray stallion from issuing challenge.

As if to gauge their intent, the destrier stallion lowered his head and pawed the ground, one heavy hoof churning the rocky turf like a spoon going through custard. Muscles bunched and flowed beneath his black skin.

"Don't move." Montisfryn's words were a whisper.

In the presence of true majesty, Eloise was quite content to sit and stare.

When they made no response to his taunting, the stallion tossed his head and, in a clear show of indifference, turned toward his mares.

Eloise studied the horses grouped in a loose bunch beyond the stallion; each had a padded cloth secured over their back. "Why do these mares have blankets? The mares in foal didn't have such protection."

She glanced up to see Montisfryn's lips compress, then ease as he replied, his voice devoid of expression. "Tis to protect them from the stallion's hooves."

For a moment, the point escaped her. Then a blush rose to her cheeks. "Oh."

As if he had heard, the stallion chose that moment to demonstrate—amply. Resisting the impulse to turn away—or at least close her eyes—Eloise refused to succumb to the fluster that threatened. It was, after all, a scene she had witnessed oftimes before, albeit never performed with such gusto. Destrier stallions, it was glaringly obvious, were bred for their staying power. Resolved to show no embarrassment, she let her gaze unfocus, not, however, before an unexpected thought flowed across her mind.

How would it feel…she suddenly felt very warm.

Beside her, Alaun frowned, the impromptu demonstration bringing vividly to mind what he could not accomplish with his own chosen mate. He did not dare approach Eloise from behind; the memory of how she had reacted on the single occasion he had was permanently etched in his mind.

He slanted a glance at her; the ache in his loins intensified. Swallowing a curse, he swung Gabriel about. "Come. It's getting late. We should return."

Side by side, the small troop at their back, they cantered through the paddocks and down onto the track to the ford.

Glancing at Montisfryn's profile, Eloise found it stern, patriarchal. "I've been thinking, lord, that twould be useful to order a second chair for your chamber, so that we may both be comfortable of an evening. Twill be winter soon, and we'll have long hours to spend so. Think you I should speak to the carpenter?"

Eyes innocently wide, she looked up at him.

Frowning, he slanted her a glance. "Lady, I have yet to hear that you will call me husband." He waited; she said nothing. With a fleeting grimace, he continued, "Tis clear you need more time—we will wait until you are ready." Looking ahead, he added, "I do not wish you to feel pressured by such things."

It was a very good thing that he wasn't looking at her, else he'd have seen the love that lit her eyes. "Aye, perhaps you are right." She hoped he wouldn't wonder at the brilliance of her smile. She looked around. "Are all these fields part of the demesne?"

His frown easing, he nodded. They ambled on through the sunshine, she questioning, he answering, their thoughts very much on each other.

High above on the roof of the keep, Elspeth hung over the battlements, studying the riders avidly. Eyes used to following the flight of hawks had no difficulty discerning their expressions.

"My lord looks content—doubtless he's tumbled her in the grass somewhere." Ignoring the gasp that elicited from Mistress Martin, the only one near enough to hear, Elspeth continued, taking a perverse delight in the consternation she knew she was causing her keeper, "I wonder if they did it while watching one of his stallions mount a mare? I would wager he took her the same way. She's smiling, too, so I warrant she's had her pleasure."

Shrugging, Elspeth turned to gauge the effect of her words. "Then again, I imagine such women are content enough to be used anyhow, for it shows their master still has need of them. Tis undoubtedly so, think you not?"

"*Mistress Elspeth!*" Martha Martin had only just succeeded in catching her breath, so her scandalized accents lacked the force of her feelings. Round-eyed, the stout, tallish woman stared at her charge as if Elspeth had just sprouted horns and a tail.

Elspeth smiled, superciliously condescending. "Nay, mistress, tis the way of the world." She dismissed her crudity with a wave. "I know well how my life is to be. Fear not—I like the scenario well enough." Folding her arms beneath her small breasts, she leaned again on the battlements and surveyed the fields. "I will enjoy being mistress of all this."

"What nonsense is this, Elspeth?" Martha Martin regarded her charge with mounting horror.

"Tis not nonsense at all, Martha—I tell you true." Elspeth crooned her words into the wind. "I'm to be Montisfryn's wife—we were betrothed long ago, when I was but a babe. Naturally, we couldn't be married ere now, for I was first too young, and then he was summoned to France. Now he's returned and we'll be married soon. He's ordered a dowager's chair for the hall, did you know?"

Martha Martin's mind reeled. She had told them, warned them, to watch their words in front of the little witch, but Sir Howell and his lady had grown so accustomed to overlooking Elspeth, to acting, indeed, as if she wasn't really there, that they had waved away her concern. Here was the result.

Sir Howell and Lady Davarost had been frank in explaining their links with the Montisfryn household when they had hired Martha to watch Elspeth some weeks before. Martha had performed a like service for others, and was aware of the possible dangers; she had suspected Elspeth of eavesdropping at the time. Lady Davarost had mentioned the suggestion that had been made at Elspeth's birth; it was nothing unusual for a young nobleman to be betrothed to his mother's goddaughter. But, as Martha had understood it, the matter had never progressed beyond a suggestion—Elspeth's oddity had become apparent at an early age.

But trying to convince Elspeth, such as she was, that there was no betrothal would be so much wasted effort. Martha knew that well enough. Saints alive, what now?

Drawing breath, she focused on her charge, only to discover that Elspeth had turned and was watching her intently.

"Do you fear I'll make trouble over Lady de Cannar?" Elspeth didn't wait for an answer. "How little you know me, Martha. Why, I'm delighted Montisfryn has shown so much understanding of my wishes that he's thought to provide us with such an excellent chatelaine. She is excellent, is she not?"

"Aye. But—"

"And you must admit, he's been particularly clever in finding one who will also warm his bed. I can only be grateful that he's realized that *I* will not be willing to do so."

Martha choked.

Elspeth grimaced. "I suppose I will have to do it sometime, to provide him with his heir." She waved dismissively. "But that can wait for later. For now, I'm perfectly willing for Lady de Cannar to continue to meet his needs."

"Elspeth, Lady de Cannar is *not* Montisfryn's mistress. Please do not even make reference to such an idea."

Elspeth's lip curled scornfully. "Think you I know not what goes on in his chamber of nights? Why, the room verily reeks of their lust every morn."

Martha briefly closed her eyes.

Elspeth's eyes grew smaller, brighter. She chuckled, a cunning expression stealing over her pale face. "They think I don't know of such things, don't they? They think I'm a mindless ninny in that regard. But I know all about it—more than you, I warrant."

Refocusing on Martha, Elspeth smiled, inviting her to acknowledge her cleverness. "I sneak out at night to the stables, early enough to be before them. Tis remarkable how many of my father's grooms use the loft for their trysts. Tis easy to watch in the moonlight." Her gaze sharpened, glowing with a feverish intensity, while her lips fell slack. "I've seen it all—from the back, from the front, standing up, lying down. Did you know one of the maids uses her mouth?"

When Martha goggled, Elspeth assured her, "Tis true." She nodded, clearly recalling the event. "Tis a most amazing sight. And then there's the other way, too. One of the grooms tells all the wenches that tis best that way so they won't swell with his seed." She cast a sly glance at her stunned companion.

Blanking her expression, Martha struggled to get a grip on the situation. She had suspected her charge of some degree of voyeurism, had, indeed, suspected Elspeth was far more active in many ways than anyone supposed, but nothing had prepared her for this.

Elated by her companion's astonishment, a natural response to so much cleverness and knowledge revealed all at once, Elspeth glowed. Slipping an arm through Martha's, she turned the unresisting woman toward the stairs, leaning close to say, "I learned all about couplings in the hayloft, Martha. I've been watching for years." Elspeth smiled, smugly superior. "Perhaps you should come with me next time?"

Martha closed her eyes and shuddered.

Chapter 17

"'Tis bitter, tis true." Taking another sip of the alewife's suspect brew, Eloise wrinkled her nose. "Yet tis strong enough. Mark the barrel for use late on a feast day—twill easily pass muster then."

"Aye, lady." Relieved, the alewife grinned. "After the second barrel, they never knows what they be supping, anyhow."

Smiling, Eloise nodded, then, senses suddenly quivering, she turned as a large shadow blocked the light.

Montisfryn stood framed in the doorway, his gaze on the alewife. "Leave us."

The woman bobbed and scurried past him; shooting a quick grin at Eloise, she tugged the door closed behind her.

Halfway across the room, Alaun paused, engulfed in unexpected gloom. Two small windows set high in the buttery's stone walls threw shafts of weak light across the earthen floor. Eyes adjusting, he strode on to halt before Eloise.

Looking down at her face, aglow with welcome, his own softened; he grimaced. "A messenger has arrived, lady. Sir Kendrick, who you know, has struck a problem in repossessing his lands which lie on my northern boundaries. He's asked for my support—I must go to his aid."

Her smile didn't waver, but the glow dimmed. "Will you be gone long?"

"Twill take two days to settle Sir Kendrick's business, but having ridden thus far, I should take the opportunity to call on my other vassals in the area before winter sets in."

"Aye." She laid a hand on his arm. "Tis the wisest course."

"I will be gone at least three days, likely more." Raising a hand, he cradled her cheek.

She turned her head and pressed her lips to his palm. "I will await your return, lord."

The invitation in her dark eyes was too tempting. He lowered his head, his lips hungry for hers.

Only too ready to meet his need, Eloise pressed herself to him, her arms stealing about his neck, eager to farewell him as a loving wife should.

With a groan, he broke from the increasingly ardent embrace. Feathering kisses along her jaw, he drew back. "Nay, lady. Tis enough."

His gruff tone contradicted his words.

"Nay, lord." With her own supple strength, she drew him back. "I want you." She took his lips again, and let her hands wander.

Alaun felt his body tighten in response. He steeled himself to resist. "Lady, I have a troop mounted and waiting."

"They will wait."

"Nay, Eloise—twill take too long to go to our chamber."

"Then take me here. Now. I want to feel you deep inside me again before you go."

It had been some time since he'd last suffered her words, yet she had clearly not lost the knack. He was hard and throbbing, aching for her now. Gritting his teeth, he tried to ease back. "I would not, lady. Tis not suitable—"

His voice suspended; his eyes widened before his lids fell. "*Saints in heaven!*"

Her fingers had slipped beneath his clothes, finding their way through the layers to his rigid staff. Long digits caressed him, nails scoring lightly, up and down, until he thought he would explode.

Confident she'd overcome his scruples, Eloise raised a hand to his cheek. "Take me now, lord." She kissed him again, then eased back a little, smiling knowledgeably. "Twill be quick enough."

On a groan, his resistance collapsed. His arms crushed her to him as he bent his head, his lips tracing the curve of her throat down to the throbbing pulse at its base. "I would not hurt you, lady."

"Nay, you will not." Eyes closed, she arched her neck to give him better access. "You have taken me quick before, if you recall. On the river bank."

Alaun recalled—very well; his hands were already tucking up her skirts. His flames flaring high, he raised his head and scanned the chamber. They were surrounded by barrels of every description, wine tuns and the massive casks in which the castle's ale was brewed. There was no suitable surface on which to lay her; the barrels that were high enough had too great a girth.

There was no possibility of turning back—she'd set his fires too well. He groaned. "Lady, I would have you remember this was your idea."

"Aye, lord—I take full responsibility." Her teasing smile suggested she did so very gladly.

He lifted her. For a moment, he held her, her softness poised above his hardness; she gazed down into his eyes as she wrapped her long legs about his hips. He lowered her slowly, impaling her inch by slow inch.

Lids falling in time with her descent, Eloise felt him surge the last fraction to embed himself inside her. She couldn't breathe. Her body quivered, straining, muscles paralyzed by a need she could neither suppress nor assuage. On a half-sob, she buried her face in his shoulder and clung. He lifted her, then eased her back, setting a rhythm that accelerated rapidly.

Reassured by the slickness of her heated sheath, Alaun loosed his reins and let his body have its way. She gave herself completely and he took all she had to give, sinking deep into her luxurious softness, feeling her cling, muscles tightening, then easing as she loved him. Slender and supple in his arms, she gasped and trembled as the tempo rose.

Engrossed in the swelling symphony, Eloise didn't realize he had walked to the wall until she felt its hardness at her back. Hands gripping his shoulders, fingers biting deep, she raised her head and braced her heated body against the cool stone. Each powerful thrust rocked her; she gasped his name as she felt the tension rising. Then his lips were on hers, his tongue surging against hers, plunging deeply in time with his body.

They burst through the wall of flames simultaneously, flying high, propelled by purest passion. They clung together as sensation peaked, senses engulfed, no reality beyond their fusion.

Then all was silent.

Breaths mingling as they struggled for air, their gazes locked, gold drowning in the dark.

The tide slowly ebbed, leaving them sated and whole.

Sharing gentle, slightly sheepish kisses, they disengaged, fumbling as they readjusted their clothing until they were once more lord and lady.

Roland was watching when they finally emerged into the light of day. Seated atop his palfrey, he had whiled away the time since the alewife had left in a discussion with Sir Humphrey, Montisfryn's castellan, also one of the party. Neither he nor Sir Humphrey, nor any of the twenty men-at-arms arrayed at their backs, had the slightest doubt over what had transpired behind the buttery door. Such was the privilege of command.

With amused tolerance, Roland stretched and stifled a yawn. And wondered, not for the first time, how long it would be before his cousin and the lady were wed. The whole castle—nay, the entire estate—was waiting for the word. Watching as the pair strolled into the sunlight, eyes only for each other, their garments peculiarly precise, he couldn't believe the celebrations would long be delayed.

Alaun paused in a patch of sunlight to look down at the woman by his side. "Take care while I am absent, lady."

It was an order—she knew it. She smiled at his frown. "Aye, lord. I will." Then her glance turned mischievous. "But I doubt not that you have left me well-guarded."

"Rovogatti does not go with me. If you need to go beyond the inner bailey, he is yours to command." He hesitated, then added, "Watch for my return, lady."

"I will. Every day." Her eyes met his, saying far more. Then she raised her chin. "Fare you well, lord."

His eyes scanned her face, touched her eyes for one last moment, then he turned away.

Eloise watched as he crossed the courtyard, pulling on his riding gloves before swinging up to Gabriel's back. Taking up his reins, he spoke a word of command and wheeled; the walls rang with the echo of steel-shod hooves as he and his troop rode out.

* * *

Two days later, Eloise was sitting with Lanella; Maud had taken the opportunity to go for a walk. Both Eloise and her prospective stepmother-in-law were embroidering; Eloise could not comprehend how, with her hands half-paralyzed, Lanella yet managed to turn out such exquisite work.

"Habit," Lanella had replied when asked.

Today, however, Eloise had persuaded Lanella to tell her own story. Lanella had commenced with her girlhood on her father's manor near Gloucester, and progressed by easy stages to her marriage.

"Aye, we were happy," she admitted. "Very happy." For a moment, she seemed sunk in pleasant memories; after a quick glance, Eloise didn't intrude. Then Lanella sighed, a soft smile on her lips. "Indeed, it took some time before I realized exactly *how* happy."

Eloise frowned. She snipped off a thread. "What mean you by that?"

Still smiling, Lanella scooped up her needle. "You must remember I was very young when we married, and I was Edmund's second wife. I assumed he had married me for my dowry, and to provide a mother for Alaun." Her smile grew misty. "It took me years to realize that Edmund's reticence, and his overly smothering care of me, were not, as I'd mistakenly thought, the attitudes of a man toward a young bride he regarded as a daughter." She chuckled. "I can still remember how bewildered I was at his anger—nay, *fury*—the day I rode out with only five men as escort."

Eloise stilled, her needle frozen in midair. "He was angry?"

"Oh, not just angry." Her eyes on her work, Lanella's smile grew broad. "Quite beside himself. Ranting, raving—it made no sense at all. I had only ridden down to the market."

Eloise blinked, then frowned at her stitching. "The incident had a greater significance?"

"*Much* greater, although I did not know it at the time." Lanella reached for the shears. "It took me *years* to break down his resistance, and it wasn't as if I was not warming his bed nightly, either."

She smiled wryly. "I daresay they are all the same, these poor men of ours. They are trained to regard any soft emotion as a danger, a vulnerability they must hide at all costs. When love comes upon them, they cannot admit it, nor put it into words. Tis to their actions we women must look—tis forever how they give themselves away."

Staring blankly at her work, Eloise made no answer.

Lanella sighed. "Twas ever so, right to the end. If I was not precisely where Edmund expected me to be within his carefully orchestrated protection, twould be the devil and more to pay. But twas love that made him so—once I realized, I could hardly resent it."

When Lanella fell silent, Eloise made no move to prompt her. Together they sat, haloed by weak sunshine, fingers busy, both absorbed with thoughts of love.

* * *

On the morning of her fourth lordless day, Eloise strode the battlements of the keep, briskly impatient. Her gaze raked the pale ribbons of the roads to the north, but discovered no sign of horsemen riding in. The day was overcast; the wind tugged at her braids and snapped the pennon on the flagpole high above.

With a humph, she stopped at one corner, tucking a wayward wisp of hair beneath her crespine. Her mood was not improved by her tiredness; she had had but little sleep over the past three nights. For some mysterious reason, succumbing to slumber without a certain large male body sprawled beside her was now exceedingly difficult.

She was perfectly certain he would not have been similarly afflicted.

Grimacing, she leaned against the battlements and looked out. She hoped he would come today. Aside from anything else, her courses were due—any day, although, as was her habit, she hadn't kept track; the womanly curse made itself known without her needing to remember it. By her vague calculation, it was more than twenty days since they had left her father's castle, which meant that, if Montisfryn didn't arrive soon, she wouldn't be able to greet him as she—and he—would wish.

Which would certainly put a pall on their private celebrations.

She had decided, finally and absolutely, to call him husband. Self-delusion had never been her strong suit—if she had entertained any doubt that she loved him, completely and utterly, the past four days had eradicated it.

She had missed him—dreadfully. And now, thanks to Lanella, she had the proof she'd needed of the nature of his regard for her. She had already begun to suspect, but Lanella's words had lifted the veil from the truth. He loved her—even if he never got the words out, she was strong enough to live with that. As Lanella had said, actions spoke louder, and more convincingly, than words.

Now all that remained was to tell him.

Just as soon as he got back.

With a last darkling glance at the empty roads, she gave a muted snort, and headed for the stairs.

The afternoon brought the first truly chill winds, driving puffy gray clouds across the sky. She retired to the stillroom, secure in the bowels of the keep and blissfully draft-free. There, she found Roseanne carefully measuring leaves into a mortar.

"Tis the ointment for wounds, lady," Roseanne said, as Eloise made her way to the bench.

"Ah, yes. Be sure you grind the amaranthus flowers well. They do not work efficiently otherwise."

"Tis a puzzle to me, lady." Roseanne stopped to brush back her tousled curls. "You call this amaranthus, yet am I sure tis the flower of love-lies-bleeding."

"Aye, tis confusing sometimes." Eloise reached for a bottle of herbs left to slowly infuse into oil. "There are many names for the most useful herbs. I call amaranthus so because I learned my lore in a convent where Latin was much used, but tis the same thing, call it what you will."

Roseanne attacked the leaves with vigor. "If tis all the same to you, lady, I would use the simple names. Aside from all else, twill remind me for what the herb is used."

"Tis not a bad idea." Eloise peeked into the mortar. "While you finish that, I will strain the extracts, and then we'll go through my box."

A companionable silence descended as they worked side-by-side. Small lamps were set high on the walls; they burned a fine oil which gave off little smoke to foul the hanging herbs. With leaden skies outside, the lamps were all lit; flickering light played over the scene. The soothing aromas of lavender and rosemary permeated the air, wormwood, rue, and other aromatics reaching scented fingers through the dominant tones.

When their chores were completed, Eloise lifted her camphorwood box down to the bench and opened it. Roseanne pulled up a stool and sat.

Eloise had brought her herb-box to the stillroom because she was no longer sure it was wise to leave it largely untended in their chamber. At first, she had thought the changes in the furnishings were no more than mistaken memory, but then the chess pieces were no longer in checkmate as she and Alaun had left them. She had noted the position on the night after he had left, when she'd retired alone to their room; last night, the pieces had been moved. And her herb-box had no longer been square on the shelf, as she had left it.

Bilder and the maids were always most careful when handling anything in that room, but the chamber lay empty for much of the day.

Her conclusions had sent a shiver down her spine. She'd resolved to remove her herb-box—it contained potent and therefore dangerous remedies—to the stillroom, where the contents could be dispersed among the range of less powerful simples.

"These are the medicaments I carry when traveling, each for a good reason." Unpacking the box, she named each packet of leaves, flowers, or bark, and described its use.

She had finished with the packets and had just started on the ointments when Elspeth wandered in.

Despite a wish not to react, Eloise stiffened. Turning, Roseanne frowned intimidatingly.

"Pay no heed to me." Elspeth waved an airy hand. "I just thought to inspect this area today."

Roseanne bridled; Eloise glanced at her warningly, then, her calm mask in place, resumed her recitation of the manifold uses of agrimony paste.

Despite her occupation, Eloise remained supremely conscious of Elspeth as the younger woman ambled about the room, blankly staring up at the drying herbs, then examining the bottles on the shelves.

Inwardly, Eloise grimaced; the sense of unease Elspeth always invoked in her was deepening by the minute.

Elspeth edged nearer, then nearer, overt interest gradually claiming her.

Eloise broke off and fixed her with a frosty glance. "Is there something you need, mistress? A dose of something, perhaps?"

Elspeth blinked, her pale eyes unreadable. "Nay." To Eloise's disquiet, the girl licked her lips. "But I would listen to your discourse. Tis quite fascinating, I vow."

Roseanne made a rude noise.

Much as she agreed with Roseanne, Eloise felt compelled to encourage the first sign she had seen that Elspeth had any interest whatever in remedying the deficiencies of her upbringing. "Very well, but please sit." She pushed forward the other stool. "You distract me when you wander so."

True, yet Eloise was honest enough to acknowledge her ulterior motive. Elspeth was rarely still, fidgeting and flitting about constantly; with luck, she would find the constraint of a stool too fatiguing, and flit somewhere else.

But Elspeth surprised her, sitting preternaturally still, even stiller than Roseanne, as Eloise continued her lecture. Elspeth's pale blue gaze remained vacant, yet oddly intent, as if hearing of diseases and cures enthralled her. By the time Eloise had described all her ointments and started to lift out the vials of syrups and oils, she was resigned to Elspeth's presence.

"This is syrup of wild poppies." Eloise held up three tiny vials of golden liquid. "Twill bring on sleep, but must be used judiciously. Tis not as strong as the Eastern poppy, but if too much is given, then the person may sleep unto death." Laying aside the vials, each holding a small thimbleful, she recited the details of the preparation, then passed on to the next vial—oil of betony.

Slack-lipped, Elspeth sat on her stool, no hint of expression in her empty eyes.

Quelling a shiver, Eloise set forth her most potent remedies, wishing there was one that would ease her chill.

* * *

Her cure came in the guise of her lord and lover, who returned to his castle with the setting sun. Summoned by a single clarion note blown from the top of the keep, his household turned out en masse to greet him. He rode straight to the steps of the keep. The courtyard filled with the usual pandemonium, grooms rushing up to claim the horses, squires hastening to retrieve weapons from the saddles.

He looked well, Eloise thought, as she stood, proudly contained, inwardly joyous, at the top of the steep steps. The wind had ruffled the heavy locks of his hair and brought color to his cheeks. He dismounted, greeted Edmund with a nod, then he was coming up the steps, taking them three at a time. His expression as he joined her was set and impassive, but his eyes burned.

"Lady." He grasped her arm, forcefully turning her into the hall. "I need a bath. Immediately. I would have you tend me in our chambers."

"Aye." Surprised, Eloise felt his coiled tension via his grip on her arm. "But are you and your knights not hungry, lord?"

He glanced down at her. "I am famished, lady, and the others will be, too. Supper can wait."

Eyes widening, realizing that whatever else had to wait, he would not, she gathered her wits and signaled her staff. He released her to give her orders, but immediately she had done, he summoned her with a glance to where he had propped against the lord's table, listening to his lieutenants' reports. Brusquely approving the decisions they had made in his absence, he dismissed them, then briefly conferred with Edmund before turning to her.

"Come, lady."

Her elbow once more locked in a viselike grip, she kept her expression as impassive as his as he guided her to the stairs. Once upon them, she felt compelled to ask, "What of Lanella?"

"She will survive without my greeting until I am in suitable case to visit her." From his position on the stairs below Eloise, he lifted his eyes to hers. "'Tis your welcome I crave, lady. Would you deny me?"

"Nay, lord." She smiled as they gained the upper corridor. "I am merely enacting the role of your chatelaine in reminding you of your other duties."

"Then allow me to remind you of *your* other duties, lady."

Without further warning, he swept her into his arms, locking her against him as his lips captured hers. He claimed her mouth ruthlessly, storming her senses, taking all she had to offer and demanding more.

The hard body she was pressed against left her is no doubt of the urgency of his need. They were both trembling when he finally raised his head.

Eyes closed, he rested his forehead on hers. "I have missed you, lady."

"As I have you, lord."

After a moment, they drew apart and walked to their apartments, not touching, neither daring to stir the smoldering embers, not until they were alone.

He stopped in the anteroom to speak with Bilder.

Eloise went straight to the bathing chamber, a small room off the bedchamber; beyond it lay the garderobe. A convoy of servants were trudging up a narrow service stair to upend steaming pails into the large wooden tub. She dipped her fingers in. "More hot water."

While the order was obeyed, she fetched two linen pouches stuffed with herbs and tossed them into the tub. The scents of pennyroyal and peppermint wafted into the air, carried on the rising vapor.

When the tub was filled to within a foot of its lip, she called a halt, reserving two steaming pails by the hearth. A blazing fire threw light and heat across the room, driving the chill from the now scented air. Satisfied, she returned to the anteroom.

When she appeared in the doorway, Alaun dismissed Bilder and, golden flames leaping in his eyes, swept her back over the threshold. He heeled the door shut as his arms closed about her.

Their second kiss was every bit as frantic as their first.

"I need you now—the bath can wait."

His raspy growl brooked no denial. She knew she should object— theoretically. Practically, he was impossible to stop. As the backs of her legs met the bed, she knew very well she wasn't about to argue.

They fell on the silk coverlet in a wild tangle of limbs, rapidly resolved as he pushed her skirts to her waist and swung over her, spreading her thighs as he lowered his body to hers. She lost her breath on a gasp as, with one powerful thrust, he joined them. Then, holding above her, he started them on a wild lovers' ride.

And a very wild ride it was.

He had never loved her so forcefully, his passion usually harnessed until the last moment. This time, he had but the barest control, driving into her with long, surging strokes that made her arch wildly as she matched him, crying out as he took her over one peak, then straight on to the next.

Only when she was sobbing for breath did he lower his head to hers. His lips found hers and covered them, stealing what little breath she had left. Then his tongue took her mouth, rapaciously plundering as his body relentlessly claimed hers. She was his—dually branded by the heat of his tongue and the searing thrust of his staff. He pushed her higher, probing deeply, setting fire to her very soul.

She shattered. In the same glorious instant, she felt him explode deep inside her.

Oblivion, deeper than it had ever been, claimed her.

Utterly relaxed, every nerve in her body unraveled, she didn't stir when Alaun left her. She didn't know that, for long moments, he stood by the bed, sipping from a goblet, his gaze roaming the beauty he'd claimed. Even when he lifted her and stripped her, she did no more than murmur sleepily.

Smiling, he laid her back on the bed. Strength returning, he dispensed with his garments then, as naked as she, he lifted her in his arms and walked into the bathing chamber.

Eloise came back to life as his large hands cupped her breasts, gently, rhythmically, soaping them. Warm water lapped about her, a soothing soporific. She was nestled against his chest, her bottom on the tub floor between his thighs, his legs a cage on either side of hers. Eyes half-closed, she murmured his name, and felt his lips at her temple.

"Be still, lady. I am washing you."

With a soft chuckle, she let herself drift into the dreamy realm of aftermath, held there by the gentle strokes of his large palms. With exaggerated care, he straightened one of her arms, then the other, soaping each limb and the curves of her shoulders. Then he cupped water and dribbled it over her, rinsing away the suds.

Floating in a sea of warm sensuality, she made no demur when his hands drifted lower, the soap cupped in one palm. He made her lean forward to deal with her back, then urged her to slump against his chest again, running his hand in slow circles over her taut waist. Then he reached down and cupped a hand behind one knee, slowly drawing her leg up so he could soap her toes.

She giggled, then caught her breath as his hands followed the smooth curves back, over her knee. He stopped there, and she breathed again. He repeated the treatment on her other leg. Even in her dreamy daze, she possessed wit enough to wonder what came next.

He leaned back, reclining with his head on the tub edge, and eased her over, settling her atop him, her cheek pillowed on his shoulder. She lifted heavy lids to find his gaze, warm and deeply golden, on her face. Then he bent his head and kissed her, slowly, languorously, until she sighed into his mouth.

Apparently satisfied, he lifted his head and gave his attention to the back of her waist. Mesmerized, not by his eyes but by the slow, purposeful strokes of his hands, she lay quiescent in his arms, and let him touch her as he would, let him bestow soapy caresses beneath the warm water, his hands traveling over the firm globes of her bottom to gently caress the cleft between and the sensitive backs of her thighs.

Trapped in a dream world of total surrender, she felt him lift her, turning her again, pillowing her head once more on his shoulder. The long sweeps of her thighs were next in line for his ministrations, slow sensuous strokes that left her skin tingling.

She mumbled something, what she hardly knew. He bent his head and pressed a kiss to her temple as his hands drifted to her hips. With deliberate strokes he circled her hipbones, then let his hands drift inward, one splaying across her belly as the other rose to deposit the soap on the edge of the tub.

Senses overwhelmed by the constant stimulation, she didn't protest when, beneath the water, he hooked his feet around hers and drew her thighs wide. Then he cupped her, blunt fingers parting her, tracing each fold, each hollow, each crease. She quivered. He hesitated as if gauging her state, then the hand across her belly tensed, holding her firmly while with his other hand he continued to explore her in inexorably increasing intimacy.

Each stroke, each sliding movement, impinged on her senses with startling clarity. Her skin was tingling, alive to every touch—of the water, of his hands, his fingers. The lap of the water at her breasts was a lover's caress, the teasing rise and fall over her peaked nipples an excruciating pleasure. The increasing pressure of his fingers as he probed her softness brought her untold delight.

Adrift, she swam in a sea of sensation, opening herself to his practiced caresses, letting him love her as he would. Slowly, her inner tension wound tight and she arched against his hand; he murmured softly, erotic images in his words as his breath fanned her cheek. He held her immobile, forcing her to lie quiescent beneath his hands. With shattering patience, he coaxed her to a long, extended climax that dragged his name from her lips and left her panting in his arms. They closed about her, holding her safe, secure, his forever.

When, untold minutes later, he tried to rise from the tub, she forced herself fully awake. "Oh, no."

Supple and slippery, she turned. Spreading her hands over his chest, she pushed him back into the water. "Tis my turn now."

The look on his face was one to treasure. She could see the memory of what had occurred the last time he had let her have her way with him flash through his mind.

One brow rising, Alaun forced himself to relax against the tub. "Lady-witch, I love you well, but there are aspects of our present situation that I think you have not fully considered."

"Oh?"

She already had the soap in her hand. On her knees between his thighs, she fell to soaping his chest.

"Aye." He let his lids fall, watching her from beneath his lashes. "Think on this. If you touch me to arouse me, as is in your mind to do, I will want to quench my fire inside you. And if I come above you in this tub, you will surely drown."

She blinked, then frowned, her hands slowing.

"And if you are to ride me—" He broke off, lips curving in a knowing smile. "Ah, lady-witch, you have not the strength to meet me that way, not after twice reaching ecstasy."

Her frown black, her expression disgruntled, Eloise shot him a baleful glare. Not too much consideration was required to tell her that he was right—in all respects. She had only enough strength left to keep herself upright. Flat on her back, she stood some chance of holding her own, but any other position would have to rely on his strength, not hers. "I vow tis most unfair, lord."

A great chuckle rumbled through his chest, sending ripples across the water. Under his lashes, his eyes gleamed gold. Raising a hand, he caressed her cheek. "Nay, lady-witch. You may wash me—but then we will adjourn to our bed."

He was as good as his word, letting her wash him thoroughly, an act that filled her senses with him and her body with a bone-deep longing. While she did, he told her of his visit to Sir Kendrick and three of his other vassals, more, she suspected, to distract himself than her.

When she was finished, he urged her to her feet. Standing beside her, he rinsed them both; water cascaded down his body, over gleaming skin stretched over firm muscle. As he stepped from the tub and turned to help her from the water, she saw him as a golden god, heavily aroused, the firelight gilding his skin, the flames of the fire in the hearth less bright than the glow in his eyes.

He wrapped her in a towel and gently dried her, dropping stray kisses on her temples and lips. Only when she insisted did he allow her to dry his back, legs, arms, and chest, while he dried the rest of him. Then he lifted her as if she weighed nothing and carried her back to their bed.

Shut away from the world behind velvet walls of scarlet and gold, laid on soft furs and scarlet silk, she was supremely conscious of the heavy beat of her heart as she watched him watching her. He sat on his knees on the bed beside her, clearly lit by the candles in the sconces of the bedhead. His hands lay relaxed on his thighs; his gaze roamed over her, unhurriedly taking stock, as if he would commit every inch to memory. His gaze lingered on her belly, taut above the dark triangle of curls, then slowly rose to her breasts, full and aching, and thence to her face.

A slow, knowing, confident yet mysterious smile broke across his face.

"What about supper?" she murmured, conscious of a conflict in her roles.

"Nay, lady-mine." His golden eyes met hers. "I would forgo it in favor of having my fill of you."

Moving with his customary slowness, he lay beside her, placing one finger across her lips when she would have spoken further. "Nay, lady-witch. No more words. I would love you without distraction."

He did, hands, lips, and body moving in orchestrated worship as he surrounded her with his love. Each caress was slow, deliberate, an act of devotion, every touch designed to heighten their mutual pleasure. Their progress down the longest road they'd yet taken to fulfillment was smooth, formal, ceremonial, each phase stretching and blending into the next, the transitions undetectable, the mileposts marked only with sighs or muted gasps.

Never had he loved her so deeply, so completely, without any vestige of restraint. And he demanded the same depth, the same intensity from her. She gave it without reservation.

When they finally joined, she could neither see nor hear, speak nor think, and she knew he was the same. Their hearts beat as one as they moved in concert, in perfect harmony, alive to the symphony of their senses, trapped within them.

The sunburst that claimed them was greater than any before. Cataclysmic, formed of their fire, nothing could withstand its heat. Willingly they gave themselves up to its flames; it melted them, fused them, then forged from their souls an entity greater than either, born of their love, tempered by their passion.

The furnace slowly cooled; they drifted back to earth, subtly altered, never to be the same, more completely one than even their conscious minds could know.

Chapter 18

Sated, replete, Alaun slept dreamlessly. Asprawl beside the woman who was his wife in all but legal fact, his contentment lay heavy upon him. So sunk was he in oblivion that, when the presentiment of dawn beckoned him to wakefulness, for once his mind refused it heed.

Dawn broke; the castle rose. Still he slept on.

Eventually, the strident sounds percolating through the shutters penetrated his slumber, prodding him toward consciousness. His mind responded, but reluctantly, sluggishly.

His body was another matter.

The soft curves pressed to his side were instantly recognizable. Dulled and distant, his wits were still wrapped in the fogs of sleep when he shifted, setting his chest to the warmth of her back, pressing his loins, already aching, to the smooth globes of her bottom.

She murmured sleepily and stretched her long legs. He trapped them with his, moving instinctively, conscious thought yet beyond him. She was lying on her side; he pressed his knee between hers, anchoring her lower leg.

Coming up on his elbow, he muzzled the soft skin beneath her ear as his hand pushed over the sweet curve of her waist, then rose to capture her breast. The ripe flesh filled his palm, swelling at his touch. His fingers sought and found the peak, caressing it to marble hardness. That done, his hand drifted downward; he trailed kisses over the sensitive hollow between shoulder and throat, then, with his teeth, he grazed the taut line of her neck as his knee nudged her upper leg higher, opening her to his touch.

The clouds about his mind thinned as his fingers delved, seeking her response. When her honey flowed freely, slick on his fingers, he held her pouting lips wide and, almost shuddering with relief, sheathed his throbbing staff in her softness.

And woke up.

His eyes flew wide as he realized what he'd done.

He froze, fighting the almost overpowering urge to ride her. "By the saints, lady, I am sorry." His anguished accents made it clear he was. Appalled, he tried to draw back—only to feel her long fingers wrap about his thigh, holding him to her.

"Nay, lord—why so? You have not hurt me." Eloise had been awake from the instant he'd touched her—she was keen to continue. "We have never tried it this way before."

"But..." He sounded dazed. "You do not like it when I am behind you, Eloise."

"Nay, tis not so." She smiled. "I do not fear you, and I know well who it is who beds me."

A half-smothered groan fell on her ears.

"As for this position"—she wriggled her hips experimentally, feeling him rigid within her—"I have yet to form an opinion on the matter. Tis pleasurable enough thus far. Perchance, if you were to demonstrate its benefits, I would like it very well."

More of her words—she would kill him if she continued. Nevertheless, Alaun felt forced to say, "Lady, you do not have to do this."

She tried to glance back at him, but couldn't. "Tis my pleasure to please you, lord. Know you not I would do anything you wish?"

Anything? He discovered he wasn't breathing and hastily rectified the omission; he was lightheaded enough as it was. Chest swelling, he hesitated, then pressed a kiss to her shoulder. "Do you mean that, lady-witch?"

"Aye." She shifted tentatively against him. "But you will have to teach me the way of it, lord, for I know not how to be mare to your stallion."

He couldn't hold back his groan. St. George forgive him—he couldn't even think while buried inside her. "Aye." Closing his eyes, he drew back, then surged deep. "I will teach you." Leaning over her, he gently nipped her neck. "Twill be a most pleasurable lesson for us both."

He made sure it was. At first, he rode her while she lay half prone, rocking her in the curve of his loins, letting her grow accustomed to the sensation of his rigid staff passing into her from behind. He watched her carefully, sensing the rise of her passion, the slow coiling of the tension inside her. Time and again, just before the critical point, he drew back, penetrating her no more than an inch, enough to tease, but not enough to push her over the edge.

Once she had drawn back from the precipice, he sank into her again, her softness closing about him like a glove.

When he hung back the fourth time, denying her release, Eloise had had enough. Sinking her nails into his thigh for emphasis, she protested. "Nay, lord—I want you deep. Now."

His lips nuzzled her nape.

"If you truly want me deep, lady-witch, you will have to lift your pretty arse."

"How?" The word was a demand, not a question.

Without withdrawing from her, Alaun drew her to her knees. After a moment's discussion, she elected to rest her elbows on the sheets, declaring the angle more comfortable. He didn't argue, knowing she would thus be better braced against him. Curling his hands about her hips, he anchored her before him. His knees inside hers, he drew back.

His first deeply probing thrust elicited a satisfying moan. Soon, she was sobbing in helpless delight, her breath expelled in sharp little gasps as, again and again, he withdrew and thrust deeply, nudging her womb. The head of his staff pressed against her inner portal; he closed his eyes, lost in the wonder of her.

Passion held them so tightly, neither heard the door latch lift.

Beyond the bed curtains, weak sunshine streamed in, lighting the room. The heavy anteroom door edged noiselessly inward, revealing a slight figure.

Eyes gleaming, Elspeth took in the fully curtained bed, rocking slightly, then she quickly entered and closed the door. On silent feet, she approached the foot of the bed. With nimble fingers, she sought the gap between the curtains, then applied her wide, pale eye to the slit.

Lips parted, excitement mounting, Elspeth looked upon the scene within. Licking her lips, she devoured the naked back before her, all rippling muscles and straining sinews, tight with lust and passion. His buttocks flexed as he thrust deeply into the woman kneeling before him.

Elspeth shivered. It was even better than she'd imagined.

Time and again, she had tried to catch them at it, but Mistress Martin shared her room and was a very light sleeper. Then, too, there was his grisly old squire who slept in the anteroom, and, finally, the obstacle of his stiff and horridly squeaking door. She had been stymied by that door for years, prevented from even watching him sleep. Until now, she had only been able to examine the room when no one else was about.

But today, the fates had smiled. The pair had slept in; his squire was in the bailey, and Mistress Martin had gone to speak with Elspeth's father. And the lady herself had had the door fixed, removing the last hurdle.

A shuddering moan fell on Elspeth's ears and she sucked in a breath. Her slack lips worked; her eyes glowed feverishly. Very well did she remember the looks on her father's maids' faces as that one particular groom had used them. As Montisfryn was apparently using his chatelaine. Twould give Elspeth great satisfaction to see the same expression on the proud lady's face. Another deep thrust eliciting an even more shattering moan decided her.

Releasing the curtain, Elspeth moved silently around the bed. Carefully, she picked out the gap in the side curtains and, after a moment's consideration, knelt down, then peeked in.

The face she saw was blissful, eyes closed, pleasure in every line. Not the slightest hint of pain marred the lady's flushed countenance. Shocked, Elspeth looked back—and smothered a gasp. Outrage welled as she watched how they joined. Twas wrong! Twas—

In the instant in which she would have spoken, it all came clear in her mind. Of course, Montisfryn wouldn't spill his seed inside his chatelaine.

Elspeth calmed, breathing deeply. He was so large, very likely the woman had not yet stretched enough to accommodate him there, so he was using her otherwise to gain his pleasure—that was all there was to it. The lady's pleasure was incidental; he probably wouldn't bother to give her release, but merely gain his own.

Reassured, Elspeth settled on her knees to watch.

But what she saw did nothing to ease her mind.

As he felt the end draw near, Alaun moderated the force of his thrusts; releasing Eloise's hips, he reached forward to fondle her breasts. They filled his hands, sumptuous and swollen, the peaks hard as pebbles as he rolled his palms over them. She gasped his name on a sob of sheer pleasure. His breathing ragged, he bent to place a string of kisses along her supple spine, damp with the dew of their exertions.

She was heated and flushed, so full of their fire that she pulsed hotly about him, threatening to scald him. Sensing her rising climax, he wrapped one arm about her hips, holding her hard against him as he picked up the pace, arching over her as he drove deep, and then more deeply still. The muscles of his thighs locked, anchoring their position. Taking his weight on one braced arm, with his other hand he sought the tight bud of her desire, hidden beneath its hood. He found it, caressed it, then trapped it between thumb and finger. Gently, he squeezed in time with his thrusts.

She screamed his name and melted about him. Two driving thrusts brought him to where she hung, suspended, caught in the passionate web they'd spun.

Then release swept her; her body pulsed strongly about him. Gritting his teeth, he held still, savoring each rippling caress before surrendering to the inexorable tug; in an orgy of short, pumping thrusts, he filled her with his seed.

With a long, guttural groan, he collapsed, sweeping her knees from beneath her so that they fell together, his body sprawling protectively over hers. He kissed her nape; her fingers stroked his thigh. Closing his eyes, he let oblivion take him.

The bed curtains fell shut.

Elspeth rose.

Her pale eyes opaque, she drifted from the room.

* * *

When Eloise awoke, she was alone. A slow smile lit her face; she rolled onto her back and stretched her arms high. She felt *glorious*! After dallying to savor her memories for one, last minute, she pushed back the covers, and the curtains, and rose.

To find the sun already high and the morning well-advanced.

Quickly donning chemise, cote, and hose, she went through to the garderobe. Returning to the bedchamber some minutes later, she discovered a plate bearing a cup of ale and two pieces of fresh bread placed prominently on the chest by the door. She grinned. Clearly, Alaun had remembered her when he'd broken his own fast, and had sent a maid with the plate to spare her sensibilities.

Sipping the ale, she found it slightly sweet—not too much so, but she made a mental note to mention it to the alewife. Nibbling on the bread, she crossed to the corner where her surcotes hung. Selecting one of grass green wool, she laid it on the chest, absentmindedly supping ale and munching bread while she finished lacing her cote.

Finally, she dragged the surcote over her head and smoothed it down, then adjusted her braids and set her fillet in place. Satisfied her appearance was all that it should be, she opened the door and headed for the hall.

She had yet to tell Montisfryn of her decision.

As she stepped onto the dais, the usual bustle greeted her. Maids bobbed curtsies; the two pages seated at the high table with their slates doffed their caps. The chaplain smiled at her, then turned back to his charges.

Looking around, Eloise blinked. The hall receded, then returned. Her throat felt thick, as if from breathing smoke. Her head felt odd, too.

Puzzled, she glanced at the maids gathered about the fire; none showed any signs of discomfort. Wondering if, perhaps, she'd been more affected by Montisfryn's attentions than she'd realized, she cautiously headed for the entrance hall. A few minutes of fresh air would doubtless clear her head.

The area above the steep steps was momentarily empty. Emerging into the weak sunshine, she blinked; raising a hand to shade her eyes, she struggled to lift her lids against the glare. The buttery, directly opposite, seemed a long way away. Frowning, she squinted, trying to bring it into focus.

Down on the cobbles some yards from the steps, Alaun was speaking to two of his sergeants when both men looked up, their gazes going beyond him, their expressions blanking in surprise. He glanced back—and saw Eloise weaving on her feet at the top of the steep stone steps.

In that instant, she turned and saw him.

Eloise smiled and raised her hand—at least, she thought she did. Her limbs didn't seem to be responding as they should; leaden, listless, they dragged her down, making her peculiarly clumsy. Even more puzzling was Montisfryn's expression; he was looking at her with concern, even fear, in his face. Then, with an oath even she could hear, he started toward her.

She realized, then, that there must be something behind her. Some danger. She wanted to turn around and see, but she couldn't get her feet to move. She looked down to see if there was some obstruction to account for it, and felt herself lurch crazily.

Frightened, she hauled herself upright. Her breath stuck in her throat. Eyes wide, she stared down at Montisfryn. He'd reached the bottom of the steps.

She blinked; gray clouds obscured her vision. She blinked again, and the clouds turned black. A roaring grew, filling her ears.

Alaun caught Eloise as she fell, a virulent oath on his lips as he hoisted her up and swung away from the precipitous steps. "Edmund!" With that bellow, he plunged into the hall, striding through, leaving confusion in his wake, spreading it before him.

He stopped by the fire, intending to ease Eloise onto one of the hurriedly vacated benches. Only then did he realize just how deep was her faint. She lay limp, lifeless in his arms. With a curse, he turned toward the stairs.

Roland appeared by his elbow. "What?"

"She fainted." Alaun paused, mind racing. "Get Meg."

"At once." Clapping him on the shoulder, Roland signaled the two pages, frozen, round-eyed, over their slates.

Alaun started toward the stairs. Bilder popped up, took one look at his burden, and raced up ahead of him. Jenni, summoned from the workrooms, hurried up behind, fretting already.

Bilder propped the doors wide; Alaun strode straight to the bed, so recently the setting for their intimacy. He waited while Jenni and Bilder, both pale but composed, drew back the heavy curtains and straightened the sheets. While they did, he looked down at Eloise's face, examining it closely. It told him nothing. Her lids remained down, sealing her away.

Dear God—what had happened?

When Bilder and Jenni drew back, he stepped to the bed and gently lowered Eloise, laying her straight, her arms at her sides. With hands that shook, he removed her fillet, releasing her braids.

He stood back.

It was an effort to draw breath, to expand his chest against the iron band that had clamped about it. Bilder glanced at him, then motioned to the robin; together, they slipped out.

There was a bustle in the anteroom and Roland appeared, Lanella in his arms. "Meg's on her way."

"What happened?" Lanella demanded as Roland set her down in the chair.

"She...seemed to faint." Closing his eyes, Alaun pressed a fist to his forehead. "I caught her just before she fell down the keep steps."

"But why did she faint?" Lanella's eyes were filled with worry.

He shook his head.

"Put me *down*, you great oaf!"

Alaun turned as Meg made her entrance cradled in a hulking archer's arms. The man deposited her carefully on her feet, and got a swipe about his ear for his pains.

"You put me down when I tells you, do you hear? I can still walk—I'm not that old yet."

Alaun bit down on his ire. "Meg, my lady has fainted. I would have you see to her."

Meg's eyes blinked wide. "Her? But she's as healthy as a horse."

His face hard, expressionless, Alaun waved Meg to the bed.

Meg went, slowly, as if she couldn't quite believe the reality of the slim figure laid out on the sheets. She drew near the side of the bed and reached out a gnarled hand to touch Eloise's cheek. Meg blinked, her old eyes widening even more. Her hand lingered, as if she was reluctant to believe what her senses were telling her, then she shifted her fingers to the slim column of Eloise's throat.

Her habitual rumbustiousness flown, Meg glanced at Lanella. "If you would, lady, I would have your opinion, too."

Subdued, Lanella summoned Roland to her aid. He carried her to the bed, and set her beside Eloise's still form.

"Just touch her face and hands, lady."

When Lanella did, Meg asked, "Seem they too cool to you?"

Lanella glanced up. "Aye. Certainly too cool."

"And her heart. I can just feel it here, in her throat, but if you touch under her breast you should feel it."

Lanella did, and her face grew paler. After a moment, she lifted her head. "Surely tis too slow?"

Meg grimaced. "Aye—so I'm thinking."

The old woman looked at Alaun, her bright eyes worried as they searched his. "But what think you, lord? You should know more certainly than any other."

It was a battle to breathe. Alaun forced himself to the bed, then laid his fingers across Eloise's brow. The smooth skin felt like marble, cool, almost chill. He knew her heartbeat as well as his own; pressing his hand beneath her breast confirmed beyond doubt that her pulse had weakened dramatically. He dragged in a breath that shook. "Her breathing is also too shallow."

Her chest was barely moving.

Lanella was frowning. "Was she well this morn, or is this a sudden thing?"

Alaun scrubbed his hands over his face and looked at Meg. "She was well and still asleep when I left her an hour ago." He was sure for he'd woken to find himself slumped over her. He had turned, taking them to their sides, cuddling her while he'd sought for the words to confirm his hopes. She'd smiled in her sleep and mumbled something, then had snuggled back down to doze. She'd been warm and very much alive.

Now she was slipping away from him.

And he felt *helpless*.

"Did she have any food or drink?"

Meg's question halted his incipient panic. "I know not," he replied. "We'll have to ask."

"What about that?" Roland pointed to a plate and cup on the chest.

Frowning, Alaun crossed to see. "It was not here when I left." He wiped a finger across the plate. "Crumbs. Bread—same as we had." He picked up the empty cup and sniffed it. "Ale." It didn't smell quite right.

"Bring the cup here, lord." Meg beckoned from the bed. "'Tis likely that was how it was given her—few poisons act so fast eaten."

"Poison!"

Alaun turned at Lanella's gasp. Her eyes were wide; shock etched her face. Roland went to her, but she refused to let him lift her. She held tightly to Roland's sleeve as she stared, first at Meg, then at Alaun.

He felt her gaze; for a long minute, he studied Meg's stoic expression, then, resigned, he faced Lanella. "'Tis likely. I know of nothing else that would act so—unless 'tis some odd woman's problem, but that you and Meg would know. I believe 'tis poison that has made her so."

"But—" Lanella struggled with the question that was already high in his mind. "*Who?* Why? No one here has any reason to wish her harm. 'Twas plain she was to be your wife—the people have taken her to their hearts."

Tears stood in her eyes.

"There must be something we don't know," Roland said.

"Be that as it may," Meg interrupted forcefully. "'Tis the what, rather than the who, that we need to know first—and the sooner the better. If you will give me that ale-cup, lord?"

Alaun yielded it without a word.

And watched as Meg inserted a finger, wiped it around the pewter cup, then, closing her eyes, placed that finger in her mouth.

Lanella hissed in shocked surprise.

Meg sighed and opened her eyes. "There's no taste I can sense through the ale, but 'tis too sweet. If old Carrie has a bad brew, 'tis sour or bitter, not sweet."

Roland beat him to the question: "But what does that tell us?"

"Why, that 'twas not just any old potion or herb-juice that was added." Meg looked at Alaun. "Our lady was poisoned with a syrup—and only the likes of her has money for to use sugar like that, nor yet the time to make such."

Alaun turned his head. "Bilder!" Instantly, the squire appeared in the doorway. "Find Roseanne."

"Try my chamber," came from Roland.

A quick discussion established the advisability of tracing the source of the cup and plate. Sitting on the bed, one of Eloise's limp hands on his knee, trapped beneath one if his, his anguish concealed behind a mask of stone, Alaun explained their fears to Edmund, who had arrived, his face grave, moments before.

The steward paled, but squared his thin shoulders. "I'll go at once to the kitchens. Cook does not dispense ale freely other than at meals, so tis likely she'll know who has requested ale this morn."

Grim-faced, Edmund strode out, passing Roseanne as, hesitantly, she edged into the room. Her eyes were wide and still blinking away sleep, her hair tousled, her chemise all awry where it showed above her gown.

"You wanted me, lord?"

His face was a graven screen behind which violent emotions surged. "Aye." Rising, Alaun walked to the bed's end to face Roseanne. "My lady has been poisoned. Meg thinks twas with a herb syrup."

For an instant, he wasn't sure Roseanne understood him, then her gaze flicked to the still figure on the bed. Her eyes widened, then, pupils dilating, rose to meet his.

"Nay, lord." Roseanne backed. "Twas not me, I swear it!"

Alaun blinked, then frowned. "Nay. I do not suspect you." With an effort, he drew patience to him. "You had no reason—had, in fact, many reasons to wish her well, did you not?"

Roseanne nodded. "Aye. She has been good to me, lord."

"And she's taught you something of herbs. You're the only one here who might guess what it is she's been given."

Roseanne looked doubtful. "I know but little, lord. She has only just started to teach me, and that mostly in the simple remedies. I know not much of her more potent drafts."

"But you know more than we." Alaun fought for calm, desperation very near his surface.

Meg snorted. "Stop dithering, girl! Just come and take a look at her—no one's going to bite you if'n you can't guess what it might be."

Literally pushing Alaun aside, Meg beckoned to Roseanne; she took the girl's arm as she came forward and hustled her to the bed.

"Now see—she's chilled and her heart is slow. What herbs give that effect? I know tis not valerian—does not give the chill. But what else makes a body so?"

Almost reverently, Roseanne touched one of Eloise's cold hands; her brow furrowed. "Tis none of the simples she has taught me, certainly. But she has many others in the stillroom—she warned me some are dangerous."

Muttering a curse, Alaun swung to Roland. "I want a lock on the stillroom door. Immediately." After the horse had bolted maybe, but who knew what else might come? Besides, giving an order for some specific action was something he could actually do.

Roland left, but returned within a minute; no doubt Alaun's sergeants were waiting in the corridor. The whole castle would be tense, expectant, hanging on the outcome of events in this chamber.

Roseanne was still frowning, Meg still hovering. Alaun struggled to harness his impatience, his desperation, the urge to roar and bellow that this could not be—that they had to fix it and make her better—immediately. Now.

Lanella was still perched beside Eloise, her eyes fixed frowningly on the pale, still face. "Tis almost as if she was asleep—deeply, deeply asleep."

Roseanne's head came up; she stared at Lanella. "Syrup—syrup of poppies!"

Flushing in triumph, Roseanne swung to face Alaun. "Twas only yesterday she showed it me—three little vials that she unpacked from her case. She said twas not as strong as the Eastern poppy—though I know not what that is—but twas used to bring on sleep."

Roseanne paused, clearly summoning more of her memories. "She said it must be used judici…judici…"

"Judiciously?" Lanella asked.

"Aye—that is it. It means carefully, does it not?"

"Aye." Grim-faced, Alaun kept his gaze on Eloise's slim figure, on the fractional rise and fall of her breasts that told him she yet lived.

"She also said that if too much was given the person may sleep unto death."

Silence fell, engulfing them all in the dread embrace of that one word.

His gaze on the proof that life still remained, that death had yet to claim her, Alaun was the first to break it. "We know not how much she was given. Tis possible she will sleep, and then awake." He looked at Roseanne. "But if twas only yesterday the vials were unpacked, it seems unlikely that any save you and she would know they were there."

.Again, it was obvious Roseanne wished herself elsewhere. She shot a glance at Old Meg.

Meg frowned at her. "Tell all you know, girl. Spit it out—he'll not eat ye, whatever it be."

With another nervous glance, Roseanne ventured, "Tis that we were not alone when the lady unpacked her box and told me about each of her specifics. Mistress Elspeth was there—she asked to stay and listen, and the lady allowed it."

"Elspeth?" Lanella's face showed her surprise—then her shock as the implication registered. "Oh, no—surely, no. Why, there's no reason for her to dislike Eloise."

"Not if you discount jealousy."

It was Roland who'd spoken. Alaun turned, lifting a brow.

Roland grimaced. "You no longer notice, but Elspeth always looks at you as if she owns you. I make no claim to know what goes on in what passes for her mind, but I would wager she resents Eloise's position here, at least with respect to you."

Alaun's expression darkened. "You should have warned me!"

"But Elspeth's never shown any signs of doing anyone harm before!" Roland ran a hand through his hair. "I hoped she would be gone soon—I would have spoken if I'd suspected her of this."

For a pregnant moment, Alaun held Roland's gaze, then he sighed and dropped his challenging stare. "Aye, well. I should have noticed myself."

Meg glanced up as, compelled, he returned to the bed. She yielded her place to him, fluffing her shawls over her old shoulders. "Tis my thought, lord, that we need to be sure tis the poppy juice and how much she had."

Taking Eloise's hand, he nodded. "Roland—accompany Roseanne to the stillroom. If the vials are still there, mayhap we have got this wrong." He had to own to a difficulty in casting Elspeth, incapable Elspeth, as a murderess.

But Roland and Roseanne were immediately replaced by Edmund with further proof of Elspeth's likely guilt.

"The cup is the one sent to Mistress Elspeth this morning—Cook is sure for there's a small dent in the side. Cook remembers the incident for twas long after breakfast. Mistress Martin came down, saying that Mistress Elspeth was hungry, and had asked for bread and ale."

Feeling increasingly numb, Alaun nodded. Across the bed, his gaze met Lanella's, shocked and already grieving. But he couldn't yet grieve—wouldn't let such a negative emotion take hold. Eloise still lived, still breathed—there'd been little change since he'd brought her in. "Fetch Mistress Martin."

Edmund left.

As the minutes slid by, Alaun found it more and more difficult to focus on Elspeth's guilt or otherwise, on his duty as lord to determine it. His mind felt sundered, torn in two, the larger part centered on the still figure on the bed. All that mattered was that she lived—he cared for nothing else. All he wanted was to sit with her, holding her hand, willing her to live—doing whatever it took to ensure she did.

But Mistress Martin was discovered in conference with Sir Howell; Alaun had, perforce, to resume his investigation.

"Where is your charge, mistress?"

Mistress Martin blinked. "She has gone hawking, lord." She hesitated, then added, "Her groom is reliable."

Stony-faced, Alaun asked, "I understand you fetched bread and ale at Elspeth's direction this morn."

"Aye. Twas mid-morning, but Elspeth swore she was in dire need."

"And you took it to her and she consumed the bread and ale?"

"Nay." A frown clouded Mistress Martin's face. "When I returned to our chamber, she was gone. I left the plate and cup on the table and went to find her. She does that frequently—slipping away—just to annoy me."

"And you found her?"

"Not immediately. Twas only when she returned for her gloves before riding out that I saw her again—a half-hour or so ago." Martha Martin looked around and saw nothing but grave faces. "Is there something amiss, lord?"

Alaun kept his temper shackled although it cost him dear. "We have reason to believe that your charge has poisoned Lady de Cannar."

Martha Martin paled. "If I may ask how she did this thing, lord?"

"Ale was given to my lady this morn. We believe the poison was in it."

Alaun watched as Martha Martin considered his words, her expression grave. "Perhaps I should see if the cup and plate I delivered to Elspeth are still in our room where I left them."

He shook his head. "Cook has confirmed that the cup found here was the one she gave to you."

"Oh, I still can't *believe* it!" Lanella wrapped her arms about herself and rocked. "How *horrible*—how will I tell Lucilla?"

"Do not worry, *maman*. If tis proven that Elspeth has done this thing, as seems very likely, twill be I who will tell my godmother."

His tone, unfortunately, did little to soothe Lanella. Agonized, she shook her head. "I know Elspeth's strange, but oh, *how* could she do such a thing?"

Alaun shut his eyes. He didn't have strength to spare to comfort Lanella—he had to keep it all for what was to come, for what might yet have to be faced. This morning, all had seemed won—victory had been his. Now, his whole life hung by a slender thread, by the almost imperceptible rise and fall of his lady's chest—and death hovered, waiting to take it from him.

"Lord, I crave your indulgence."

It was Mistress Martin who spoke. Alaun opened his eyes. "Speak, mistress. If you have any light to shed on this matter, now is the time to reveal it."

She nodded. "My duty is not straightforward, lord, for I am employed by Mistress Elspeth's parents, yet tis my belief that while we are resident here, I owe you some degree of loyalty, too. Thus it is that I see myself free to speak."

He nodded briefly, acknowledging her difficulty, absolving her of any charge of disloyalty.

Martha Martin clasped her hands tightly and cleared her throat. "Twas only a few days ago that I realized twas so, but Elspeth believes herself betrothed to you, Lord de Montisfryth. Such is her state that, from my considerable experience in handling such as she, I know well tis impossible to convince her otherwise. If I had known her mind had settled thus, I would have spoken strongly against her coming here, and would certainly not have agreed to act as her keeper in such circumstances. I have endeavored to bring this matter to Sir Howell's attention for the past three days; I regret he would not view the matter with the seriousness I felt it deserved."

Alaun was thunderstruck. "There has never been talk of a betrothal between Elspeth and myself. How came she by this idea?"

Mistress Martin paled. "Sir Howell and Lady Davarost told me…"

Alaun saw red. "There has been some mistake—"

He was cut off by Lanella's groan. "There was, there was. My pardon, Alaun, but twas so long ago, and came to naught—your father and I never thought to mention it. Forgive me, but I never imagined…" She broke off, her eyes on Eloise's still figure.

Seeing the tears in Lanella's eyes and the fear in her face, Alaun hauled hard on his temper. "Nay, *maman*, do not blame yourself. But tell me now, if you please. What is this about?"

Pressing her lips together, Lanella blinked rapidly. "Elspeth was born while you were away with Gloucester—that's why you never knew. Lucilla was so happy, and when your father and I went to the christening to stand as godparents, we discussed the possibility. It seemed a fair match at the time— your father was not an earl, remember." She paused, then continued, "But Elspeth's strangeness soon became apparent and we talked of it no more. And it was just talk, Alaun—no more, I swear."

"Aye." Mistress Martin nodded. "Tis what Lady Davarost said. But tis not as Elspeth choses to interpret it, and that is the crux."

For several moments, Alaun considered, then, lifting his gaze, fixed it on Martha Martin. "Are you saying that Elspeth is beyond reason—that she cannot discriminate fact and fantasy?"

Mistress Martin hesitated, then said, "Tis more that she accepts only certain facts and will not see any that do not fit her picture. She's incapable in that. Her world is her own creation, but is based on some real facts. The others her mind supplies. Such as she now is, she cannot be brought out of her world because, for her, *it* is the real world and ours the fake."

"You're telling me that she's insane—of unsound mind?" His voice had assumed the tones of a judge.

Mistress Martin bowed her head. "That is my belief, lord. I fear her actions this day must confirm it."

"What will you do?" Lanella, eyes wide, fixed her gaze on his face.

Alaun looked back at the bed, to where Meg sat wedged in a corner by the bedhead, the fingers of one hand pressed to the pulse at Eloise's throat. "For now, Elspeth must be confined. Twill be time enough to decide her fate, and hear all the evidence against her, once we know if my lady will live." Or die. He couldn't bring himself to say the word aloud.

"If it please you, lord, Mistress Martin and I will see to Mistress Elspeth."

Alaun turned at Edmund's words, and nodded curtly. "If you would."

The older man hesitated as if he would say more, but then turned and ushered Mistress Martin to the door. They left, conferring in hushed tones in the anteroom before, their strategy settled, they went to find Elspeth.

Alaun ignored their whispers, his mind focused on Eloise. She still lived, but for how long? Lanella was sobbing quietly into a kerchief; Meg's face was unusually grim.

Then there was noise without and Roland entered, Roseanne close behind. Alaun lifted his head and looked his question.

His expression bleak, Roland met his gaze. "We found the vials. They were in Elspeth's chamber."

"How much was given her?"

Roland closed his eyes, then opened them. "All three vials were empty."

For a moment, Alaun was blind, although his eyes remained open. Then, moving slowly, he turned and walked to the bed. He stood beside Lanella and looked down at the pale face on the pillows, calm, perfectly composed, yet lacking the light of love and laughter that had been there when he had left her that morn.

"So she will die."

Chapter 19

There was no sound in the room bar Lanella's soft sobs, then even those ceased.

Alaun stood, his heart like stone, trying to grapple with his conclusion. His brain felt numb; his body chilled.

"No."

Strangely, the denial came from Lanella. She sniffed, then resolutely wiped her eyes. "Not necessarily. I—oh, how I *wish* I had paid more attention years ago—but surely tis true that most strong potions have antidotes?"

She looked at Meg; Alaun followed her glance.

Meg pursed her lips, then nodded. "That has been my experience, lady." She turned to Roseanne. "Did she mention any counteracting potion?"

But Roseanne sent their hopes plummeting with a shake of her head. "Nay, she mentioned no such thing."

Lanella, however, refused to give up so easily. "Mayhap not specifically, but I think tis a thing called a stimulant we need. Twould be strange if, capable as she is, she did not have one made up." She directed an imperiously imploring look at Roseanne. "Come, girl—you said she described to you all she had."

"Aye, but more in the way of what illnesses each mixture would cure."

Meg snorted. "Think only of the syrups or elixirs or potions. Did she have anything to help fainting? Or tiredness?"

Roseanne brightened. "Fainting, aye." Then her brow clouded. "But she said twas really a strong remedy for leth-ar-gy, whatever that be."

Alaun glanced sharply at Lanella. "Are you saying we can use another potion to counteract what she was given? To make her heart beat faster and her breathing better?"

Lanella nodded. "Tis likely. If we can but pick the right one."

"Can you remember what she said about this potion for lethargy?" Meg looked sternly at Roseanne. "Twill be important if we are to use it."

Luckily, when it came to matters of memory, Roseanne was confident. "Tis mostly oil of rosemary, with extract of hawthorn berries and extract of foxglove leaves added. She said twas truly powerful, and no more than a drop should be given on the tongue. If too much was given the heart would race, and might seize or burst."

Meg snorted. "Aye—sounds right. I have heard of oil of rosemary."

Alaun raised a brow.

Meg sniffed. "Some men use it to enhance their performance—it increases breathing and vigor. The hawthorn berries and foxglove leaves are likely for the heart, but from all I've heard, the warning is meet—tis a mighty powerful specific."

Alaun closed his eyes, looking inward for strength. They were suggesting walking a tightrope, juggling two powerful potions, one against the other—hoping they got it right. The only one who would know for certain was the patient, and if they made a mistake, she would die. Along with the child he was sure she was carrying. To entrust such precious lives to their inexpert doctorings went wildly against his grain.

But if he didn't?

He opened his eyes to find Lanella and the others watching him.

"This needs must be your decision, Alaun." Lanella looked grave. "Tis going to be risky, but tis my opinion the stimulant will be needed." She glanced at the figure beside her. "She's already very low."

He had no choice.

He looked at Roseanne. "Go fetch this oil. Roland—go with her."

They left immediately, returning ten minutes later with a vial of greenish liquid. Alaun took it and held it to the light. Inwardly, he grimaced. If it was as they thought, he held her life—and that of their child—in his hand.

The rest of the day passed painfully slowly. Noon came and went; food was brought on trays, but lay largely untouched. Lanella remained in the chair by the fire, built up to throw as much warmth as possible into the room. They'd covered Eloise with furs, trying to ease her chill. But her coldness came from within; she remained deathly pale, her skin cool to the touch.

Alaun roamed the room, unable to leave, too restless to sit. Meg and Roseanne took turns sitting by the bed, fingers on Eloise's pulse, checking her shallow breathing. They had yet to administer any of the green oil; they'd agreed to wait until her condition weakened in the distant hope that it would not. Jenni, round-eyed and subdued, crept in and out of the room, but there was little she could do; Rovogatti fetched her away. Roland and Bilder remained in the anteroom, ready to carry out any orders. Edmund looked in every hour, to learn what news they had and carry it to the people waiting in the hall and the baileys.

As the day wore on, a pall of silence descended on castle and town. Few had not seen their lord's chosen lady and exclaimed at her beauty; in his people's eyes, she was a fitting mate for him—proud, graceful, and imperious. They'd nodded and winked, and warmed themselves with thoughts of the nuptial celebrations. Now, they did only what had to be done, and that silently, gathering in groups to discuss the latest news in hushed tones.

And to dwell on the manifold iniquities of one scrawny witch, who they, one and all, abominated.

Quite how that news got out was never learned, but castle folk were too close a community for any secret to remain so for long. Alaun learned of the threat when Roland, his expression devoid of its habitual joie de vivre, re-entered the bedchamber.

Roland came close, speaking low so Lanella wouldn't hear. "Rovogatti's without. He's just come from the outer bailey. There are murmurings and more—threats against Elspeth. Edmund and Mistress Martin caught her when she rode in, and have locked her in her chamber. Mistress Martin is with her. With your leave, I'll set a troop about the guest wing. There's no saying what might occur..."

Roland couldn't continue.

Alaun nodded. "Aye."

Roland clapped a hand on his shoulder, then turned away.

"Roland?"

Roland glanced back. He read the thoughts behind Alaun's eyes with ease. "I'll take command of the castle. You must remain here in case your decision is needed."

Alaun nodded again; Roland left.

Afternoon leached into evening—it was then the deterioration came. Eloise started to sink, her heartbeat dropping away, her breathing barely detectable.

Meg had been watching her.

Summoned to the bedside, Alaun looked down at the deathly pale face on the pillows. "Give her the oil. Two drops. Now."

Meg cast him a startled glance, but what she saw in his eyes made her hold her tongue. She administered the oil. They waited, watching, their entire existence focused on the slim, silent figure.

She responded very slowly, the increase in her breathing the first thing to show, then her pulse quickened.

The relief was so great it bowed his shoulders. He sank onto the bed, head lowered, eyes closed, breathing deeply.

After a moment, Meg spoke. "Lord—tis just the beginning. We'll have to watch her very close from now on, for we know not how long twill be before the effect of the oil wears off. When it does, tis likely she'll sink very fast."

Numb, he nodded.

Meg and Roseanne shared the watches of the night. Roland fetched Lanella away, carrying her back to her apartment under protest. Alaun insisted; Lanella looked gaunt. She was not, in truth, very strong, although she'd certainly improved since Eloise had come.

The thought drew his mind back to the bed from which he'd strayed but little through the hours. Eloise hadn't moved since he'd laid her there; her face was an emotionless mask. A death mask.

He shook the thought aside. He would *not* let her go so tamely.

Throughout the night, he remained by her side, her hand in his, his fingers on her weak pulse. As the hours dragged by, he forced himself to look ahead, to the plans he'd made, to actions already taken. He refused to think of defeat. The messenger he'd dispatched that morning should reach Westminster on the morrow, to inquire of the chancellor, who knew him well, as to the king's precise whereabouts. Edward had expected to depart from Calais by the end of September. It was likely his liege lord was already in the country, hopefully not far distant.

The thought of making formal application to marry Eloise de Versallet, the widowed Lady de Cannar, had occurred only to be dismissed. Despite Edward's edict to wed, his liege was not above making political and capital hay out of such a request. A personal petition delivered directly to His Grace stood a much better chance of rapid affirmation.

His gaze resting on Eloise's face, Alaun swore he wouldn't wait on the outcome of any lengthy deliberations. If she was spared this night, he would wed her soon; Edward and his minions could come to terms with the fact in their own good time.

They almost lost her three times.

As Meg had foretold, when the effect of the stimulant wore off, Eloise's decline was abrupt and acute. Two drops more, administered on the back of her tongue, seemed barely enough to anchor her to life. But the second time it happened, her response to the rosemary was more pronounced, although still slow. Her heart pounded heavily and false color appeared in her cheeks.

Meg, who had come at his call when Eloise had faltered, settled herself against the bedhead and blinked owlishly at him. "The effect of the poppies is wearing off. If she again needs more rosemary, twill not be safe to give her more than one drop."

Reluctantly, he agreed.

Dawn was still some way off when her breathing again sank low. Meg was there and gave her the agreed dose.

Then they waited.

Her pulse was thready, close to faltering; the furs did not stir, so shallow was her breathing. Still they waited. He was steeling himself to order another drop, knowing the danger yet frantic at the thought of losing her, when the furs lifted fractionally. He waited, his own breathing suspended, until it happened again. As blessed relief swept him, he lifted his eyes to

Meg's. He nodded, and they both relaxed.

He didn't leave Eloise—could not—too terrified that death would take advantage of his absence to claim her. The first hints of dawn were glimmering through the shutters when he realized the pulse beneath his fingers was stronger, although she'd been given no more stimulant.

Lifting his head from where he'd pillowed it on his arm, he looked up, into a face that, while still very pale, seemed to have eased. Her features no longer held the sharpness of a marble effigy; her usual light color had yet to return, but when he glanced at the furs over her chest, elation swept through him. The furs lifted regularly and discernibly, the steady rhythm one he recognized at some deep, intimate level.

She was with him again—back from the dead.

He looked further and saw Meg asleep in her corner, her old fingers still curled about Eloise's other wrist.

Slowly, he rose and slipped away from the bed, wanting to shout his joy, his relief, to the world, yet also needing to savor the moment alone, privately, acknowledging the inescapable, that without Eloise, life would be worthless, colorless, devoid of all happiness.

She was the center of his existence—and she'd been spared.

He opened the shutters and leaned on the stone sill to look out on his familiar world. The rising sun broke through wispy clouds; it lanced through the river fogs, transforming them into veils of shimmering gold. The air was crisp, clear, scented with wood smoke and the tang of the nearby forests. Closer at hand, the smell of baking wafted from the kitchens, along with the usual clinks and clunks as the castle awoke to the day.

Closing his eyes, he drank it all in, the sounds and smells of castle life. He gave thanks to the saints for Eloise's deliverance, that all he could sense, his life, yet had meaning. He felt the hot prick of tears behind his lids; he couldn't even remember when last he'd cried.

* * *

In mid-morning, Alaun convened what was, in effect, a baronial court in Lanella's chamber. Everyone involved in the drama was present, except the two principals. Eloise was still sleeping, although it was clear her slumber was now more natural. With Meg's assistance, he had stripped Eloise of her surcote and gown, and had wrapped her in a thick bed-robe before laying her back beneath the furs. She'd moved and murmured as she often did, snuggling against him while in his arms. Meg had cackled, as reassured as he.

Elspeth remained under lock and key—and guard. Rovogatti presently stood outside her door while Mistress Martin attended the deliberations.

"I find it all very hard to understand." Sir Howell Davarost, never an imposing sight, looked shattered. His weak face had crumpled; he looked helplessly about, as if hoping someone would rescue him from his plight.

Stoically, Alaun suppressed his contempt; he had expected neither sense nor support from that quarter. "The matter is beyond question, Sir Howell." They'd heard evidence from all sources, from the cook who had filled the ale-cup, to the archer who had seen Elspeth emerge from the stair to the stillroom with something clutched in her hand. Bit by bit, they'd traced what had occurred; it only remained for Alaun to decide what to do.

To pass judgment on his stepmother's goddaughter.

Lanella looked peaked and drawn; Alaun knew he looked haggard.

"As I see it, tis clear." He fixed Sir Howell with a steady gaze. "Elspeth Davarost, daughter of Sir Howell Davarost, of Davarost Manor by Worcester, poisoned my chatelaine, Eloise de Versallet, the widow of Raoul de Cannar, with intent to take her life. By the evidence of our collective experience, and by the testimony of Mistress Martin, hired by Sir Howell and Lady Davarost as keeper of their daughter, it seems certain that Elspeth Davarost is of unsound mind."

There was no murmur of dissent, only a pervasive expectation.

"That being so, I do hereby banish Elspeth Davarost from all lands I hold of the king. Once she leaves, she is never to return, on pain of death."

Lanella paled, but said nothing; Sir Howell shifted uncomfortably.

"As Mistress Martin has advised that Elspeth is likely to resist my injunction to leave, to the extent of acting in a manner likely to cause herself and others harm, I myself will lead the escort that will deliver her to Davarost Manor."

Murmurs broke out, a soft protest from Lanella, who would appreciate what it would cost him to leave Eloise at that time, a more robust protest, a curse, in fact, from Roland, who would not have him subject his temper to such strain. Sir Howell, of course, looked relieved; someone else was, after all, going to sort things out.

Alaun held up a hand to still the arguments. He had other reasons for journeying to Worcester, but did not intend discussing them. "We leave in an hour." Davarost Manor was some twenty miles distant. "After delivering Mistress Elspeth to her home, I will travel to Worcester to pass the night with my uncle, the bishop, before returning on the morrow." His gaze swept the room. "Humphrey, you'll take command here; Roland, you'll accompany me. We'll take a troop—I doubt we'll need more."

Roland looked like he wanted to argue, but nodded curtly.

A commotion beyond the door drew all eyes. At Alaun's intimation, Roland strode over and looked out. A minute later, Roland turned, pale and ready to move.

Alaun was already on his feet when his cousin's eyes met his.

"Rovogatti's been found with a broken head in Elspeth's chamber. The guards in the courtyard heard screaming, then all was silent. They sent one of their number up to check—he found the door wide and Rovogatti senseless."

"Turn out the garrison. Find her." Alaun threw the order at Humphrey and Edmund as he headed for the door.

Roland was waiting in the corridor. Without a word, they ran for Alaun's chamber.

Alaun charged through the door into his anteroom. And pulled up short.

A knife in his fist, Bilder was rising from where he'd been sitting, polishing a helmet in front of the bedchamber door. "Lord?"

Heaving a sigh of relief, Alaun clapped Bilder on the shoulder. "Elspeth's escaped, but clearly she has not come through here." Alaun turned to Roland. "Check the keep, and the lock on the stillroom door."

Roland nodded and left.

Alaun hesitated. He should go down and join the search, but the need to check on Eloise, to see if she'd awakened—and to calm his still prowling fear—waxed strong. Jenni was sitting with her, keeping watch now the worst was past. Turning to the bedchamber, he paused to tell Bilder, "I'm leaving within the hour to escort Mistress Davarost home. You'll accompany me. I'll be visiting my uncle—pack suitably. We'll return tomorrow."

"Aye, lord."

Alaun lifted the latch, and was about to shove the door open when it swung inward. He stared, then saw the marks of the carpenter's adze along its edge. Putting out a hand, he pushed the door wider, noting as he did the traces of fat on the barrels of the hinges. He swallowed a curse as the door opened—silently.

He stepped into the room, shutting the door behind him before turning to the bed.

The figure sitting in the chair drawn up by the side of the bed was not little Jenni. Straggly red tresses showed on either side of the chair's back.

One glance told Alaun the robin was nowhere in sight—that, impossible though it seemed, Elspeth was sitting calmly beside Eloise.

Rage poured through him, welling up, engulfing him, leaving a red haze before his eyes. He'd purposely avoided meeting Elspeth, knowing how he would feel when he did. Now, having had the occasion sprung upon him, base instinct took command. On silent feet, he approached the chair.

She neither heard nor sensed him.

From directly behind the chair, he looked down on Elspeth's head, on the slim column of her throat. He could snap it so easily. By his sides, his hands reflexively flexed, long fingers curling.

Almost of their own volition, his hands rose. He glanced at the bed. Eloise hadn't stirred; she lay curled on her side, one hand tucked beneath her cheek. Her breathing was deep and steady; the light flush of sleep shaded her cheeks.

The sight of her face, the serene perfection of her features, hauled him back from the brink. Killing Elspeth in Eloise's presence would be tantamount to sacrilege—he couldn't contaminate their love with such an act.

Slowly, very slowly, he forced his hands to the carved knobs ornamenting the top of the chair, and gripped them tightly. Bowing his head, he breathed deeply, willing the killing urge away.

'Elspeth heard his harsher breaths; she turned and saw him.

He raised his head—she smiled.

Inwardly, he shuddered. Why hadn't he seen the taint so clearly visible in her pale eyes? Because he, like everyone else who knew her, had grown used to her abominations, and hadn't been looking for the change that showed that she had passed beyond the pale. She had tried to kill—had felled Rovogatti simply because he stood in her way. And where was the robin?

But first, before he could consider anything else, he had to get Elspeth away from Eloise.

He forced himself to speak calmly. "Come, Elspeth—we're shortly to leave for your home. You will need to pack."

Her smile was delighted; she rose and turned to him. "I was just explaining it to her."

He made no comment, but stepped back, gesturing to the door.

Elspeth walked toward him, talking rapidly, breathlessly, excitedly. "I told her I wouldn't permit her to bear any babe of yours. I'm to be your lady, as everyone knows, and I will be mother to your heirs. You needn't deny you've grown infatuated with her to the point of gifting her with your seed—I witnessed all last morn—but I will not permit it. I have told her that, as her potion proved insufficient to kill her, I will allow her to leave. I will not tolerate her presence here when we are wed."

Smiling ingenuously, Elspeth halted before him. "Tis a pity for she is an excellent chatelaine, but we'll find another. And you may take another mistress—one to whom you will not become attached—perhaps from the women in the castle? There are many whores here—the little French one is very inventive. You would probably enjoy her."

To his intense relief, Elspeth stopped there. He stared down at her, horribly, unwillingly fascinated. Had she really crept in and watched them last morn? With the door as it was, she could have done so. Did she really imagine...such questions were pointless. He glanced at the bed.

Eloise was still asleep.

Inwardly sighing with relief, he waved to the door. "Come. We must hurry."

He kept sufficient space between them so she couldn't touch him; that he couldn't have borne. He opened the door and she preceded him into the anteroom, much to Bilder's consternation. Alaun signaled Bilder with his eyes; the squire came to attention, his gaze fixing on Elspeth.

"Elspeth, how did you get in there?" He asked the question in as calm and restrained a tone as he could manage.

Elspeth preened. "I had to talk to her so I used the service stair. I never knew it was there until I heard them clearing the bath while I was watching you last morn."

"And where is my...chatelaine's maid, the one who was sitting with her?"

"Oh, her." Elspeth shrugged. "I called her to the bathing chamber and tied her up. She was no trouble."

His temper very nearly broke free; he restrained it with difficulty. When he was sure he had it under control, he looked at Bilder, then at Elspeth. "I am giving you a direct order, Elspeth. Do you understand? You must not disobey. You will wait for me here."

With that, he returned to the bedchamber. One glance sufficed to reassure him that Eloise hadn't stirred. He strode to the bathing chamber, and found Jenni bundled in a corner, bound with towels and cords, bruised and frightened, tears streaking her small face.

"Tis all right," he soothed, as he lifted her and cut the cords, then tugged at the knotted towels. "Your lady is all right."

"That...that *witch* was here!" Jenni's hissed words testified to a depth of hatred he hadn't expected in one so timid.

"Aye—I have taken her out. Now listen, Jenni, for I must leave within minutes to take Mistress Davarost away. I'll return tomorrow. Take care of your lady whilst I'm gone. Rovogatti..." Alaun paused, not wishing to frighten the robin more. "Rovogatti will be here, too, so he will help if there's need." It would take more than a knock on the head to put the rugged Genoese out of action.

"Do not worry, lord. I will watch over her." Rubbing her chafed wrists, Jenni bustled through the doorway into the main chamber. She peeked at the bed. "She still sleeps—did the witch disturb her?"

"I think not." He looked long and hard at the slender figure in the bed, then glanced down at the robin. "I must leave now, Jenni."

"Aye, lord. Fare you well and may the saints send you swiftly home."

He nodded. And forced himself to go.

In one respect, his prediction fell false. Rovogatti was not incapacitated, yet neither was he staying behind. One look at the Genoese's set face, and Alaun didn't order him to do so. With Rovogatti in such a mood, Elspeth would have no chance of serving them any tricks.

He didn't take any chances on the ride. Their departure from castle and town was watched by many—in unnatural silence. If Elspeth had possessed any normal sensitivity, she would have cringed from the threat implicit in the quiet crowds—one reason he was determined to get her away without delay.

The twenty miles to Davarost Manor were covered at a furious pace, much to the discomfort of Sir Howell and Mistress Martin. The former warbled complaints to which no one gave heed; the latter bore it stoically. On her flighty mare, Elspeth was wedged between the troop's mounts, a burly sergeant before her and Rovogatti directly behind; when she pertly tried to insist on riding at the head of the column next to Alaun, he refused her so curtly she instinctively recoiled.

Thereafter she kept silent, until they were cantering into the courtyard of Davarost Manor. Then, from her prattle, it became abundantly clear that she believed they'd returned to her home to be wed. Alaun left her with her father and Mistress Martin and strode in to see his godmother.

Lucilla, Lady Davarost, had little in common with her husband. A handsome woman, she managed the manor and Sir Howell's interests with an eagle eye, and otherwise devoted her attention to her ever-increasing brood.

Alaun laid the matter of Elspeth's transgressions plainly before her. Lucilla was deeply shocked, and manifestly remorseful and apologetic. Alaun accepted her regrets, tendered to himself, Eloise, and his people. Without quibble, Lucilla accepted his edict banishing Elspeth from his lands, assuring him that Elspeth would be confined, and would cause no further trouble. After assuring Lucilla in return that she and the rest of her offspring would always be welcome at Montisfryn, Alaun took his leave.

His visit with his uncle, the Bishop of Worcester, was a more relaxing affair. Alaun and his men arrived late, but, always keen for news, the bishop made them most welcome. Restricting himself to recounting the events surrounding the fall of Calais while they supped, surrounded by his uncle's servitors, Alaun waited until they retired to the privacy his uncle's sanctum to broach the real purpose of his visit.

His uncle grimaced as he considered Alaun's question. "Legally, you need not. Politically, however, I believe you should. Edward's unlikely to be thrillingly happy with you if you do not, despite his edict."

Alaun heaved a disgusted sigh. "Aye—so I thought."

"Mind you," his uncle continued, "as there's no impediment to this marriage, if there was any reasonable reason, twould not be untoward for you to go ahead without the king's assent, given he has not forbidden the match outright."

"He'll not do that. He's beholden to both myself and the de Versallets over this last campaign, and will be keen to keep our support. Tis the likelihood of extended negotiations I like not—you know how Edward and his treasurer think. And the lady is exceedingly well-dowered."

"Oh, I quite see your point. You would rather marry her this year than two years hence."

"Exactly." Alaun eyed his uncle squarely. "So what constitutes a 'reasonable reason'?"

The bishop rolled the thought around as he savored his mead. "The easiest way would be to get the lady pregnant—that would certainly constitute reasonable reason. The Church would then support you—we're very keen to have as many legitimate souls in our cure as possible."

Alaun felt his lips lift for the first time that day, his usual confidence resurfacing. "That matter is already in hand. How far along does this reasonable reason have to be?"

The bishop waved airily. "Not far at all. Enough to be obvious. Once that much reason exists, tisn't likely to go away, so there's no call to hang back—the wedding can go ahead, and little matters like Edward's consent can be sorted out later."

"Good!" The tension—the fear, the panic, the chill terror he could not name—that had gripped him for the past twenty-four hours receded even further. Eloise would be his—legally, morally—as much his as his lands and equally under his protection, in a month, two at the worst. Hopefully sooner.

The bishop smiled benignly. "Is that all you wanted to know?"

"Aye." Alaun reached for his goblet. "My other questions have all been answered."

* * *

When the door closed behind Montisfryn, and Jenni resumed her seat, Eloise finally allowed her senses to sink back into the billowing clouds that beckoned. Her mind was able to function, yet her body would not awake. It had required a huge effort to lift her lids when she'd heard Elspeth's voice—fear had lent her the strength to do so.

The sight that had met her wavering gaze had hardly been reassuring. The scrawny witch had been sitting in Alaun's carved chair, where previously Eloise had sensed Jenni's soothing presence. Her robin had disappeared—which was probably as well considering some of the things Elspeth had said. Eloise had closed her eyes, but her mind had listened, appalled by Elspeth's depravity. Even more appalling had been the witch's vision of the future. Thankfully, Alaun had come and had taken Elspeth away, and had brought Jenni back.

It was safe to sleep again.

Eloise awoke in mid-afternoon, fully restored, well-rested and ravenous. While she satisfied her hunger, doing justice to the feast Cook had instantly sent up on being informed of her need, she quizzed Jenni on what had occurred. "The last I remember was feeling ill and going out onto the keep steps."

"You swooned, lady, and would have fallen down the steps, but the lord reached you just in time. He caught you up and brought you in. Twas very shocking for us all."

"Hmm, yes." The mists parted; she recalled Montisfryn's face as he'd run toward her. "He brought me up here?"

"Aye—and stayed with you all night. He didn't leave until it was clear you were on the mend."

"Ah." She had a dim memory of being held in his arms not so long ago. Frowning, she picked up a sliver of apple. "What happened between?" Elspeth had said she had poisoned her, and when Eloise had awakened, she'd tasted rosemary on her tongue.

Jenni shifted on the stool. "I can't rightly say, lady. The lord was here, and Lady de Montisfryth, too, until late. They didn't call for me till morning."

Eloise nodded and let the matter slide—she would learn the truth when Montisfryn returned. Until then, Lanella could no doubt ease her curiosity.

But, "She's not well, lady," Jenni informed her. "Maud said the strain of yesterday, and this morn when she farewelled Mistress Elspeth, fair brought her low. She's laid up, and Maud said as she hoped she'd stay quiet until tomorrow."

"Aye—I'll not disturb her. Who else is here?"

When Jenni told her, Eloise did not hold back her grimace. Not even Roland. She felt close enough to Edmund to question him on most subjects, but Jenni had said he hadn't been present through the evening and night, and she didn't wish to pry in ways that might strain his loyalty.

So she would have to bear her questions in patience.

Giving orders for the bedchamber to be aired and freshened, she doffed the heavy bed-robe in favor of a fresh scarlet cote and surcote, and went up to the top of the keep.

The servants she passed smiled hugely, nodding politely, clearly delighted to see her recovered. On the battlements, the guards saluted her. Her smile broad, she paced the walks, the brisk breeze blowing the last remnants of sleep from her mind. She leaned on the battlements and looked out over the fields and forests.

And remembered leaning thus on her father's battlements and thinking of her dreams. Dreams she'd lost all hope of realizing until Montisfryn had arrived and proved her wrong.

He'd vanquished her memories and laid them to rest.

He had made her the lady of a large and prosperous establishment; he would be back tomorrow to stand, strong and protective, by her side. As for children, with time, by the saints' grace, they, too, would come.

And, to crown all, the last vital ingredient—the one that would breathe life into her dreams and protect them against the chill winds of fortune—was theirs.

She loved him—and she knew he loved her.

Triumphant, her spirits soaring, she breathed deeply of the crisp autumnal air. The last rays of the setting sun lingered gently on her face, reminding her of his gaze.

Tomorrow, when he rode in, she would not let him distract her—not until *after* she had called him husband.

Chapter 20

Triumphant anticipation held Eloise in thrall—up until the moment a messenger in the de Versallet livery stood before her in the hall and declared: "I bear greetings from your father, lady. He, together with your brothers William and John, lies west of Gloucester in company with the king. They're much engaged in chasing outlaws, but your sire sees an end to that in two or three days. He would visit with you, lady, and sends word the king accompanies him. Our sovereign is much inclined to visit with his vassal and late comrade-in-arms, the Earl of Montisfryn."

Eloise simply stared as the glorious scene she'd spent all afternoon rehearsing faded from her mind, consigned to oblivion by grim reality. She blinked; the hall, and the expectant faces of her new household, all seated for supper, crowded in.

Suppressing the almost overwhelming urge to curse her father, she forced a smile and waved the messenger, one of William's squires, to a position in the hall.

"Tis a great honor, lady." Edmund, seated beside her, was all gratified anticipation. "Edward's not visited for many years, not since the lady's illness came on."

"Aye." She tried to sound enthusiastic. "But there's much work involved." Her mind was racing, weighing possibilities, likelihoods, and certainties. The urge to curse her father grew. She turned to Edmund. "Tis very likely that with the aftermath of my illness, while I may be awake through the night, I will need my rest tomorrow. Think you, if I write instructions for what needs doing for the king's visit, you could relay them to my people on the morrow?"

"Assuredly, lady."

One point settled. There was much yet to organize.

After all she'd been through—Raoul and the years of loneliness—she was not about to let her sire ruin her one great scene.

* * *

She left before dawn, passing through the barbican the instant the drawbridges were lowered and the gates swung wide. The flickering torchlight worked to her advantage, allowing her to pass as a maid sent into town on an urgent errand. Exiting the town gates was easy, the town guards having no responsibility for castlefolk.

After a night spent with parchment and ink, drawing up a long list of orders for the household, then slaving over the letter she'd left for Montisfryn, she was ready to let the strong little cob she'd extracted from the stables play out his friskiness in a lively gallop. The road leading south lay before them, empty at present; she kept to the well-beaten surface as long as she dared—only when the sun was well up and the walls of Leominster rose ahead did she leave the road to cut southwestward.

A few comfortable nights and peaceful days at Claerwhen would see them clear of Edward and her father. She had suggested Montisfryn explain her absence on the grounds of an urgent summons to attend the deathbed of one of her more august teachers—a weak excuse on which to absent oneself from one's sovereign's presence, but it would have to do. There was no reason Edward should have any burning desire to meet *her*, after all.

The cob coped well with the rougher terrain; she congratulated herself on having chosen him. Jacquenta was too well-known; if she had taken the mare, Montisfryn's guards would have stopped her and, albeit with the greatest deference, would have checked with Humphrey before letting her through. And Humphrey would not have let her leave. He would have insisted, terribly politely, that she wait for Montisfryn himself. And, of course, pigheadedly arrogant male that *he* was, he would definitely not have let her go.

From her point of view, it was impossible to stay.

If she did, Edward and her father would insist she marry Montisfryn the minute they learned that she was sharing his bed. Given the normal standards of castle gossip, that meant approximately an hour after they arrived. As Montisfryn was already under edict to wed, the chances of refusing were nil. Not that *he* would balk.

But if she allowed such an event to come about, he would never believe that she, of her own will and desire, had agreed to call him husband. And if *he* didn't believe that, *she* would never hear the words she was determined, someday, to wring from him.

Even should he return to the castle before the king arrived, and she told him then, there was no way to hide her knowledge of Edward's impending arrival. Montisfryn would think she had agreed solely to avert Edward's otherwise inevitable reaction.

Not because she loved him.

If there was one point she was determined to make clear, it was that she *did*.

After the king and her father had departed, Montisfryn would come for her. Free of all possible coercions, she would tell him—clearly, unequivocally, unambiguously—that she loved him and was prepared to call him husband from that day forth.

Nothing and no one—not even the king—was going to deprive her— and Alaun—of that.

Hopefully, he would understand why she hadn't taken an escort.

She grimaced. Then fell to considering the best way to distract him.

The Welsh hills loomed on her right. Her goal was the hamlet of Vowchurch, guarding the bridge over the River Dore. By her calculations, she would gain Claerwhen's walls by mid-afternoon; imagining her reception, she rode on.

* * *

Having left Worcester at daybreak, Alaun strode up the steps of his keep an hour before noon. The courtyard was a-bustle, his servitors busy about their business; pleasing aromas wafted from the kitchens, presaging dinner. All was peaceful, serene, well-ordered.

Gaining the top step, he raised a brow at his steward, waiting, alone, to greet him. His chatelaine, presumably, was still resting.

That supposition was quickly confirmed.

"She was very well last night, lord. Fully recovered. But she warned she did not expect to find sleep easily through the night, and would likely lie abed this morn." Edmund went on to detail the king's projected visit, de Versallets and all.

Reaching the hall, grinning, Alaun clapped Edmund on the shoulder. "I could not have had more welcome news."

He was tempted to announce that the festivities surrounding the king's visit would include his marriage, but he swallowed the words. Edward was ever unpredictable—and Alaun had yet to discuss the details with Eloise.

That thought sent him to their chamber. He opened the door and saw, as he'd been warned to expect, the bed with its curtains closed.

The sight didn't fool him for an instant; he *knew* she wasn't there.

Smothering an oath, he wrenched the curtains aside. His disbelieving gaze fell on the silk coverlet, neatly laid, the pillows undented. Propped against them lay a packet of parchment. Grabbing it up, he read his name inscribed in Eloise's neat hand.

With a vitriolic curse, he broke the seal.

As he read her message, his scowl deepened.

"How is she?"

Glancing up, Alaun saw Roland peering around the door. "Gone."

"*What?*"

Eloise's precise lettering covered sheet after sheet. Confusion increasing, Alaun sifted through the pile. "Apparently, she's gone to visit at Claerwhen until the king and her father leave. I'm to send for her once they've gone."

Roland's bewilderment mirrored his. "Doesn't she like Edward?"

Alaun uttered a frustrated growl. "This makes no sense!" He reached the end of the missive, only to be informed that Eloise would explain all when next she saw him. Exasperation overflowed. "By all the saints, *now what?*"

"I hesitate to mention it, but this isn't going to look good when Edward arrives with old Henry in his train." Roland caught his eye. "If we leave now, you can reach Claerwhen on her heels, and sort it out, soothe her feathers or whatever. Then she can be here at your side when Edward rides in."

"Precisely my thinking." Alaun was already reshuffling the pages, scanning each carefully. "I wonder how many men she took...with...her?"

Alaun stilled. For the space of three heartbeats, he remained utterly frozen. Then, slowly, he raised his head until his gaze met Roland's.

There were times Roland literally gave thanks that he'd known Montisfryn from the cradle. It helped take the edge from the instinctive fear that gripped anyone forced to witness the transformation from sleepy lion to roaring predator, from lazy arrogance to contained, but raging fury.

"Send to the gates. I want the men who allowed my lady to pass unescorted this morn in the hall immediately."

Roland didn't reply—he leapt to obey. No one dallied when Montisfryn employed such flatly lethal tones.

Alone, Alaun closed his eyes, willing his fury and the cold terror that fueled it back under his control. Opening his eyes, he flung the pages of Eloise's missive back on the bed and strode to the door. "This time, lady-witch, when I catch up with you, I *will* beat you."

He growled the vow through clenched teeth. Even as he made it, he knew it would be broken, but the sentiment, expressed, relieved a little of his ire.

"Don't bother unpacking," he snarled at Bilder as he marched across the anteroom. "We're leaving immediately for a few days chase."

"Hunting, lord?"

"Aye." He knew his smile was feral. "Hunting." A lady-witch. With a view to taming.

He slammed out of the room and stalked down the corridor.

Roland returned to the hall as the guards were filing out. The matter of punishment had been straightforward—the guards were supposed to verify the identity of every person who passed through the gates; they should certainly have questioned a lone woman leaving before dawn.

Roland caught Alaun's eye. "I've a troop mounted and waiting."

Alaun rose. "Humphrey, you're in charge. I doubt Edward will arrive before I return, but should he do so, you'll bid him welcome in my stead, and offer him the comforts of this hall. Lord de Versallet, also—he's my lady's father."

"Aye, lord."

Grave and concerned, Humphrey accompanied them outside.

Alaun had Gabriel's reins in his hand when a messenger, the gold leopards of England leaping on his livery, thundered into the courtyard. The man threw himself out of his saddle and presented himself with a flourish.

"My lord earl! Edward, King of England, France, and Wales, bids you come to his aid!"

Alaun scowled. "*By St. George's dragon!* What now?"

The squire looked taken aback.

"L-lord?" he faltered, then he gamely recovered. "His Grace has been engaged in fearsome battles with outlaw knights and other nefarious brigands. He has pushed up from Southampton, where he landed fresh from Calais, and has joined with Lord de Versallet in sweeping all northward before them. From Gloucester, His Grace summoned the Earl of Oxford to strike from the east. Now, he summons you to join him, sweeping the area clear as you come south."

Edward's strategy was clear. With the Welsh mountains to the west, the outlaws would be trapped, and forced to yield. Alaun sighed. "Aye, well." He turned to Humphrey. "Turn out the garrison. I'll take two companies with me, both with a full complement of archers, all mounted. A third company, likewise supported, to follow with the wagons."

Even as he spoke, his men were scattering, the troop already mounted dismounting and racing off to don half-armor. Bilder had already disappeared back into the keep.

"As for the rest—" Alaun continued with instructions for his vassals, concluding with, "Summon Sir Eward and provision wagons to his instructions from the castle stores. I expect this to take no more than three days, but he had better bring provisions for a week. Knowing Edward, if these outlaws are lunatic enough to try for Wales, he'll have us up on the passes playing catch-me-who-can."

Humphrey grinned.

The messenger looked shocked.

Straight-faced, Alaun dropped a hand to the lad's shoulder. "You'd best hie to the kitchens and recoup, squire. I do believe that was the longest royal summons I have ever received."

Humphrey choked, but the squire looked pleased. He bowed and hurried off.

Alaun turned, one brow rising. "*Fearsome* battles? With *nefarious* brigands?" He shook his head. "I must remember to ask Edward about those."

Half an hour later, they rode out, harness clinking, squires leading the heavy destriers scattered through the ranks. The noise as they clattered over the cobbles brought the townsfolk to their windows. They cheered and waved. Acknowledging the greetings, Alaun felt impatience gnaw at him even as premonition touched chill fingers to his nape. Gabriel, infected with his mood, sidled and tugged at the reins, literally champing at the bit. Catching Roland's cautious sideways glance, Alaun favored him with a blank stare.

Roland was clearly relieved at being spared worse.

As soon as they were clear of the town, Alaun deployed his force in a wide arc to east and west of the road, reaching to the foothills in the west, and to the edges of the forest in the east. That done, he delegated command of the sweep to his senior household knights and, with Roland's original hand-picked troop, spurred ahead. The squires leading the destriers fell behind as the palfreys thundered down the road.

They passed through Leominster at a trot and continued south.

Alaun had intended going straight to Claerwhen to make sure of Eloise before heading south to join the king. However, when Hereford hove in sight, lit by the westering sun, he saw the familiar golden leopards flying above the gates. The sight filled him with disquiet.

A disquiet that grew as they entered the city to find it awash with Edward's guardsmen and de Versallet vassals. The king had moved north very swiftly.

The outcome was predictable.

"Lost them!" Edward's fist slammed into the table before him. "They must've slipped sideways, though the lord knows to where. We'll know soon enough. The scouts have been out since noon."

Lounging at one end of the small table, Alaun saw no benefit in comment.

Edward eyed him narrowly. "I suppose you're going to tell me I was too impatient?"

Alaun raised his brows. "Me, sire? Never. Where's the need?"

Edward's roaring laugh filled the room.

"Be damned to you, Alaun." Edward smiled, hazel eyes slightly rueful, then abruptly, he sobered. "But this is more your country than ours. I'm grateful you came so promptly."

Alaun inclined his head. "As it happened, sire, I was coming this way on other business." He lifted his tankard and took a long draft, using the moment to slam a mental door on his burgeoning fear.

Naturally, Edward was curious. "What business?"

Alaun let his gaze rest on the only other occupant of the small chamber. Henry de Versallet returned his regard from the other end of the table. "The matter concerns a piece of property recently made into my care."

Henry's eyes lit, but his expression turned commiserating. "Difficult matter?" he suggested.

Alaun allowed his lips to curve. "In some respects." He turned to Edward. "Your Grace, I would respectfully petition you as regards this property."

Not at all shortsighted, Edward was intrigued. "How so?"

"Before I make the matter plain, Your Grace, I would remind you of the duty you laid upon me when last I took my leave of you."

It took Edward a moment to recall the point. "To secure the March, and—*to marry*?" Edward sat up, his long nose all but twitching. "You wish to present a candidate for my approval?"

Alaun inclined his head. "Aye, Your Grace." There would be no better time—Edward would shortly have need of both him and the de Versallets.

"Well?" Edward sat back. "Who is this lady?"

"She's the daughter of another of your vassals, sire. A widow."

Edward frowned. "A widow?" He pulled thoughtfully at his beard. "You know, Alaun, I'm not saying anything against this lady, mind, but widows have a nasty tendency to have developed damned sharp tongues. I have often remarked it."

Henry quietly choked.

It took no effort at all to look wry. "Aye, sire, you have the right of it. Tis my sorrow and a burden, but..." He shrugged. "There are compensations."

Edward roared; Henry had yet to get his breath back.

"So it's like that, is it? You've developed a taste for the wench and wish to commit yourself for life? Ah, well—it comes to us all, and you've escaped a damned sight longer than most. Come, then—who is she?"

"Eloise née de Versallet."

Edward sat up. Totally sober, he favored Henry with a long look, then turned back to Alaun, hazel eyes narrowing. "What is this, eh? A conspiracy?"

Alaun raised both brows. "Nay, sire—how so? Until your summons arrived, I never knew you, or Lord de Versallet, were here."

Having rapidly assimilated his present position, Edward looked unconvinced. "Just good management, hmm?"

A shrug seemed the wisest answer.

Edward cleared his throat. "This widow—to whom was she married?"

Henry answered. "De Cannar, sire."

Startled, Edward swung to face Henry. "*That one?* The one who's been your chatelaine for the last some years?"

Henry nodded. Edward slowly turned back to Alaun, his gaze intensely suspicious.

Unaffected by the king's scrutiny, Alaun waited.

Eventually, Edward humphed. "What I want to know is how you got close enough without losing anything vital. From all I've heard, the lady's a potent source of frostbite."

Alaun's smile felt brittle. "Tis a matter of technique."

Edward's reply was decidedly brusque.

"Am I to take it you approve, Your Grace?" Half-answers would avail them naught.

Edward grumbled into his beard; he cast a darkling glance at Henry, whose expression remained utterly guileless, before muttering, "Aye—though tis a fine thing when such decisions are demanded at such short notice. I like it not."

Alaun inclined his head. "You have my promise not to repeat the offence, sire."

That got Edward laughing again.

Under cover of their sovereign's mirth, Henry raised his goblet in a silent toast, gray eyes gleaming.

"Where is this lady, then?" Edward demanded. "You said something about being made over as property—is she at Montisfryn?"

Meeting Edward's gaze, Alaun struggled to quell his anger. "Not at this moment, sire." He let his lids veil his eyes. "Lord de Versallet gave her into my care some weeks ago—you will doubtless hear of the event—twas over a tournament."

"Aye?" The mere mention of a tournament brought a glow to Edward's eyes.

Alaun nodded. "She's now chatelaine at Montisfryn, pending our marriage. Unfortunately, she has an exceedingly unsuitable and long-ingrained habit of which I have yet to break her. Rest assured I shall do so. However, such as it is, the lady is presently at Claerwhen."

"Claerwhen, heh? But what is this habit of which you so disapprove?"

Alaun felt his expression harden. His fingers clenched on the handle of his tankard. "She slipped from Montisfryn, purposely tricking my guards, and hied to Claerwhen—on her own."

For a long moment, Edward simply stared at him. Then the king erupted.

"Damnation!" Edward thumped the table. "You had better break her of this habit soon, my friend, for I won't have it! Here am I, striving to rid the countryside of these thieving jackals, while some witless woman worth more than my mint flitters about the fields like a newborn lamb trying to find a wolf!"

With a dramatic gesture, Edward turned on Alaun, hazel eyes glinting. "I'm exceedingly glad, Montisfryn, that you've taken on this arduous task. I intend to hold you to it. You'll keep this woman under control—by St. George and all the saints, if you can't do it, no one can!"

"You have my word on it, sire."

"Humph! Yes, well—make sure that you keep it." Edward, color high, paused for a gulp of ale.

It was clearly a propitious time to change the subject. Alaun leaned back in his chair. "But how is it a mere band of outlaws has attracted Your Grace's attention?"

Edward waved a hand. "Tis not just any mere band. There's far more involved here than that."

Effectively distracted, Edward settled his elbows on the table. "Apparently, this group decided that, while the rest of us were winning booty in France, they would help themselves to some on this side of the Channel. A little matter of intimidation, then payment demanded from the wool merchants to ensure their pack trains reached the coast. The courts have been inundated with pleas. The burghers are complaining, the merchants, the weavers—even the shippers. Tis half a crisis, have no doubt. But the odd thing is, this crew has been mighty efficient, always concentrating on the most productive areas. You know how the clip varies—these jackals always seem to know where the pickings will be richest. The merchants are justifiably uneasy."

And Edward needed the continued backing of the merchant guilds to further his prospects in France. Alaun saw it all—no further explanation was needed.

"Their leaders are landless knights, which explains their success until now."

Alaun raised his brows. "So tis not a disorganized rabble that we face?"

Edward shook his head, his resurfacing grin one of wolfish anticipation. "Nay—we should have good sport, by all accounts. De Vere should be here soon—his column has been sighted to the east."

Noise of an arrival filtered through the door.

"Hah!" Edward set down his tankard. "My scouts, no doubt."

But it was Roland who entered, followed by a thin cleric. They made obeisance to Edward; catching Alaun's eye, Roland shook his head, then spoke to Edward. "Forgive the intrusion, sire, but we have news."

"Aye?"

"The outlaws you seek are encamped before the convent of Claerwhen. They've surrounded the gate, and are attempting to gain entry. This is Father Laertis, an envoy of the Bishop of Hereford. He was visiting the convent and slipped out to summon assistance. We came up with him just beyond the outlaws' pickets."

Edward was frowning. "But what the devil were you...?" His words trailed away.

Alaun felt Edward's glance, but kept his gaze on Roland. His face, he knew, was expressionless. "Did you see her?"

Roland wetted his lips. "I didn't—but Father Laertis did."

The cleric took up the tale. "A lady fitting the description of the one these knights seek rode into the outlaw camp an hour or more ago. She was alone and was within their pickets before she realized. They have her in the leader's tent."

Alaun swore—one short, eminently expressive oath—then he clamped a lid on his fury.

"Did you see this leader?" Edward asked the cleric.

"Aye, Your Grace—a dark, heavy-jowled fellow. I have recently seen him about the town, but have never heard his name." Father Laertis drew himself up. "Sire, I was on my way to beg the bishop to send relief to the ladies of the convent."

The situation was guaranteed to appeal to Edward. Through the haze of his rage, Alaun heard the king say, "You may leave the matter in my hands, Father. Convey my greetings to the bishop, and assure him the convent will be relieved within two hours."

The good father looked confused. "But, sire—tis barely more than two hours till dusk."

Edward rose. "Aye, and Claerwhen is less than an hour away. Come, Montisfryn, de Versallet! We'll finish with this lot by nightfall!"

* * *

As Edward ordered, so it occurred. John de Vere, the Earl of Oxford, rode in at Hereford's northeastern gate—and rode straight out by the west one. His forces formed the rearguard of an aggressively intent, highly skilled small army that descended on the sleepy hamlet of Vowchurch and, unchallenged, crossed the Dore. Once on the far bank, the generals paused to take stock. At Alaun's suggestion, Roland was summoned to where he and the others conferred on a small hillock.

As Roland came up, Edward was speaking, squatting to draw in the dust. "From memory, the rise yonder forms the rim of a large depression. The convent stands at the far side, built out from the cliff beyond. Tis my thinking the outlaws must be encamped directly beneath the walls—here." Edward made a mark in the earth, then glanced up at Roland. "Is that so, de Haverthorne?"

"Aye, sire." Roland accepted the stick from Edward and filled in the outlaws' position. "Tis my feeling this leader has not much experience in tactics, sire, for he's drawn up his force very tightly—from here to here—and set his pickets close in—about here."

Alaun pounced on that. "So they'll not have seen us yet?"

Roland agreed.

Edward grinned ferociously. "Tis easy, then—we'll deploy about them. De Vere, you take the left, de Versallet and I will hold the center and I'll send Nick Dreythorne to command Montisfryn's men on the right."

That last command was not one Alaun had expected. Straightening, he raised his brows at the king.

Edward's hazel eyes met his, then he clapped him on the shoulder. "Take a small force and strike direct for the leader's tent. Leave the battle to us, my friend, and concentrate your energies on getting your lady out of it."

Grim-faced, Alaun nodded.

The Earl of Oxford was frowning. "One moment, sire. What if, in order to escape our approach, the brigands force the walls of the convent?"

Edward snorted and pulled on his gauntlets. "The walls of Claerwhen are amongst the strongest in the land. I should know—Philippa extracted the price of reinforcing them from me some years back."

"But what if they use pitch-arrows to set the buildings within ablaze—to act as a diversion?"

"The buildings within are all good stone and slate. That damned convent is in better order than any castle standing—except his." Edward jerked a thumb in Alaun's direction. "And before you suggest that the good ladies might not approve of us bloodying their walls, let me tell you that old Maude de Lacey, who is presently Mother Superior, would be more likely to order up hot pitch and firestones than swoon at the sight of battle. Nay—quibble no more. Let us have done."

Thus relieved of his major command, Alaun left the other commanders to coordinate their attack. Summoning ten of his most experienced men, he and Roland headed off on foot. The wagons had caught up and were quietly rolling across the narrow bridge; to right and left, the king's forces were already deploying along the riverbank, ready to advance.

Alaun and his men toiled up the short incline, cresting the ridge well to the right, where a wood gave them cover. Slipping stealthily beneath the trees, they silenced the pickets stationed within the wood, then moved on, only stopping where the trees gave way to grassed pasture. The largest tent, one of dun-colored canvas, stood a hundred yards away.

Alaun could not take his eyes from it. He knew how easy it was for someone to be killed in the chaos of battle. Fear such as he had never known gripped him; black terror filled his soul. A deathly chill clutched his gut, slowly permeating to his bones. Beneath his helm, his lips moved in silent prayer.

Still as a statue in the shadows of the trees, despite the desperate compulsion riding him, he waited for the approach of the king's forces.

* * *

Within the dun-colored tent, Eloise sat bound on a stool, her back to the central pole, a gag over her lips, a bruise throbbing high on her cheekbone. Her head ached, but beyond that and her less than comfortable position, she was conscious only of growing impatience. Fear had no purchase in her mind; her captors would have thought her insane had they known that she considered them nothing more than nuisances sent by the saints to plague her.

She already knew salvation was at hand. Her only worry was that whoever Montisfryn had sent to verify that she had reached the convent safely would bring Montisfryn himself, and possibly Edward and her father, too, down upon the outlaws—and her.

It would be nice to be saved, but for what? Montisfryn would be furious, and Edward and her father equally irate, although possibly not for the same reasons.

Such thoughts made her head throb even more; determinedly, she banished them. She would worry about such dangers when they arrived.

"I don't like it."

The black knight Eloise had seen in the grounds of Gloucester cathedral paced back and forth across the tent. "That damned witch of an abbess is up to something."

"You worry too much, Cedric." His strangled-voiced clerkish friend lounged on a stool by a table. "In his usual impetuous way, Edward is probably halfway to Shrewsbury by now. The ladies of the convent will, I'm sure, see the sense in sharing their provisions in return for their colleague."

The clerk's sharp gaze rested on Eloise; after a moment, it shifted, fixing on the black knight's ogreish visage.

"It would be wise to bear in mind, Cedric, that Lady de Cannar is presently our most valuable asset. Not only will fear for her gain us provisions enough to dare Wales in winter, but if we play our cards right and keep her in our hands, we may well turn a nice profit."

"Nay—I like that scheme not. We should leave her here." Sir Cedric thumped the table as he passed. "Taking her will keep de Versallet, at least, on our trail, and what if, as she claims, Montisfryn seeks her? His forces are considerable—he will crush us like ants. All we have are a handful of hedge-knights."

"Afraid?" The strangled voice sneered. "I thought you boasted you could take on any knight spurred and not fail."

The sneer was returned in full measure. "In single combat, aye, but we are not talking about honorable, chivalric fighting here, Master Driscoll. If we engage with any of the king's vassals, the fighting will be bloody and furious—and we will not prevail. I did not join your enterprise to have my skull crushed by some knight's mace."

Master Driscoll. It was the first time Eloise had heard the clerk's name. She had yet to fully understand what these men were about, but Master Driscoll was at the heart of it.

When she'd ridden into their midst, surprised but not alarmed as there had been nothing to show if they were friend or foe—and she'd never imagined a foe camped outside her convent gates—these two had been all but at each other's throats. Apparently, they had tried to storm the convent, only to discover how impregnable Claerwhen was. Eventually learning who she was, and that she was known to those within, after some discussion, they had dragged her before the walls.

Summoned to the walks high above, Mother Maude had looked down at her, and had clicked her tongue. "What are you doing here, Eloise?"

She'd explained, only to have Mother Maude bend an exasperated glare upon her.

Sir Cedric, standing beside her, thumbs hooked in his belt, had raised his dark voice. "Open your doors and let us provision our wagons, lady, and we will return your daughter to you."

"Nay, Mother! Do not. They will not kill me—I'm worth more to them alive." She hadn't anticipated Sir Cedric's reaction, but a blur at the edge of her vision had had her moving away—his blow had not landed full on her jaw. It had felled her nonetheless.

"*Cease*, sir knight! Lay another finger on the lady and you will *rue the day!*"

The furious words had fallen, ringing, from the battlements above, giving even Sir Cedric pause.

Senses swimming, Eloise had glanced up to see her erstwhile Mother Superior shoot a contemptuous glare at the burly knight. Then the wily old lady had turned to Master Driscoll. "This matter will require discussion. I'm Mother Superior here—although my word is final, I am bound to consult the wishes of the community. I will go and confer, and return with our answer."

With that, Mother Maude had departed, leaving Eloise blinking up at the vacant battlements, recalling that, not only did Mother Maude rule with absolute authority, but that the river and Vowchurch could be seen from the higher levels of Claerwhen's towers.

The only explanation for Mother Maude's words was that help was close at hand.

Chafing restlessly against her bonds, Eloise wondered when it would arrive.

When it did, she was one of the first to know. The tent pole to which she was bound started to vibrate. A surge of nervy excitement rushed through her. Destriers were approaching—lots of them.

* * *

In the shadows of the wood, Alaun breathed deeply, his eyes on the line of Edward's advance. Mounted knights came over the ridge, trotting forward to enclose the outlaw encampment in a semicircle of burnished steel. To shouts of alarm and the usual rush to don armor and seize weapons, the line drew inexorably closer, locking the outlaws against the convent walls. The knights halted just out of bowshot of the hastily drawn up defenders.

Still, Alaun waited.

An order was barked, and archers, his own men on the right flank and the massed archers of the king, de Versallet, and de Vere on the left, stepped forward. Sheets of arrows rained down, felling the outlaws' bowmen before they'd received orders to mass and fire. Panic rose within the outlaws' ranks, then a brawling voice was raised, cursing the waverers back into line.

Lifting his head, Alaun located the source; a huge, black-armored knight, who had emerged from the dun-colored tent.

Beneath his helm, Alaun's lips curled in a snarl. The warrior-impulse to go after the leader was strong, but was a river ripple compared to the tidal wave of instinct that compelled him to Eloise's side. His eyes returned to the dun-colored tent, then he glanced at the men behind him. "We secure and hold the tent at all costs."

They nodded.

Alaun turned to see the king's archers retire, revealing the knights, now dismounted. Limited by the convent walls, the field was too circumscribed for a mounted charge. Instead, Edward's massed men-at-arms raised their voices in a bellowing roar, the names of their commanders joining those of all the saints as they strode forward, eager to dispatch their foes.

Alaun waited until the first wave had broken over the outermost outlaws and the battle was fully engaged before raising his arm, his sword gripped in his fist. "On!"

Despite their lack of numbers, his men were used to such fighting; in a tight wedge, they drove through the ranks of the outlaws like a hot knife through butter, leaving corpses in their wake.

The outlaw leader, large and black, remained behind the innermost ranks, watching the battle, gauging the tide. He had yet to join the fight, but his huge broadsword hung ready in his fist. Twenty yards from the tent, Alaun's force fanned out to encircle it. In that instant, the black knight turned and saw them.

With a bellow, he summoned a small group held in reserve in the lee of the convent walls close behind the tent. They rushed forward, interposing themselves between Alaun's party and their objective. Cursing, Alaun and his men redeployed to meet the unexpected attack. The outlaw line to their left collapsed, pushed in by knights of Alaun's household eager to support him. As a result, he was caught up in the melee, surrounded on all sides, too busy defending, then crushing, to immediately press on to the tent.

Around and about them the battle raged.

Pulling his sword from the chest of a pikesman, Sir Cedric de Croilly stepped back and rapidly took stock. Desperation's cold claws were already deep in his flesh. His forces would shortly fail—he would be handed over to Edward, a king who took great delight in making examples of those of whom he disapproved. And traitorous knights sat high on Edward's list of abominations.

There was but one slim chance of altering the outcome. Cursing darkly, Sir Cedric turned and fought his way back to his tent.

* * *

Inside the tent, Eloise sat her stool, every muscle rigid, her eyes fixed on the slim dagger that had appeared in Master Driscoll's white fingers. Fear caressed her nape; panic threatened. She ignored both emotions, her only thought to survive.

"Such a pity, dear lady, that it has to come to this." Master Driscoll rose from the stool and paused to resettle his garnache. "But you can see that it wouldn't do to leave you alive to identify me?"

With an empty smile, he started toward her.

For the hundredth time, Eloise tested the bonds at her back. They held fast, her wrists crossed behind the tent pole. Her feet, however, were free. She would have to try to trip Driscoll once he drew near. Eyes wide, her every sense concentrated on the man approaching, death in his hand, she didn't even blink when the tent flap was thrown aside.

"What are you about?"

Sir Cedric's snarl had never sounded so sweet. Eloise dragged in a quick breath.

His eyes on Driscoll, who had swung to face him, Sir Cedric brought his sword forward. "I thought you said she was our greatest asset? You wouldn't be trying to cover your tracks at my expense, would you, Master Driscoll?"

Driscoll backed, but was caught off guard when Sir Cedric brought his sword flashing up. The clerk screamed, clutching bloody fingers as the knife went flying. Sir Cedric backhanded him viciously, sending him sprawling across the table.

"Don't move." Sir Cedric scooped up the dagger.

Driscoll's features were livid. "What do you think you're about?" He put a hand to his cut lip. "Edward will never let you go."

"He'll let me go to honor a fight."

Moving behind Eloise, Sir Cedric sliced through her bindings.

Before her sigh of relief could even reach her lips, he hauled her to her feet. He released her only to wrap his left arm about her neck, locking her head in a vice. The point of Driscoll's dagger, now in Sir Cedric's fist, pricked her throat.

As he backed toward the exit, dragging Eloise with him, Sir Cedric sneered at Driscoll. "You gave me the idea yourself, old man. I can beat any knight born in single combat—and the lady is my ticket to the fight."

With that, Sir Cedric half lifted, half swung Eloise through the tent flap.

Straight into the hell of battle.

The noise was deafening. It had been loud in the tent; now, without even the canvas to mute the roar, the din fell on Eloise's senses, nearly driving her to her knees. Sir Cedric tightened his grip, holding her up before him, the knife poised to pierce her throat if she struggled. He halted in front of the tent, where a small area remained clear at the epicenter of the melee.

Her gag still in place, Eloise looked wildly about.

"Halt!"

The roar erupted directly beside her ear. She felt the blood drain from her face. The fighting had degenerated into so many individual combats, knights, pikesmen, and men-at-arms intent on slaughtering each other in a seething cauldron of flailing broadswords, swinging maces, and jabbing daggers and pikes.

The scene was one of nightmarish vignettes, the dead crushed beneath the feet of the living.

"Hold! Or the lady dies!"

Chapter 21

"*Hold hard!*" The cry was Edward's. It was taken up by his commanders and relayed along the lines. Gradually, the clamor subsided, the warring parties obeying the call, stepping back, lowering weapons, warily eyeing their opponents as, chests heaving, all fought to catch their breath.

"What goes on here?" The fiery Plantagenet strode through the ranks, clearing a path with one heavily protected arm, knocking aside any who did not hurry out of his way. Edward halted ten yards before the tent, his bloody broadsword in his right hand; Montisfryn shouldered forward to come up alongside.

Eloise felt faint, relief slipping like a drug through her veins.

Alaun glanced at Edward and met the king's hazel gaze.

"Where in hell have you been?" Edward's voice was low, muted by his helm.

Alaun grimaced behind his. "Unavoidably detained by an unforeseen obstacle. It's dead now."

Edward grunted. For a long moment, he eyed the man hiding behind Eloise's skirts. "Well?" Edward demanded, the word loaded with contempt. "You perceive me all ears, sirrah."

"I propose a trade. The lady's safety—"

"One moment." Edward raised his visor. "I warn you—do not ask for liberty, for I will not grant it. Not for any man above the rank of sergeant. For the rest, I am willing to parley."

Sir Cedric's lip curled. "What care I for such?" The question produced a stunned silence. "I ask for myself your safe-conduct into exile. For the rest—you may have them."

The contempt of Edward's men was open. As for Sir Cedric's own followers, they all turned and, recovering from their shock, were only restrained from advancing on their blackguardly commander by Edward's intimidating presence.

Openly disgusted, Edward studied the rogue knight. "You seriously believe I'll allow you to walk free without facing judgment for your crimes?"

Sir Cedric's prompt response made it clear he did not. "I'll agree to be judged by combat—single combat against your chosen champion."

Above her gag, Eloise's eyes widened.

Alaun noticed, and gave mute thanks for the gag. "Accept," he advised Edward in an undertone.

"Think you can take him?" Edward's eyes remained on the black knight.

His eyes locked on the blade glinting at Eloise's throat, Alaun's reply was a feral growl. "Twill be a pleasure."

"Save something for me." Then Edward raised his voice so all could hear. "In order to secure the safety of the lady, I agree to abide by the outcome of single combat between yourself and my named champion. Should you prevail, you'll have escort from my domains. Should you lose, I will pass judgment upon you. Agreed?"

"Agreed." Sir Cedric removed the knife from Eloise's throat, but caught her arm, his gaze shifting to his erstwhile companions-in-arms. "But first, disarm your prisoners."

Edward snorted, but gave the necessary orders. The remaining outlaws, disgusted and disillusioned, were ready to surrender. They were removed, and a circle of knights formed about a flat area some yards from the tent.

Eloise saw her father and William come shouldering through the crowd, followed by the Earl of Oxford and Edward's commanders, Sir Nicholas Dreythorne and Sir Hubert Neville. Together with Montisfryn, they conferred briefly with Edward, then the king turned and approached, Roland beside him.

"Surrender the lady."

Sir Cedric released her.

Edward's eyes narrowed on the bruise on her cheek. "Are you well, lady?"

Tugging the gag from her lips, Eloise bobbed a curtsy. "Tolerably so, Your Grace."

"Go with Sir Roland, lady."

"Your Grace, I beg—"

"Go...with...Sir Roland." This time, Edward enforced his command with a royal stare.

Eloise met it, and would have disregarded it had Roland not said, "Nay, lady—tis pointless. He will fight, and you will not change that."

Turning to glare at him, she found herself surrounded—by her father and brothers, as well as Roland.

"Stop arguing, sister," William tersely advised. "Be thankful

Montisfryn has allowed you to watch—myself, I would not have permitted it. And I daresay any or all of us might yet have second thoughts about humoring his views."

Eloise snapped her mouth shut. And glared at them all.

"The combat will commence immediately." Edward's voice rang clearly over the sea of heads gathered around the circle. "I declare Alaun de Montisfryth, Earl of Montisfryn, my champion this day. The judges will be myself, the Earl of Oxford, and Sir Nicholas Dreythorne. Are the combatants ready?"

"Aye." Montisfryn, his broadsword gripped in one mailed fist, stepped into the ring. He saluted Edward.

Sir Cedric was slower, but took his place. "Aye."

Edward waited, but Sir Cedric offered no salute, apparently engrossed in studying Montisfryn. Disgusted, Edward waved. "Let the combat commence!"

Wedged behind Roland and William, with her father and John behind her, Eloise had to crane her head to keep the fighters in view. The two men circled, Montisfryn moving with his habitual, deceptive slowness. Then she looked at Sir Cedric—and swallowed. Black-visaged, black-garbed, shorter than Montisfryn, but heavier, the traitor-knight would be no easy conquest. "Sir Cedric was very convinced he could beat any knight born."

Both Roland and William heard her. In concert, they turned their heads to stare at her, as if unable to credit the idea that *she* could doubt Montisfryn's ability.

She put her nose in the air. "Doubtless, he'll soon learn otherwise."

A sword clanged, and saved her from further embarrassment; Sir Cedric had launched his attack. Within minutes, it was clear that he believed Montisfryn overly slow on his feet. Dancing about, Sir Cedric rained blows like an out-of-control thresher, but found no opening. Then Montisfryn struck back; Sir Cedric's shield shuddered. The sheer force of the blow made the onlookers wince. From then on, the combatants traded blows more evenly, but it was clear that that first thundering response from Montisfryn had rocked Sir Cedric's confidence. He backed away; Montisfryn simply stood stock-still and waited for him to return. Sir Cedric did, only to receive another hellish wallop that shook him to his knees.

A cheer went up from the watching crowd, but Montisfryn didn't press his advantage. He stepped back and waved Sir Cedric to his feet.

Eloise couldn't believe her eyes. "Roland—why did he do that?"

"'Tis an insult of sorts," Roland hissed. "To show his contempt for the villain."

The villain was trying to kill him—and he took time to issue subtle insults. Eloise drew in a deep breath and held it. "Oh," was all she allowed herself to say.

The clash of steel refocused her attention. Sir Cedric had lumbered to his feet—and swung directly into the attack, broadsword swinging furiously.

"Foul!" came from Sir Nicholas Dreythorne. "Attempt to trip."

Eloise gasped and pressed forward. The autumn sun was sinking, its dying rays lancing along the swinging blades, red-gold fire gilding the sharp edges—bringing home to her that this was no tournament bout. These swords were not blunted; this was a fight to the death.

Her heart lurched as Montisfryn took a sheering blow on his upper left arm. He disengaged, but as he turned, she saw a thin trickle of blood bead on the polished surface of his armor. Her heart contracted to a painful lump; unconsciously she pressed a hand to her chest, her eyes never leaving the scarlet-surcoted figure in the center of the ring.

Both men had taken cuts, but neither seemed to notice. Sir Cedric fought with increasing desperation. Montisfryn remained as ever— invulnerable, unshakeable, grimly resolved.

She knew the moment the tide turned. There was something in the set of Montisfryn's powerful shoulders, in the increased, yet rigidly controlled power in his swing, that heralded the end. It came in a brief flurry of expertly executed blows that felled the traitor-knight, first to his knees, then, when he attempted to strike at Montisfryn's mailed legs, to his back.

Stretched out on the scuffed earth, Sir Cedric lay panting, snarling, a beaten, but still vicious cur; his great barrel of a chest heaved as he looked up through his visor along the length of Montisfryn's broadsword. The tip rested at his throat, pressing threateningly through the links of his gorget.

His arm shortened for the final thrust, Alaun raised his visor and glanced at the king.

Edward strode forward; a deathly hush descended. He stopped by Alaun's side to look down at the traitor, then glanced about him. "Hear ye. I, Edward Plantagenet, by God's grace ruler of this realm of England, do hereby pronounce sentence on this man, convicted by his own words and actions of visiting mayhem on our people. He demanded and we graciously permitted trial by combat. The outcome is clear to all. Thus do I condemn this man, no longer knight, to death." Edward reached out and, without shifting the blade, took Montisfryn's broadsword. "And by my own hand do carry out the sentence."

From her position, all Eloise saw was the downward thrust of Edward's powerful arm.

There was a moment of grim silence, then the tension faded; murmuring, the men about the ring dispersed, their attention shifting to all they needed to do before night fell.

Alaun met Edward's eyes. They exchanged a look of grim satisfaction, then Edward uttered a short laugh and clapped Alaun on the shoulder, handing him back his sword before turning aside as others hurried up.

With a brief sigh, Alaun turned away from the still twitching corpse— just in time to catch Eloise as she flung herself at him. She tried to hug him, an impossibility given he was fully armored, even while she railed at him.

"*You* did not have to be champion—there were any number of others who could have fought—William, for one. Tis not wise to be forever putting yourself forward. Are any of those cuts deep? How many are there? This one is bleeding. Tis senseless—"

"*Cease*, lady!"

The bellowed words achieved their objective. Stunned, she blinked up at him.

He scowled at her. A whirlwind of emotions was rampaging through him—the aftermath of a fear that came close to terror feeding a rage so raw he could not comprehend it, all mixed with the crazed lust of battle, all drowned by a bone-deep longing to sweep her into his arms. But if he gave into the latter, his armor would bruise her.

Holding her silent with his gaze, he tugged off his gauntlets and handed them to Bilder, who had already relieved him of his sword, then hauled off his helm. Wordlessly, Bilder took it, handing it on to a younger squire before setting fingers to the buckles of Alaun's plates.

His expression granite-hard, Alaun lifted one hand and caught Eloise's chin, tilting her head to the fading light. "Where came you by this bruise, lady?"

Barely able to breathe, Eloise tried to see through the storm clouds hazing his golden eyes. His gaze was merciless, yet his eyes were dull.

"And I have yet to hear your explanations for how you come to be here, why you left Montisfryn against what you knew to be my wishes, and with no escort of any kind." Eyes narrowed, he towered over her, his expression unyielding. "Which last is a point we will discuss in considerable depth later, make no doubt."

The undiluted promise in his words sent a shiver of sensation squirming down her spine. Lifting her chin from his grasp, she reached for the buckles of his armplates. "I left a letter in which I explained my actions. Tis not my fault did you not read it."

"That epistle?" He snorted derisively. "I read it. Your reasons did not feature. Even had they done so, they would not serve to excuse you."

There was a resolution in his eyes which she wasn't certain she appreciated. "We can discuss such matters later. Tis your injuries I would see to now."

Finally freed of his plates, Alaun planted his fists on his hips. His hands were shaking, so great was the urge to touch her. If he did, in his present state, the consequences would be beyond his control. He gritted his teeth. "I understand it not, lady, why, if my injuries so concern you, you do not heed my orders. Think you on this—tis the *third* time I have fought for you."

The words shook Eloise. She looked up and met his turbulent gaze. Her lips softened and she looked down. "I am sorry if I have again been a burden, lord."

"You are *not a burden*!"

Startled by the force behind his words, she glanced up to see him cast a mute appeal heavenward. He looked down, impaling her with golden spears.

"You are *mine*! Tis time you understood that."

She blinked—and realized that the man standing by Montisfryn's shoulder, facing away yet near enough to hear every word, was none other than Edward Plantagenet. She shot a startled glance at Montisfryn. "Aye—I am your chatelaine, lord."

He did not take the warning well.

His eyes slitted. His expression harder than granite, his voice deep and low, he growled, "Lady, do you seek to deny what lies between us?"

Inwardly, she quivered; outwardly, she cast a pointed glance at Edward's back, then glared at Montisfryn. "I know not what you mean, lord."

A muscle in his jaw flickered. He glanced up, over her head, then looked down at her again. "My pavilion is being erected yonder. I will explain it to you there."

His eyes told her very clearly what would happen once they reached his pavilion. She lifted her chin. There was yet a chance she could salvage the situation. "Nay, lord. My father is here and I would visit with him, and the king—"

"The king is here, and has a few decrees of his own to make."

Eloise bit back a gasp, her eyes flying to Edward's. He had turned, and now joined them. She sank into a curtsy, then drew herself up, frostily regal.

Edward eyed her with scant approval. "You, lady, have caused me, your father, and Montisfryn much concern. Tis not meet that you continue unwed. As Montisfryn is already under edict to marry, I will see you two legally joined this night."

Stunned, Eloise felt her eyes grow wide. Her jaw had dropped; she rapidly retrieved it. "*Nay*, sire!"

Large, protuberant hazel eyes, not as gold as Montisfryn's, blinked at her. Slowly, Edward leaned forward so his face was level with hers. "Nay?"

Fleetingly, Alaun closed his eyes, wishing he could shake them both. Gritting his teeth, he reopened his eyes, no longer caring if his emotions showed.

"Tis not a matter open to royal edict, not in my case." Eloise was sure of her ground; chin high, she held it without a qualm. "I say naught to your wish to see Montisfryn wed, but *I* will not marry him."

She glanced at Montisfryn; what she saw in his eyes rocked her. Her breath caught in her throat. Distantly, she heard herself falter over the words, "At least, not at your command."

Edward's expression was incredulous; Alaun doubted his sovereign had ever been thus plainly denied. He watched as Edward blinked, owlishly, stared at Eloise for several long moments, then straightened and turned to him.

"I shouldn't have interrupted. For the Virgin's sake, take her away and explain it to her. Clearly."

Alaun smiled grimly. "Aye, sire. I will see to the matter immediately."

Edward humphed. He turned as one of his knights hurried up, speaking rapidly, indicating a rumpled figure being helped from the dun-colored tent.

Once more favored with the king's back, Eloise was determined to cling to the slim hope that remained. "Lord, I would visit with my father—"

"Nay, lady." Montisfryn looked down at her. "We will have this matter out in my pavilion." His eyes were beaten gold, his glance razor sharp. "Now."

The last word was imbued with sufficient force to shake her confidence and rob her glare of its sting.

"So that's how it was." Gesturing to an approaching figure, Edward glanced back at Montisfryn. "The brigands knew which of the regions and merchants to target because they'd kidnapped one of my senior clerks."

Eloise blinked.

Edward turned to welcome said clerk. "How now, Master Driscoll—did you suffer much at these scoundrels' hands?"

Approaching from beyond the king, Driscoll couldn't see Eloise; she was shielded by both Edward and Montisfryn. She risked a glance around Montisfryn, and saw the clerk make deep obeisance to Edward.

"My days of captivity have not been easy, sire." Driscoll sighed, artistically weak. He looked around, shaking his head. "I pray you, sire, allow me to retire at once to Hereford. I am not a man of war, and like not the atmosphere of this place."

Edward looked a little taken aback, but, as ever in victory, he was willing to be gracious. He opened his mouth.

"Sire—a word, if I may."

Edward cast an impatient glance over his shoulder. "I am busy, lady."

Eloise met the royal gaze calmly. "You are about to be taken for a fool, Your Grace."

The comment had the desired effect. Edward bristled, an intimidating sight. Montisfryn glanced down at her, but made no move to check her. A fact of which Edward took due note. Head erect, buttressed by Montisfryn's unquestioning support, Eloise waited patiently.

"You had better explain yourself, lady."

Gracefully, she inclined her head. "When last I saw this man you call Master Driscoll, he'd been struck by the false knight, Sir Cedric—you can see his cut lip—to prevent Master Driscoll from killing *me,* so that later I would not be alive to identify him as the instigator of the plot."

The calm pronouncement riveted all attention.

Master Driscoll, who had paled on hearing her voice, peered at her from behind the king.

Edward turned back and surprised him. "How answer you this charge,

Master Clerk?"

Driscoll smiled, visibly shaken, yet dismissively confident. "The lady is distraught, sire. Tis well known the female mind can be temporarily unbalanced by seeing acts of violence. She's hysterical and knows not what she says."

He glanced at Eloise, an unctuous smile on his lips—and quailed.

Even Edward, following his gaze, was impressed.

"That, sire, is a *vile calumny!*" Eyes blazing, Eloise looked down her nose at Driscoll as if he was a species of rodent. "I have *never*," she declared, "been hysterical in my life. There are many here who can vouch for that."

Edward raised his eyes to Montisfryn's; Alaun answered the silent question with a nod.

"Be that as it may," Eloise swept on, "my evidence that this man, Master Driscoll, was not only in league with these outlaws, sire, but the instigator of the scheme, lies not just on my observations of today, which I will come to in good order. I first came across Master Driscoll while at Versallet Castle. I overheard a conversation between him and Sir Percival Mortyn, in which he instructed Sir Percy to mass his men in the Savernake. I did not, at the time, comprehend the significance of what I had heard and spoke to no one of it, but perhaps Sir Percy is among the knights you overpowered here today, and might be persuaded to tell his story?"

Edward nodded to a hovering knight, who immediately went to find out. Turning back, Edward asked, "When was this, lady?"

Eloise hesitated. "During the tournament recently held by my father, Your Grace. Some…"

"Four sennights ago," Montisfryn supplied.

She looked her surprise. "Is it that long?"

He cast her an inscrutable glance. "Aye."

"There were other meetings you witnessed?" With a raised finger, Edward summoned a pair of guardsmen.

"Aye. The next was at Gloucester cathedral. While my lord was conferring with the priest, I chanced to look through the chapel windows, and saw and heard Master Driscoll approach Sir Cedric. Master Driscoll spoke of settling an agreement to their mutual advantage."

Driscoll viewed her with distaste, a muscle twitching above one eye. "She has plainly mistaken me for someone else, sire."

Haughtily, she raised a brow. "Can you prove you were not in Gloucester that day?"

The clerk's color rose; he controlled himself with an obvious effort.

"When I rode into their camp this afternoon, Master Driscoll and Sir Cedric were hand-in-glove, discussing means to gain entry to the convent to raid the stores. They hauled me before the walls and used threats against me to try to force Mother Maude to open the gates." She paused to smile sweetly upon the hapless clerk. "Which is why Master Driscoll is so anxious to quit the scene, for Mother Maude can testify that he acted in amity with Sir Cedric, not as one forced."

"Tis not so, Your Grace." Master Driscoll was sweating freely, but was clever enough to keep his head. "I behaved as I did only under the gravest threats. Besides"—he drew breath, visibly calming—"the guardsmen who found me can testify—I was bound in the tent. See here." He drew one hand from his robe. "Here is the rope with which I was bound. I was not a willing conspirator."

Edward raised a brow, then turned to Eloise. "How say you, lady? Is it possible you're mistaken? Tis difficult for a man to tie himself."

She smiled. "Perhaps, sire, if you would summon those who found him, we will have the matter clear."

Driscoll blanched.

Eloise glanced up; Montisfryn stood, reassuringly large, at her shoulder. He met her gaze, then looked forward, wordlessly instructing the guardsmen about the clerk to draw closer.

The three guardsmen who had searched the tent came quickly, saluting as they halted before Edward.

"You found this man in the tent yonder?"

The eldest of the three replied, "Aye, sire. He'd been tied to the tent pole."

"If I may, sire?" When Edward nodded his permission, Eloise asked, "When you entered, were the clerk's hands still tied?"

The guardsman blinked. "Nay, lady—he'd fallen from the stool having freed himself."

"How?"

"Your pardon, lady?"

She gestured to the rope Driscoll still held in his hand. "Master Driscoll has said that this is the rope with which he was tied—take it." The guardsman did. "Now tell me how he came to free himself. Look at the ends of the rope."

In the fading light, the guardsman examined the rope. "Tis sawed through, lady. With a dagger, most like."

"Aye, tis so. Where, then, is this dagger?"

The guardsman looked at her, then at Driscoll, then, lastly, at Edward. "Sire, there was no weapon of any kind in the tent when we entered. We searched."

Edward turned to Master Driscoll. "Well, Master Clerk—where is this dagger with which you freed yourself?"

The clerk's eyes were shifting, darting about. "I..." With jerky movements, he went through the pretense of searching his robes. His face was ashen. "You can see how I cut myself with it." He held out his fingers. "It must have fallen somewhere, sire."

"Nay—the dagger that sawed that rope was seen by many." Eloise kept her voice calm and unemotional. "Tis Master Driscoll's, sure enough. Twas the dagger with which he intended to silence me, that Sir Cedric struck from his hand, and then held at my throat in full view of you all. Tis presently on Sir Cedric's corpse, most like. But before he pulled me from the tent, Sir Cedric used the dagger to cut that rope from about *my* wrists."

With a dramatic gesture, she stretched out her arms; the long sleeves of her cote drew back to reveal the rope burns scoring her slim wrists.

Even in the deepening twilight, the marks showed clear.

With a contemptuous smile, Eloise held the clerk's eyes. "Come, now, Master Clerk. Your skin is almost as white and delicate as mine. You say you were tied by Sir Cedric. Do not be shy—show us the proof."

For an instant, Driscoll looked at her as if she was a witch. Then he turned wildly—straight into the embrace of the burly guardsmen.

"Take him away—make sure he remains alive." Edward smiled—a gesture full of teeth. "You're just what I need, Driscoll, to convince Parliament that I have their interests at heart."

"Sire!" The man sent in search of Sir Percy returned hotfoot. "Sir Percy's unconscious, sire, but others confirm tis as the lady says—twas Driscoll recruited them."

"Good—that will relieve Lady de…Cannar from having to go to London. Briggs?" Edward turned to his secretary. "You heard it all, didn't you?"

"Aye, sire."

"Excellent. Write up the depositions. Then convey this felon to the Tower. In irons. Lay the whole story before the parliamentary secretaries. I'm sure they'll have a nice charge drawn up and heard, all ready for me to pass judgment upon when I return to Westminster. See to it."

They had to carry Master Driscoll away.

Edward turned to Eloise. "We are indebted to you, lady, and thank you for your courage. Twas not a little thing to speak so."

She held his gaze calmly. "Nay, sire. Twas my duty, and I have much experience of legal matters."

Edward's lips twitched. "Indeed?"

"And speaking of duty, sire, I would ask a boon."

Suspicion bloomed in Edward's eyes. "What boon, lady?"

Hands clasped tightly before her, she drew breath. "You spoke just now of an order to wed, sire."

Edward laughed. "Nay—ask it not. Your lord is before you. I cannot grant your boon without rescinding one I have already made him. Besides"—his hazel gaze sharpened—"your manner here this hour has convinced me tis as I said—you should wed. Tis to cheat my realm to have you otherwise—your proper station is at your lord's side, keeping his castles and bearing his sons." His glance slid to Montisfryn. "I admit tis a tall order." Straight-faced, Edward glanced back at her. "But I expect there'll be compensations."

Eloise glared at him.

Edward pretended not to notice. With a regal wave, he dismissed them, adding as he turned away, "De Versallet and I will discuss the settlements; my clerks can draw up the necessary documents. I will expect you at supper. You will wed thereafter."

Incensed, she opened her mouth; Alaun clamped a hand over her lips.

"Nay, lady. Have done." Stony-faced, he drew her around, then forced himself to release her, retaining only a firm clasp about her elbow. His muscles were flickering, restless beneath his control; waves of emotion rippled through him, steadily eroding his will. He'd endured all he could. He started toward his pavilion, set up before the wood amidst those of the other commanders. The king's great tent stood beside his.

Eloise had to hurry to keep up with his stride. His grip on her elbow was too tight, but she didn't think to complain. Now that he was touching her, she could sense the passions surging through him—and knew she would get but little chance to divert them. Little chance to avoid verifying Edward's clear assumption—which would destroy any chance of dismissing the king's injunction. Leaving her with no chance of convincing Montisfryn that she loved him!

His tent loomed before her. Abruptly, she dug in her heels.

Too late.

Montisfryn flung aside the tent flap and swung her through the opening. He let the flap fall as he released her, leaving them enclosed in candlelit gloom.

Quickly, she crossed to the space before the central pole. She swung about—and saw him strip off his surcote, then shrug out of his mail tunic, flinging the garments at Bilder. The squire scurried out. With a fluid movement, Montisfryn pulled off his padded gambeson; his shirt went with it.

Then he lifted his head and his gaze transfixed her. She didn't need better light to know what was in his eyes. Slowly, he stalked toward her.

She swallowed. The candlelight shifted over the contours of his chest, glinting on the fine curling hairs. Instinctively, she backed. She avoided the pole, only to feel his armor chest behind her thighs.

Eyes wide, she put out a hand. "Alaun—"

He didn't stop.

He reached for her, one hand framing her jaw, the other wrapping about her waist. He hauled her against him and his lips came down on hers.

Fire.

It raged through him and poured through her.

It seared the breath from her throat, then raced hungrily through her veins. Molten passion erupted, flowing swiftly.

Her thoughts crisped to ashes. Her lips parted under his; he stole her breath, then gave it back, hot and searing. Ruthlessly, he claimed her mouth, branding her with flame. His hand was on her breast, fingers hard about the firm mound. Protected by gown and chemise, her nipples crinkled tight; the unrelieved ache drove her wild.

Bringing her hands up, she framed his face, and kissed him back hungrily, greedily, suddenly as desperate as he to sate their volcanic need.

Abruptly, he pulled away, trapping her between his thighs and the chest, his fingers busy with her laces. His chest was rising and falling rapidly; boldly, she spread her fingers across it, caressing the wide muscles, the sleek contours that had always fascinated her. They shifted at her touch. He met her gaze, his own heavy-lidded, the flames roaring in his eyes. His features were hard, passion-driven. He looked down at his fingers, his lips twisting.

She reached up and drew his lips to hers. They kissed long and deep; the caress only served to fuel their raging hunger. Then, abruptly, they were at the eye of the storm, that brief moment when they could catch their breath before the maelstrom caught them again. Dragging in a shaky breath, she laid her head against his shoulder. His lips pressed to her temple, then he rested his head against hers.

Alaun closed his eyes and breathed deeply, inhaling the scent of her, the rich perfume of her hair, the subtle scent of her arousal. "By the holy Virgin, I thought I'd lost you."

The words were little more than an agonized growl. He struggled to master her laces; he was shaking, aching, weak with need.

"Nay—I am here. You will not lose me thus easily." Eloise placed her hands over his and felt them quiver. She glanced up, into his flame-etched eyes. "There's no need for this."

Smoothly, she took over, unlacing her gown.

Alaun let his hands fall; he closed his eyes and dragged in a deep breath, struggling to hold back the tide. "Nay," he replied. "There is—need and more." He opened his eyes, and knew they were blazing. "I love you, lady." He shook as he said the words. "And I cannot *bear it* when you are not safe within my care."

Eloise's hands stilled. She looked up—and felt like she was falling through some trackless void. His gaze, golden and burning, held her. "What did you say?"

Her question was weak—lips twisting, he brushed it aside along with her hands. Her bodice was open to her waist; he pushed the halves wide. "Nay—I have no gift for sweet phrases. Let me show you."

"Don't—" She was too late to stop him ripping her chemise. She resigned herself to going to her wedding naked beneath her gown. Then his hands were on her flesh, urgent and demanding. Her lids fell as she leaned back, her hands dropping to rest on the chest behind her as, an ageless smile on her lips, she offered herself to him.

He gorged himself on her bounty, and they were back in the flames once more. The fire raged and took them; they welcomed it. Their lips met again, urgency building, coursing through them.

A cough came from beyond the tent flap.

"Lord?"

His heart thudding in his ears, in his veins, in his brain, Alaun lifted his head in disbelief. His eyes met Eloise's—she looked as dazed as he felt. He had to clear his throat before he could speak. "Aye?"

Bilder's voice reached them, hesitant but clear. "The king sent to say as he was waiting on your presence."

Beneath his breath, Alaun swore, then called, "Aye—my compliments to His Grace. We'll join him in a moment." With a smothered groan, he dropped his forehead to Eloise's.

Only to hear her curse the king and her father in terms she must have learned from her brothers—she'd certainly never heard them from him. He lifted his head to look at her.

Eloise saw his surprise—and groaned herself. "You don't understand. Tis what drove me from Montisfryn." She dropped her head against his shoulder and tightened her arms about him.

"Edward and your father?"

She nodded. She was heated—so was he; she could feel him, rigid and throbbing, against her stomach.

"That much I'd gathered." He pushed back a wisp of her hair. "What I have yet to hear is the reason behind your flight."

She sighed. "Nay—tis no great matter now. They've spoiled it—and I will *never* forgive them." The last was a vow.

For a long moment, Alaun just held her, trying to ease the empty ache inside him, then he sighed and touched his lips to her temple. "Nay—if it truly bothers you to marry me, I will speak to Edward. With his permission, we can wait yet awhile."

She looked up, frowning as her eyes searched his. Then she grimaced. "Nay—that is not it." She cast him a disgruntled look. "Tis that I wished to tell you myself—without being '*forced*' to it—that I would gladly call you husband."

For an instant, he held her gaze, then he closed his eyes and drew her hard against him. "Tell me anyway," he commanded.

Eloise responded—to his deep growl and the feel of him hard against her. She twined her arms about his neck and stretched up to touch her lips to his. "That I love you—husband?" She felt him quiver. "I will say it as many times as you like, but will you believe me?"

He opened his eyes and frowned at her. "Why would I not?"

She grimaced. "Nay—you will never be certain that I'm not simply making the best of the situation."

She felt the beginnings of his laugh before she heard it. Incredulous, she stared at him, then tried to pull back. His arms tightened about her.

"Nay, lady-witch." He smiled down at her, delighted, leonine assurance in every line. "I've known for an age that you love me."

She frowned. "Nay—you are merely saying so, so that I will not be so difficult."

Grinning, he shook his head. "I have known at least since Hereford."

"Hereford?" She searched her memories. "Nay—I said nothing."

"Not in words, but your actions, believe me, were explicit enough."

She blushed.

Alaun laughed and crushed her to him. He found her lips with his, claiming his right, staking his possession. His hand rose to cup her breast; the crest was already tightly ruched even before he drew his fingertips across it.

They were both breathing raggedly when he lifted his head. "Nay, lady—you have given yourself to me again and again—think you I knew not what you offered—what I gladly took?" He searched her eyes. "Yet I did not know if your love was yet strong enough to allow you to call me husband."

She looked long into his eyes, her own glowing darkly. "My love for you is vast, unending—all-powerful."

Silence held, then, slowly, he bent and touched his lips to hers. "As mine for you is infinite, unchartered." Drawing back, he grimaced. "And stronger than I sometimes like."

Her smile brimmed with triumph. "Twill be pleasant to spend a lifetime charting our passions."

"Aye." He shifted against her. "And exploring them."

Eyes radiant with love met his. For a long moment, he luxuriated in the dark depths, in the glow that warmed him to his bones, then she smiled her witchy, ageless smile and drew him back. He kissed her long and deep; she moved against him, seeking, giving. Offering. He couldn't resist—he took. And their fire roared again.

The effort required to lift his head, to break their kiss, left him dizzy.

Their eyes met. They were both breathing rapidly. Their bodies, pressed intimately together, told their own tale.

Eloise licked her throbbing lips. "Edward is waiting."

"Aye."

She focused on his lips, strong and firm—and remembered what they felt like upon her. The emptiness inside was a physical ache. She could feel him against her, could feel the urgent compulsion building between them. Again she licked her lips. "There's no time to get undressed."

His lips curved.

She forced her gaze upward. His eyes burned bright, a constellation of suns.

Alaun looked down—at her face, at the passion, fully-flowered, in her eyes. "Lady, do you love me?"

"With all my heart."

"Then turn around."

Without hesitation, she did.

* * *

In the king's tent but yards away, Henry de Versallet sat musing at the board. The supper dishes were spread before him, cooling. In a chair to his right, Edward, King of England, sat waiting.

Carefully hiding his smile, Henry reached for his wine cup.

Without warning, a low moan shivered through the night.

Startled, he and Edward exchanged glances.

A second moan, softer, sobbing, fell on their ears.

After that, he and Edward exchanged no more glances.

Ten minutes later, Montisfryn escorted Eloise into the circle of candlelight, his expression that of a lion who had feasted well. As for Eloise, her features were soft, her skin still flushed, her dark eyes aglow. She was smiling—and leaning heavily on Montisfryn's arm.

After one raking glance, Edward shifted uncomfortably and waved them to their seats.

Awash with sated pleasure, Eloise paid scant attention to the talk about her. Supper dishes came and went; she partook of them absentmindedly. She heard Montisfryn and her father discussing the settlements; she murmured an assent when asked. To her surprise, her father suggested their marriage be formalized on the morrow in the chapel at Claerwhen.

Blinking, Eloise brought Henry into focus where he sat opposite her. She heard Montisfryn support the notion—Edward humphed and agreed. Eloise's gaze met her father's; she gifted him with a brilliant smile.

Henry's eyes misted over. Hiding behind his goblet, he silently invited his Elaine to witness his achievement, and give them her blessing.

The supper party was not prolonged. As Montisfryn raised her, Eloise heard Edward make some pointed comment, something about waywardness and its rightful reward. The allusion escaped her. She smiled serenely as she made her obeisance.

Escorted through the night back to the now familiar scarlet-and-gold pavilion, Eloise sighed as the dimness enveloped them. Montisfryn led her to the side of the bed. She was about to turn, to go into his arms, when he stayed her, his hands firm about her waist. He stood behind her; she felt his breath, then his lips, touch her ear.

"Did you take note of the king, lady?"

"Nay." She smiled dreamily. "Did he say anything to the point?"

"He was displeased to learn of your unattended flight, as was I. Tis a matter we must settle ere we go further."

There was a note in his voice that suddenly made concentrating easy.

"Nay." She spoke slowly, her mind rapidly marshaling her defense. "I've already agreed to take an escort with me should I venture beyond your castle walls."

"Aye, so you agreed—yet were you alone when you rode up before Claerwhen. How explain you that, lady?"

She grimaced. "Twas a difficult case, lord. I acted as I thought best. I could not take an escort—you must see that." When, standing silent in the darkness behind her, he said nothing, she asked, "Would you have me not act, even when I feel I should?"

"Nay—all I ask is that you take an escort should you leave my walls, and that you do not venture forth without leaving word of your destination."

Her breath came more easily—at least she'd left a note. "But what of your commanders, lord? There are times they might not understand my reasons for riding forth."

"Aye, very likely." Alaun's lips twisted as he drew her back against him. "I will give orders that, should I be absent, you are to be provided with an escort of whatever size my commander thinks suitable for your venture, but otherwise you are answerable only to me for your actions."

She relaxed against him, her head on his shoulder, one hand stealing up to touch his cheek.

He slanted a glance at her. "But in return, lady, I would have your solemn vow not to ride alone again. Ever."

In the shadows, her eyes met his.

Eloise smiled. As far as he was able, he was offering her total freedom. "You know I will not. Ever." She tilted her face up and back, inviting his kiss. He took her lips in a slow, easy caress, then lifted his head, still holding her firmly before him.

In silence, he looked down at her; she felt her heart thud. "Lord?"

"We now have to deal with your punishment, lady."

She looked forward. She was leaning against him; his hands at her waist held her gently. Slowly, her lips curved. "And what is that to be, lord?"

Alaun heard the assurance in her voice, and smiled, too. "There are many who would say that your willful acts justify my taking my hand to your rear."

He felt her chuckle.

"Nay—but your hand is frequently on my rear, lord."

He tightened his hands about her waist and blew gently in her ear. "Should I beat you, lady?"

"Nay, twould not benefit either of us."

"Aye, so I think. I have it in mind that a different form of chastisement would best suit us."

Eloise was intrigued. "And what is that?"

"There are three parts to your punishment." He bent his head; his lips traced the line of her throat. "Do you remember the fantasy I had you enact for me outside Gloucester?"

She shivered. "Aye." How could she not? Just the thought of what he had done sent warm flushes through her.

"Tomorrow, you will be my wife in truth—twill henceforth be your duty to play that role in all my fantasies." The hands at her waist shifted, drifting upwards until each cupped a breast. Long fingers unerringly closed about her nipples. "Whenever and wherever I decree." His breath fanned her check. "As frequently as I wish."

She had to moisten her lips before she could speak. "You have more fantasies?" Her body arched lightly as his fingers played.

"Hundreds."

His hands went to her lacings, swiftly undoing them. She had to concentrate to control her voice. "And what else must I do?"

"You must dutifully inform me of any fantasies you have."

Lifting her arm, he started on the buttons closing her sleeves. She studied his face, the clean, hard planes, the wide forehead. "In words?"

He met her gaze. His lips curved. "Not necessarily. But you must make your meaning—the full breath and scope of your vision—clear."

She nodded. "What else?"

He didn't answer immediately, apparently too engrossed in helping her from her clothes. Only when she stood naked, breathing too fast, her skin set alive by all the subtle, delicate caresses he'd bestowed along the way, only then did he come to stand before her, placing his hands once more about her waist.

His gaze, golden and smoldering, locked with hers.

Then he smiled, somewhat crookedly. "Tis in my mind that you'll have punishment enough in bearing my sons, lady. They are likely to be large." He glanced down, letting one hand sculpt the trim lines of her belly and hips. "And you are not so very big."

"Nay, lord." She pressed close. Reaching up, she laid her fingers on his lips. "Never ask me to look on the bearing of your babes with anything other than joy." Stretching up, she replaced her fingers with her lips. His arms closed around her, gently at first, then they tightened as desire took hold.

When she eventually drew back, his eyes were ablaze.

Alaun closed his eyes and touched his lips to her forehead. "I am glad to hear you say so, lady, for tis a punishment you will not escape."

His words were soft, gentle; he wondered how she interpreted them. He took her lips again, and her mouth, his hands roaming her curves with proprietorial candor. She gave of herself freely, as she always did. Abruptly, he drew back and wordlessly urged her to the bed.

Eloise went readily. She slipped beneath the furs, then lay back and watched him undress. Muscles rippled beneath his tanned skin, the long line of back, buttocks, and legs smooth as a sculptor's wish. He was a golden god—and he was hers. Her lips curved as he joined her.

Stretching out beside her, Alaun looked down at her face, features soft, full of love. She didn't know—she did not keep track of the days. His hands found her; she murmured, reaching for him. For an instant, he held back, wondering whether to prompt her. Then he smiled—and bent his head to kiss her. Let her surprise him with her news.

Eloise went eagerly into his embrace, her body seeking his even as his sought hers. She—they—had triumphed; tonight would be their celebration. He had said more than she had ever hoped to hear; she wouldn't care did he never say the words again, just as long as he showed her—frequently.

He seemed fascinated with her belly, tracing its contours as if gauging the possibilities. She smiled.

"You've met William, lord?" She murmured the question, her lips against his ear. "My mother had the same build as I. I doubt not that I will bear your sons easily."

Alaun glanced at her face, one brow rising. "I would not announce that with such confidence, lady, else Edward thinks I've been too lenient with you."

The smile that curved her lips was unutterably, heart-stoppingly feminine. "Nay—tis easy enough to compensate." Her lids veiled her eyes. "Tis simply a matter of making your fantasies more frequent, more...demanding." Her gaze fixed on his lips.

Inwardly, he groaned; desire surged.

She felt it—she reached up and drew his head to hers. Her lips claimed his; their flames flared high. She arched against him, inciting, inviting his possession, her legs tangling with his as she artfully writhed.

He pressed her back to the bed; he would have covered her, but she stayed him, pushing him back, one hand on his chest, her witchy smile on her lips.

"Nay, lord." She turned to come up on her knees before him. "Come—plant your seed deeply, as do your stallions." She glanced over her shoulder; her eyes gleamed. "Long, strong—and *very* slow."

He shut his eyes. Groaned aloud. What could he say?

Shaking his head, he opened his eyes—and without further ado, obeyed.

Epilogue

Montisfryn Castle
July in the 23rd Year of our Sovereign Lord, Edward III (1349)

"'*T*is done." With a satisfied sigh, Eloise shut the lid of the chest of baby clothes she and Jenni had been sorting.

"I will get Bilder to move it to the nursery when he returns, lady."

"Aye." Eloise smiled at her little robin, not so little now. Swollen with her first child, Jenni's cheeks were still rosy, but she'd lost the ability to flit.

A commotion—distant shouting—intruded on their peace. Eloise frowned. "What is that racket?"

Moving to the window, she leaned out, but her view of the private gardens and the river and forests below told her nothing. Then, from around the corner of the keep, came the sound of men's voices, and the stamping and snorting of horses. A thrill shot through her, down to her toes. "Jenni…?" Then she recalled she could no longer ask Jenni to run down to the keep steps.

"Aye, lady?"

"Nay, never mind." Ears straining, her pulse quickening, she caught the sound she was waiting for. She glanced at the child lying sprawled on the hearthrug.

The afternoon sun slanted through the window to burnish tumbled golden locks. Her son lay sweetly oblivious, one thumb jammed in his mouth, long lashes casting crescent-shadows on his downy cheeks. Although swathed in puppy fat, the long limbs and heavy bones of his sire were already discernible.

The door burst open. Montisfryn strode in.

He halted inside the threshold, his gaze transfixing her. His strongly cast features told her little, but the glow in his eyes was unmistakable.

He turned to dismiss Jenni; a knowing smile on her face, the robin was already at the door.

Eloise reached him as the latch fell.

"I didn't expect you," she finally managed to gasp, when he released her lips to pay homage to her breasts. "Not for days."

"There were fewer problems than I anticipated. We rode back through the forests." Alaun drew back to survey the bounty he'd recently reclaimed from his son. "There's a fine boar and a stag for your larders, lady." He grinned. "And some plump pigeons as well."

Her breath hissed in as his thumbs caressed the sensitive peaks of her breasts. She shook her head. "Tis not food I am hungry for, lord. Think you, I have been without sustenance for more than a week."

He laughed. "And what of me, lady? My fire has been untended for just as long."

Dark eyes glowed from under heavy lids. "Come, then, husband—and let me quench your flame."

Husband. He closed his eyes and savored the word, even as her knowing fingers savored him. When she'd razed his defenses and added her torch to his blaze, he gathered her close; his lips on hers, he backed her to the bed. He lifted her, laying her on the scarlet coverlet, then glanced at his heir. "Will he wake?"

"Nay." She stretched languorously and held out her arms. "He's only just gone down. We should have an hour or so before the little tyrant awakes."

"Ah, well." He smiled lazily down at her. "Twill have to be quick, then."

It was not, of course, for they knew well how to savor the timeless moments, to stretch the brief minutes of glory, to give, and take, and give again, until they lost themselves wholly. Completely.

Later, content to his marrow, Alaun reclined against the pillows. He was naked; equally naked, Eloise lay curled in his arms. About them, the sheets and covers had been reduced to a froth of white linen and scarlet silk. Their clothes lay like so many discarded leaves, littering the floor.

But the storm had abated; peace reigned about them, the golden afternoon rich and replete. His gaze rested on his son; he had yet to become inured to the fascination of their creation.

Eloise wriggled in his arms, pressing her ivory curves more fully into his loins. He chuckled and pressed a kiss to her temple. "Tis just as well he's a sound sleeper."

She blushed and slanted him a haughty glance. "I am not that loud."

"Aye, you are." He blew gently in her ear. "But tis a wondrous sound, that of a lady-witch in ecstasy."

She blushed even more, then narrowed her eyes at him. "If you do not stop teasing me, I shall be quiet."

He couldn't stop his laugh. "Like the night before we were wed?" Her cheeks were now rosier than Jenni's. He cuddled her close and whispered in her ear, "I did tell Edward you had tried most valiantly to spare his sensibilities when he complained the next morn."

Horrified, Eloise stared at him. "You didn't?"

He answered with his lazy lion's smile.

Thoroughly discomposed, she humphed—and snuggled deeper into his arms.

Even now, nearly two years later, she could recall the events surrounding her second marriage with crystal clarity. The sheer happiness of that time was something that would remain with her forever.

"What are you smiling at?"

She glanced up, into glowing golden eyes. They showed his emotions so clearly—passion, desire, anger, fury, and every nuance between—strong, powerful emotions, each had their particular shade. Love filled his eyes now, deep and tender—the purest gold.

Her smile deepened. All her dreams had come true.

"I was thinking of our wedding. Twas a good time, lord."

"Aye, and we've been blessed with many good times since."

His gaze shifted to their son. She grinned. "Strange. At the time, you seemed very much in two minds over whether you had overdone my punishment."

He shuddered and closed his eyes. "Nay—do not remind me. I am not looking forward to your next time." Even as he said the words, his hand curved about her gently rounded belly. Her next time was seven months away.

She smiled, but didn't laugh. Her confinement had shaken him badly; it was the first and only time she had seen him distraught, defeated, weak.

"I do not like seeing you in pain, lady."

She lifted a hand to his cheek. "Tis not so bad. And I would not forego it if it meant foregoing the result." Her gaze brimming with maternal pride, she surveyed her first-born. "He's growing well, is he not?"

"Aye. We'll have him a warrior in no time."

She frowned. "Tis my belief, lord, that he should learn his letters before he learns to wield a sword."

"Nay, lady. He is warrior-born and bred."

"Aye—and at barely one, his favorite sport is riding atop your destrier. I do not believe you need encourage him to knightly pursuits, lord."

Naturally, he took that as a compliment, smiling delightedly. She shook her head and gave up.

He gathered her close, resettling her in his arms. "I have been thinking that we should visit Versallet Castle—perhaps next month? We have not seen your family for well-nigh a year, and I will not have you traveling once you are big with child."

Her head on his shoulder, she gazed at the scarlet canopy. Her family had visited shortly after Robert's birth. "Julia's with child—did I tell you?"

"William will be pleased. And relieved. Tis high time."

Wriggling around, Eloise chuckled. "Nay—tis *usually* so in my family. Twas why I was so surprised at our own good fortune."

Alaun managed to still his twitching lips, but his eyes betrayed him.

Eloise frowned, and settled her elbows on his chest. "Now what is so funny in that?"

"Nay, lady—do not ask. But your news inclines me even more to visit with your father."

She narrowed her eyes. "Why?"

He smiled. "Tis merely a matter of assessing the outcome of the wagers he and I engaged in. Tis my belief I've had the best of the exchange."

"How so?"

When he lay smiling smugly upward and said nothing, she prodded his chest.

He grimaced and absentmindedly caught her hand. "You recall that, on the occasion of your first marriage, your father won a Montisfryn stallion from me?"

"Aye."

He shifted his gaze, trapping hers. "And at our next crossing, I won you from him."

"So?"

"Your father could never breed the champions he desired from that Montisfryn stallion, because he lacked the right mares to hold the seed. I, on the other hand, came away with a de Versallet wife who demonstrably holds my seed to good effect."

She grabbed a bolster and thumped him mercilessly. Laughing, he defended himself, then captured her hands, holding her above him to watch as she tried to glare through her laughter.

"I do not appreciate being likened to a mare, regardless of how much you may fancy yourself a stallion."

"Oh?" He let his eyes go round. "But, lady, tis *you* who most frequently use the terms. When *I* speak of mares and stallions, tis actual horses to which I refer."

She would have hit him again had he let her. Instead, laughing softly, he spread his arms until she collapsed on his chest. Their lips found each other's without conscious direction for a long, easy caress. She pulled her hands free of his and used them to frame his face; he wrapped his arms about her and the kiss went on and on.

When, eventually, she raised her head, he arched a brow at her. "Anyway, tis my memory, lady, that you once said, in this bed, that you would be anything I wished."

Eloise looked down at him, her dark eyes radiant. "I'll be anything you wish—your wife, your lover, your partner, your helpmate." Her eyes softened, searching his. "A mare on which you may get your champions. I

care not, lord—as long as I have you."
Golden fire reached for her and held her close.
"Forever, lady-witch."

For information on all Stephanie's published books, visit her website at

http://www.stephanielaurens.com

For alerts as new books are released, plus information on all upcoming

books, please sign-up for Stephanie's Private Email Newsletter, either on her

website, or at: http://eepurl.com/gLgPj

Or if you're a member of Goodreads, join the discussion of Stephanie's

books at the Fans of Stephanie Laurens group.

You can email Stephanie at stephanie@stephanielaurens.com

Or find her on Facebook at

http://www.facebook.com/AuthorStephanieLaurens

Author's Note

I have always been fascinated by medieval life. Steeped as I have been for the past 40 years in Regency-era England, I found the contrast represented by medieval life intriguing. If the Regency era is the modern era stripped of technology, then the mid-medieval period is the Regency era stripped of all creature-comforts, a time in which there existed even fewer distractions from the emotional crises of life, and even thinner veils of civilization behind which such clashes were screened. All the most powerful emotions—passion, desire, anger, greed, and all the others—are closer to the surface, more raw, more intense.

I spent over a year researching England in medieval times, reading countless academic texts, and ultimately attending a university summer school on medieval life. Those studies led me to focus on the mid-14th century, a time of pageantry, of tournaments, chivalry, and armed campaigns. It was a time when noble ladies stood as regent for their husbands and ruled their lands and people whenever those lords were absent—which was frequently, and often for years. Life in castle and town was colorful and communal, and there was, necessarily, a greater balance of shared responsibility and standing between the sexes through this time.

Consequently, the mid-1300s seemed a time well-suited to a Stephanie Laurens' romance—a time when our heroine as well as our hero could believably have been forceful, intelligent, headstrong, and willful, and proactive on the widest stage.

Most factual details described in *Desire's Prize*—details of castle life, Edward's campaign, the tournament, herb lore, the journey, even of the city of Hereford in that time—have been drawn from academic sources. All else is purely the product of my imagination, albeit informed by said sources. Two specific details might have surprised. First, the notion of a lightning bolt killing a fully armored knight is drawn from fact. During Edward III's campaigns in France, both the English and French armies lost hundreds of knights to lightning strikes, and it was common practice not to wear full plate armor unless battle was imminent. Added to that, the country with the greatest frequency of lightning strikes per annum is, in fact, England. The use of the term "booty" might also strike readers as anachronistic, but that word, used in the sense of valuable goods seized in war, predates the historical period in which this book is set, and was the term so used in this time.

In terms of chronology of writing, this work was completed after Captain Jack's Woman, and before Devil's Bride. In terms of characters, therefore, Alaun and Eloise fall between Jack and Kit on the one hand, and Devil and Honoria on the other. Discerning readers will detect the echoes in that all three works are based on the emotional challenges encountered when two exceptionally strong characters fall in love.

If you enjoyed DESIRE'S PRIZE, you might enjoy Stephanie's pre-Victorian-era romance-mystery series, THE CASEBOOK OF BARNABY ADAIR NOVELS.

WHERE THE HEART LEADS

The first of the Casebook of Barnaby Adair Novels, in which Barnaby Adair, previously seen in *The Truth About Love*, *What Price Love?*, and *The Taste of Innocence*, meets his match in Penelope Ashford, who previously appeared in *On A Wicked Dawn*.

From Where the Heart Leads:

In any modern society, justice needed to be seen to be served evenhandedly, without fear or favor, despite those among the ton who refused to believe that Parliament's laws applied to them. The Prime Minister himself had been moved to compliment Barnaby over his latest triumph.

Raising his glass, Barnaby sipped. The success had been sweet, yet it had left him feeling strangely hollow. Unfulfilled in some unexpected way.

Certainly he'd anticipated feeling happier, rather than empty and peculiarly rudderless, aimlessly drifting now that he no longer had a case to absorb him, to challenge his ingenuity and fill his time.

An intriguing man
Handsome, debonair, and deliciously dangerous, Barnaby Adair has made his name by solving crimes within the ton. When Penelope Ashford appeals for his aid, he is moved by her plight—and captivated by her lush beauty.

An undaunted lady
More than a pretty face in a satin gown, Penelope has devoted her will and intelligence to caring for London's orphans. But now her charges are disappearing. She turns to Adair for help, never dreaming she'll discover in him a man who matches her appetite for life and passion.

Where the heart leads
As Barnaby and Penelope unravel the mystery of the missing children, they uncover a shocking trail that leads to the upper echelons of society, and a ruthless criminal who is ready to destroy all they hold dear, including their newfound understanding of the irresistible intrigues of the heart.

Soon to be followed by:

THE PECULIAR CASE OF LORD FINSBURY'S
DIAMONDS
(SHORT NOVEL)

Coming mid-Janaury, 2014

Penelope Adair, wife and partner of amateur sleuth Barnaby Adair, is so hugely pregnant she cannot even waddle. When Barnaby is summoned to assist Inspector Stokes of Scotland Yard in investigating the violent murder of a gentleman at a house party, Penelope, frustrated that she cannot participate, insists on a detailed report—and promptly arranges a private dinner party so that she and Griselda, Stokes's wife, can be duly informed of their husbands' discoveries.

But what Barnaby and Stokes uncover only leads to more questions. The murdered gentleman had been thrown out of the house party days before, so why was he returning? And how and why did he come to have the fabulous Finsbury diamond necklace in his pocket, much to Lord Finsbury's consternation. Most peculiarly, why had the murderer left the necklace, worth a stupendous fortune, on the body?

The conundrums compound as our intrepid investigators attempt to make sense of this most baffling case. Meanwhile, the threat of scandal grows ever more tangible for all those attending the house party – and the stakes are highest for Lord Finsbury's daughter and the gentleman who has spent the last decade in darkest Africa striving to resurrect his family fortune so he can aspire to her hand. Working parallel to Barnaby and Stokes, can our would-be lovers find a path through the maze of contradictory facts to expose the murderer, disperse the pall of scandal, and claim the love and the shared life they now crave?

THE MASTERFUL MR. MONTAGUE
(FULL LENGTH NOVEL)
Coming end April, 2014

THE CURIOUS CASE OF LADY LATIMER'S SHOES
(SHORT NOVEL)
Coming mid-June, 2014

LOVING ROSE: THE REDEMPTION OF MALCOLM SINCLAIR
(FULL LENGTH NOVEL)
Coming late July, 2014.

About The Author

#1 *New York Times* bestselling author STEPHANIE LAURENS began writing as an escape from the dry world of professional science, a hobby that quickly became a career. Her novels set in Regency England have captivated readers around the globe, making her one of the romance world's most beloved and popular authors.

DESIRE'S PRIZE is her fifty-third published work. All of her previous works remain available in print and all e-book formats.

Stephanie lives with her husband and two cats in the hills outside Melbourne, Australia. When she isn't writing, she's reading, and if she isn't reading, she'll be tending her garden.

Readers can email Stephanie at stephanie@stephanielaurens.com

Or find her on Facebook at
http://www.facebook.com/AuthorStephanieLaurens

Or if you're a member of Goodreads, join the discussion of Stephanie's books at the Fans of Stephanie Laurens group.

For information on all Stephanie's published books, visit her website at
http://www.stephanielaurens.com

For alerts as new books are released, plus information on all upcoming books, please sign-up for Stephanie's Private

Email Newsletter, either on her website, or at: http://eepurl.com/gLgPj

7333021R00180

Made in the USA
San Bernardino, CA
03 January 2014